Praise for *In Bed with the Earl*

"Exceptional . . . This series launch is an intoxicating romp sure to delight fans of historical romance."
—*Publishers Weekly* (starred review)

"Sizzling, witty, passionate . . . perfect!"
—Eloisa James, *New York Times* bestselling author

Praise for Christi Caldwell

"Christi Caldwell writes a gorgeous book!"
—Sarah MacLean, *New York Times* and *USA Today* bestselling author

"In addition to a strong plot, this story boasts actualized characters whose personal demons are clear and credible. The chemistry between the protagonists is seductive and palpable, with their family history of hatred played against their personal similarities and growing attraction to create an atmospheric and captivating romance."
—*Publishers Weekly* on *The Hellion*

"Christi Caldwell is a master of words, and *The Hellion* is so descriptive and vibrant that she redefines high definition. Readers will be left panting, craving, and rooting for their favorite characters as unexpected lovers find their happy ending."
—*RT Book Reviews* on *The Hellion*

In the DARK
with the
DUKE

OTHER TITLES BY CHRISTI CALDWELL

Lost Lords of London

In Bed with the Earl

Sinful Brides

The Rogue's Wager

The Scoundrel's Honor

The Lady's Guard

The Heiress's Deception

The Wicked Wallflowers

The Hellion

The Vixen

The Governess

The Bluestocking

The Spitfire

Heart of a Duke

In Need of a Duke (A Prequel Novella)

For Love of the Duke

More Than a Duke

The Love of a Rogue

Loved by a Duke

To Love a Lord

The Heart of a Scoundrel

To Wed His Christmas Lady

In the DARK with the DUKE

CHRISTI CALDWELL

Ⓜ Montlake

Text copyright © 2020 by Christi Caldwell Incorporated
All rights reserved.

Published by Montlake, Seattle

www.apub.com

Amazon, the Amazon logo, and Montlake are trademarks of Amazon.com, Inc., or its affiliates.

ISBN-13: 9781542021265
ISBN-10: 154202126X

Cover design by Juliana Kolesova

Printed in the United States of America

For Lindsey:
In you, I've been so very lucky to have an editor
who not only believes in my work
but also helps make sure it "sparkles."
I'm so grateful for all you do.
Thank you for always being there to discuss my
characters and plot points and everything in between.
Lila and Hugh are for you!

One fist to the gut.

One to the eye.

A third to the throat.

And that's how one dies.

—*The Fight Society*

Prologue

Covent Garden
London, England
1810

The rules were clear.

They were simple.

Always land the hardest, sharpest blow. The decisive one that, when properly dealt, ultimately kills.

And that ruthlessness was what brought the nobility 'round. After all, they would turn out coin for the cruelest of pleasures, and those cruelest pleasures were what kept Hugh Savage alive.

Or they had. Until tonight.

Hugh jabbed a fist out, punching swiftly at the air. From the reflection in the cracked beveled mirror, he caught sight of his visitor before the man even spoke.

"You do know what you have to do?"

Hugh met that question with nothing more than another practiced blow that hissed in the quiet.

The desperate ones always wanted a damned meeting. As if they had something meaningful to contribute. Ultimately, Hugh had come to realize, those lessons were more about the obnoxious nobs convincing themselves that they had some control over the matchup, when really, the two men in the ring were the only ones who mattered.

Restraining the fury pumping through him, Hugh let his fist fly, coming so close to the mirror his knuckles brushed the glass.

Jab-Jab-Jab.

Yes, the last thing Hugh, a bare-knuckle fighter, needed was a lesson. And certainly not from the man who'd come here as a coach. He might come from the highest ranks of London high society, but in these streets, Hugh was king of the ring. He faced the lord. Nearly forty years older than Hugh's fifteen, the man was smaller by three stone, shorter by a foot, and stupider by a lot. Hefting his shirt overhead, Hugh tossed it aside, and the color drained from the fine gent's fleshy cheeks.

A clamor of cheers and cries went up outside the doorway, in the room where even now the latest contest ensued. Over that din, Hugh could still make out distinct sounds: The audible swallow of the masked lord as he took in Hugh's scarred and marked chest. The rapid bobbing of the gent's throat. The scratch of fabric as the gent clenched and unclenched his jacket.

"I know how to fight," Hugh said, speaking his first words since his handler had sent him back to ready for his match. "And even if I didn't, the last person I'd take tutelage from is one like you."

Surprise brought the old man's eyebrows flying up over the tops of the fabric obscuring his face.

Hugh smiled coldly. They were always startled by his crisp tones. Always unsettled, as though they'd stumbled upon an anomaly, a fine-speaking person who had no place in these parts.

But despite Hugh's flawless King's English, none would ever dare dispute or question that this was the only place he belonged.

The old lord managed to find his voice once more. "I want him dead. I've got a sizable sum on you."

That was the plan, then. The Fight Society, which had begun as a ruthless underground children's bare-knuckle ring, had evolved as the competitors had gotten older, and the spectators had begun to thirst for more bloodshed. More violence. More danger. More *everything* except mercy for the street rats made to *tussle* for their enjoyment.

Bare-knuckle fighting had devolved into matches to the death—boys who'd never really been boys, forced to scuffle like dogs in the street, with not even a meal tossed to the most ruthless to emerge triumphant.

I have to get out . . . I have to get away from this . . .

"Did you hear me, boy? I want him dead."

"My lord, if you'll excuse us for a moment."

As one, Hugh and the masked nobleman looked to the owner of that voice—Dooley, the hated handler.

The gentleman stomped over to the lead handler. "The boy's not being agreeable," he said, jabbing a finger to the ground, punctuating each word. "He's a stubborn, shameful one, and—"

"And also one of our best." Dooley flicked a flinty stare over a still-silent Hugh.

The mask that concealed nearly the whole of the patron's face pulled around his fleshy lips.

While that pair spoke in angry but hushed whispers, Hugh practiced several swift uppercuts.

They wanted control of every exchange. Of every duel. Of every outcome. To hell with all of them.

And to hell with this life that wasn't a life.

"If you'll excuse me, my lord?" Dooley was saying.

The nobleman cast another look Hugh's way. He wanted to say more, but apparently he was not as dumb as Hugh had originally taken him for.

The moment he'd taken his leave, Dooley closed the door behind him and turned the lock. "You disapprove."

It wasn't a question, and even if it had been, Hugh wouldn't have answered Dooley.

"You're too good at what you do to hate this life," the head of the underground operation said, almost conversationally. "Every last one of the combatants out there would kill to possess your skill, Savage."

Savage. It was the only surname he'd ever known. One he didn't remember being given, and as such, he may as well have been born with it. Either way, the name was an apt one.

"Killing's what they do anyway," Hugh pointed out jeeringly.

Every muscle in his body went taut and strained and pulsed as the realization hit him.

We. Not "they" . . . *we.*

For tonight, Hugh would be expected to take part in that same barbarism. If he wanted to live, that was.

Sweat slicked his skin.

It had been inevitable.

This moment.

This exchange.

He'd known this night was coming. He'd just managed to convince himself that Dooley believed Hugh's value as a fighter was greater. That it would spare him from being thrust into a death match.

"Here." The other man tossed something at him. "You asked for these?"

Hugh caught the strips of thinly cut, white linens. There was no such thing as honor in the rookeries. Men took any advantage they could. It was why, without compunction, he sat and proceeded to loop his thumb and wrap behind one hand.

"Does that really work?"

"It worked for the Greeks and Romans," he muttered. The cloth wraps protected a boxer's bones and skin. It was a strategy not known by the other fighters in the streets.

"Interesting."

There was an absurdity to the casual nature of their exchange, one so at odds with the fact that, in mere moments, Hugh would leave this room and either meet his end or turn himself into a murderer.

Dooley probed him with his gaze. "What do you know about the Greeks and Romans?"

A lot. It was another detail he couldn't explain about his past; however, while he may be forced to fight, he'd not give anything more to this man. Any of them. Hugh checked to see that he had adequate tension in his hand. He tugged the linen and then made a fist, testing to be sure it didn't constrict his movements too much. "Is that what you're here to talk about? Ancient civilizations?" He looped the linen around his wrist, then paused midway through the third loop to glance over at Dooley. "If so, perhaps you'd want to talk about the mere mortal Cronus, how he castrated and took apart his father, Ouranos's, brain?"

The handler paled. Hugh's meaning had not been lost.

Dooley quickly recovered. "Or mayhap we focus instead on how Zeus cut that foolish lad into pieces for ever daring to think he could have vengeance on a god?"

A god.

Hugh's lip curled in a sneer. Was that what the other man took himself for? But then, in a way, in this world, wasn't he? Dooley and the lords who ran this ring ruled all.

The only difference? This hell would never dare be mistaken for anything but a Devil's paradise.

"Either way, Savage, I've not come to argue with you." Dooley strolled over. "Not on fight night. Not when you'll require your every wit about you."

Hugh wasn't one who'd ever dare believe Dooley's words were born of any real concern. Nay, he and the others here, they were commodities, ones who could be dispensed with as easily as a street peddler hawked her basket of eggs or bread.

His hands larger than most, Hugh wrapped them with the second strip of linen, taking care to smooth the cloth free of any wrinkles or lumps.

"It's . . . taken a turn. I know this might come as a surprise to you, but I'm not one who necessarily . . . approves of the new direction."

Hugh made no attempt to mask his contempt. "Because you're so *concerned* about us boys?" And now girls who'd been brought in to take part.

Dooley scoffed. "My concern is the profit to be made." Wandering over, he stopped so that he didn't have to crane his neck so much to meet Hugh's gaze. "Training fighters is costly. But more, it is time-consuming. If we're losing even two boys a night, it's too many. That's two more I'll have to find and train, and even then, they'll never have the same skill as you lifelong fighters."

Hugh's gut clenched. Aye, that was precisely what they were.

Dooley released a belabored sigh. "Alas, try telling that to the lords who run this place. And I?" He shrugged. "I merely answer to them. Just as we all do to the peerage. I can suggest the best practices with which to make money in this venture, but I cannot make them do anything."

Hugh sneered and went back to his wrappings. "Of course, you'll always do precisely as they want." Those masked five who ran the ring. The aristocrats whose money and perverse thirst for gladiatorial fighting had seen the creation of the Fight Society. They were the ones responsible for the children pickpockets and orphans plucked from the streets and whatever hospital they'd called *home* to take part in this hell. Dooley, however? Powerless as he was compared with the leaders of the ring, he still bore a like responsibility for all that happened here.

Hugh felt, but didn't bother to look for, Dooley's disapproving frown. "*Tsk. Tsk.* I'm not totally heartless."

Not totally may as well have been the same as *completely*.

"I've invested heavily in you. You? You are special, Savage."

6

Despite his resolve not to give any of his tormentors the benefit of a glance, at those words, Hugh couldn't resist looking up.

Dooley's gaze was slightly unseeing as he stared across the preparation room. "I've never seen anyone fight like you. You don't sound like a street rat. But you fight like one. You are unique, and that deserves to be protected."

That.

Not he.

Not Hugh.

As always, he was inanimate to these people. An object to be used for their whims and pleasures. They were all just pieces upon a chessboard, being shifted and shoved about, these men controlling each ultimate move and outcome.

Just as they had tonight by sending Hugh into the gladiatorial match.

I'm going to be ill . . .

The shouts and cheers from the arena were growing to a crescendo.

The time was near.

It is all coming to an end . . .

Tired of dancing around whatever had brought Dooley here, he asked, "What do you want?"

"See." The handler wagged a finger. "This is what I was speaking of. You possess an intuitiveness . . . in the arena but also in every exchange." He let his arm fall to his side. "But I'm intuitive as well. Your opponent tonight is a new one. The Assassin. I want you to end him tonight."

"Isn't that the expectation, regardless?"

Dooley's stare held Hugh's. "I'm telling you that is what you *need* to do."

Sitting up straighter, Hugh focused on the double meaning there.

"I've no doubt you'll win, Savage," Dooley said, studying him contemplatively.

Aye, because he didn't lose. As such, that would be the expectation this night from the nobs who ran this ring, and from the spectators who came and threw wagers down on the combatants.

"If . . . ," the other man said, bringing Hugh back to the moment, "you want to."

Hugh went absolutely stock still.

Dooley knew.

"I know," the other man confirmed.

And Hugh fought the inner tumult that not even the secret he carried for tonight's match should be something he owned. That the handler had gathered his intentions. He'd been robbed of even this. He couldn't staunch the tide of bitterness.

"There's nothing you can do about it," Hugh finally brought himself to say. This decision was his own, and that was enough. It would have to be.

"It would . . . be a shame if you never fought again. After all"— Dooley gave a dismissive flick of his fingers—"it is what you *do*. But losing you tonight without having something out of it?" Dooley shook his head.

And that would be Hugh's triumph.

"You smirk. You think you've won in deciding what you'll do this night," Dooley murmured, walking a measured circle around Hugh. "Except you've not considered the possibility I might be able to do something for you . . ." The handler let that dance in the air between them. "First, the only one who can take the Assassin down is you. The other boys"—*and girls*—"they don't stand a chance. If you don't do it, no one will, and my crop will be wiped clean."

His *crop*.

"Do you understand what I'm saying?"

"You're wanting me to kill him so he doesn't kill the rest of the boys and girls." Bragger. Maynard . . . and others. They were the ones whose lives would be on the line if Hugh didn't act this night. "All the children earning you coin?"

Dooley nodded slowly. "Yes, that's it."

"What's in it?"

"For you, don't you mean?" Dooley flashed another of those even, pearl-white smiles. "Finish the question, Savage . . . What is in it for you?" He clipped out each syllable. "Always be in it for yourself."

Aye, it was, simply put, the way of all East London.

All levity faded from Dooley's previously even features. "You take down the Assassin . . . kill him . . . and I'll see you with a *significant* prize."

"Oh?"

"A purse of twenty pounds."

It was a veritable fortune.

Hugh went back to adjusting the fabric on his hands. "Your coin? It isn't of any use to me." He spread his fingers the same width apart, testing the movements he'd use in about a quarter of an hour's time. "Caged like an animal, your money does me no good." For Hugh and the others . . . money served no purpose.

"But what if the cage is sprung . . . And what if you've the chance to . . . escape . . ." Dooley left that last word dangling and twisting in the air.

Escape . . .

It was a dream Hugh had let die long ago, so long he'd believed himself immune to feeling anything when so much as hearing it.

Every last hope, however, came roaring back to life, as lifelike and overwhelming in their intensity as they had been when the door had been accidentally left unlocked and he'd stepped one foot outside.

Only to be caught half-in and half-out of the doorway.

The bloodying he'd been given for trying to escape had beaten out any other attempts.

"I see it in your eyes, Savage. You don't know what to say. You want what I hold out, and yet you fear that I'm playing some . . . game with you."

Hugh tried to make himself remain still under that unerringly accurate read of every last thought running through his head.

Dooley proved relentless, drifting over, further tempting him. "Think of it. No more sleeping in a locked room. Looking up at the sky. 'Savage' can go away, and you can return to being . . . 'Hugh' again."

Hugh.

His throat convulsed. "I'll never be him again." His voice came out like a ragged growl. "Savage" was the only name he'd wear. The only one that fit any longer. And now, forevermore.

"Yes, well, that might be true, but if you win this one fight, it will be your last." Dooley left that there.

And then Hugh . . . would be free.

He tried to breathe, but his chest was tight, his lungs forgetting their basic function as he all but strangled on a sentiment he'd thought long dead: hope.

The sky. Walking free without answering to anyone. Never again using his fists.

His hope, however, was sprung from death.

Hugh's gaze locked on his white wrappings.

For his freedom was contingent upon killing this night.

But by Dooley's words, Hugh wouldn't be the only one to benefit by the Assassin's death. Maynard, Bragger, and all the other boys who'd been locked up would be spared from squaring off against the monster Dooley described.

Liar. This isn't about them. It's about you . . .

Aye. He conceded that point to the jeering voice in his head. It was about him.

"I'll do it," he said quietly.

"Wise decision." Dooley's thin lips curved ever so slowly; the soft candle's glow shone off the handler's unnaturally sharp incisors, giving him the look of Satan who'd just struck a deal. "Wise decision, indeed. You won't regret this."

Dooley proceeded to rattle off instructions. "After the fighting, when everyone is back in their rooms"—*cells. Prisons the same as Newgate is what they are*—"I'll knock once. The door will open. You've the count of five to be out and through it. A sack will be there. You'll take it, and that will be it."

Dooley stalked off, but the moment he reached the door, he stopped and glanced back. "Oh, and Savage?"

Hugh drilled him with his eyes.

"They won't simply accept your loss. They'll look for you. I suggest you see yourself far away from this place. Far away." With that ominous warning, Dooley left.

Once alone, Hugh stared at the empty rooms.

This would be his last night. Never again would he have to throw a fist or beat a person unconscious. Or break a bone.

And yet, when he waited for the rush of overwhelming relief . . . it did not come.

For Hugh was unable to shake the sense that he'd made a deal with the Devil this night.

And once locked into an agreement with the Prince of Darkness . . . there was no going back.

Ever.

Chapter 1

THE LONDONER

Yet another Lost Lord has been discovered. Another
child, kidnapped. Another life and future forever
altered. For too long, the nobility has believed itself
immune to such dangers and threats. Only to at last
discover no one is truly safe . . .

V. Lovelace

London, England
1828

The world was on fire.

Lady Lila March, however, seemed to be the only one to have realized as much for nine years now.

And still, not everyone was suitably aware of the peril.

At that present moment, it was her widowed sister, Sylvia, who demonstrated an absolute lack of concern for life's dangers.

Though in fairness, not very many years ago, in her naivete and innocence, Lila hadn't been all that different from her sister.

"It w-was t-terrifying," their mother, the dowager Countess of Waterson, wailed. "A-absolutely t-terrifying."

Having long ago mastered the art of dwelling in the shadows, Lila stood in the farthest corner of her brother's parlor. She hovered alongside the drawn curtains and made herself invisible to her mother, sister, and Constable Lockwood, that trio at the center of the room.

It wasn't the first time Lila had witnessed her mother's tears. The countess had been free with them over the years. Generally, they'd been brought forth to try and elicit cooperation from her daughters at the start of their London seasons. Even given all the tumult and turmoil the March family had faced, this was the only time she'd seen genuine crystal drops.

"You're making more of it than there was." Lila's only sister, her elder by two years, spoke with a calm that did little to quiet their last living parent.

"I'm making . . . I'm making . . ." The dowager countess never managed to get the words out. Instead, she broke down into another blubber of tears. "Th-that woman was trying to t-take him. I-I saw the way she was s-staring."

And as quick as the tears had come, rage took their place. Their mother turned a sharp glare on the constable who'd been summoned. "How are you people allowing this to happen?"

This . . . as in the kidnapping of innocent babes and children. Ever since the public had learned that first one, and now, according to the papers, a second heir to the peerage had been sold and traded to a gang leader from the street, the stories had gripped Polite Society and the papers.

"Not every woman or man who admires a babe is intent on kidnapping them. Please, tell her that," Sylvia implored the constable.

Alas, all business and no-nonsense since he'd arrived, the handsome man in a sapphire suit and bowler hat didn't look up from his notes.

The same notes he'd been scribbling in his book since he entered the parlor to face an overwrought countess and her even-keeled daughter.

In a display of complete desperation, Sylvia turned to the silent Lila. "Please, Lila. *You* tell her she's being unreasonable."

That managed to bring the constable's attention up and over . . . and Lila remained stock still, feeling exposed. Mr. Lockwood peered at her, and she made herself stay motionless under that scrutiny until he went back to his work.

Her sister pressed her with an imploring gaze.

Except Lila couldn't give Sylvia what she sought. Nothing about this world in which they lived was safe, and she'd only be exposing a sibling she loved to greater peril if she offered false assurances.

Their mother ultimately answered for Lila. "Your sister won't do that because she knows I'm right. There's nothing natural about what has happened to these babes of the *ton* . . . and I'd not s-see your son fall to th-that same f-fate." And just like that, the dowager countess dissolved into another noisy, blubbery fit.

"And how long did this woman follow you?" Mr. Lockwood asked her.

Even across the length of the room, Lila detected her sister's audible and exasperated sigh. "She *wasn't*—"

"Easily for the better part of an hour," their mother cut in. She resumed wringing her hands. "It wasn't natural, I say. There was nothing natural about it. How she was staring . . . How she was looking at the babe."

"He is an adorable babe, Mother," Sylvia said exasperatedly. "Why should anyone not admire him?"

Yes, her sister was correct on that score. Nearly two years old, Vallen had the same dimpled cheeks and charm his late father had possessed.

The constable finally lowered his notebook. "And you've never seen this woman before?"

"I'm here," Sylvia snapped when the constable put that question to the dowager countess. "You might ask me."

At last, he flicked a gaze over to Lila's sister. "I'll ask whomever might answer the question," he said coolly. "And by your own assessment, you didn't see a reason for concern. The dowager countess, however, did." Turning dismissively, he glanced back to the matriarch of the family.

And their mother launched into a lengthy—and nothing if not impressive—cataloging of the woman she believed had been following her and Sylvia and Vallen.

Lila returned her attention to the slight crack in the curtains that opened out to the world below. Bustling with people moving about their daily activities. Horses being ridden past. Carriages rumbled by. And for so very long, Lila hadn't been part of any of it.

Nor, given the evil that had resurfaced in the papers, those tales of stolen children and murdered families, did she wish to be.

Just then, an enormous pink lacquer carriage rolled to a stop directly in front of her family's townhouse. Even had she not detected the immense gold crest emblazoned upon it, the garish color of the conveyance would have been enough to identify the occupant.

A servant scratched once at the door and then entered.

"Pardon," Lila's maid said, dipping a curtsy. "Lady Annalee has arrived—"

"We are not accepting guests at this time," the countess cried out. "And certainly not that scandalous creature. Send her on her way." With a finality to her tone, she turned back, gesturing wildly as she once again spoke to the constable.

Lila's maid, however, loyal as the day was long, looked to her mistress.

Lady Annalee, her former friend, had in her request to visit become insistent in ways that Lila didn't understand . . . or deserve. "I'm not accepting visitors," Lila said quietly.

Adelle dropped another curtsy, backed out of the room, and drew the doors shut.

Lila shifted, peeking out once more at the outrageously clad figure below. Alive and vibrant and grinning from ear to ear, the lady couldn't be more different from Lila. But then, that hadn't always been the case . . . Once, they'd been so very much alike.

Just then, Annalee glanced up. From around the wide, garish silk hat she wore, she caught Lila's gaze.

"That is all?" the countess was saying, pulling Lila's focus back to the present threat. "There is nothing else you'll do?" she demanded of Mr. Lockwood.

"There's nothing to do, my lady. The information you've provided?" The constable snapped his book shut. "A blonde woman with a frayed dress and gloveless fingers?" He tucked the small leather notebook into the front of his jacket. "You may as well have been talking about any Englishwoman. I will, however, conduct my research, if you wish—"

"I don't wish," Sylvia said tersely.

With that, he dropped a bow. "Is there anything else . . . ?"

"There isn't," her sister snapped. "You can leave. Now."

The moment he'd gone, their mother exploded into a bundle of frenetic energy and movement. "The gall of him. Well, either way, we needn't worry because you and Lila will be joining me and Clara and Henry."

Lila's stomach lurched. She didn't visit the country. Not any longer. She didn't leave this townhouse. "No."

"Absolutely not," her sister said simultaneously. "Lila is welcome to join me at my townhouse when you depart for Clara's confinement, but I'm *not* retiring to Kent."

The dowager countess ceased her aimless pacing and took a path over. With every elegant, graceful step that carried the older woman closer, the swell of panic threatened to choke Lila. "It is no safer here than it is in the country," her mother said.

Lila winced.

"Mother," Sylvia chastised. Sweeping over, Lila's elder sister, her protector from childhood, all but placed herself between Lila and the countess. "That's hardly any manner of reassurance."

"Mother is correct," Lila croaked. "It's not safe here." She wetted her lips. "It isn't safe anywhere."

Sylvia favored the both of them with a pitying look. "What happened today? It was not a threat." And in that she revealed just how very different Lila and she were . . . how differently they'd both come to the other end of tragedy.

"Perhaps it wasn't," Lila gently allowed. "But mayhap it was."

Sylvia threw her arms up.

"No one is properly alarmed by this situation," the countess said. "No one, aside from Lila and myself."

"What do you mean, no one is alarmed?" Stomping over to the stack of papers resting on the marble-topped parlor table, Sylvia grabbed them up and waved them around with both hands. "The only information in the papers is *about* the Lost Lords." She tossed them to the floor, where they landed with a sharp *thwack*.

"Yes, yes. Of course they are," the countess said with an angry slash of her own hand. "But only because they fear the return of those children and their lost status." Her eyes darkened, and when she spoke, her whisper was filled with such terror that gooseflesh pebbled Lila's skin. "But not the real danger."

Sylvia glanced to Lila. For help? Lila couldn't be the voice her sister sought. Not in this, the first time she'd ever really agreed with their straitlaced mother. Lila let her gaze fall to the floor, earning another frustrated sigh from Sylvia.

"Given your feelings for the country, you are welcome to remain with me at my townhouse," Sylvia said to her. "But I'm *not* leaving," she added for their mother's benefit.

"There's no reason for you to stay in London," the countess cried. "Since Norman's death, you don't even attend *ton* events." And then she pressed a fist to her mouth in a belated attempt to catch the gasp that escaped her.

Sylvia winced.

"Sylvia," their mother said frantically.

"It is fine," the elder of her daughters said with a tight shake of her head, then marched across the room. Suddenly, she stopped at the threshold of the room and looked back. "You're right," she said evenly. "I haven't gone to any functions. I don't go to balls or soirees." She'd not shed her widow's weeds, but in her willingness to go out during the day and bring her son to the park or visit shops, she was still more alive than Lila. "But if I run off to hide in the country, all because of some baseless fears, then I never will. Then I'll be—" Sylvia stopped. But she needn't have. Her meaning was already clear.

She'd be no different from Lila.

"Mother. Lila," she said, dipping her head.

And as her middle sibling rushed off with their mother hot on her heels, Lila couldn't even be hurt.

Lila had hidden herself away from the world . . . And now, by her sister's revelation this day, Sylvia intended to reenter the living. And what was more, she'd do so without a proper worry over the dangers that faced them all.

Restless, Lila bent and began stacking the newspapers.

As she did, the inked words flashed before her eyes, replaced by the other paper to cover it.

Dark deeds . . .

Stolen children . . .

Evil . . .

Danger . . .

As she knelt on the floor, the words on the top paper held her locked in place.

Lila didn't know whether her sister or her mother were, in fact, correct. What she did know was that there was a threat, and if . . . *when* . . . peril eventually came, be it the danger written about in these papers or another unknown one, her sister would be lost. And because of it, Lila's nephew would, too.

Lila added the last and final paper, *The London Inquisitor*, to the top of her pile . . . and paused.

For her sister had been incorrect. There were apparently additional stories outside the tale of the Lost Lords that merited society's interest . . .

THE SAVAGE GENTLEMAN

"Savage Gentleman," she muttered to herself. Those very words a contradiction. She stood, and unwittingly, her gaze went back to that article.

> Whispers abound that Savage's Fight Society's greatest, most skilled bare-knuckle fighter, Hugh Savage, will return to the ring for one of his far-too-infrequent matches. Never felled by a single fighter, he remains a legend.
>
> Though there is speculation that talks of the Savage Gentleman's return are merely a ploy to raise revenue and increase membership, the hope remains that he will step into the arena soon . . .
>
> M. Fairpoint

Wistfully, Lila reread the column several times. Certainly, this Mr. Hugh Savage had never known the terror that gripped Lila still.

What must it be to possess a skill whereby one needn't live with fear? Where one was capable of looking after oneself and not holding one's breath in anticipation of inevitable doom.

She didn't move for several moments.

Why couldn't she possess that same skill? Why couldn't she be the one to take control and ownership of her fate and, while she remained here in London with Sylvia and Vallen, ensure that she was capable of caring for them?

Her heart pounded a little harder in her chest . . . as in that moment, a plan was hatched.

And with it, hope born . . .

Chapter 2

Hugh Savage's abhorrence of violence made his role as proprietor at Savage's Fight Society a peculiar one.

Those men born to the streets, however, didn't really come into this world with any real choice.

Principles and honor didn't stave off hunger. They didn't offer shelter from a country as stingy with its sun as it was with its charity. Nay, as an orphan who'd spent his earliest days in the streets, Hugh had never been given a choice. Not truly.

As such, he'd done what every last man, woman, and child in the rookeries did: he'd survived.

From when he was a boy scrabbling with other boys and girls and whomever his handlers had him face in the ring, to when he'd become a young man marching across the Continent to face down Boney's forces, fighting was all he'd ever known.

And it was all he'd ever know.

A swell of cries went up as the men around Savage's Fight Society surged to their feet, crowding about as the current fight neared a crescendo. "Get him! *Get him!*"

When Hugh had first started with the arena, those shouts had ravaged him.

In time, however, he had taught himself the skill of, if not blocking out, managing to mute those shouts. In those earliest days here, when the memories had been crispest, he'd struggled to disentwine the feral sounds of this place from those of different fields of carnage.

Nay, he'd learned very early in both the roughest corners of East London and the fields of the Peninsular War, and then Waterloo, nothing good came from waging war.

Lands were torched. Lives lost. And in the end, the ones left standing bore the imprints of battle as scars on their skin, and the intangible sickness that couldn't be seen in their ravaged minds.

In the midst of the pandemonium unfurling in the fighting ring, which was more warehouse than arena, Hugh caught a flash of brown fabric that whipped ever so slightly outside the back window before it went still.

He narrowed his eyes.

What soldiers *did* walk away from battle were left with heightened senses. He could hear the crunch of brush, crushed under footfalls that weren't silent enough. The squelch of mud. The softest whisper.

And there also came an amplified sense of sight: the ability to be face-forward but also watching out of the corner of one's eye at the same time.

A burnt-umber hue—a shade of brown so near a perfect match to the mud-spattered windows that anyone else would have missed it.

Homing his gaze on that whisper of cloth, he stared, unblinking . . . until a spring breeze gave that fabric life again, and it flapped and fluttered in the night.

The article may as well have been a calling card announcing the person who failed so mightily at stealth.

"Rip 'is goddamned 'ead off." The high-pitched cry sounded above the din.

Motionless, Hugh waited. All the while his gaze was on that window and his quarry, he surveyed the area around him. Be it on the battlefields of Europe or the streets of Covent Garden, a man who didn't manage to keep at least five paces ahead of his enemies ultimately succumbed.

The two proprietors, Griffin Maynard and Samuel Bragger, who were engrossed in talking, gave no indication that they were aware of anything but the business they discussed. Throughout the warehouse, the boys they employed from the streets hurried around them, collecting bets still being tossed down on the two fighters.

Just then, Maynard quit the arena, and Bragger started over to Hugh.

Child fighters together, Maynard and Bragger had been the ones who'd given Hugh his work here. He owed them in ways no man wished to be indebted. But as a soldier learned in the heat of battle, survival came first, pride a distant second to that most important task.

If it hadn't been for the pair of them, he'd have been like every last member of the king's regiment, who'd returned to all-too-brief, empty praise and hungry bellies. After all, in the same way grand parades didn't provide shelter at night, accolades didn't stave off hunger. They'd given him shelter and food, and then more importantly . . . work.

Hugh did another sweep.

Gone.

He may as well have imagined that flash of fabric at the back window, and yet neither was he so naive as to fail to trust what he'd seen.

Bragger stepped between Hugh and that window.

"I think we might have company," Hugh said the moment his partner joined him.

"You're right," Bragger shouted over another swell of noise from the crowd.

Hugh's senses went on alert.

Bragger grinned. "We've got 'im."

The voyeur briefly forgotten, Hugh was incapable of focusing on anything beyond those three words: *We've got him.*

There could be any number of men Bragger spoke of. And yet Hugh knew. The past was about to be resurrected, and Hugh thrust back into the world he'd sought to bury.

"We've got 'im," Bragger repeated as if Hugh hadn't heard the first pronouncement. Because neither Bragger nor Maynard—nay, no one in these streets—could ever expect Hugh to feel anything more than a vicious bloodlust for revenge. "Angus located him."

"How?"

"'eard from 'is contacts on the street that someone was settin' up a new fight club. The bastard 'ad already gotten started recruiting fighters."

"Dooley."

"Aye, Dooley."

And while his partner talked, Hugh's gut churned.

Long before Hugh had returned to the rookeries, the men who'd become his partners, Bragger and Maynard, had begun hunting down the ones responsible for the hell they'd endured and seeing they paid with their lives . . . or by suffering other, worse fates. They could have been the most profitable club of any kind—gaming or boxing—in London, and yet all their funds, collectively, had gone to getting the answers and information to take down the five ringleaders of the Fight Society—four of whom had fallen.

And whenever they needed more funds for their search? They dragged Hugh out as the main attraction he was. It was a role he hated, but a task he completed for everything his partners had done for him.

Fighting and more fighting. That's all there ever was or would ever be as long as they remained buried in the past of the Fight Society.

But now? It was Dooley's turn to pay for his crimes.

All because he'd come back to carry out the same evil he'd once perpetuated against them. Because it was never enough. The world craved a good fight, and because of it, there was always coin to be earned and a surplus of men willing to sell their souls to perpetuate that violence.

And I'm no different . . .

For once they had the information they sought from Dooley, Bragger and Maynard would kill him, and then they'd move on to the final leader of the Fight Society, who would also pay the price with his life. It was a revenge Hugh, savage bastard that he was, should gleefully take part in, and yet, God rot his soul, he couldn't.

Vomit singed the back of his throat, and he swallowed convulsively.

Bragger gave him an odd look. "Are ya listenin' to me? 'e's 'ere."

Hugh peered once more at the window, and made one more attempt to avoid the revenge no doubt being meted out. "I thought I saw someone lurking—"

"It's a damned patron," Bragger said impatiently. "Let's go."

Let's go.

There it was.

An order.

And the decision was made for him.

Hugh and Bragger started through the arena.

Neither man stopped until they'd made the steep climb to the private suites above the ring.

The office was none other than a training room. With ropes and metal bars covering the walls and windows, it had more the look of a torture chamber. But then, torture was synonymous with fighting.

"Savage?" Bragger asked impatiently, prompting Hugh to move once more. He eased the door open and slipped inside.

All at once, Hugh's past rose up to meet him.

The man, as finely dressed as any lord, lay prone on the floor, blood covering the whole lower part of his face, a steady stream leaking from his right nostril and running down his fleshy jowls. His rounded cheeks had already been painted a palate of blue-and-purple bruises. And yet, even nearly obscured by Maynard's handiwork, Hugh recognized him.

Recognized him all these years later.

After he'd slipped out of his cell and nabbed his purse, Hugh had hightailed it from the rookeries and thought never to see Dooley or any of those connected to the Fight Society again.

Because that had been the hope. That was what had given Hugh the strength to carry out that act of evil in a ring full of rabid spectators.

And his stomach pitched and roiled, threatening to revolt just as it had on that long-ago day.

"Savage . . . ? . . . *Savage* . . . ?"

Hugh snapped back to the moment and found Bragger giving him an odd look. "Ya all roight?" he asked out of the side of his mouth.

No. Hugh managed a nod. "Aye."

Just then, Maynard buried his boot in their old handler's ribs.

Dooley released an animallike cry, one that harkened to the days when they'd been in the midst of battle and Dooley had been the one on the sidelines.

And it was surely some deficit of Hugh's character that as Bragger smiled, Hugh had to fight the urge to look away from the merciless beating being doled out. That lack of relish on his part a reminder that he was as much a traitor now as he'd been then.

For everything in their pasts and in their histories said Hugh should want this moment as much as Maynard and Bragger had salivated for it. That he should relish the blood of their enemies running upon their hands.

"Please," the gentleman whimpered, looking up. His once broad, powerful Roman nose, now crooked and broken, poured blood still, turning his puce-colored waistcoat black.

Funny, as a boy fighting like a cock or a stray dog, how much bigger and older Dooley had seemed to Hugh.

The rapidly brightening bruises marring the older man's cheeks stood out in stark, vivid splotches as all the blood left his face. Only, he wasn't old. Not really. Though just ten or so years older than Hugh, the other man had always seemed older. Frailer. Back when he'd been using young boys on the streets as ruthless fighters for the perverse pleasures of wealthy lords and merchants, Dooley and the still unidentified man who'd turned boy on boy. Making them into killers, all in the name of entertainment for twisted clients with aberrant tastes.

Silently, Hugh pushed the panel closed behind him and his partners, and made himself say something. "Dooley." Ultimately, he'd managed nothing more than a name.

Hope shone through the battered man's pain-glazed eyes. "S-Savage."

"Ah, looking for 'elp, are ya?" Bragger made a *tsk*ing sound. "I'd say you've quite placed your hopes in the wrong people. Ain't that roight?" he asked.

Their other partner, Maynard, a bear of a man, nearly two stone bigger than either Hugh or Bragger, answered for the pair. "Quite so."

"Jesus," the older man whispered, looking like one facing Death himself. And no one said the cruel weren't clever, for Dooley was wise enough to know death was precisely what the trio before him represented. They'd been out for his blood since boyhood, and had brought him home to feast.

"I never took you for a godly man, Dooley," Hugh said quietly.

"I'm sorry." Dooley's lower lip quivered. "I'm s-so sorry."

"No," Hugh said, coming closer to the trio in the middle of the room. "You're not. That is, not sorry for what you did." He stopped over the sprawled handler, and despite himself, he couldn't resist the wave of pity at the state in which the man now found himself. And the fate he was about to meet.

"And not sorry enough to end yar ways," Bragger said coolly.

Deaf in his left ear from too many blows to the head, Griffin Maynard called out too loudly, "Forgive me for gettin' started without the both of ya."

Bragger propped a shoulder against the door. "Worry not, mate. Plenty of Dooley to go 'round." He cracked his knuckles. "Plenty of flesh to go 'round."

The greying gent whimpered and buried his head in his hands, the shaking digits immediately washed red with blood.

Maynard grinned widely, displaying a bottom row of uneven teeth, and again set to work beating Dooley.

Hugh's stomach roiled.

There was no end . . . not to this. There would never be an end. After they'd dealt with Dooley, there'd only be another to be brought forward in the name of vengeance. And then when they had their revenge, those linked to Dooley and his cohorts would come for them. On and on it would go.

Forcing a casualness he didn't feel, Hugh grabbed a sturdy oak chair and seated himself close to their prey on the floor.

Maynard paused to wipe sweat from his brow. "We've been looking for ya," he said conversationally, as if he didn't even now wear the other man's blood on his knuckles.

"Not just 'im," Bragger pointed out.

A study in false contemplativeness, Maynard rubbed at his chin, leaving a streak of crimson in his wake. "No, that's true."

Burrowing his face into the hardwood floor, Dooley whimpered, the high-pitched sounds better suited to a wounded beast.

Or a child forced to fight another child . . . a child broken and battered from too many fists and knocks to the temple.

Hugh tightened his jaw. "You've done an impressive job of hiding." So why had he come out now? *Why?* he silently railed. "Was the fortune you made off our backs"—*and souls*—"not enough?"

Bragger joined Hugh and Maynard so they formed a circle around their former tormentor. "Rats always come scurrying from their hiding places," Maynard said from his place at Dooley's head.

The handler looked up at the giant of a man towering over him and squeezed his eyes shut.

"I wanted to h-help you," Dooley sputtered.

Bragger laughed, a cold, deadened chuckle that none would ever dare confuse with any real amusement. "'elp us? *'elp us?*" There was a slightly desperate pitch to that word echo.

Dooley scrambled onto his arse and sought to back away from the ring they formed. "You were begging for scraps. Pleading for coin."

Aye, they had been. Part of Mac Diggory's gang of boys, they'd stolen and begged for the Dials' most ruthless man. In the end, they'd been sold to Dooley and dragged to another part of London, where they'd been robbed of far more than food or monies. They'd had their very souls ripped from them. It was why, when he'd had the chance, Hugh had grasped the only way out for boys in these parts—serving King and Crown.

In the name of respectability, honor, and a new beginning . . .

His gaze locked on a point over Dooley's head.

What a naive fool he'd been. When the erroneous assumption was that a man from the streets was wholly incapable of naivete or innocence.

"Ya bought us. Made us slaves," Bragger was saying. Fire and fury blazed from his eyes. "Didn't even get to keep a coin. Kept us locked up, ya did. Boys." The other man's throat worked in an unexpected crack in his armor. "Girls."

Of their trio, Bragger remained the one most trapped in that shared part of their past, and hell-bent on revenge at all costs. But then he was the only one of their trio with any blood family: a sister who'd been a fighter and then disappeared. Had he a family, perhaps Hugh would have felt the way the other man did.

"They were orphans, too," Dooley whined, lifting his hands up beseechingly.

As though it had been a privilege . . . And Hugh proved that savage part of his soul couldn't be disentwined from who he was, from a primal hungering to take the other man apart . . .

"Yar going to pay for it," Maynard snarled, surging forward.

Dooley shot a hand out. "N-not all w-was bad, though. You must say that. W-why, you've built a *liiiiiiife*," he cried out, and eyed the wrist Bragger had snapped with a single well-placed slash of his hand.

Writhing and twisting, Dooley rolled onto his enormous stomach and sobbed and screamed incoherently. The raucous cheers from the patrons below melded that bloodthirsty revelry with his cries of agony.

Hugh made himself stare at the pathetic heap rolling around the floor. To acknowledge that suffering. For even as Dooley's crimes merited punishment, evil only begets more evil. Until a person found one-self drowning in violence.

As though he'd identified his mark, the weakest of the group surrounding him, Dooley stretched his untouched hand out. "Please h-help me, Savage . . . *Heeeelp* . . ."

Hugh's stomach knotted.

"Oh, sir, pray don't kill him . . . Help me . . . Won't you heeeelll—ahhh . . . ?" The blast of a close-range musket blew away the remainder of that distant entreaty.

"Savage? Savage?" It took a moment for Maynard's voice to penetrate through the echoes of gunfire in his mind.

Hugh forced back the distant sounds from a different battle and concentrated on the one before him.

"Ya all right?" his partner asked.

Had any of them ever been all right?

"Fine," he said tightly.

When Dooley's screams dissolved into quiet, shuddery sobs, Hugh curled his hands. Wanting to end this. Needing to. "We want the name of the ringleader."

So they could have their *revenge*. His partners, however, had failed to realize a truth Hugh had come to long ago: they'd never be free. They'd always be haunted, and then after Dooley and the final person, the mastermind, was found and dealt justice, there'd only be more blood on their hands.

Dooley squeezed his eyes shut, and his enormous Adam's apple jumped. "I can't."

Hugh and his partners shared a look.

"Ya can't?" Bragger pressed. "Or ya won't?"

"B-both. I cannot give you a name because I don't h-have it. Do you truly believe a fine one from the *ton* would deal with a plebeian like me?"

Leaning down, Bragger caught the other man by his shirtfront and dragged him up so that their noses touched. "And . . . what of Val?"

"Val?" Dooley echoed.

"Valerie," Bragger repeated.

Memories of Bragger's sister, the fourth of their group, merged with the stranger who'd darkened the back entrance of his club.

Another person he'd betrayed and failed. When he'd been caged with the other children, Hugh had seen them protected. And when he'd gone? Val had disappeared. An all-too-familiar guilt swirled in his chest, just one more debt he'd pay to the men before him.

When Dooley remained tight-lipped, Bragger shoved him hard to the floor.

And it was surely a deficit of his character that Hugh had tired of the violence and death and suffering.

Leaning down, Hugh dragged the battered and bloodied Dooley up so their noses touched. "Don't play games with me," Hugh warned in lethal tones that set the man to trembling all the harder. Didn't Dooley know he made it worse for himself? "Now we won't ask you again; give us the damned name."

The not-so-confident-or-strong-now bastard cried out. "I've no idea where that one is." Dooley struggled to get himself onto his knees. He held his hands out, the left wrist dangling at an awkward angle. And the old bastard must have thought better of it, for he drew his limbs close to his sides. "Been missing now for years," he said on a rush. Dooley glanced among them. "You have to believe me. I don't—*ahhhhhh*," he cried out again as Maynard jabbed him once in the temple.

"That's another mistake on your part," Bragger said, his face revealing the vicious delight he took in the other man's suffering. "We don't have to do anything." He leaned down, sticking his face close to Dooley's. "Not anymore."

Dooley caught Hugh's eyes on him, and mayhap he saw the internal struggle Hugh waged, for he stretched his hands up beseechingly toward him. "Please. I'm telling you the truth. I don't know who was responsible for the Fight Society, and I don't know where Valerie Bragger is."

Maynard and Bragger came closer.

"What do you think?" Bragger asked in hushed tones, and Hugh would have to be ten times a fool to fail to know that this was a test of his loyalty . . . to the group. To justice. Nay, not justice—vengeance. Though those two words were thought to mean entirely different things, they were ultimately the same. One was a fine and kind word to imply one was in the right.

Hugh spoke carefully. "Dooley was certainly not the brains or the money behind that long-ago operation." He ensured that the bastard in question couldn't detect their exchange. "He's a link to whoever was in charge."

Bragger's brows shot up. "You're suggesting he's absolved?"

Hugh's skin pricked from the attention his partners turned on him. Having been gone from the group for almost ten years serving the King's Army, there could be no doubting he was the outsider of their trio in every way. And his loyalty was always in question.

The object of their debate stretched his neck, straining to hear.

Angling his shoulder so that their old handler couldn't read his lips, Hugh spoke. "I didn't say that." Anything less than consigning the man to death would be viewed as a betrayal or failure on Hugh's part. "Not at all."

"What are you saying, then?" Maynard asked impatiently.

Hugh carefully considered his words. "I'm merely suggesting he's of far greater use to us alive." For there was no doubt from the hatred simmering from their eyes that both of his partners were of a mind to end Dooley once and for all. Here. Now. Hugh, however? He'd sent enough men, both the innocent and the soulless, on to their makers. *Though it wasn't really just men, was it?* That jeering voice wreaked havoc on a conscience that hadn't been killed either in the rookeries or facing down Boney's forces. Hugh lowered his voice so that the pathetic mass on the floor couldn't make out his words. "Angus was sloppy in bringing him here. Hire someone whose work this is. Someone who knows how to track people."

"A damned constable." Maynard scoffed. "Ya think the law would be on the side of a fucking street rat over the lords this one protects?" He jabbed his thumb back toward Dooley.

No, Hugh wasn't so foolish as to believe their sort would ever be seen on the side of right.

"I'm saying hire someone who's beholden to us," Hugh said with a pragmatic calm his partners never evinced. "Someone who is skilled at finding the information we seek that we'll never have access to because of who we are."

"An investigator," Bragger said flatly.

"Aye. Connor Steele." Everyone in these parts knew the man's name. "He's the best . . . and he's from these parts."

Bragger's brow furrowed.

"What are you saying?" Dooley implored, and Hugh silently cursed the other man for not knowing when to remain silent.

But then desperation made a person do stupid things.

Hugh knew that . . . and had witnessed that firsthand—remembrances that would haunt him until he drew his last breath.

"I don't know about any damned investigator," Maynard said, but Hugh caught the determination in the other man's tone, the one indicating he'd very much made up his mind about Dooley's fate. "Perhaps a bit more time with me and Bragger might jog some of those forgotten details."

A vicious grin brought Bragger's lips up. "Allow me the honor."

Hugh tensed his mouth. "I'll see to the arena."

With that, he started for the door, Dooley's cries trailing after him. "Please, Savage. Tell them to spare me."

Please, sir, spare me . . .

"No. No. *Noooooo.*" Dooley's screams pierced through the slap of flesh against flesh. "Please. *Pleaaaaaaase doooooooon't.*"

An ungodly screech trailed close behind as Hugh pulled the door shut behind him, leaving Dooley to his fate.

Chapter 3

THE LONDON INQUISITOR

Savage's Fight Society remains a marvel and a mystery.
The battles fought within those walls too uncouth, too
uncivilized to ever write of. And yet, all society wishes to
enter and learn for themselves ... But only the smallest
few are granted entry ... to meet the legendary fighter,
the Savage Gentleman ...

M. Fairpoint

There were nineteen and a half steps.

It was a peculiar number, not even. Not complete. Just nineteen and a half stairs that led to the back of Savage's on one side, and the business across the way—a bakery, now closed.

But then, everything about the building and its location was peculiar. The front, level with the street, gave the appearance that Savage's Arena was only one floor. And yet, the moment one wandered close to the back of the building, the steps leading down below to an alley—and the two lower levels of Savage's—were visible.

Lingering in the shadows of the rookeries in the dead of night, they were odd details to note, and yet they were also easier for Lila to focus on than the fact that she stood fifteen paces away from the arena owned and operated by London's most ruthless fighter—Hugh Savage.

Shivering from the cold night, she burrowed deeper into her cloak. Since her hired hack had brought her here earlier that night, she'd been unable to bring herself 'round to facing Savage just yet, and she continued her study of the building.

Savage's was hardly the manner of place to command notice. Neither, however, was the end-unit establishment run-down. Ivy clung to parts of the uneven brick facade. Hanging out front over a narrow entryway door was a crude wood sign with one word painted upon it: SAVAGE'S. The block-shaped letters had been done in a stark red, with crimson paint having dripped down. The apostrophe and lowercase *s* were smaller in size and added as if an afterthought. As if the proprietor sought no approval or validation as a reputable business.

Somewhere in the distance, a lone dog yapped. Those barks cut out and then gave way to a vicious growl, met by another, deeper one, as somewhere in the night, two animals waged a battle of their own.

I can do this . . .

This was not the first time she'd gone out in search of what she wanted. Why, almost two years ago, when she'd made a forcible effort to reenter the living, she'd sought out music lessons from the notorious madam and former performer Clara Winters. And not only had she proven she still had strength enough to venture into the world—even if it had been at night—she'd also rediscovered her love of music.

And in being here? What she stood to gain by visiting Hugh Savage represented something even greater—the ability to look after those she loved.

Each reminder sent strength back into her spine.

Yes, she *could* do this.

Why, Lila had survived the masses attempting to tear her apart. She wore the marks upon her body still from a crowd trampling over her as if she were as insignificant as a bug crawling upon the earth.

That reminder was at last what compelled her to move. Bypassing the front windows she'd peeked within earlier, she started for the steep stairway that led around the back of the three-tiered building. Lila gathered her brown skirts, held them slightly aloft, and began her descent.

One.

Two.

Three—four.

She fixed on counting each uneven step as a way of rechanneling her focus.

And with every rise and fall of her worn leather boots, the tension in Lila's chest eased, and a lightness took its place. There was a buoyancy that lent a frenzied cadence to her steps.

And then her feet touched the bottom.

Hands on her hips, she peered back at the stairs she'd just descended.

She'd done it! She'd left the protective fold of her family's household, hired a hack, journeyed to the rookeries, and battled back her demons.

After making her way to the windows that looked into the arena, she wiped a small space in the filthy glass, and then, with her nose against the window, peered inside.

Her brows came together. A crush of spectators crowded about; they tossed their arms up, shaking their fists as they cheered for a pair of men who approached the center of the room.

A bell rang, and those men . . . those fighters proceeded to trade jabs and blows. The shorter, stockier of the pair let fly a quick punch, but the spectators surged, concealing that inevitable strike.

Lila's smile froze on her face.

There were so many people.

So . . . *many.*

Her skin went clammy.

Screams from a time long ago crashed about her in a cacophony with the shouting on the other side of those murky panels.

And Lila bit her lower lip until the metallic tinge of blood flooded her nostrils and senses.

"Kill 'em," someone bellowed in a booming voice that shook Savage's dirtied windowpanes.

"Stand down! I'll kill the lot of you . . ."

Lila spun so quickly she staggered, and came down. She shot her hands out, managing to keep from pitching forward on her face. She balanced on her haunches and stared at the now slightly ripped gloves. Under that smooth leather, her palms grew moist. Perspiration dotted her brow and wound a path down her face as she was once more that girl in Manchester.

Another wave of shouts went up from the establishment five paces away, and she bit the inside of her cheek to keep back a moan.

The noise.

Sweat slicked her skin, and she concentrated on breathing.

And yet, as fresh as the memories were still, she may as well be trapped in the past, where darkness dwelled and screams ricocheted like the recoil of gunfire. Repeating over. And over.

Do not think about it.

Do not let the thoughts in.

Because when she turned herself over to these memories and emotions, there was no saying how long she'd be trapped in that hell . . . and she could not afford to lose her wits, particularly here. Not when her visit to this place represented a pathway to being the protector her sister and nephew needed.

Lila concentrated on drawing in small, slow breaths until the memories retreated.

She'd not expected the noise. Nor, for that matter, had she expected at this early-morn hour there'd be a crowd within.

For if she had, she couldn't have come. Not even in the name of protecting her nephew or sister.

Closing her eyes, Lila spit; her saliva darkened the stone, and she stared at it to give herself something to focus on rather than the nausea churning in her gut.

"Kill 'em . . . Kill 'em dead!"

The screams from Manchester melded with the rougher Cockneys of Savage and his patrons. They all rolled together so that Lila couldn't untangle which voices belonged to her past, and which to this moment.

She clamped her hands over her ears, curling her fingers hard into her head in a bid to claw out those distractions. They were ones she didn't need now. Not ever, really, but certainly not now.

Time crept by, and through it Lila warred with herself, searching in a vacuous void for strength and courage.

She'd been wrong. She couldn't do this.

This is a mistake.

Chapter 4

The stranger had returned.

And it *wasn't*, as his partner had predicted, a patron.

Hugh stiffened. The voyeur's pale, whitewashed face stood in stark contrast to the mud-splattered windows, long in need of cleaning. He sharpened his gaze on his subject.

Many of the spectators who set foot inside Savage's were as fascinated as they were repelled by the violence on display between fighters.

This would not be the first time someone had thrown up at the establishment.

It would, however, be the first time a *woman* got sick outside that window, watching a match.

The arena erupted into another roar, calling Hugh's attention back to the fight in progress. And by the way the small, scrappy fighter, Robert Tibbs, stumbled around on his feet, the match was nearly at an end. That hint of an end only added to the fervor belting throughout the room.

A shout rose out higher than the others in the arena. "Punch 'im, you bastard. Knock 'im on 'is arse."

Not taking his eyes from the stranger, Hugh started through the crowd.

His quarry had ducked away from the window, but the fabric of her cloak continued to announce her presence.

He shouldered his way through the squeeze of spectators.

The patrons remained wholly engrossed in the bloody battle before them. His lips curled in a cold smile. That was, however, the way of the world. When they focused on their pleasure, everything else was forgotten.

Hugh reached the back of the arena and let himself outside.

A cool blast of air hit him in the face, at odds with the stifling heat from within, as bloody welcome as it always was, following his escape from the din.

Some men flourished amidst the shows of violence that played out here night after night. From the moment he'd traded his years of service to the King's Army for a life in this hall, Hugh had been the anomaly to every last man to walk through these doors: he abhorred the crowds that assembled. Everything about this place, the raucous screams and shouts, harkened back to another place . . . another time . . .

Outside, away from the din, there was freedom.

At least for now.

Part of him more than half expected the late-night guest had already gone. That she'd been one of many curious passersby, looking to steal a glimpse of what unfolded in Savage's.

He immediately found her.

The moonlight did her no favors this night. The perfectly formed circle hanging in the sky cast a bright glow over her.

The fabric of her cloak was fine, the quality and cut belonging to no one who dwelled in these parts. The footwear that peeked out from under the hem revealed serviceable, sturdy boots better suited to a maid. As such, with her back to him as it was, her station remained a mystery. As did her age.

As did her presence here.

Eyes closed, she leaned against the side of his building like one who needed the support of the structure to keep herself standing.

No. She wasn't of these parts. Not with her inability to detect a man standing just paces away. Not with her complete obliviousness.

Then, as if making a liar of him and everything he believed, she opened her eyes and pushed the hood of her cloak back. Just a fraction, but enough to reveal the sizable scar that slashed down the middle of her forehead. Like a jagged bolt of lightning, the mark, faded white, revealed the injury to have been a long-ago one. Nay, hers wasn't the flawless skin belonging to a lady.

"Hullo," she said quietly, speaking like one who'd known he was there the entire time and had bided her time, had waited for the moment to greet him.

And with just two syllables flawlessly delivered, crisp and clear, she confirmed one of the questions he'd had this night—she wasn't from the rookeries.

Or . . . mayhap, with her proper King's English, she was like Hugh . . . an oddity in these parts.

He edged a stare over her. The woman was a riddle, a mystery cloaked in the night's shadows, and the only thing more dangerous than a woman of known origins was a mysterious woman of unknown ones. "Evening." Reaching into his jacket, he withdrew the matches from inside and struck one of those unpredictable ends.

It sparked, a large bright flame formed, and he touched it to his cheroot. Shaking the match, he dropped it to the cobblestones and stomped it under his boot.

"What are those?"

It took a moment to register she was making small talk.

"Matches."

And Hugh, who'd become adept at reading all people, found himself wholly unable to make out a single thing about this peculiar stranger before him.

Cries went up from within Savage's, and the lady whipped her head back toward the fight unfolding. Swiftly jerking herself away from the window, she slumped against the building once more. Her breath hitched, a noisy little sound that could have been a gasp or hiccup.

"You going to be sick on me?" he asked around his cheroot.

"No." Her voice emerged faint and pathetically weak. "Well, not on you, per se."

He sought for a hint of a jest, but by the waxen hue of her skin and the way she clenched her eyes tight, she spoke plainly. Hugh took another draw from his cheroot. He'd had plenty of moments like the one now facing the young woman before him. In this place, too. It was one of the reasons he'd begun smoking cheroots in the first place. When the past got all mixed up in his mind with the present, and his breath came fast like this woman's before him, he'd used cheroots to pace his breathing.

Joining the mysterious stranger, he came forward with the cheroot out. "Here."

The young woman hesitated and then deliberately pushed the hood of her cloak back.

Her lashes fluttered, as if it were a struggle to open those lids, and then she did.

Hugh froze as he took in the details which her hood had previously concealed. Her eyes. It was her eyes he noted first. They were a spellbinding blend of gold and copper and peach, a brown that didn't know which to settle on and so had melded every variation in between.

"What am I to do with that?"

Pulled back from that fanciful musing, he took a final draw before offering it over once more. "You smoke it."

He expected her—a woman more refined than the sort he kept company with—to turn her nose up in distaste, but then . . . she was here, wasn't she? As such, unsurprisingly, the young woman collected the cheroot and brought it to her mouth. Hesitating, she looked up at him.

"Inhale." He demonstrated the motion.

She took a pull, and then color blazed to life on her cheeks as she descended into a paroxysm of coughing. As she choked, he surveyed the area for others. Only shadows graced the back of his establishment. She'd come here . . . alone. For what purpose? To steal a look at the barbaric fights inside? She'd certainly not be the first. Those of her lofty station had a perverse interest in how the other half lived. Hugh and his ilk were oddities for their viewing pleasure.

The moment she'd managed to get the rise and fall of her chest settled into an even cadence, she took another small inhale. This time, she coughed only lightly.

"Thank you," she said softly, as if she were thanking a fine lord for a cup of tea and not one of East London's most ruthless street fighters for a scrap of smoke. She made no move to return his cheroot. Instead, she puffed away on it like she'd been doing it the whole of her life.

He passed an assessing gaze over her. He couldn't make out her form, which was swallowed by the folds of her heavy-looking brown cloak. But he'd place her somewhere near twenty-five. Not a child. A woman grown.

From within the arena, cheers erupted as another winner for the night was crowned.

There'd be no break between matches. They three—he, Bragger, and Maynard—made their coin by the number of fights, and any rest in action meant a decline in profits.

When he looked back at the odd nighttime visitor, he found her with her eyes clenched shut once more, puffing away at his cheroot. "What brings you here?" When she clearly had no wish to be.

It was a sentiment he connected with all too well. In fact, mayhap that was why he remained chatting with her now.

His question managed to bring her eyes open once more.

She stared not at Hugh but rather the flaming tip of the cheroot. "I'm looking for someone."

Ah. With that, the quiet stranger directed her attention back to his window.

She craned her head back and forth, skimming her gaze over the crowded arena. "Do you know the people in there?" Her breathing rasped loud in the night.

So it wasn't simply the cat's curiosity that had brought her out. She sought one of the patrons. If it wasn't a morbid fascination with stealing a glimpse of the ruthless world at play behind the panels of Savage's that brought strangers here, it was the quest to rescue a *respectable* family member from the den of depravity and evil. "Some," he allowed. It was an absolute lie. Hugh knew each and every man who stepped within the doors of Savage's. "Is it a brother?" he hazarded.

There were several beats of silence before the young woman seemed to register that question. "Hmm?" Even so, she made no attempt to answer him. Her cheeks whitewashed, she just continued on with her distracted but determined search.

"Are you looking to bring your brother home?" He paused. "Or is it a husband?" After all, she was of the age that she'd be married by now, to some fancy merchant, perhaps.

"I . . ." This time, she quit her exploration and looked back in Hugh's direction. That vague blankness of her earlier stare had returned. Her eyes belonged to the haunted. Hugh knew. They were the same ones that had been reflected back in a mirror every day of his life. "No." She took one more effortless draw of his cheroot and then held out that half-finished scrap. Taking it back, he folded his arms and took another draw of his own, then languidly exhaled. He eyed her over the cloud of white. "I don't have family in there."

And yet her search of the fighting ring was purposeful. Patience with her, her presence here, and their exchange at an end, he took a step toward her. "What's your name?"

She eyed him warily. "My name is Lila."

Lila. That was all. Delicate and soft, it rather suited the ashen figure lurking outside his place. "Lila *what*?"

"It doesn't matter." The chit had a healthy modicum of unease. It's likely why she hadn't already been killed in her jaunt through the rookeries. Neither was she a coward. She jerked her gaze back to the fighting ring.

Aye, it mattered. "You're lurking 'round a fighting ring in the rookeries? I say it does." Nor did she get to go invading his territory and thinking she had a right to any secrets.

He'd hand it to her—any other person would have been run off in a rightful terror.

She hesitated but remained fixed to his cobblestones.

"Go home, Flittermouse." He crushed his cheroot under the heel of his boot and ground it into a loose cobblestone. "You don't belong here."

"Perhaps not, but neither can I leave."

Her threadbare admission held him in place. Hugh faced her once more. The young woman tangled her fingers in the fabric of her heavy brown cloak. "I'm looking to speak to someone." Her shoulders shook slightly as she stole a glance over her shoulder at the inside of the fighting ring. "He's in there. As I said before. He's n-not a relative." She spoke quickly, whipping her gaze back as if she couldn't bear the sight of the violence unfolding within. Nor should she. Only the hardest men with the most deadened souls knew what to make of those displays of savagery. "Just someone I have business with."

Interesting. And he found his lips pulling at the corners; the muscles of his mouth strained and protested that foreign movement. A smile. Who would have believed him capable of that damned expression anymore? "Trust me, Flittermouse. There's no one in there you have business with." Be they the street fighters who honed their skills and practiced them upon the other street fighters or the lords who tossed good coin to watch those bloody displays, neither of those sorts were ones she could or should have any dealings with. "Get out of here before you find yourself hurt," he said with a gentleness that would have earned the unending hilarity of every last man inside that fight club.

If possible, her already pale cheeks turned two shades whiter, leaving her eyes wide, stark brown pools of terror. "I can't," she whispered, her voice haunted.

It wasn't his business. *She* wasn't his business. Nothing good could come from some fancy lord's daughter or wife or sister darkening his doorway. But it was also wiser to know just why she'd come, and whom she sought. "Who are you looking for?"

"One of the proprietors."

He straightened. What business did she have with Maynard or Bragger? "Which one?"

She wetted her lips. "Hugh Savage."

Well, this proved even *more* interesting. Hugh hooded his eyes and kept his features in a careful mask. She wouldn't be the first person to assume that Hugh was a proprietor here. Previously "Bragger's," they'd changed the name to Savage's as a nod to their lead fighter, who put spectators in their seats. Beyond the use of his name, Hugh had no claims to this place. "Trust me, you do not have any business with him." That he could say with a definitive certainty.

"No," she agreed. "Not yet. But . . . I intend to. There's something I have to speak with him about." Hope flared in her painfully revealing and also too-clever eyes. "You know him."

"I didn't say that," he said, noncommittal, and not missing a beat.

"You're here," she pointed out. She waved at the building behind them. "You must know the men in there. Particularly the owners of the place? There are three of them?"

Hers was a question, one that he ignored. "I know Savage doesn't take business meetings with strangers." He flicked a gaze over her. "And particularly not with women when he's in the middle of a fight. As such"—he cocked his head toward the stairway that emptied out onto Whitechapel—"I suggest you don't waste your time with him."

Instead of taking the very pointed directive, she returned to the window. Angling her head left and right, she surveyed the crowd on display in the fighting ring below. "Is he one of the fighters in there, then?" she asked, desperation underscoring her words.

"He doesn't want your kind about," he said, flatly ignoring her question.

With that, he stepped around her and started back toward the fight club.

In a startling display of temerity at odds with her earlier terror, the woman rushed over and blocked his path. "You can't speak for what he wants or doesn't want."

"Trust me," he said coolly. "I feel comfortable saying I can. Hugh Savage is a ruthless bastard." A memory flashed across his mind's eye. Flickers of passages. Moments. Spliced apart. Different fields. All running with blood. "He's cut men down, for sport and not." As he spoke, the color continued leaching from her high cheekbones. Pressing his advantage on her fear, he went on speaking. "As a rule, he doesn't deal with women. And especially not polite ladies who've no place being where you are now."

Instead of being driven back by the frost in his tone, the lady stepped closer. Her eyes lingered on his beard, and she peered intently at him. "It is you," she whispered. "You're *him*."

Hugh silently cursed.

The crowd roared again as a winner was announced. Which meant it was also time for the next match to commence. "What do you want?"

The lady dampened her mouth, the pink flesh of her tongue darting out, tracing the seam; it was a display of unease that, at the same time, proved erotic, drawing his focus to that flesh disproportionate in size—a slightly fuller upper lip, a narrower bottom. Yet interesting enough to command notice. Much like the woman herself.

"I want to hire you."

It took a moment to register her words. "You want . . ."

"To hire you," she said on a rush, and then reaching inside her jacket, she tossed a heavy purse at his feet and took a hasty step away.

And a memory slipped in . . . of a masked woman on the arm of a patron at the fight society. From behind the black velvet strip concealing her identity, her eyes gleamed. *Clink-Clink-Clink. Kill him, you filthy street bastard.*

That husked voice of long ago would haunt him until he drew his last breath.

"Did you just throw money at me?" he asked on a steely whisper.

The lady troubled at her lower lip. "I . . . yes. I did."

He stared down at that little velvet sack brimming with coin. Fury slithered around inside. "First, Flittermouse, don't ever throw money at me, is that clear?" he asked, gliding toward her, and she continued retreating. "Ever."

In her haste to get away from him, the damned lady didn't reveal so much as a hint of awareness of her surroundings.

Hugh shot an arm out, and she released a cry, her arms coming up protectively about her head.

Cursing, Hugh caught her around the middle just as she would've toppled backward.

Horror wreathed her pale features.

He stuck his face close to hers. "Second, I don't fight for pay." These days, every bare-knuckle match was born of loyalty, each fight fought for the benefit of his partners, the pair who'd taken him in. Beyond that, he'd not an interest anymore in maiming or killing another soul. Turning them about, he directed her slight frame toward the street. "Now, get out."

The woman stumbled a step, then caught herself.

Hugh headed for the door.

"You misunderstood," she called back. "I don't want to hire you as a fighter." There was a pause.

"Good night, Flittermouse," he said, not breaking his stride.

"Please!" Panic brought the young woman's voice creeping up several notches. "I want you to teach me how to fight."

Chapter 5

THE LONDON INQUISITOR

No one can beat Hugh Savage. In his history of fighting, no one did. As such, there's not been a match worthy of mentioning since he left the ring.

M. Fairpoint

Lila had managed the seemingly impossible: to stop Hugh Savage in his tracks.

Only, with his broad back to her and the memory of his icy rage, it had all become jumbled in her mind as to whether she actually *wanted* Hugh Savage to remain.

Lila's heart hammered a sickening rhythm in her breast.

She'd angered him. The bold slash of his lips, turned down at the corners in a scowl, had left no doubt as to his feelings. Everything inside her said to flee.

And yet she'd done it. She'd not only found Hugh Savage, but she'd spoken with the notorious fighter and put her request to him. Some of it anyway.

And she was still standing. For nine years, she'd hidden from the world and avoided interactions with men of all stations, only to find herself capable of coming to the rookeries and requesting the services of a man known for his lethality.

No, she'd not brought him around to agreeing to work with her. In fact, since her pronouncement, he'd not so much as uttered another word, neither accepting nor denying her request for services. But she hadn't fainted or fled, and somehow she'd spoken evenly with him, and with that came a triumphant thrill inside.

He turned back. "What did you say to me?"

A lone cloud moved overhead, obscuring the moon and dousing Hugh Savage's face in shadows, and there was something even more terrifying about engaging him in the dark. For at least with some light between them, she could see the threat before her. She could have it illuminated and wasn't left with the panic of guessing at his sentiments.

Twisting her fingers in the fabric of her cloak, Lila hovered where he'd all but thrown her moments ago. "I came here to learn about what you do."

"What I . . . do?"

She tried—and failed—to make anything from that echo of a question. Clearing her throat, she went on. "In . . . there." Not bringing herself to look at the place behind them, she gestured vaguely with her palm. "And I'd like to ask you to provide me with basic instruction."

He shook his head.

"On how to fight, that is." Even gentlemen like her brother-in-law, who'd trained at boxing, could be taken down. But this man? "According to the papers, you're undefeated." Learning from one such as him would see her equipped with the skills she needed to care for those she loved, when she had failed not only herself but also the friend she'd dragged along with her to Peterloo.

Did she imagine the upward tilt of his lips? Or was that more of the night's shadows at play? For when the cloud cover lifted and the earth again bathed him in pale-white light, not so much as a hint of emotion flickered across his face.

"This is certainly a first," he murmured.

Nay, Lila didn't expect it was customary for a lady of the peerage to journey to the rookeries and put such requests to the legendary street fighter. Why, before her sister-in-law, Clara, proprietress of the Muses music hall, Lila had never known that a woman could ever be anything other than a wife . . . or an unmarried spinster. "I don't see why that should be the case," she said softly. "Too often women find themselves prey—of their husband, of brigands on the street. Why should they not seek you out?"

"Because women generally have sense enough to know not to tangle with the Devil," he said on a silken whisper.

He was trying to terrify her.

And it is working . . .

Refusing to give in to the warning bells clamoring loudly in her mind, urging her to flee, Lila made herself look at the monster of a man across from her. Truly look at him. Not unlike her, he bore the marks of life. But he'd never been taken down. Not as she had. And he'd also triumphed to become king of this underground empire. "You don't look like any Devil," she finally said. "You may as well be any man, Mr. Savage."

A cold laugh shook his frame. "And that is why you'd be wise to go, Flittermouse. You wouldn't know danger if it leapt out and took a bite of that pretty face."

There were two erroneous statements there:

One, he assumed she knew nothing of danger. He was dead wrong on that score.

And two, he'd called her pretty.

Mayhap the dark of night concealed her enough to hide the marks upon her own skin. Or mayhap he hadn't looked closely enough at her. Scarred upon her face and legs as she was, none would ever dare mistake her for any degree of pretty.

"No, you're not so very scary, Mr. Savage," she murmured. For one who had lived on the streets, he sounded a good deal more like the gentlemen she'd once conversed with, once upon a lifetime ago, during her first—and last—London Season.

His eyes thinned, forming narrow, impenetrable slits. "Why do I think you're trying to convince yourself as much, Flittermouse?"

Mayhap because Lila was, and Hugh Savage was correct in that she merely sought reassurance in his clipped tones. The ones that were familiar, and if not safe, safer than the harsher, coarser ones that haunted her still. Either way, she'd come here to begin a new future and didn't intend to be turned away. "I'm prepared to offer you a sizable sum."

It was the wrong thing to say. A foolish reminder of the misstep she'd made moments ago. Hugh Savage's gaze slipped from her to the bag—forgotten until now—on the ground between them. When his eyes again found hers, that steely, unforgiving smile hovered on his lips. "I don't give lessons. Ask one of your male relatives."

She held a palm up. "I don't have a family member who might teach me." Her brother, Henry, had spent most of his life being proper and never engaging in anything that might be deemed dangerous or scandalous. With the exception of his recent marriage to a former courtesan, he'd lived an otherwise dull and sheltered life. And even with that, he'd never dare support the manner of venture which Lila intended. "Those I know are people who've largely lived sheltered existences," she settled for.

"Stick to those people," he said bluntly. "Trust me, Flittermouse, you don't have any business around these parts. You wouldn't know what to do with anything but 'safe.'" He shook his head. "You wouldn't *want* to deal with anything except safe."

"You are correct on that score." She couldn't stop the painful twist of her lips. "Both of them." Only, Hugh Savage made assumptions about what Lila had—or had not—endured. He assumed hers had been a sheltered existence. That fateful day in Manchester, however, had shown her just how much out of her control the actions of the world around her were. "Furthermore, I believe that is the point, Mr. Savage." As a girl she'd been insulated from danger. "That is why I've come to you." It had taken but one fateful day to realize no one was immune to peril; it could and ultimately did visit those of every station. As such, "safe" wasn't what she required. It wasn't what she needed. But it was what she intended to help make the world. "Mr. Savage?" She paused. "Is that your real name?"

"Does it matter, Lila-With-No-Last-Name?"

Fair enough. "I don't suppose it does," she allowed.

"You're a woman who wants to learn to fight. Do yourself a favor and visit Gentleman Jackson's clubs."

Gentleman Jackson had taught her brother-in-law—and in those lessons had failed Norman. Nay, it had to be the Savage Gentleman, one who'd neither failed nor been felled.

What she needed to learn couldn't be taught by some gentleman. She'd equip herself with the skills to look after those she loved, as she'd been unable to do for her friend that day at Peterloo. "He doesn't possess the manner of knowledge I require." She shook her head. "It has to be you."

"Me."

His statement didn't have the uptilt of a question, and yet she nodded anyway. Lila needed one who'd learned how to survive in the roughest of worlds. Hugh Savage hadn't just managed to live but rather had thrived, the king of an empire on the fringe of civilization . . . As such, he could survive anything.

"There're three owners here; how'd you settle on me?" He pinned a hard stare on her, and she shifted under the force of it. "It's because they call me the Savage Gentleman, isn't it?"

She prayed the dark concealed the guilty blush heating up her cheeks. "No."

"No," he said flatly.

When she'd come here, seeking him out, she'd not allowed herself to think she'd secure anything but his agreement.

Either way, she'd been overconfident in the outcome of this meeting.

"It has to be you," she said softly.

For there were no other options. Not in terms of learning from the most skilled. Her brother-in-law had boxed . . . and been killed for it. Her brother had been beaten and nearly killed in the streets. Gentlemen ruled the world. But they didn't know anything about it. Not truly.

Oh, with their tutors since the nursery and their Oxford educations, those high-ranking members of Polite Society knew the laws and the rules of society. But they didn't know anything outside that safe, protected sphere they moved so comfortably within.

No, those privileged peers didn't know how to live a life of any real meaning, and more importantly, they didn't know how to survive. She recognized a survivor, and only wanted to learn from one.

Hugh Savage remained on the steps, staring back at her with such a piercing intensity that it should have roused a deserved terror.

Anything could happen to her here. *Anything.*

And certainly at the hands of a man rumored to have killed for fun. An admission Hugh Savage himself had made. So why didn't he inspire the same fear in Lila that nearly every other person incited?

Why, when he was more than a foot taller, his garments straining under heavy muscles, and his skin scarred and marred with ink, did she feel . . . comfortable? Unwittingly, her gaze went to the slight gape in his shirt, the place where a cravat should be, but where instead only bronzed skin, tufts of hair, and crimson-and-black ink peeked out.

"I'm not a bare-knuckle instructor," he finally said.

"I'm not looking for an instructor, per se, but rather, a fighter to teach me what he knows." About strength. About how to not be knocked down, and about how to help people who *were.* How to take down a man who'd hurt those she loved or those who needed protecting. Or herself.

"That's an instructor," he said flatly. "And if I was," he went on as if she hadn't spoken, "I'm not going to be doling out lessons in the night when my ring is in the middle of a fight, Flittermouse."

Flittermouse.

There it was again.

And Lila decided that was it . . . That peculiar term of endearment was what made him . . . human . . . and not a monster, and what made her able to face him here alone. "I see." She fiddled with her skirts. "I'm sorry for having taken you away from your boxing match."

"Fight. It's a fight."

Did he think that clarification would unleash panic in her heart? It was a reminder of how little he or the whole world knew of her, or the hell that all people, regardless of station, were capable of enduring. "You have my assurance that I'll not interfere with the regular course of your business affairs. Until another time."

"There isn't going to be another time."

He might think that was the case. She gathered up her purse and started from the alley. Mr. Hugh Savage had been clear he didn't want company in the night when he was in the middle of his work.

That was fine.

She'd cede that, but she had every intention of securing his assistance.

Some thirty minutes later, Lila found her way back to her sister's home, and not even bothering with a sleep that would not come, she made her way to Sylvia's library.

Freeing the clasp of her cloak, she released the garment and set it down along the back of a leather button sofa. The floorboards groaned and creaked as she walked, assessing the row of floor-to-ceiling shelving. She silently mouthed the name of each title as she went through the still-unfamiliar inventory.

"Flittermouse. Flittermouse," she repeated quietly. Why had he called her by that name?

She skimmed row after row, and stopped.

A General System of Nature by Carl Linnaeus.

Lila plucked the book off the shelf and read the title page. Tucking the tome under her elbow, she resumed her search.

Mr. Sav—nay, she'd not think of him by that surname. Hugh. Hugh was a good deal less intimidating than having a name such as Savage. Either way, the man should have been a good deal more specific as to when his fight business took place. Though in fairness, she very well should have asked him at which point he concluded his nightly business. Nay, instead, she'd proven as tongue-tied and meek as she'd been for so long, struggling to get out a proper question past the fear that too often paralyzed her.

"Weak ninny," she mumbled under her breath. Lila grabbed another book by Linnaeus, *Animalia Paradoxa*.

Setting it aside, she continued on in her search. Lila filled her arms and took up a place on the sofa beside the now cold hearth. Stretching out her legs, she lay down and made quick work of the written words. That ability to read swiftly and recall the details upon the pages was a skill that had come from all the books she'd read over the years. As such, she dropped completed book after completed book back atop the sloppy pedestal table, and became fully engrossed by the next.

Bat, called also by us lapwing, and—

Lila abruptly sat up.

Flittermouse. The flittermouse is a four-footed beast of the ravenous kind. It much resembles a mouse . . .

During the winter, bats cover themselves with their wings and hang asleep in dry caves. During the summer, they hide themselves in the day, and flutter about in the evening . . .

Lila's fingers curled reflexively, her short nails leaving little crescents upon the pages. That was how the world saw her . . . Her family. Polite Society. It was also how Lila had seen herself for so long, too. She knew precisely what she'd become, and why . . . and that knowing had brought her both to a plan for her future, as well as to Hugh Savage's establishment.

But there was something in knowing that the man whose assistance she now sought should have so quickly, and so adeptly, formed that same opinion after just a handful of moments when she'd embarked on the bravest—albeit stupidest—act she'd taken part in since Peterloo. "Flittermouse," she muttered.

"You're awake."

Lila gasped; the book tumbled from her fingers and hit the floor with a sharp *thwack*.

Sylvia hovered at the doorway, dressed in her black widow's weeds, just as she'd been for the two years since her husband had been killed. "May I join you?" her sister asked when Lila still didn't say anything.

"I . . ." She'd rather Sylvia didn't. Nor was it simply guilt that drove that desire. "Of course." Sylvia and Lila had been the best of friends the whole of their lives, but after Peterloo Lila had forgotten how to be around her family. She'd forgotten how to be around all people. The only exchanges she had some success in navigating were those she was in control of. Because then she could prepare and script, and there came less uncertainty than existed with spontaneous meetings.

As Sylvia claimed the edge of the upholstered rosewood chair, she paused to gather the book Lila had dropped.

From the corner of her eye, Lila's gaze snagged on her damning cloak. Keeping her gaze fixed on Sylvia, Lila pushed the article onto the floor behind the chair, where it landed with a noisy rustle.

Sylvia whipped her head up. "What's a flittermouse?"

Befuddled, Lila shook her head.

"I thought I heard you mention it when I entered."

"I . . . uh . . . they're bats. I'd never heard of them before," Lila lamely settled for. Hoping her sister wouldn't press her further. Grateful when she didn't. Relieved when Sylvia instead set the book aside.

Sylvia's expression was wistful and more than slightly sad.

"I received this today." Reaching inside the pocket of her dress, she drew out a note. "It's an invitation," she said as Lila took the thick ivory vellum.

Pleasure Ball,

"While we Live, Let us Live . . . !"

Lady Sylvia

Is requested to attend the masquerade at Barton's Hall on Thursday, 26th of May, current at eight p.m.

"While we Live, Let us Live . . . !"

Lila's lips quirked up in a sad smile. They were perfect words for a family who'd been riddled by grief. "Your in-laws," she said needlessly, refolding the invitation.

Leading host and hostess of Polite Society, the Marquess and Marchioness of Prendergast had retreated these nearly two years since their eldest son's passing.

"I was angry at first," Sylvia confided. "How dare they think to host a gala so very close to Norman's death, and then it occurred to me . . ." Her sister studied the invitation in her hands. "It *is* nearly two years."

Then it dawned on her—*this* was why her sister had sought her out. This wasn't about Sylvia's in-laws, but rather Sylvia herself.

A range of emotion tugged at Lila's breast: joy for her sister, who'd been so very bereft since she'd been widowed and was now just finding her way out. But there was also . . . a bittersweet sadness to it. A sense of being left behind, as her sister and the world continued on and carried on while Lila remained shuttered in the shadows. Hiding from her demons.

And curse her selfish soul, there'd been solace in Lila not being alone in her misery.

She looked up. "And what do you think about the marchioness throwing their masquerade?" That garish, lavish, glittering event everyone sought an invitation to. Lila had attended but once, and long, long ago. Then, the event had been so very exciting; she and Annalee had been carefree and overjoyed that night. Now, the idea of those crowds and the raucous noise of the revelers was enough to leave Lila sick.

Annalee, however, was even more vibrant than she'd been then.

"I know what you're thinking," her sister said, a defensive edge to her tone that brought Lila back to the present. "You think they shouldn't have something so extravagant." Sylvia stared sadly at the empty hearth. "It was Norman's favorite event that they hosted."

"Do you . . . wish to go?" Lila asked, holding her breath, dreading the answer.

Tears filled Sylvia's eyes, and she angled her head toward the hearth. "I don't know." When she looked back once more, the moisture had gone, and all that remained was the perpetually sad glimmer within their blue depths. "I mean, I shouldn't. It would be wrong to attend . . ." She paused and looked to Lila once more. "Wouldn't it?"

Her stomach lurched. *Oh, God . . .* Her sister wanted her to join those wild festivities.

Scratch-Scratch-Scratch.

They both looked to the doorway.

"You said to come whenever the little master awoke, my lady," the young nursemaid said, coming forward with Sylvia's babe.

Sylvia was already out of her seat. "There you are, my love," she greeted her son. She stretched her arms out and scooped the plump child from the girl's hands. Her sister cooed, and the little boy answered with a giggle. "Ma-Ma-Ma."

As the maid dipped a curtsy and left, Lila stared on, a silent observer to mother and babe. And from the distance came memories of another mother and another child.

"Please, take her. Take her with you . . . Take my chiiild . . ."

"Lila?" Sylvia's hesitant query cut through that terror.

I'm here. I'm in London . . . Not safe. But here. That litany rolled around her mind; it stabilized her heart until the organ beat a normal cadence. "I'll do it," Lila blurted before her courage deserted her.

Sylvia didn't so much as blink.

"I'll join you at the marchioness's masquerade," Lila confirmed.

Her sister clutched a fist to her chest. "I . . . I . . . am so very happy."

One of them was.

And as Lila sat there, watching as Sylvia and Vallen played, there was only one certainty . . . Lila had let Annalee down by not being strong enough to save either of them. She'd not fail anyone else. She needed to be strong and prepared, not just for herself but for all those she loved.

Hugh Savage had been insistent that he'd not help her. With Sylvia's impending plans for them, however, Lila had no intention of accepting anything but his capitulation.

Chapter 6

"Ya were weak with Dooley."

That morn, as he went about cleaning the arena, Hugh knew better than to rise to Maynard's baiting. "I didn't see much reason to add a beating to him. Killing him before we get the information you seek isn't going to get you anything more than another dead body."

"Us."

Hugh glanced up from the benches he was wiping down.

Maynard settled a hard, narrow-eyed stare on him. "Don't you mean 'us'?"

"Aye. Us . . ." Because that was the truth. After he'd returned from war, hungry and begging for coin, they'd rescued him. That was a debt that could be paid only after he helped where he could to bring the rest to justice . . . and in that, hopefully atone in even a small way for Valerie's disappearance.

"We're afraid yar gettin' rusty," Maynard said, stretching his left arm across his chest.

"Losing yar edge," Bragger chimed in from across the room.

Their words . . . their discourse in harmony, even with the pair standing at the opposite ends of the arena, couldn't be a coincidence.

Warning bells jingled.

"I train daily," Hugh said carefully.

Bragger and Maynard exchanged looks.

Folding his arms at his chest, Bragger spoke. "Training ain't the same as actual fighting . . ." That booming echo pinged around the empty hall.

His partners converged, both stalking over until they flanked Hugh.

"Bragger ain't wrong. Ya *ain't* 'ad a turn in the ring, Savage. In . . . 'ow long's it been?"

"Two weeks, now?" Maynard provided when Hugh didn't respond.

"Three," Hugh murmured. It'd been three weeks since he'd been asked to step into the ring and beat another man into oblivion. A twenty-one-day *reprieve*. For that's all it ultimately was . . . a reprieve. This one had been longer than the others, and he'd managed to convince himself that maybe he was done. That they'd stop thrusting him into the ring and absolve him of his debt at last.

"Hmph," Bragger said, noncommittal. "That's a long time to not step into a ring. Join me, Savage." Those three words would never be misconstrued as anything other than the order they were.

Aye, because that's what he did . . . he answered to these men.

No different from an indentured servant, paying off a debt that could never be paid.

Hugh made one more attempt. "I've got the cleaning to see to," he said. The upkeep of the arena had been the other thankless job that had been passed on to him upon his arrival years earlier. Aside from the occasional street urchin they'd pay a few pence to, that work had stayed in Hugh's hands. Even so, it was far preferable to fighting.

Maynard spit out a mouthful of saliva, staining the floor Hugh had just swept. "Cleaning is a waste when ya still 'ave good foighting years in ya."

Hugh ignored him. Instead, he dusted a rag down a crude bench soaked in spirits that some spectator had spilled. *Except, is Maynard really wrong?* Fighting was all Hugh knew. He hated what he was. Attempting to escape that lifestyle, he'd walked away before, and only found himself mired in even greater death and misery.

Ultimately, Bragger cut right to it. "Profits are down. If we're going to 'ire Steele loike ya suggested, we're gonna need to pay 'im."

"It wouldn't be wise to expect I'm to be the only draw. There've got to be others." Some poor romantic fool who glorified the *sport*.

Maynard's mouth tensed. "But there aren't *now*, Savage. Not any fighter who's going to draw patrons in."

Hugh's stomach muscles knotted.

There is no way around it.

They'd not rest until he stepped into the ring and battered another desperate man for a bloodthirsty crowd's pleasure. He'd contentedly clean spit and blood off the floor before putting himself through that. But what other choice did he have?

He couldn't walk away. He'd done that years ago, and left Maynard, Bragger, Valerie . . . and so many others to their fates. And upon Hugh's return . . . how had the pair of proprietors responded to that past betrayal? Not with resentment or loathing. Instead, they'd taken him in. They'd been there for him at his worst.

"Let's 'ave a go with me in the ring," Bragger repeated. This time, it was a clear command issued, and the evil that surely ran in Hugh's blood jeered him for wanting to turn and unleash all the frustration at his failings and ties that bound him into a fight.

And what was worse? This hungering to face the bigger, broader man. Because of the hold he had over Hugh. Because of the debt Hugh would always owe him. But then, that was the soul of a fighter, no matter how much one might wish it, or how much one disavowed the battle, there were moments when the primal instincts reared and a man couldn't separate himself from what he was.

Bragger grinned as Hugh shed his jacket and shirt, tossing them at a nearby hook.

It was hard to say how many times and to how many men Hugh had sold his soul, but there was no doubt Bragger had been one of them.

Whether he liked it or not, he was indebted to them for the future they'd saved him from, and the one they'd given him.

Hugh joined the other fighter at the center of the ring.

Head back, one arm held closer to his body, the other lead hand extended, Hugh kept a careful eye on his opponent.

No matter their size, the trick to besting a man in any fight came down to one specific detail—attention.

Focus. Concentration.

It was a fact not known to most of the fighters who battled with their bare knuckles on the streets or in fighting rings.

All of it.

The pain.

Jab-Jab—Uppercut.

The loss.

"Ya 'ad any thoughts about wot we could do to turn our profits around?" Bragger asked as they stepped around each other. His raised arms and focused gaze belied the conversational quality to his tone.

Hugh didn't take his eyes off Bragger's elevated fists. "I'm sure you've had thoughts yourself." He landed a sharp jab to the other man's flat stomach.

Bragger grunted but remained otherwise unfazed. "Aye, Oi 'ave. Ya'll fill the arena. Ya always do."

And there it was. Even expected as it'd been, Hugh was caught off balance.

Bragger pounced, shooting a fist out and catching him in the jaw.

Staggering under the force of that blow, Hugh swiftly righted himself and then danced away from his opponent, giving himself a moment to recover.

Once he had his legs under him, he danced back toward the middle of the floor. "The ring's mismanaged." It had been since Hugh had set foot inside years earlier. It was also Bragger's weakness. This place. For all hope of Bragger finding his sister was tied to it.

The head proprietor growled and came hard at Hugh with a swift series of rapid uppercuts.

Hugh angled back, skirting those blows. "You're giving money to any thug in the street who'll get information about the Fight Society. Those men . . . and women . . . fleeced you along the way."

Again, Bragger charged Hugh, this time landing a solid fist to his gut.

The air left Hugh on a sharp hiss.

Triumph lit up the other man's eyes, and he pressed forward.

Spinning away from him, Hugh turned himself over to the fight.

Hating how easy it came. How easy it would always come.

He let a punch fly, connecting with Bragger's nose. The appendage instantly spurted blood, a crimson stream his partner didn't even bother to brush away.

Blood rushed to Hugh's ears, pounding hard in time to his rapid breaths and the thundering of his heart. And as if from a distance came the sharp cries of another.

Or mayhap it was Bragger?

It was all confused in his mind.

"Charge the field . . . Charge the field . . . they're on the attack . . ."

Sweat dripped from his brow and streaked down his face. His eyes stung; his opponent's visage blurred before him. And he landed blow after blow.

Bragger's almost creepy laugh blurred with the cries of those in a field slicked with blood. The innocent, cut down all around him. Men he'd cut down in the heat of battle until he'd realized too late the sins being committed that day.

Breathing hard and fast, Hugh unleashed all his fury. All his rage and horror, turning it loose upon his opponent.

For as long as he was immersed in this world, a fighter was what he would always be—a monster, not a man. *Jab-Jab.* Not with the crimes he was responsible for. *Jab-Jab.*

Hugh blocked the overhand right with his elbow and forearm. He threw three quick, sharp uppercuts that would have felled a smaller, weaker man than Bragger, but managed only to stun him.

The other man grinned and dealt four rapid jabs to Hugh's ribs.

"You ain't human." Bragger grunted, dancing away from Hugh. "That's why ya 'ave to foight. Who can do wot ya can?"

You don't look like any Devil . . . You may as well be any man, Mr. Savage . . .

What would his predawn visitor think if she saw him now? There was only one certainty: the sight of him in the ring would send her running faster than any of the harsh words he'd hurled at her. For the nickname he'd given her, the flittermouse had been more of a tigress. And Hugh was captivated still by—

He grunted as Bragger took advantage of his distraction and landed a heavy blow to his chin.

"'e's in yar 'ead, isn't he?" Bragger asked, slightly out of breath, finally revealing his first hint of tiring.

There could be no debating who the other man spoke of: Dooley.

That was the difference between Hugh and his partners—they were stuck in the past of their earliest days fighting. Hugh's demons spanned continents and the countryside of England.

Hugh came faster, barreling forward, landing blow after blow to Bragger's stomach, kidneys. Left cheek. Right cheek. In the distant recesses of his mind, he registered Maynard cheering him on.

"Take 'im down . . ."

Maynard's voice became a distorted echo of Hugh's former commander.

God rot his soul.

If he'd ever had a soul to begin with.

Hugh missed a step, and Bragger's fist connected in a rapid one-two-three with his belly.

Stifling a groan, he stumbled, and then quickly righting himself, he danced out of the other man's reach.

From the sidelines, Maynard burst out laughing.

Rap-Rap-Rap.

Musket fire came in a staccato beat.

Bringing his arms back up into position, he and Bragger matched steps, and Hugh tunneled all his energy, all his attention, on his opponent.

Pacing himself, he waited for a window . . . and then found it. He threw a punch; twisting it over, he struck the other man with the palm of his hand. Bragger swayed on his feet. Before Hugh drew his fist back into position, he pressed his advantage, raking his nails across Bragger's face.

With a sharp cry, Bragger went down hard on his arse, sprawling onto his back.

Hugh came to a stop over him. His chest heaving, he looked down at the bloodied, beaten man staring up at him.

"Yar ruthless." Bragger smiled and then spit out a mouthful of blood onto the floor. "And that's why ya need to foight." And beast that the other fighter was, he rose as if from the ashes and came at Hugh once more.

Hugh shot an elbow up, catching Bragger's fist before it collided with his cheek. The other man wouldn't quit. He'd consign Hugh to this.

Jab-Jab-Jab-Jab.

He landed four quick uppercuts to his opponent's chin.

Aye, his partner called him ruthless, and he had the right of it. Violence was more a part of Hugh than his own skin. And he hated the other man for being correct. Because there was no way out of this.

Out of the corner of his eye, he caught sight of his other partner.

Hugh didn't blink.

Maynard stood in the doorway speaking with—Hugh frowned—a woman. A young woman, wearing an altogether familiar brown muslin cloak, stood beside Maynard.

Motionless. Pale.

As she watched Hugh and Bragger battle, she'd a similar look to the one she'd worn in the early morn, when she'd been about to vomit outside the arena.

What in hell?

Dirty fighter that he'd always been, Bragger threw the inside of his forearm, catching Hugh in the temple and knocking him to his knees. Ignoring the triumphant laughter at that dirty play that combined with a ringing in his ears, Hugh leapt to his feet. He'd taken too many knocks to the head. There was no other accounting for the sight before him now.

Lila's horror-filled gaze remained locked on him and Bragger.

Aside from his and Bragger's rapid breathing, only silence echoed in the arena.

She'd been adamant Hugh wasn't a monster. She'd been so damned certain in her convictions that she could have almost tricked Hugh into thinking he was something other than he was.

But there was only one certainty after this moment with her here, deathly still and silent, her cheeks ashen: he'd effectively disabused her of every false notion that had brought her here—*twice* now.

Why did that simple reality make him want to snarl and hiss like the bloody beast he was?

Maynard broke the quiet. "Ya've got company, Savage."

"What do you want?" he barked.

He expected her to run.

He should have known better by now, that this one would never do what was expected of her.

"Hullo, Mr. Savage," she said quietly. Her horror-filled eyes went to the bloodied man alongside Hugh—Bragger, keenly taking in Lila and the entire exchange.

Hugh needed to get her out of here.

The surest lesson he'd secured about his partners over the years was that they'd weigh a person and gauge what use they could get out of them. Hugh had proven no different. Lila would be the same.

"Wot 'ave we 'ere?" Bragger purred, a silken drawl.

"No one." Hugh was already striding across the room to place himself between the damned lackwit and his partner. "She was leaving."

"I-I'm not." She peered around Hugh's shoulder. "My name is Lila."

The head proprietor touched a finger to the brim of an imagined hat. "Friend of Savage 'ere?"

"Yes."

"No." Hugh's curt denial blended with her affirmation. He gritted his teeth. The only thing missing in this farcical exchange was a damned curtsy. "We're not friends." Hugh didn't have any. And that also went for the two men taking in his and Lila's exchange like vultures assessing their prey. Taking her hard by the arm, Hugh dragged her several steps.

"You're hurting me."

"You know how you avoid that?" he asked between clenched teeth. "You don't come here." Even so, he lightened his hold.

Several paces away, Maynard took in every nuance of Hugh and Lila's exchange. Half-deaf, the other man would never pick up every word, but any word was too much.

"Forgive me for distracting you," she said in hushed tones that weren't quiet enough.

Out of the corner of his eye, he caught the grimace Maynard and Bragger shared.

Aye, because everyone in the rookeries knew distractions were costly and weren't allowed in these parts. It was the first and only time he'd ever been accused of that sin, because quite simply, Hugh had never allowed himself anything less than clear focus. "I wasn't distracted," he bit out between tight lips.

"You're just being polite," she demurred. "I saw you look my way, and then that gentleman—" The young woman's choice of words earned guffaws from Hugh's partners. She looked over at the both of them. "I'm sorry—I don't know your name."

"Bragger, ma'am." And damned if the notoriously ruthless street fighter didn't have a bemused smile in his voice. A smile? Impossible. The blighter found mirth only in the presence of absolute brutality.

"Thank you." Lila shifted her attention back to Hugh. "As I was saying, once I was admitted and you saw me, Mr. Bragger felled you."

Hugh's sore jaw worked several times. "I'm not being polite." That would be the first time he'd been accused of that sentiment.

"Yes, well, given that you're bellowing, I'd certainly say you are not. I was referring to—"

"What in hell are you doing here?" he snapped.

Lila the Flittermouse jumped, then spoke on a rush. "You told me to return when you weren't seeing to business so we might continue our discussion."

So they might continue their discussion? What in hell? Hugh considered Lila. If she had so much as half a brain in her head, she would have dashed off.

"I failed to anticipate that you'd still be working. We should have settled on a time when we last met."

Silence hung in the fighting ring.

It was the more loquacious of their trio that broke the impasse. "This isn't working," Bragger called, pulling the young woman's attention from Hugh over to him.

"I . . . it certainly seems like fighting."

"Aye, it is." Bragger toweled off his face. "But this?" He grinned coldly. "This is pleasure."

This is pleasure . . .

To every other man who stepped through these doors, including the very ones who owned it. Except for Hugh. This place, an empire of almost nothing, was as much a curse as a blessing.

Lila shivered; at that slight tremble, her muslin cloak rustled noisily. "Thank you for that clarification."

Bragger chuckled. "Proper lady, this one is."

"I don't have dealings with the nobility," Hugh Savage said coolly. "I don't trust them."

"Ahem." The flittermouse cleared her throat and settled her focus on Hugh. "As I was saying, I've come so that we might resume our discussion."

Bragger grabbed a towel from the wall and tossed it over to Hugh.

"That wasn't a discussion," Hugh said, wiping the blood and sweat from his face.

"Then what would you call it?"

Hugh ignored her question. "And that was your takeaway last evening, Flittermouse? That I wanted you around?"

She nodded. "Just not in the evening, during your fight-club hours."

It appeared he'd not been so very clear with the woman, after all.

From over her shoulder, he caught Bragger's keen gaze watching them. "Get out."

The young woman brought her shoulders back. "I . . . I don't think I will."

"Not you," he gritted out between clenched teeth. "Actually . . . *yes, you, too*. All of you, get out."

Both of his former fighting foes took themselves off, laughing uproariously as they went. Lila folded her hands primly before her, but remained affixed to her spot.

She'd not fled.

Even as she should have. Even as she'd seen the violence Hugh had told her he was capable of.

It proved the greatest twist of irony that he'd managed to run off two of the toughest street fighters in East London . . . and the flittermouse remained. "I can't decide if you're brave," he muttered, "or stupid."

The young woman shoved her hood back. "I far prefer the former." Her gaze fell to his bloodstained knuckles, and he balled them tightly at his sides.

"Well, the only thing to convince me it isn't the latter is if you leave." When she made no move to heed that order but rather stared on, transfixed, at his hands, he snapped, "Now."

"I'm afraid I cannot"—this time, she directed those words not to the digits that had unleashed ruthlessness this morn, but rather at his naked chest. Her already enormous brown eyes formed perfect moons in her face. With a little squeak, she directed her eyes up at the ceiling—"do *thaaat*," she said, her voice pitched several shades higher, emerging slightly garbled.

He gave his head a bemused shake. Leave it to Lila the Flittermouse to be more fazed by his damned naked chest than the evidence of earlier bloodshed. Being an object of horror wasn't an unfamiliar one. Women had alternately been gripped with a perverse fascination by his heavily scarred body or had run off screaming. "Not at all shocking, the flittermouse squeaks," he taunted.

Lila took that for the challenge it was. She lowered her head until their gazes met. She didn't steal so much as another glance at his naked chest, but neither did she run, and it answered that question he'd been asking himself since they'd met several hours earlier: she was brave. "They are bats."

Of their own volition, his brows drew together. What in blazes was she on about?

"It is just, following our meeting last evening—"

"This morning." And any other woman, nay, person, for that matter, would have been soundly sleeping following the hours this one had kept. "It was several hours ago."

"Yes; be that as it may, until our meeting I was unfamiliar with the term 'flittermouse,' and I assumed you were placing me in the mouse persuasion." She spoke with her hands, punctuating certain words and inflections. "However, my research revealed the flittermouse is not at all like a *mouse* mouse."

Hugh had suffered any number of blows to the head over the years; some had knocked him out cold. Some had left him with a headache months after. Never in any of those instances had he felt more turned around than he did in this moment. With this woman. "A . . . '*mouse* mouse'?"

"As in related to the mouse family."

There were any number of things he should say to the lady in this instant, all of them pertaining to her leaving, and yet he could manage only one question: "You went home and . . . researched the *flittermouse?*"

She gave her head a little nod. "There were only a few hours before our meeting."

He shot a glance at the doorway his partners had disappeared behind. "We don't *have* a meeting, Flittermouse." As it was, his partners already questioned his commitment to their cause. The last thing he could afford was having them think he was taking on a distraction in the form of . . . of . . . whatever in hell she was here for.

"I've not learned everything there is to know about the flittermouse," the oddity went on as if he'd not spoken. "What I *did* discover, however, is really rather fascinating, if you care to know?"

"I don—"

"According to ancient Chinese culture, the bat is a symbol of hope and joy."

Apparently, no invitation was needed. Reaching into the satchel that dangled from her wrist, she withdrew a small leather book and held it out.

When he made no move to take it, she carried on. "In fact, the Chinese word for bat—*fu*—is nearly identical to the word for 'good fortune.'"

"Trust me, Flittermouse," he said dryly. "I've known you for twelve hours, and the idea of you and good fortune? They don't go."

A slight frown marred the place between her eyebrows, highlighting the tip of the scar at the center of her forehead. And he, who'd not once in the whole of his thirty-three years bothered with questions about how a person came by their marks, found himself wondering how this woman had. It didn't fit with her fine speech and garments.

Clearing her throat, the young woman flipped her book open and turned quickly those pages. "Bats also are representative of 'Five Blessings' or *wufu*," she said. "Long life, wealth, health, love of virtue, and a peaceful death."

Hugh folded his arms at his chest. "By that, one could make the assumption that your being here represents death."

Her frown deepened, and she spared a look down at her peculiar volume. "I—I'd not thought of it *that* way," she allowed. "However"— she turned her book around to face him—"I believe you're failing to note the other more interesting—"

His patience snapped, and he surged forward, startling a gasp from her. She lost her grip on her book, and it clattered to the floor.

The woman did have some modicum of fear left, then. "I don't want to know about your damned encyclopedia of knowledge on bats. Do you know what I would like?" He didn't allow her a word edgewise. "I'd like for you to turn and walk your pretty little arse outside my club so that I can return to my business." He didn't want to school her or anyone else on how to kill or maim. Nay, the last thing he sought was more blood on his hands. Hugh stuck his face close to hers. "Are we clear?"

She dampened her mouth, the crimson red of that plump flesh standing in stark contrast to the ghostly pallor of her skin. Fear leached from every part of her almost elfin face, and came through in each puff of her quickened breathing. "You haven't hurt me." Her response came out so faint he barely discerned the words there. "I've now met you two times, and on both occasions you've been less than pleased with me."

God, she was exhausting. "That's a goddamned understatement."

"Precisely." And with each word, strength returned to her voice. "You've hurled insults, and you are one accustomed to using your fists, and yet at no time have you attempted to hurt me." She squared her shoulders. "As such, the conclusion I've arrived at is that: one"—she lifted a single digit—"you're not a man who'll put his hands upon a woman."

His stomach muscles twisted in a pained vise. Nay, he wouldn't. But there'd been others who had . . . He gave his head a slight, clearing shake. "And two"—she stuck up two fingers—"many of your responses have been mere bluster."

Mere bluster. And yet, another first had been dealt him this day. He rubbed distractedly at his chest. "My God, that's a brave bet you've taken."

Lila nodded jerkily. "Yes. Yes, it is. But the benefits of my braving your displeasure far outweigh those of my running off in fear." She motioned to his tattoos. "And it is going to take a good deal more than you rubbing at your well-sculpted chest to scare me, Mr. Savage."

He managed his first smile that morning. "'Well sculpted,' am I?"

A pretty blush climbed her cheeks. "You don't strike me as one who searches for compliments or doesn't know precisely who you are or what you look like. Therefore, yes, you are very well sculpted. Like a statue." She tacked on that elucidation like an afterthought that required being spoken.

Hugh ceased rubbing at the dagger pointed to the place his heart should be, and for the third wonder since their first exchange, he discovered another unexpected fact about himself: he was capable of going hot in the face. How very confident she was that she stood in the presence of an honorable man. It was a mark of both her naivete and her stupidity.

But then, what did it say to him that he was even now considering the request she'd put to him? "Very well," he said curtly. Stalking over to the hooks along the back wall, Hugh grabbed his white lawn shirt hanging there and waved it toward the bar where drinks were served to patrons at night. "Have a seat and say your piece, Flittermouse."

Chapter 7

THE LONDONER

The nobility has pretended too long that they are immune from the world's evil. It is time for a reckoning, one where Polite Society acknowledges the danger that exists. And this story of the latest Lost Lord merely serves to illustrate that the *ton* is as guilty of sin and darkness as those born outside its illustrious ranks . . .

V. Lovelace

Given everything Lila needed to learn and the fact that she still had to convince Hugh Savage to help her, her attention really *should* be on the arena she'd managed to gain entry to.

Alas, as she approached the row of stools at the bar, her eyes were riveted by just one thing in Savage's . . . or rather, one person—Mr. Hugh Savage.

Nor were her thoughts fixed on his earlier display of violence, as they should have been, but rather on him as a man. Hugh Savage was nothing short of a breathtaking display of manhood.

Where mortals were made of mere flesh, this specimen of the gods dripped muscles. From biceps that bulged to the corded sinew over his flat belly, there wasn't an ounce of spare flesh upon him. Jagged scars covered him like a canvas, and that flesh not marked by old wounds and injuries bore renderings in black and red ink.

And she expected she should be horrified. That would be the proper ladylike response. Only, he wore imperfections like a Michelangelo masterpiece.

With her gaze she traced those renderings on his flesh, and desire stirred low in her belly, fanning like a warm flame.

He again smirked, and for one horrifying moment, she believed that he knew the wicked wandering of her thoughts. That he'd caught how very mesmerized she was by his physique. "Do I have to throw you into your seat, Flittermouse?" he asked as he pulled his shirt on over his head. "Or do you think you can manage it?"

"I can . . ." *not manage anything in this moment.*

Hugh stuffed the tails of the lawn article into the waistband of his trousers. Her mouth went dry . . . not with fear, but with raw and very real desire. And it was so foreign, so new, feeling *anything* where any person was concerned. But this? This burning heat low in her belly proved the first reminder in nine long years—she was alive. Gloriously and joyously alive.

She'd believed herself altered in every way after Peterloo, only to find she was as capable of desire as any woman. And that proved a heady discovery.

He gave her an odd look, effectively quashing that all-too-brief joy.

Embarrassment painted her cheeks red. "I can do it," she blurted. Except she lingered there, watching as he wiped the blood from his hands. "Do you do that often?" At his questioning glance, she clarified. "Fight."

His mouth hardened. "What do you think?"

She wetted her lips. "I think . . . you conduct yourself . . ." Precisely as the papers had painted him: as a ruthless street fighter, known as the

Savage Gentleman for his fine talk, but who could bring a lesser man to his knees. "I think you conduct yourself like one who fights often."

"Then that's the answer."

But was it the true one? "So you and your partners, in addition to running your club—"

"It's an arena."

"Where boxers fight?"

His eyes sharpened on her face. "Do you have a notepad? Are you some reporter wanting to know about the owners of Savage's?"

Lila touched a hand to her chest. "N-no. I'm not."

He continued on relentlessly. "Have you come to talk about how we run our establishment?"

He was mocking her. "Perhaps we should get to the heart of my visit."

"Let's."

Holding up the hem of her cloak and dress, she attempted to hoist herself onto the high seating.

And failed.

Hugh pressed his eyes closed, and his mouth moved as if in prayer, which, if she was hearing him correctly, also contained intermittent curses, too.

Suddenly, he shot his enormous hands out.

Lila gasped and brought her arm back to land a reflexive blow, but it merely grazed the air above his shoulder as he set her in her chair.

The notorious fighter smiled mockingly at her; the half tilt to those impossibly hard lips said he'd caught her response and found humor in her futile attempt at properly throwing a punch.

Lila tightened her jaw. She wasn't one to be hurt or offended by Hugh Savage's response. In fact, that pathetic attempt on her part accounted for her presence here even now. "I take it you caught that."

"Your punch?" he asked drolly, coming around to the other side of the bar. "Just the opposite."

And coward that she was, Lila was besieged with relief at the distance he'd put between them. "Yes." Lila shifted on her bench, and caught the edge to keep from sliding off. "Which brings us back to my reason for being here."

"You want to be a street fighter?" he asked, bringing a bottle out from behind the counter. He held the brandy aloft.

"No. No," she said, and waved off his offer of spirits. "Women aren't bare-knuckle fighters."

His expression darkened. "Just because you haven't seen them, doesn't mean they aren't. Women fight."

Women fight.

He spoke of a world of primitive violence and chaos.

Lila's gaze slid to that ring where he'd been embroiled in battle just moments ago.

"Get off me . . . Please, I beg you . . ." Her own pleas pealed around her mind, and she took a deep breath and forced back the memories. "I don't *want* to fight," she clarified. Rather, she wanted to be skilled should she so need it. "Does anyone really wish to?" she asked quietly to herself. As soon as the question left her, a memory slid in of Mr. Bragger and Hugh, who'd been so wholly in his element, a man born to war with his fists, and a master of it.

He pulled his lips back in another of those mirthless grins. "Did you see me and my partner? Did that look like two men who didn't wish to fight?"

"You didn't strike me as one who was enjoying himself, Hugh."

It was a realization that had come to her as she'd stood and watched him. In the same way she was haunted and hunted, she recognized those same primitive responses in this man before her.

His eyes darkened. "You don't know a damned thing, Lila." He spoke the truth, and that truth was also the reason she was here even now. "You think like a damned lady." Once more, he proved far more insightful than was safe.

"Do you expect a lady of the peerage would find herself in a hack to the rookeries, and to your club even now?" she countered, her voice climbing a notch.

"All I know is I don't trust the nobility, and you certainly don't sound like any woman from these parts," he said with a finality to that pronouncement.

"Do you have many ladies come to your club?"

"Yes," he said bluntly.

Well, *that* wasn't what she'd expected.

Steepling his fingers, Hugh stared at her over the tops of them. Studying her. Probing her with those penetrating eyes which could surely pluck the deepest secrets from the Home Office.

And throughout his scrutiny, Lila kept herself absolutely still. That state having been the one skill she had mastered these past nine years. It was the surest way to not attract notice, and to be certain one remained safe from harm. All the while, her pulse pounded at the deep mire of lies she found herself diving into.

He finally let his hands fall. "Why don't you get to whatever it is that's brought you here *again*?" Lila remained silent, searching for words. "Don't you have a family?" he asked with more gentleness than he'd shown in any of their previous exchanges.

And because of that, he deserved the truth. "I do."

"One that cares about you?" His question came without inflection.

"Very much so." She fought the twist of sadness in her chest. Most any other noble family would have committed their daughter to an asylum, had she descended into the state Lila had. At the very least, those powerful peers would have forced one such as Lila into marriage, foisting her on some dissolute lord who didn't mind having a recluse wife.

"Tell me why a woman like you needs to learn how to fight."

"All people should know how to protect and defend themselves, Mr. Savage," she said quietly. "I expect you should know that as well as anyone."

He shifted a gaze over her face, and she went still under that scrutiny. That all-knowing stare landed on the vivid scar she wore in the middle of her brow. Lila clenched her fingers, burying them in her lap. God, how she abhorred that mark. For the imperfection it was. And for the memory that had been stamped upon her skin of that once glorious August day.

"You're going to have to provide more than that, Flittermouse," he finally said.

He wanted her to offer him more details? Aside from her sister-in-law, Clara, she'd never shared any part of that hellish day in Manchester with anyone. Nor did she even know if she could.

Nervous energy hummed inside her.

Cries—her own, and other men's, women's, and children's—all screamed around the chambers of her mind.

"Help me . . . Please, God . . . Pleeeeease. I'm here . . . Please . . ."

Lila struggled to swallow.

Shimmying down from her stool, Lila gave her back to Hugh Savage. "I witnessed the evil this world is capable of," she said hoarsely. She made herself face him once more. "And I only know that I can't move about it once more without knowing how to protect those I love from it."

His heavily muscled frame went whipcord straight. "You're in danger, then?"

Warmth chased away Peterloo's demons. This was why he was the Savage Gentleman, then . . . One who was truly ruthless wouldn't have given a damn whether a stranger to him was in peril. "I'm not in immediate danger from anyone," she assured. Rather, she'd come to appreciate that everyone was always at risk.

Some of the tension went out of him.

She went on. "I want to equip myself with the skills to protect those I love." Lila held his gaze. "I won't share more than that. Though

I expect you have your own secrets, Mr. Savage, and I'd not press you on yours, either."

"Ah, yes, but I've not asked you for anything."

Lila nodded. "Fair enough."

"And is there a husband or protective relative whom I can expect would show up on my doorstep?"

"I've no family who would come here." It was a lie by omission on her part. If Henry and Clara discovered her gone, they would track her to Hugh Savage's and force her back to Mayfair. But they wouldn't because they weren't here. And by the time they returned, she'd be done with her lessons, and Mr. Hugh Savage would be only a memory.

⁓

Mere moments ago, he'd considered himself half-mad.

He'd been wrong.

There was nothing "half" about it. He was completely and totally mad. There was no other accounting for the fact that he'd entertained Lila for as long as he had, or that he actually was considering her request.

I witnessed the evil this world is capable of . . . And I only know that I can't move about it once more without knowing how to protect those I love from it . . .

It had been those words that had given him pause. The ones that had confirmed beyond any shadow of a doubt that she was no part of the peerage. Those men and women didn't know a thing of toil or struggle. And they didn't have the haunted eyes this woman before him did.

This woman, who now implored him to teach her to fight. And yet ironically . . . "There's nothing I can teach you," he made himself say.

Nor did that rejection come from a need or desire to get rid of her. The truth was, he'd never really trained to fight. He'd never instructed anyone to fight. Everything he'd learned had come from being tossed into a ring and battling other children.

Her face fell.

"I don't teach people how to fight." And he never would. The last thing he wanted to do was turn out more fighters on the world.

She stretched a palm across the scratched and nicked bar surface and gripped his forearm. "There must be something I can do or say?"

"Is that an offer, Flittermouse?" Hugh looked pointedly at where she touched him, her unwitting caress slight and oddly more enticing than the outrageous, bold ones of the women he'd kept company with over the years.

"Of course not." Color flooded Lila's face, bathing her slightly pointy but dainty chin, high cheekbones, and forehead in a bright shade of red . . . That vibrant blush heightened the whiteness of the scar. "You're trying to shock me."

"Are you attempting to reassure yourself with that, Flittermouse? To convince yourself I'm something other than what I am? That I'm somehow *safer*?"

She dipped her gaze down, and he followed it all the way to her clenched fists; they were curled into visible balls that had left her knuckles white. Unbidden, his eyes went to that scar once again.

It doesn't matter . . .

How she'd come by it wasn't his concern.

She didn't matter.

Hugh didn't need to be responsible for anyone's well-being. The people he did keep company with were those who were capable and adept at survival.

And his earlier resolve wavered.

The young woman caught his focus on that mark, and she tipped her chin at a proud angle, one that both dared him to ask a question and also sent him to the Devil with the fire there, all at the same time. Not for the first time, he wondered after that damned scar. Was that what accounted for her being here? Was she, despite her earlier insistence, the miserable wife to some brutal nobleman? After the violence and evil Hugh had witnessed from them over the years, nothing about what those men were capable of did or would ever surprise him.

"How did you learn to fight, Hugh?" she asked quietly, laying command to his name as no one else had ever dared. That left him vulnerable in ways he'd never been.

Hugh leaned in. "You don't want to talk about your past"—and it only fueled his questions about the obstinate woman—"and I don't talk about mine."

Hope lit her eyes. It was a sentiment he'd not seen in more years than he could remember, and he almost failed to identify it for what it was. "That is fine. I'll agree to those terms."

And he, who'd never been given any reason to believe in God, found himself closing his eyes and praying for patience. When he opened them, he found her wary-once-more gaze upon him. "They aren't terms. I'm explaining to you why I won't provide—"

"But not *can't*," she said, pouncing on that choice of words.

He spoke over her. "I'm no Gentleman Jackson. There's no program I offer to teach you or anyone to be a great fighter."

"You've never been beaten, they say."

"You make more of it than it is." The whole world did. Hugh's gaze moved beyond her shoulder. "I just survived—and there aren't lessons for that."

She scoffed. "You can teach me how to have a good stance so I don't fall if I'm hit or pushed. You can teach me how to distract or disarm an attacker." Lila came closer, and with her every word, he became further intrigued . . . by her. By what she proposed. "And you can teach me how to strengthen my body." Unwittingly her words drew his gaze down her slender frame.

He swallowed hard.

And as he stood there, considering the request she put to him, he contemplated everything he'd already come to glean about the woman in a short time. If he didn't agree to help her, she'd find another.

In these streets.

Someone who thrilled at the fight and had no compunction about raining one's fists down until one's opponent was dead and bleeding at his feet.

And she'd be taken apart by whichever street fighter she presented that request to. Nor was it cynicism on his part, but rather a whole life's worth of exchanges with those same men.

He found himself wavering, and fought against all his better judgment.

Hugh didn't help people. The last time he'd tried . . .

Please, sir, won't ya 'elp me. Please . . .

Lila stared back at him with those same haunted-yet-hopeful eyes. It was a contradictory mix of life-hardened and innocent that went together not at all, that bespoke a woman with secrets. The last thing Hugh could afford was a woman like that in his life.

Hugh came out from behind the bar, and at his approach, she stiffened.

She'd both fear him and ask for his aid. The lady must be desperate. There was no other accounting for her presence here still. Hugh bent down and rescued her forgotten book on flittermice. He weighed the small volume, his large palm dwarfing the title. "What's your name?"

"I already told you—"

"You gave me a first name. I want all of it."

She eyed him carefully a moment before volunteering, "Lila March."

Lila March.

Hugh turned it over in his mind.

Feminine and soft, and yet at the same time, direct and succinct . . . it suited her.

"I'll give you your lessons, March," he said.

Lila's long throat moved wildly. "Thank you. Thank—"

"Don't thank me *yet*. There'll be conditions and . . . Nothing is free. Nothing. Not in these parts."

She eyed him apprehensively. Her tongue darted out to trace that wide seam of her lips. Had she been any other woman, and had there been something other than unease rippling off her slender frame, the gesture would have been construed only as seductive. "Let us begin with the conditions."

"My rules. They're mine. I'm not in the business of turning out fighters. Don't go telling your friends. Don't go sending anyone else to me, thinking I'll make them into fighters to take on the world."

Something shifted in her eyes. Fear. Having known that emotion best above all others, he recognized it in this woman.

Good, she was realizing the kind of man she'd sought out.

"Next, I don't go by 'Hugh.' I'm Savage." It was a name that aptly suited him, one he might not have been born with but that his handlers had assigned to him, and that had proven apt in its assignation. "Next—"

She was already shaking her head.

Shaking her head?

"I'm not calling you 'Savage.'"

"It's *not* negotiable," he snapped.

"Is it because you think to remind me or others of your ruthlessness and the violence you're capable of?" She peered at him, those fathomless depths that penetrated as if they could see into a man's soul. Or worse . . . the field of carnage that lay at his feet. "Or," she asked pensively, "is it a reminder for you?" And mayhap with those too-apt words, she could. "Either way," she went on almost conversationally, as if they were two passersby in her fancy end of London, exchanging pleasantries on the day, "did you know the origins of the word 'savage' come from the early fourteenth century?"

"No, and I don't—"

"In fact, the earliest usage didn't refer to one who was brutal or barbaric. Its roots, *salvaticus*, are Latin in origin. In ancient times, people greatly feared the untamed land, the forests, and the woods. And with good reason," she said, "when one considers the unfamiliar and ofttimes dangerous creatures that lived there. Eventually, the word went through an evolution in meaning. It came to be used to refer to those who were indomitable and valiant. The negative connotation we now associate with your surname, in fact, didn't come until much later."

He narrowed his eyes. She'd come here, romanticizing his damned *name*?

Her etymology lesson was met with a muffled snickering outside the room.

Hugh glared in the direction of the doorway. "Get the hell out," he thundered, and there came distinct footfalls as Bragger and Maynard retreated.

"Are they your partners?" she asked.

He ignored her question, again leaving her to the erroneously drawn conclusion that he was an equal to the men who owned this place. "I've already told you, I don't answer questions about my past, and I don't want to know a damned thing about yours. I don't want to know who you belong to. How you take your tea. What your favorite color is."

She scraped a frosty stare up and down his person, and by God, even he, street-hardened, emotionally deadened bastard that he was, found himself hard-pressed not to be embarrassed by the ice there. "I don't *belong* to anyone, Hugh."

"Yes, I can see that," he muttered. He'd wager the future he'd built himself here that there wasn't a man who could tame her. "Third, if I have to deal with an irate husband or brother or father or any other damned angry male relative . . ." He let that dangle there for the threat it was intended to be.

Lila March stared at him expectantly, then shook her head. "What are the consequences?"

Damn, the Flittermouse had teeth. He clenched his jaw. "I'll see them ruined," he vowed, and the little color in her cheeks faded, leaving her whitewashed. Good. Before she entered into the arrangement, she'd better be prepared to know exactly what she was agreeing to. "They wouldn't be the first." And with what Hugh and his partners intended for Dooley and his cronies, they wouldn't be the last.

And the lady must have seen some of that lethal rage in him, for she took a step away—a steady one, but a retreat nonetheless.

"Do you truly believe if there were an irate husband or brother or father," she asked, her voice faintly tremulous, "that they'd ever dare make a public display about our being together?"

"I'm less worried about what they'd do to protect your reputation, as opposed to what they'd do to try and ruin me and my business," he said flatly.

She chewed at her lower lip. "That is a fair point," she conceded. "I assure you, H—*Mr. Savage*," she corrected when he gave her a sharp look, "there is no one who'd seek vengeance. That is not who I or my family are."

Who was she, and furthermore, who was her *family* that they'd either not know of her jaunts to the rookeries or, worse, would allow them? "Either way, I want it clear that if you're wrong, or if you're lying and you've vindictive kin, you'll pay a price."

A visible shudder racked her slender frame. "We're clear."

"Your lessons take place here, at five o'clock in the morning, daily." She didn't so much as flinch at that meeting time. One that would have had any respectable member of the peerage balking. The flittermouse proved the exception yet again. But then, given everything he'd gathered about her in the short time he'd known her, that detail shouldn't have come as any manner of surprise. "We'll begin with one-hour sessions."

The young woman absently touched the center of her head, the place where her scar stood out, even in her pale face. Catching his attention on that telltale gesture, she let her arm fall quickly to her side. "And . . . how long do you anticipate my lessons will need to run before I'm . . ."

He quirked an eyebrow. "Sufficiently able to kill a man?"

If possible, she went ten shades whiter. "I was going to say *sufficiently trained*."

Hugh scraped an eye over her; the enormous cloak hung upon her frame, giving her the look of a little girl playing dress-up. Painfully thin as she was—almost gaunt—and weak enough for a strong wind to snap, he didn't have much confidence in her stamina or strength. "I don't have much hope, Flittermouse."

She edged her chin up and dared him with that mutinous expression. "Then you must not have much confidence in yourself as a fighter; for if I don't learn, it won't be my fault, Mr. Savage."

And for the first time, there wasn't annoyance with the flittermouse who didn't know if she wanted to wilt or to be brave, but rather a stirring of appreciation. He grinned, the expression rusty, the muscles strained, and the smile altogether foreign and unfamiliar.

Lila eyed him warily.

Yes, mayhap she wasn't so very stupid, after all.

"And lastly? You're to come alone," he added. "If you bring anyone else with you, we're done here."

"There is no one."

That was it. By her own admission, there was a family that cared but was absent. An air of mystery continued to swirl about the peculiar creature. And if he'd been another man, he'd have some interest in having answers. Hugh was clever enough to know he didn't want any baggage that came with another human being. It was all a man could do to handle his own demons and secrets.

He spread his palms out. "Those are the rules, Flittermouse."

The lady gave a jerky nod. "Thank you. I will see you on the morrow, Mr. Savage."

"Ah," he said as she turned to go. "I said we're done with my rules, but we've not yet discussed payment."

She faced him with all the tangible excitement one might show for a meeting with Lucifer. Which wouldn't be an inaccurate response on the lady's part. "Payment?"

"*Tsk. Tsk.* Never tell me you thought my offer to teach you would be altruistic on my part."

"N-no." She followed his approach with those eyes that served as a window into her every fear. The lady took several steps away from him. Her back knocked against the bar. "But I . . ." Her words trailed off as he came to a stop before her. "What do you want?"

Did she refer to this moment? Or their arrangement? If he'd been a betting man, he would have bet the former. "A favor. If or when I require it."

She dampened her lips once again in that telltale gesture of her unease. "A favor."

He flashed a smile. "Worry not, Flittermouse. I don't desire you, and I've no intention of bedding you."

A blush started on the lady's neck and worked its way up her cheeks until her face was suffused with color. And he noted for the first time that she wasn't such a plain creature, after all. In fact, she was really rather . . . interesting.

"I don't need nor want anything . . . at this moment. But the time will come that I do, and I want payment made, no exceptions."

Lila hesitated, and it was the first instant since her arrival out back and her return that he saw the wheels of her mind turning in her eyes, the questioning of her decision in being here, and the peril of entering into any pact with him. "I can pay you . . ." She fished around the inside of her cloak.

"I don't want your money."

Lila withdrew her hand. "Very well. It is a deal: an unnamed favor granted at a later date."

Chapter 8

Dearest Lila,

It has been entirely too long. You must rejoin me.
There are so many joys you've missed out upon. Might
I persuade you to accompany me about town?

Your truest, longest, and dearest friend,
Annalee

When Lila had been a girl awaiting the day of her Come Out, she had dreamed about the gowns she'd wear. The satin fabrics. The soft, draped silks. She had reveled in each appointment to the modiste, where she'd shed her long skirts for a woman's garments.

Following Peterloo, she'd seen the inherent silliness in the joy she'd found in clothing. What had it all been about? From that day on, gowns had come to serve but one purpose—practicality.

It had been so long since Lila had mingled with the living, she'd long lost touch with the latest fashions worn by ladies for *ton* events. She didn't know what they donned for rides about Hyde Park or to go to the theatre, because, in short, those were places she'd vowed to never again visit.

As she scoured the many garments hanging inside the blue-and-gold-gilded armoire, she had even less knowledge as to what she should wear for her upcoming fighting lessons.

There was only one certainty: her former friend, Annalee, would know. Oh, Lila had once had all the answers for their pair. But not any longer. Now, Annalee would know precisely what to wear or not wear.

The chiming clock struck four, lending an urgency to her search.

She briefly paused. Her fingers locked on the smooth satin of a pale-blue gown with crystals dripping from the sleeves and bodice. The fabric gleamed soft and lustrous.

What would it be like, to stand before a man such as Hugh Savage in this dress . . . ?

As soon as the thought slid in, fire burnt her cheeks.

Worry not, Flittermouse. I don't desire you, and I've no intention of bedding you . . .

Lila compressed her lips into a line and shoved the gown to the back of the armoire.

What did she care whether he found her desirable? In fact, she should be relieved that Hugh Savage, the ruthless fighter whom she'd be spending close quarters with for the foreseeable future, didn't.

It is because you feel like less than a woman . . . It was because she'd become a shadow of the person she'd been, a person she didn't recognize, and with his every sneer or jeering taunt, she was reminded of the person she wasn't. Whereas Annalee had rejoined Polite Society, and she'd done so with a splash that had scandalized the *ton*. Notorious for wearing her crimson skirts, she'd shocked the world. While Lila? Lila had lived her life safely.

Shut away.

She froze in her search . . .

Her gaze caught on the last dress hanging in the Venetian armoire. That hated, stained, and ripped article.

Giving her head a shake, she tore her focus from the familiar dress and returned to the more recent, brown and grey dresses her family had commissioned at her request.

In the end, Lila settled on a dark grey that almost shimmered when the light touched it.

After she'd dressed and plaited her hair, Lila made her way through the doorway that had served as entrance to the original servants' corridors. Walled in but not closed off, they afforded Lila a secret path throughout her family's household. One that allowed her the freedom to avoid everyone's company.

The narrow space, nearly pitch black, would have once roused terror in the girl she'd been. Her eyes, however, had become adjusted to dimly lit rooms and places. Either way, time and life had taught Lila it wasn't the shadows and dark one should fear, but rather the world around them. The dark acted like a cloak, offering a sanctuary to hide within. Stepping out amongst the living, one was at the mercy of the people around one—the hungry crowds, demanding food. The guards and government, determined to oppress. In short, a world at odds, which would always be at odds, and because of that eternal conflict, there would forever be uncertainty to any person who moved about society.

When she reached the last step, Lila let herself out to the shared, narrow alley between her family and Lord Crossley's residence. She stole a wistful glance over at the townhouse. How many times had Lila run back and forth between these two homes so she might see Annalee?

Annalee, whom she'd been visiting with in Manchester, had flourished where Lila had wilted after Peterloo.

One fact remained: neither woman was the same person she'd been.

Lila kept her gaze trained forward, focusing on the flicker of light from the streetlamp ahead.

A short while later, she found her way to the hackney waiting at the end of Mount Street, just where she'd instructed him to be yesterday morning. Beneath the thin layer of black paint, the previous owner's coat of arms was visible on the doors of the hired carriage.

"Good morning, ma'am," the driver greeted in his street-rough Cockney. "Same place?"

"The same." Lila inclined her head, and opening the door, she drew herself inside the ancient conveyance some nobleman had sold off that had now become the cornerstone of the hack driver's business. She settled onto the bench, stripped of its upholstery but for pieces of pink fabric that had proven too difficult or bothersome to remove.

The carriage lurched forward and started a slow roll through London.

As they traveled, she pushed aside thoughts of Annalee and focused on her impending meeting.

I don't go by "Hugh." I'm Savage . . .

Was Savage even his surname? Or was it one he'd taken on to mark his place in the underworld of London?

Either way, in that moment as she'd rambled on with her lesson on the root word of the name "Savage," she'd not known whether she'd sought to enlighten him or reassure herself.

Though a man nearly six inches beyond six feet, his body dripping chiseled muscles and adorned in black-and-crimson paint, was hardly one to inspire calm in a lady, particularly a lady who'd made it her way to never seek out any company.

Only, if she were being honest with herself, there hadn't been solely fear on her part—an all-too-familiar sentiment she'd become quite adept at identifying. There'd been something even more powerful: desire. Heat fanned her belly, as welcome now as it had been during their meeting yesterday morn.

There was something freeing in her body's response to him. For in feeling something other than fear, Lila relished the truth that she was not a completely empty shell of a person. That if she was capable of feeling desire, then surely she was as capable of feeling joy and hope . . . and living again.

The carriage hit four consecutive pits in the street, and Lila caught the edge of the bench and gripped it hard to keep herself from pitching around.

They were nearly arrived.

To give her fingers something to do, she peeled the moth-eaten curtain back a fraction and peeked out at the darkened streets . . . until several moments later when the hackney rolled to a jerky stop outside Savage's.

Lila remained fixed on the bench.

I can do this . . .

She could do this. She'd done it before. Not in the same way, necessarily. Having journeyed to meet Clara that first time two years ago, it had been more than worth the fear she'd overcome. Lila had rediscovered a long-lost confidence: she'd found solace in music.

Now, she'd equip herself not only with simple pleasures she'd once enjoyed, like the pianoforte she'd allowed herself to again play . . . with Clara's help.

No, in coming here, in her connection with Hugh Savage, she'd learn the skills to protect those she loved.

That gave her the strength to knock.

The driver pulled the door open and helped her down.

"I'll return," she said, her gaze squarely on Hugh Savage's establishment. "You'll be paid, and well, for your patience." Collecting her hem, Lila started the remaining way to her instruction with Hugh.

Yes, only good could come from her being here. And yet, as she reached the back door of Savage's and knocked hard, why couldn't she shake the niggling feeling that she'd gone and entered into a deal with the Devil?

⌘

His partners were going to have his damned head.

Hugh yanked the panel open.

The woman on the other side was left with her fist hovering in the air. "Enough with the knocking," he snapped.

"Oh." Lila drew her fingers back and tucked them inside her cloak pocket. "I thought you may have changed your mind."

He should, but neither had he ever broken a pledge made. "So you thought to beat my door down and force your way inside?"

"No. I thought I'd press you on your intentions." Without awaiting an invitation, she swept past him, as bold as if she intended to lay siege to his fight club and name herself the proprietress.

He stared after Lila, not taking his eyes from her as she walked a small circle around his empty fight club. With her gaze, she took in the twenty-foot ring. The gallery three feet above the arena. "Are you always this damned literal?"

Her head whipped back toward him. "Yes," she said matter-of-factly before resuming her examination of the ring. "Through the windows, it appeared so very much smaller. How many can your establishment hold?"

"It's not small." His voice carried in the high-ceilinged arena. "And it can fit two hundred spectators."

She paled. "That many?"

"Aye."

"Hmm," she murmured, more to herself than him. "Do men train here and fight?"

Hugh rolled his cramped neck muscles as he entered the center of the arena. "We've a staging area for fighters before matches. There, they can prepare and practice before entering the ring."

That managed to pull her attention from the wood dais over to Hugh. "How exactly does one go about preparing for a fight?"

She'd already asked more questions than any of the boys or men he'd sparred with in his life. And . . . odd as it was, he didn't mind it. Rather, he found himself warming to a topic he'd always had a peculiar fascination with.

"The preparation is as important to a bare-knuckle match as the actual fight itself. The Spartans saw it as a way to prepare for the blows they'd receive to the head in battle."

The color left her cheeks. "That's a terrible i-idea," she said, her voice catching so faintly he would have missed it had he not been paying close attention to her every word and movement.

She'd come here, however, to speak and learn about bare-knuckle boxing; he didn't intend to sweeten his words in a bid to ease her discomfort. "Aye, a blow to the head has killed many men. But the ancient peoples were clever enough to evolve the sport. The Assyrians, Babylonians, Egyptians, Persians—they were the earliest fighters. They believed in strengthening and stretching." The last time he'd mentioned that fact, he'd met the scorn of the other boys in Dooley's Fight Society, who'd mocked him for handing out useless information that wouldn't win them any battles. Now, he searched for a hint of Lila's boredom. Only curiosity reflected back.

"And what of the English fighters?"

It was an interesting question. "What of them?" he countered with a rhetorical question. He swung his arms, alternating long, slow arcs, stretching his muscles. "By the empire's account, the greatest, most capable men on the planet?" He curved his lips in a derisive smile. "They don't want to think of fighting beyond the fists they'll throw. Those people of cultures deemed inferior to our own know a good deal more about anything pertaining to fighting than even the best English fighter." He hardened his mouth. "Men have been boxing since Kleitomachos. A good fighter knows to use the lessons from long ago. A better fighter puts them into practice." More often than not, men who showed up here with the intention of squaring off had their sights on only one goal: winning a purse.

She tipped her head pensively, sending her long plait flopping about her shoulder.

"What?" he asked.

"It's just . . ." Lila drifted closer, then stopped so there were several steps between them. Tipping her head back, she peered up. "By your own accounts, the English deride the lessons of those ancient and far-greater civilizations."

"Far greater?" It was an interesting acknowledgment most Englishmen . . . and Englishwomen . . . would not make. Hugh dropped his hands on his hips. "*Tsk. Tsk.* The king would consider such talk treason."

"The king's not here."

Nay, in the rookeries, His Majesty, the King of England, may as well have been as fictional as the bogeyman good, loyal English boys and girls went about fearing. Oh, the king owned this pit as surely as he owned the most prosperous colonies the world over, but the people here—Hugh, and every other last miserable soul—were invisible to the sovereign. Just as those who'd gone and fought for his great empire went unseen by him as well. Rage tightened in Hugh's gut. "You were saying?" he asked through that fury.

"How did you learn such things?" She continued before he could answer, before he could consider an answer. "You recite so easily information about the customs of ancient civilizations. If you're surrounded by men who deride those ancient ways, then how did *you* come by such information?"

Hugh didn't move for a moment. The simple truth was . . . even if he'd wanted, he couldn't supply her with an answer. Not one he'd understand or could explain. The only memories he had were of being a boy on the streets. The knowledge had . . . simply been there. The same way his refined speech had been. They were those incongruities that when . . . if . . . he allowed himself to think on them, brought questions about who his parents had been. "It's something . . . I picked up along the way," he said gruffly, discomfited by thoughts he'd not allowed himself in more years than he could recall.

"And you don't teach men here?"

"No teaching goes on in this place." His eyes went to the ring. "Just savagery."

From the moment he'd found himself taken in, it'd been clear his *benefactors* had only one intention for this arena.

"But if you think there are other benefits, then surely you'd train your fighters."

God, she was a dogged creature. "They aren't *my* fighters."

"Didn't you yourself say you saw the benefits?"

Aye, she asked questions like a damned gossip columnist. "I'm not the one to make those decisions."

"But you're an owner, are you not?" she asked slowly, one trying to puzzle through a mystery.

He resisted the urge to shift. "My name's on the sign," he countered, hedging. "What do you think that's for?" Hugh brought his left arm across his chest and stretched the muscles of his forearm.

Understanding blazed to life in her features. "You and your partners didn't feel it was a good use of resources."

There'd never been a consideration that they'd instruct fighters. Nay, rather, Bragger and Maynard had instead relied on throwing Hugh into the ring.

Just as they'd do all over again.

Apparently, she didn't need any input from him. An endearing little frown puckered the space between her eyebrows, that place where her scar ended. "I'd say helping people become better fighters is of tremendous value."

"But is it going to put more coin in the pockets?" They were rote words Bragger had uttered anytime Hugh had proposed anything other than fighting in the ring. Hugh, who'd spent years trying to find a place in his and Maynard's world—and who was still searching.

Just as he'd been trying to find his way since he'd gone off to war.

"That's a rather ruthless way to be," she said softly, bringing him to the moment.

"Stop with your questioning," he said tersely. Even though his partners had gone for the morn, Hugh still wouldn't risk having Lila challenge the other proprietors. The last thing he could afford was either man questioning his loyalty. "Did you come here to learn how to fight or how I run my business?"

The young woman glided over, those almost-floating steps, more graceful than those of even the finest fighter he'd seen dancing around a ring or street corner. "But there are things a person could and should do before being trained to fight?"

He nodded.

She stopped walking. "I'd have you show me that, too, then." The minx may as well have been picking out her choice of beef at the market.

She was no-nonsense. A woman who knew precisely what she wanted. A woman so very much in command of herself and her opinion, and it sent hunger rippling through him. A desire far greater than anything inspired by lust of the physical body, and more terrifying for it.

Hugh grunted. "Let's get on with it." He tossed a pair of breeches at Lila, and the pants hit her hard in the chest. "Here." He started back for the middle of the ring.

"What are these?"

"They're breeches. What's the matter, Flittermouse? Do you have a problem donning an old pair of breeches that belonged to another?"

"No, it's not that," she said haltingly. God, the minx really was a plain speaker, unable to discern sarcasm. "And, of course, I see that they are breeches. What I'm asking is what do you expect me to do with them?"

"I think it should be fairly obvious."

"Actually, it isn't."

He paused in the middle of whatever task he was seeing to. "If that isn't something you can figure out, Flittermouse, then I think we're wasting both our time with lessons."

The young woman clutched the garment close to her chest, her indecision tangible.

Folding his arms, he turned back. "Let me give you a hint . . . you put them on."

"I know I put them on. What I'm asking is why. I cannot very well go about in . . . in . . ." She waved the brown trousers at him.

He shook his head. "Breeches?"

"Precisely. I've asked you to instruct me on how to defend myself."

Chapter 9

As Lila reentered Hugh's arena, there was a jaunt to her step she didn't remember feeling in . . . more years than she could remember.

And yet, she'd felt that same surge of triumph when she managed to first bring herself to leave her family's household after Peterloo, the kind that enlivened and filled one with a giddy restlessness. Where one's emotions were a kaleidoscope of joy and nervousness, and they erupted into a state of awareness that reminded a person—she lived.

Not even that favor she'd put to Clara, the music lessons she'd managed to secure, had been as thrilling. There'd been a safety to the woman her brother had since married. She'd been a stranger to Lila, yet she'd also been the woman who'd saved Henry.

Hugh Savage was a stranger in every way.

A surly, snarling, snappish bear of a man who didn't much like her . . . or, she suspected, anyone.

And she'd not only faced him head-on . . . she'd triumphed.

Her shoulders back, Lila closed her eyes and drew in a deep breath, letting the smells of the room—bruised leather and the faint, lingering stench of sweat in the air—fill her lungs.

Tugging off her gloves, she stuffed them inside her cloak. As she unfastened the grommet at her throat, she registered the soft click as Hugh Savage shut the door behind them, locking them off from the world.

Startling, she spun to face him. How was it possible for any person of his sheer size and strength to move so silently? "Silent and quick feet," he said, starting toward her. "We'll get to that lesson." He bent to retrieve the previously abandoned trousers. "Here." This time, however, he didn't hurl them but held them out.

Lila hesitated before reaching for the cotton breeches. Hugh's fingers brushed hers, and a little electric current radiated up her arm. Heart racing, she pulled the ancient pair of breeches close.

She needn't have worried that Hugh had noted that spark of awareness; he'd already started over to the row of hooks along the back wall, lined with various articles of clothing. He lifted up a lawn shirt and inspected the slightly tattered garment before returning it to the hook in exchange for another.

And then it occurred to her . . . he was searching for a shirt . . . for her.

Which, of course, only made sense, as he expected her to wear breeches.

But now the fact that she'd undress in the same room as Hugh Savage, and then don pants and a shirt, set off a different, riotous panic in her breast. "You never did explain why I'm going to be taught in breeches, Hugh." She silently prayed he didn't hear the pitched timbre to her voice.

"No, I didn't." Her mentor held up another shirt, this one smaller and of a length better suited to a child, the quality no better than the previous one he'd considered. "Here." Loping over, he offered the garment, which Lila this time accepted from him. "You want to know why you're wearing pants when you'll only be wearing dresses in society."

"I do." Because even as it was no doubt freer, moving about in trousers, the places her family hoped she'd go and the world she intended to rejoin required her in those cumbersome articles.

"It wasn't a question," he said dryly, and she found her cheeks ablaze with heat again. How had it been possible to lose every nuance of discussion? How could one event have erased that ability to speak?

"Now, fighting, Lila, is about knowing the *feel* of one's body." He glided around her, not unlike those figures she'd seen sliding around at the Frost Fair nearly fourteen years ago, the last time the Thames had ever frozen.

"It is about learning how and in which ways to move. Touch me."

Touch me.

Her mouth went dry, and every part of her caught fire at . . .

"If you're going to learn to fight and have the strength to use those skills, Flittermouse, you're going to have to bring yourself to touch me."

"I know," she said weakly. Lila darted a hand out.

Hugh arched away from her touch, his back curved, and the muscles of his chest and stomach rippled.

She followed him with her eyes.

"Footwork is just as important as any punch you land, Lila. You cannot fight unless you know how to move your feet."

And then he moved.

Good God, he moved.

Swaying on his feet as he spoke, gliding back and forth with more mastery than any dance instructor or . . . or . . . anyone she'd ever seen waltz upon a ballroom floor. And here she'd believed herself incapable of living or feeling anything beyond fear.

"Try again," he urged, the cadence of his breathing even, when her own? Her own came ragged to her own ears.

For reasons that had nothing to do with any exertion on her part and everything to do with the man before her.

Do something.

Touch him.

Oh, God. Her heart catapulted to a different place in her chest.

Touch him?

"Well, *now*," he said impatiently, wholly unaware of the battle that raged within her.

Forcing herself to concentrate on Hugh as he dipped and shifted, she again stretched her fingers out, but he'd already spun away, anticipating and evading that touch. And as he wove about her, waltzing and gliding, her breath caught in what was far from fear and only an awareness of him and his body's skilled movements.

And when he abruptly stopped, she found herself mourning the end of that magnificent display.

"Now, until you learn the feel of your body, you're never going to learn how to use it in the ways it is intended to be used. And you're never going to properly feel anything in those skirts, Lila."

There was a beautiful poetry to his explanation, one that drove back some—not all—of her inhibitions. His words made sense in ways she'd not have considered.

"Very well." Before her courage deserted her, Lila gathered up the garments, hugging them protectively against her chest as the ramifications of what he required, and what she'd agreed to, sent a familiar panic knocking around her breast. "Where do I . . . ?" *Oh, God.* "Where . . . ?" She couldn't get the words out.

He lifted a brow. "What's that?"

He was enjoying this. *The Devil.*

But then, when one made a deal with the Devil, one found oneself burnt.

Lila lifted her chin. "Where do I change my garments, Hugh?"

He angled his head, and she followed that gesture over to the four-paneled ebony screen in the corner; the dark wood had carved into the panels the same dragon and coiled serpent that marked Hugh's chest.

"What's the problem now, Flittermouse?"

Everything.

"Nothing." The lie rolled off her tongue with a surprising ease. Maintaining the proud angle of her neck and head, she marched across the room. "There is no problem." There was really all manner of them.

The moment she stepped around the ominous screen, her shoulders sagged.

This is reckless. Absolute recklessness.

An erratic giggle worked up her throat and spilled from her lips.

"Something funny, Lila?"

Quite the opposite. "Is humor disallowed here?" she shot back, the four-paneled screen making her bold. Or stupid.

"Yes."

Hmph. Well, what was she to say to *that*?

"Get on with it, then."

Get on with it.

Before her courage deserted her. Lila started on the laces at the front of her gown. Her hands trembled so badly the velvet string slipped from her fingers. She struggled several times, and then with a silent curse, she gave up.

Laying her head against the wall, Lila concentrated on the slight cracks where the screen folded. On the other side, Hugh unbuttoned his silk black waistcoat. Her mouth went dry, and this time it wasn't fear's response that took over. Knowing that same lure as those poor moths to the flame, Lila crept over and pressed her eye against one of the folds in the panel, squinting in a bid to bring Hugh Savage into greater focus. She gasped softly.

In the short time in which she'd known him, Lila had seen the proprietor in various states of dishabille. Why, she'd even come upon him when he'd been bare-chested. But this instance? Unobserved as she was, there was something so very wicked in watching an unsuspecting Hugh Savage in his state of undress. Unapologetically, she gawked at the ripple of his muscles as he moved. He reached for the waistband of his trousers, and she leaned forward, on the tips of her toes . . .

Hugh's gaze collided with hers through the screen.

Gasping, she jumped back.

"Having doubts, Flittermouse?"

Yes, but not for the reasons he expected.

"Have you finally realized you've been reckless in coming here?"

That word echoed, Hugh's deep baritone morphing into another person's softer, delicate tones.

"It's reckless for us to go, Lila . . ."

"Lila?" Hugh called from the other side, and there wasn't the usual mockery or disdain, and just then, she found herself wishing for those safer sentiments than his concern.

The present cut through the memories of her and Annalee that August day . . .

"J-just one more moment," she returned, proud of that nearly steady deliverance.

This time, Lila managed to catch the strings of her day dress and give them a tug. The muslin garment slipped down her frame, falling in a flutter about her ankles. Stepping over it, she then tugged off her chemise.

"Does it always take you this long to undress?"

And oddly, the return of his annoyance proved steadying, and she found herself smiling. An honest and real smile. "This is actually quick," she said as she carefully laid her dress and chemise over the top of the screen. "It generally takes a lady much longer to see to her attire."

He snorted.

Lila hurriedly drew on the breeches, tying them at the waist. Belonging to a man near in height to her own, they hung a bit long at her ankles, and yet . . . she turned left and right. There was a glorious freedom in the unencumbered articles.

And saints of wonder, if Hugh Savage hadn't been correct, after all.

Grabbing the lawn shirt, she pulled the stained garment overhead and stuffed the long tails inside the waistband of her trousers.

They were freeing. Mayhap that was why men wished to keep a lady trapped in her skirts.

With her hands on her hips, Lila looked down at herself—

Gasping, she crossed her arms at her chest.

"What is it *now*?" he asked, with his usual impatience.

"I'm . . . not at all certain if . . ."

"If?" he snapped when she didn't finish her thought.

If it was appropriate. Only, she couldn't very well say as much. After all, there was nothing appropriate—in her attire, in her being here, in her discussions with Hugh Savage.

"You are certain this is the only way?" she tried once more. "That you cannot teach me in skirts?"

"I'm not going to be able to teach you anything soon, Lila. If today is any indication, your lessons are going to consist of your coming here, debating me on some damned point or another, then changing into your fighting garments, and then immediately having to change out because you wasted every bloody minute."

She wrinkled her nose. Yes, well, she supposed when he put it *that* way . . .

Furthermore, aside from one heated glance that may or may not have been part of her imagining, he'd not behaved in any way untowardly. Why, more often than not, he didn't even seem to like her.

"Have no worries, Flittermouse," he added. Lila stepped out from behind the screen. "You have my assurance, the last thing you have to worry about is me desiring y . . ." As he faced her, his words trailed off.

⁂

With Lila March hovering at the edge of that screen, there came but one coherent thought: breeches had been a bloody rotten idea. Nay, not just the breeches. The whole damned ensemble. From the thin lawn fabric all the way on to trousers that proved nearly a perfect fit for her.

It was not, however, for the reasons the young lady had feared.

And for ones Hugh couldn't have anticipated.

After all, living in the rookeries, he'd seen any manner of women in all manner of dress . . . including garments like the ones she wore now.

Never, however, had those coarser, life-hardened street figures borne the allure that Lila the Flittermouse did before him now.

Hugh worked a stare over her.

He'd not been wrong at his first perception of her: the woman was lean and barely curved, but the subtlety of that flare of her hips and buttocks proved more enticing than any overblown, fleshy frames. That thin shirt put her breasts on proud display.

And he swallowed a groan.

Lila followed his gaze downward, and it only invited his attention. She cleared her throat. "Is this all right?"

Had she been another woman of experience, born to these streets, there'd have been no doubt that with her question, she was being coy.

There was only an honesty and directness to the woman before him that enticed.

It wasn't even close to all right. Not the captivating way in which the wool garment clung to her lithe frame and accentuated her cinched waist and the slight swells of her buttocks. The threadbare article may as well have been translucent, outlining the curve of her breasts, and— she angled her arms back slightly and peeked down at herself—if one looked close enough, one could even make out the dusky portion of her nipples. He grunted. "You *cannot* wear that."

Her expression fell.

"Not because you don't look . . . not because you aren't . . ." And wonder of wonders, Hugh Savage found himself stuttering and stumbling through an exchange. If anyone were present to observe it, his reputation would have been effectively killed.

"What are you saying?" she asked with her usual bluntness.

"We need to bind you."

Her cheeks blossomed with color, bright round circles that put him in mind of apples, and damned if he didn't have a sudden taste for that sweet fruit.

"No."

It took a moment to register that the woman before him was issuing that denial. And it took an even longer moment to try and work his way back to the last words they'd exchanged.

"I'll not be bound," she said, providing that clarification he needed.

By God, he'd broken his own rule to never provide instructions on fighting . . . the same rule he'd held Maynard and Bragger to as well. And he should have chosen this insolent scrap of a woman who fought him on every damned point?

He opened his mouth to shut down this latest show of rebellion, but Lila cut Hugh off before he could speak.

"By your own admission, until I learn the feel of my body, I'm never going to learn how to use it in the ways it is intended to be used."

Hugh forced back a groan.

They were his words repeated back, and yet, when spoken in that husky, almost whispery, soft voice, it lent a seductiveness to what had merely been fighting talk.

"You . . ."

She made a face. "If you think skirts are problematic to me learning to be free with my movements, then why would binding not be?"

"Because . . . because . . ." Hugh floundered.

Lila folded her arms, plumping those small, perfectly rounded mounds, an exact fit for his palms, and desire blazed to life once more.

That was why binding was necessary, because of the damned distraction her lithe form presented. And yet . . . at the same time, the minx was right in her challenge. Nonetheless, he tried once more. "Didn't you just moments ago, yourself, say you couldn't wear these?"

"Yes." Lila flashed a small smile, a pleased-with-herself little grin. "But you made a very convincing argument."

Of course he had. *Blast and damn.* He slashed a hand toward the center of the arena. "Get in the middle of the ring. Now," he went on after she'd found a place in the middle of the room. "Your being here isn't to learn how to fight. Am I correct?"

She hesitated, that pregnant pause telling. "I don't know what you mean."

"Yes, you do. If you'd wished to learn how to box, you would have gone to Gentleman Jackson. He would have been your number-one choice, but you came to me."

The lady gave a slight nod.

"Then, a lesson about survival," he continued, taking up a place before her. "There're no rules in surviving. There isn't a respectable way to punch or not punch someone, because all that matters, Lila," he said quietly, drifting closer. The smell of her proved distracting, a floral aphrodisiac out of place with the blood, sweat, and age of the old building he'd made into an empire. "All that matters," he repeated, forcing himself through her siren's scent, "is knowing where to strike a person." He brought his hand up, and she tensed as Hugh lightly cupped her waist. "The kidneys." He glided a hand down the small of her back. "Tailbone."

Her breathing grew lightly shallow, the rasp one of desire.

Hugh dusted his other hand down her cheek, and he briefly and lightly cradled her face. "Jaw hinge." Gliding his palm back to her face, he angled her head slightly so that her neck was arched and exposed. Only somewhere along the way, what had begun as a perfunctory lesson had shifted . . . Undercurrents of sexual tension rippled as he became sucked deeper into whatever trap he'd inadvertently set for himself. "The side of the neck," he murmured, touching the underside of her arm. "The pit of one's arm." Stretching his arm down, he stroked her leg. "The kneecap," he murmured.

Her heavy-lidded eyes followed his every move.

Dropping to his haunches, he caught her left foot, encircling it in his hand. "The ankle."

"Tr-truly?" she asked, faintly breathless. "The ankle?"

"Oh, yes." A portion of the body he'd never seen beyond a place of vulnerability to be turned against one's opponent. Never, in any of the women he'd bedded, had he noted just how desirable that slight curve was where the foot met the leg.

"The . . . groin." His words came out thick.

Color spilled over her cheeks, and Hugh jumped up.

"The temple." Hugh dusted the tip of his index finger in a delicate caress along that tender spot of her head. "And the nose, of course."

She touched that pert little buttonlike appendage, drawing his eyes to the dusting of freckles, bright little flecks upon her almost ghastly-white skin.

"The eyes." He touched the corners of her almond-shaped ones. "And, of course," he murmured. Hugh cupped her nape. "*Here.* The neck." Hers, so graceful and so long. His eyes locked on the pulse hammering at her throat.

Lila tipped her head back a fraction until their eyes met, and their lips nearly brushed.

The air all but crackled from the undercurrents of energy thrumming around and between them.

Lila darted out the pink tip of her tongue and trailed it around the seam.

Hugh's eyes locked on that enticing flesh . . . and his honor, the vow he'd made to devote his life to finding and caring after another, waged with desire. He lowered his head, closer. Wanting a taste of her. Wanting to feel her passion set free, and because of his embrace.

What are you thinking?

"Time is up," he said gruffly.

"What?" Her eyes flew wide. "But . . ." Regret lit their fathomless brown depths, and he couldn't hazard whether those sentiments came from the shattered connection, or the end of their lesson. "We cannot end now. You said we had an hour."

She was impossible, and she was going to make these damned lessons impossible.

He stepped away from her, needing some space between them. "An hour, Flittermouse. An hour is what you've had."

"But we've only begun." For all the hesitancy and fear she'd shown in his presence, she proved remarkably stubborn at every turn.

People didn't challenge him. As one reviled by all, one who inspired terror in all, it was a foreign response. One that stirred an unwanted appreciation of and for the lady.

"Whatever time you waste is yours. It's not mine. I have a business to see to."

And if looks could kill, she'd have set him into a pile of ash from the fire blazing in her eyes. "That was why you insisted I change my garments. To prove a blasted point?" she said between clenched teeth.

"You do need to wear breeches and learn how to use your body."

Lila threw her arms up in the air. "But going over the twelve identifying points didn't require I change."

He shrugged. "Timing matters. It's all about timing. Consider that your first lesson."

She stamped her bare foot, endearingly sweet in her fury and indignation. "But . . . our time is limited. This cannot be an entire lesson."

"It is *how* you use your time that matters. Don't forget that tomorrow, Lila."

Lila locked her eyes on him, glaring blackly, and then stomping her way over to the screen, she slipped around the corner.

The moment she'd disappeared behind the four panels, he swiped a hand down his face.

He'd always disavowed teaching anyone how to fight. His reasons went back to his earliest days as an orphan on the street, used by Dooley to teach. And whether a person had lived or died had all fallen at his feet. As such, the moment he'd first left London, he'd vowed to never again school others in that ruthless *art*.

Not for the first time, he questioned his having agreed not only to Lila's request for lessons but also to let her in here, in this place that was sacrosanct to Hugh and the only two people in the world he'd trusted.

Though your regrets and reservations are not just about Maynard and Bragger or any vow you made to them. It was about the fact that since Lila had shed her cloak and donned a pair of trousers, Hugh had found himself besieged by a hungering that could only be dangerous. He'd not given the thought he should to the person it should be on—the last person he'd vowed to protect.

As if to lend a further edge to that silent taunting in his mind, the faint rustle of fabric as Lila removed those garments filled the quiet.

And an image slid in of her in all her glorious nudity, without lawn or linen or wool between his eyes and her delicate form.

When she emerged a few moments later, her gown and cloak were back in place, as were her serviceable leather boots. Not breaking stride, she marched to the doorway.

"Goodbye, Lila."

Not bothering with a farewell, the lady slammed the panel hard behind her.

Hugh grinned.

What he'd not expected in taking on the stubborn Lila March as a student was just how much he was actually going to enjoy himself.

Chapter 10

The following morn, making another journey to Hugh's, she was filled with the same indignation as when she'd left.

It is how you use your time that matters. Don't forget that tomorrow, Lila . . .

"'Don't forget,' he says," she mumbled, rocking and swaying as the carriage hit the same bumps and broken cobblestones of East London.

Well, today she'd not make the same mistake. She'd simply failed to know the kind of rules her instructor from the rookeries intended to play by.

When she arrived today, she wasn't going to squander any of their time, and she certainly wasn't going to give him grounds with which to cut her lessons any shorter than they already were. As such, when she'd arisen that morning, she'd donned not another dark dress for their meeting, but rather, the borrowed breeches and shirt.

She yanked the curtain aside a fraction and peered out. Clouds hung heavy in the London sky, and the streets were pitched black for it. Restless, she let the curtains fall back into place.

Does your annoyance stem from the lesson he doled out . . . or the fact that you thought he intended to kiss you and you wanted it?

Had wanted it desperately.

Which was, of course, ridiculous: both the idea that she had in that moment, with his hands upon her, yearned for his kiss, and even the idea that he may himself have wanted that embrace.

Why, not only *hadn't* he kissed her, he'd sent her promptly packing, and only after his *lesson*.

Either way, there could be no doubting the fire that had sparked languidly and then unfurled within as he'd schooled her on the twelve places to fell one's opponent.

Throughout that lesson, his touch had been perfunctory and purposeful. Her body, however, had not cared for any distinction. It had known only a wicked hungering for more of those fleeting caresses. Caresses he'd not intended to be anything more.

With a sigh, Lila let her head fall back and stared at the hood of the carriage.

How long had it been since she'd let herself feel any emotion except fear? Outrage, indignation, fury, pride—an entire maelstrom of emotions all came alive whenever she sparred with Hugh. Hugh, who didn't tiptoe about her, and who met her eyes squarely. In a world where her own family didn't know how to be around Lila, Hugh challenged her, and she felt so very alive for it.

Granted, he didn't know of her scars or the horror she'd lived through at Manchester. Nor, by his own admission, did he want to know anything about her.

Again drawing back the curtain a fraction, she stared out at the streets of St. Giles.

But something told her, even if he had known the truth, he'd not have treated her differently. Scarred and marked and cynical as he was, he'd likely known hells far greater than what she'd endured that day.

At the time, the promise she'd made to not ask Hugh any questions about his past had been an easy one to make. When she'd decided to seek him out, she'd done so not wanting to know the secrets he carried, or how he'd come to be a ruthless fighter who, by society's reports, had killed men with his bare hands. Nay, to ease her own anxieties and fears, she'd simply wanted the lessons he could impart—she'd wanted nothing of the man he was.

Now, she wondered . . . and wished to know.

How did a man who spoke refined King's English, and who wore fine garments befitting an affluent gentleman, come to live in the rookeries?

The hack came to a stop, and Lila pressed the handle, letting herself out. She jumped down. As she started for those nineteen and a half steps to the back of his fighting club, there was a spring to her step. Even with her cloak, there was a remarkable freedom of movement afforded by the breeches.

And there was also an increasing ease in leaving her household.

Nay, that wasn't entirely correct. There was a growing comfort in coming here to be with Hugh Savage. And in her speaking with someone who didn't know her as Lila the Recluse, who'd gone mad in Manchester.

Hugh didn't know Lila's history, and as such, she'd found a freedom in being someone—anyone—other than the person she'd become after Peterloo.

A lie.

A lie was what she'd given him.

A memory slid forward: a brief but telling exchange between Hugh Savage and his partner.

I don't have dealings with the nobility . . . I don't trust them . . .

She stopped at the top of the stone stairway and looked down.

It wasn't really a lie. He'd not asked her if she was a lady of the peerage.

As such, one might argue it was simply a lie of omission.

One who is a liar, that is.

A man such as Hugh Savage wasn't one who'd forgive any lie. And yet what choice had there been? Even as she attempted to reassure herself about the choice she'd made, guilt knotted up her stomach. No longer just the twinge it had been two days ago. That sentiment was growing.

Furthermore, their time together was limited. When Lila's family returned, she wouldn't be able to sneak about as she did. Yes, soon she'd be gone, and he'd never know the truth of her identity.

Neither of which, as she made her way down the stairs, eased her guilt or made her feel better . . . in any way.

Because she found she enjoyed *being* with him. Short though the time had been, she'd spoken more, and felt more, than she had in so long.

Lila lifted her hand . . .

This time, the door was opened before her fist hit the panel.

"Good morning, Hugh." Her heart lifted at the sight of him. Like all their meetings prior, he rarely bothered with a jacket, and where that had first shocked, there was a comfortable intimacy to his preferred state of dress . . . or undress, rather.

He scowled. "Are you going to come inside?" he asked, and she sprang forward.

"Yes, I . . . oh, this is one of those rhetorical questions."

"Brava, Flittermouse." He pushed the door shut behind her. "You're late."

Because I was hanging around your steps, feeling all degrees of guilt. Unable to meet his eyes, Lila made a show of removing her cloak. "I'm here now." She set the garment down over the low ledge that separated the seating from the arena and faced him. "And another thing." She rested her hands on her hips. "I've told you, I'm not a mouse. I'm not a bat. I'm a woman."

"Aye, that I see." His lashes swept down, an inky-black blanket that obscured his eyes but still couldn't conceal the burn of the stare he raked over her.

And all her indignation went out the proverbial window as she had confirmation to the question she'd had upon leaving . . . he desired her.

Because she was the Earl of Waterson's sister, none of the boys in the village had ever been anything but respectful around her. When she'd just turned eighteen, a woman by society's standards, her life had fallen apart. As such, there'd been no stolen looks or heated touches. Moments of passion and excited pitter-pattering of a heartbeat from a mere glance had been just more gifts taken from her. All that had remained after Manchester was a scared, scarred mouse of a woman.

Hugh's gaze scorched her from the inside out, touching her to the quick, and she reveled in a new discovery: she was a woman, and even flawed and marked and weak as she was . . . this man desired her.

"Shall we?" he murmured, his baritone washing over her like so much warmed chocolate.

"Yes," she whispered.

"All right, then," he said, no-nonsense, walking to the center of the arena.

Humiliation scorched her, and she gave thanks that he'd not noted her response to him.

When he looked back questioningly, she affixed a grin.

"Why are you smiling like that?"

Oh, God.

"Like what?" she asked through her teeth.

He peered at her. "Odd-like. Silly and"—*Oh, that was really enough*—"dazed."

She bristled with indignation. *"Dazed?"*

"Like you took a punch to the solar plexus."

Yes, well, Hugh Savage did have that effect on a woman. "Given your edifying lesson on the use of time, I hardly think a lengthy discussion on what I do with my lips merits."

The blue of his eyes turned a shade very nearly black.

What in her words was behind that sudden darkening, or was it just his customary annoyance?

Lila shifted on her feet. "What *now?*"

He grunted. "Let's begin."

She joined him in the middle of the arena.

"If you'd sought out your Gentleman Jackson—"

"He isn't *my* Gentleman Jackson. Nor—"

"Pay attention," he chided. "Jackson follows the rules he created: only use one's fists in a fight." Hugh sneered, his disdain palpable. He lifted his arms into perfect ninety-degree angles and sank his weight back over his legs, demonstrating a fighting form. Hugh threw a punch at the air, and she took a reflexive step away. "They teach boxing as a gentleman's sport. They erase the ruthlessness from bare-knuckle fighting to cater to those fine lords because of their nobility. They don't have to scratch and claw in the streets to survive. Their existences are safe, unthreatened."

Their nobility . . . Their existences are safe, unthreatened . . .

Lila stared blankly on as Hugh displayed several more positions of a gentleman's fighting pose.

That was what he believed. That was, in fact, what most of the world did—the peerage included. Peril didn't come to the wealthiest, ruling elite. Nay, they were safe. Insulated. Protected from the horrors of existing.

They—Hugh included—didn't think women like Annalee . . . or Lila . . . or any of the other men and women who'd fallen or been scarred at Peterloo, could ever know what it was to suffer.

That when the world had been set ablaze, she'd been trampled and dragged.

Hold the line . . . Hold the line . . .

Mooove, you whore . . .

"Lila?"

A heavy palm settled on her shoulder, and gasping, she brought an arm up to fend off the attack . . . that, this time, didn't come. She struggled through the quagmire of the past, creeping back to the present.

She was here. Not in the open fields of Manchester, running from slaughter, but here in the rookeries.

Oddly safe, in the place where one would expect there to be a greater peril than in St. Peter's Field.

"Hugh," she said dumbly. At some point, he had ceased his lesson . . . and offered this quiet concern in place of his usual annoyance. Her eyes pricked with tears, and she blinked several times in a desperate attempt to hide those drops. A man such as him would only look with loathing upon that weakness. "Forgive me." A lone tear trickled down her cheek, and she discreetly dashed at it. "I was distracted."

He caught her chin in his hand, angling her face toward his.

Damn him for not allowing her to keep her tears a secret. *What did you expect? That Hugh Savage should show you any mercy?* She tipped her head back and dared him with her eyes to say anything about the telltale sign of misery.

And then he flicked the pad of his thumb out and wiped the damp trail the tear had streaked down her cheek.

Lila sucked in a soft, little breath at that gentle caress . . . and the unexpected tenderness from him.

His gaze went to that hideous scar that ran down the middle of her forehead, and for one horrifying moment she believed he intended to ask after its origins. He moved a callused finger along the jagged slash of skin. Time had faded it, but every day she woke up, every day she looked in the mirror, it was there, a visible reminder of her foolishness. Her ineptness. "In a battle, Lila," he said softly, "you don't use your fists. You use your nails. Your feet. Even your goddamned teeth in order to survive."

She waited for him to release her, but he didn't.

And more, she didn't want him to.

Her heart began to pound . . . not at those remembered horrors of yesteryear, but because of this man. And his touch.

The air crackled and sizzled with the same volatile thrum that had rolled through St. Peter's Field. But at the same time, differently. This was not born of danger but rather some other unbridled, raw, and powerful emotion.

Hugh's gaze slipped over her face, and she remained absolutely still; her eyes, however, moved a similar path along his.

The slight scruff upon cheeks that had missed their morning shave. The crooked angle of a nose that had been broken undoubtedly too many times.

She continued her search lower.

And then stopped, lingering on a number inked upon his chest, revealed only because of the slight gape in fabric. Of their own volition, her fingers came up, and she found herself caressing that mark. *Him.*

"Sixteen," she murmured. That same number so significant to the date that had changed everything.

The muscles in his chiseled face rippled; the energy all around them continued to pulse with a harder, more unremittent pounding.

"Why do you have this here?" she whispered, breaking the rules he'd laid out, but unable to care. Because she needed to know. About the mark. About him.

"I don't answer questions." His breath rasped against her mouth.

And then his lips were on hers.

At last.

And it was, all at once, everything she'd hungered for, and nothing she could have ever prepared for or dreamed of.

Nay, it was him. This man. *His* kiss.

It was The Kiss she'd never thought to know for the sheltered life she lived, only to find life did still exist in glorious color.

He licked at her lips, like she was some confectionary treat he was both discovering and savoring. And she groaned.

Or mayhap that little rumble belonged to him because her lips thrummed and trembled.

Lila curled her fingers into the soft fabric of his shirt; a wall of corded muscles rippled. Because of her. Her touch. And she thrilled at the discovery of her own feminine power.

He deepened their kiss, the bold slash of his lips, over and over again, and Lila couldn't make sense over why women worried after their reputations or sin and scandal when there was anything so glorious as this.

Her heart was pounding wildly.

Hard and fast and loud.

Wait . . . Confusion rooted around her brain—it *wasn't* her heart.

It was . . . heavy footfalls.

Hugh tore his mouth from hers.

"You have to go," he whispered roughly against her mouth.

Lila tried to blink back the haze of desire and confusion. Go? Go where? She couldn't leave. She didn't want to leave. Not him. Not this moment. "But . . ."

Sprinting across the room, Hugh gathered up her things and tossed them into her arms. Then, taking her by the hand, he steered her to the door.

Lila dug her heels in. "My hour is not up."

"Something has come up," he gritted, grabbing the door handle.

She refused to budge. "But . . ."

"What's the meaning of this?"

Her words trailed off as she turned and caught sight of the men who'd greeted her two days earlier. "Oh." This was why he was sending her packing so quickly. At her first encounter with his partners, they had been all mocking condescension. Now, a dangerous fury poured from Maynard's muscle-hewn frame.

The taller fighter, Bragger, looked at them. "What the hell is she doing here?"

Quietly cursing, Hugh positioned himself between her and his partners. "She was—"

She stepped out from behind the shield of his body. "I was receiving lessons."

The pair of surly fighters glanced at one another, and then both turned those street-hardened stares upon Lila and Hugh.

Chapter 11

Bloody hell, this was bad.

Tension hung over the room like a palpable force.

It was certainly not the first they'd brimmed with barely suppressed fury. It was, however, the first time that rage had been directed Hugh's way. What in hell were they doing here? The arena was quiet from four thirty to nine o'clock.

Bragger's eyes formed razor slits, the knowing glint indicating the other man knew precisely what he'd been thinking. But then, nothing was truly Hugh's. He owned nothing. And he owed everything to the very man who set the rules of this arena.

Maynard looped his thumbs into the waist of his trousers. "Handing out lessons, is he?"

Aye, talking over him, cutting him from the discourse—this was very bad, indeed.

Bragger continued his cold scrutiny, and Hugh reflexively positioned himself squarely in front of Lila, blocking her off from the other man's fiery rage.

Again, she stepped out from behind Hugh. "He is."

Of course the spirited minx wouldn't know better than to let it be.

"Lila," Hugh warned. He spoke in hushed tones reserved for her ears. "We'll continue another day." Because nothing good could come from her staying here, and certainly not in her debating one like Bragger. "Now—"

"You're done here," Bragger stated with a finality that brooked no objection.

Lila frowned. She moved her focus over to Hugh. "But the papers say you're a part owner. Are you not? Because if you are, I don't see why—"

"Why is she still here?" Bragger called over, his low baritone echoing around the empty arena.

Hugh pressed his eyes closed and prayed for patience. "It is a minority partnership." One that saw him with the least earnings raked in after fights, but if he lost that, he'd be the same pathetic, poor bastard in a tattered crimson uniform, wandering the streets with his palms extended, pleading for handouts.

"But surely whatever that amount in fact is, you've the ability to make a decision as to how you spend your time?"

"This isn't the time to discuss my damned percentage share."

"What the hell are they talking about?" Maynard puzzled aloud.

"Perhaps I can reason with him?" Lila continued.

"No." He'd spare her that effort. "You're wasting your—"

Lila lifted a palm like a lady calling out for a hackney. "Mr. Bragger, is it? Mr. Savage and I"—she swept that hand toward Hugh, bringing his partners' gaze swinging his way. As if there were another Mr. Savage she might somehow be referring to. And he resisted the urge to yank at his shirt—"we'd some time remaining—"

Bragger cut her off. "I meant, you're done here, completely. Not this lesson. All your lessons. Any of them. That's not the kind of business we're in." With that, his partner angled a shoulder dismissively. "See her out, Savage."

Aye. He'd no intention of reneging on the agreement he'd come to with her but knew enough that it wasn't in his best interest to dispute his partners over it. Hugh reached for Lila's hand.

She stared at his fingers, then lifted that disapproving gaze to him. With a distinct slowness, she edged away from his touch.

And not for the first time in his life, he found himself humbled . . . from the sense of his own inferiority. For now Lila, who'd sought him out, making him out to be someone more than he was, had seen his worth, too. On the heels of that red-hot shame came a stinging fury. With his partners for commanding his days. With her. With himself for caring about her and her ill opinion. He set his jaw. To hell with her and her judgment. She knew nothing about him or the debt he owed. "We're done," he said, reaching for the door handle.

"We have a v—" Bragger went on.

"I'm not leaving."

And with that, Lila managed what had otherwise been an impossible feat: she'd gone toe-to-toe with Bragger and effectively silenced the ruthless warrior of the streets.

He took a step toward her. "What did you say?"

"Lila," Hugh said curtly, lightly taking her by the arm.

And with a breathtaking display of courage, she tipped her chin up. "What gives you the right to decide whether or not Mr. Savage provides me with instruction?" Good God, if he weren't so exasperated by her stubborn refusal to quit, he'd have been further entranced by her.

Entranced?

Hugh rocked on his heels. Where in hell had *that* come from?

Maynard whistled slowly, and gave his head a slow shake.

Bragger smiled coldly. "Everything gives me that right. Everything."

"But—"

"Lila." Hugh caught her by the wrist. Bragger wasn't one to be crossed. None of them were. But the other man's reputation had him as one who'd ruined men . . . and women alike. "You have to go."

And she must have seen something in his eyes, for this time when he opened the panel, she lingered just one moment more . . . and then left.

"Angus is here," Maynard announced the moment the door panel had clicked shut.

"Angus?" Hugh echoed.

A cool smile played on Bragger's lips. "Angus, the man who's been our eyes and ears in London. The man helping us find Val." Val. Hugh's stomach muscles knotted up. Val, whom he'd not given proper thought to since Lila had begun coming around. "I trust you've not forgotten Val?" Bragger asked, accurately following those guilty musings running around Hugh's head.

"Come on, now," Maynard murmured. "Angus is waiting."

"Where is he?" Hugh asked tersely. Nor did he think for one moment they were done talking about Lila's presence here. It was, however, a temporary reprieve he welcomed.

Cocking his head, a laconic-even-for-him Bragger led the way. Maynard, always one to avoid conflict within their group, avoided Hugh's eyes and fell into step beside him as they joined Bragger.

For years, their every focus had been on locating the ones responsible for their suffering . . . and on finding the lost member of their group. It was what had fueled them all. Their purpose had come in getting justice.

And now?

And now, you're spending all your time and thoughts on some woman you've only just met . . .

They found Angus waiting in their offices. A former member of Savage's, the sturdy Scot possessed a lion's mane of unkempt red hair to match his equally unkempt beard. How it was someone of his six feet five inches and broad size managed to sneak around the underbelly of London remained a frequent wondering of those in the Covent Garden, but was understood by the same boys—now men—who'd become adept at foot skills.

Angus sipped at his flask, that carved of wood piece he'd not been without since he'd beaten his handler and taken the flask as a trophy.

"I've got information fer ye," he announced without preamble. He swiped at his damp beard and then stuffed the wood flask into the front of his jacket.

Hugh's heart hammered. "What did you find?"

"First, congratulations are in order. Ye did a guid job oan Dooley." He flashed a grin missing several teeth. "Th' dobber didne lae his hoose fer three days."

Hugh went motionless.

"Och, aye, the day he left an' Ah followed heem."

His heart hammered. Dooley, who'd been hiding for years, had grown sloppy. But then, fear did that to a person. "Where did he go?"

"White's."

Maynard chuckled. "Of course 'e did."

And for all the missteps he'd made, and underestimations, in this, Dooley hadn't proven so damned foolish, after all. "It was strategic," Hugh explained. "He knew it was a place where we were sure not to be." Some lords hid in London's underbelly. Those who'd made Hugh and the others' lives a living hell had chosen to hide in plain sight . . . in their world . . . a world Hugh, Maynard, Bragger, and Angus would never dare enter.

"Did he exit alone?" Bragger asked.

Angus lifted one broad shoulder. "He ne'er exited. Loch a ghost, he was."

"Or he used the back exit," Bragger said dryly.

"Nae. He's a ghost coz Ah went aroond tae his apartments an' thaur was nae trace ay heem."

Hugh cursed. *Bloody hell.* Dooley was being protected by the nobility.

The burly Scot scowled. "Whit is it?"

"You won't find him," Hugh said quietly. "The nobility? They'll protect one another from our sort."

And yet . . . there'd been a reason for his sudden resurrection. Ten years they'd been searching for Dooley. Ten years scouring all of East London and asking throughout the most lethal, perilous streets. Dooley represented the one sure link to the fight club they'd been forced into. He stopped abruptly. "You're going to need someone with links to the peerage."

Angus sputtered. "Ahm doin' finn enough."

"It's not your fault," Hugh said, softening the blow. "Whomever it is set Dooley loose to see if we were still a threat." In their haste, they'd played right into their enemy's hands.

"At least the bastard knows we intend to destroy him," Bragger said, cracking his knuckles.

"That'll be all," Maynard said to Angus.

The other man hesitated, and then nodding, he took his leave.

"What now?" Maynard asked quietly.

Silence met that question.

"It's as I said, you're . . . we're going to need someone with a way into that world." Until then, they'd be circling, clueless as they'd been for all these years.

"If 'e's used Dooley as bait once, 'e'll do it again," Maynard murmured. "We were rash before. Won't make the same mistake twice."

His partners, however, were so bent on revenge that they let it get in the way of reason.

"And if he doesn't reemerge this time?" Bragger asked, removing a cheroot from his pocket. "We've waited years to get even this close to the bastard." He touched the edge of that scrap to a lone candle lit on his desk, and then inhaled from the cheroot.

"He will," Hugh said. He had to. And then it would be done.

"There remains one other bit of business to discuss." Bragger took a long draw from his cheroot, all the while glaring at Hugh over that scrap. He exhaled out the side of his mouth.

Aye, there was not to be any escaping the discussion.

"What was she doing here?"

"Lessons, wasn't it?" Maynard asked, dropping a hip against Bragger's table.

Hugh kept his face a careful mask through their baiting. "I didn't see any reason to refuse her."

"We're this close to bringing down the ringleader of the Foight Society." Bragger brought his thumb and forefinger so close they nearly touched. "And yar 'ere, entertaining a woman?" He sharpened a hard stare on Hugh. "There's only one woman we're focused on." A muscle tensed at the corner of Bragger's mouth. "Or we should be. Ya 'aven't been, though, 'ave ya?" He glanced to Maynard.

"'e 'asn't," the other man agreed with a nod. "Not the first toime it's 'appened, either, is it?"

Guilt scissored through him. It would always be there. Remorse. Shame. Regret. For having put himself first, and left so many others to perish.

"Seems like that's just another person Savage has gone and forgotten." Bragger flashed another icy smile. "Instead of keeping our energies focused on where they should be, 'e's busy with some fancy piece he doesn't know shite about."

"This is the closest we've been to finding the ones who tortured us . . . and Val," Maynard reminded.

That deliberate pause and slight emphasis sent the blade of guilt twisting all the more. Val and justice were where all his energies belonged. What kept him from providing his partners the assurances they sought? Why couldn't he just inform Lila March their arrangement was off? "I've given my word," Hugh said firmly. "And it won't interfere in what we're doing here."

Bragger shrugged. "Damned straight it won't." Ice filled his eyes. "And let us be clear, ya 'ave a debt to pay. Ya ain't a partner."

Hugh stiffened. It was the first time that truth had been stated aloud.

"We're done with this discussion about yar visitor. I don't want her in this arena."

Hugh steeled his jaw. "She's not a distraction." *Liar. You've thought of nearly nothing else except her since you came upon her in the alley 'round back, and given not a single thought to those we intend to have vengeance on.*

"It's done, Savage," Bragger said curtly. "We can't afford to 'ave people about we can't trust."

With that, the proprietors left.

The other men were right. Lila March represented nothing more than a distraction. As such, it should be altogether easy enough to sever his ties.

So why did the idea of ending it with the spirited minx leave him oddly bereft?

Chapter 12

After their explosive moment of passion and then ultimate discovery by his friends, Lila hadn't known what she was expecting when she returned for her lessons with Hugh the next morn.

Nay, she'd ruminated about all manner of possibilities: stilted awkwardness. A heated tension born of remembered passion.

What she'd not expected, however, was to find him waiting outside, his arms clasped behind him, at the top of the nineteen and a half steps where they'd first met. As if he'd been waiting for her arrival, as if he were restless for a mere glimpse of her.

Her heart hammered, and a smile pulled at her lips as she came to meet him.

"Good morning, Hu—"

"This isn't going to work."

Lila's legs ground to a halt under her, and through the clamoring confusion in her mind came but one word: "What?"

"You can't be here." He stole a glance around. As if fearing they were even now being watched. And it was a staggering moment of truth . . . discovering that even a man such as Hugh Savage was capable of disquiet.

That vulnerability made him real in ways that he'd not been before now. It made him even more into one whom she could relate with and connect to.

Lila arched an eyebrow. "Are you trying to get out of our arrangement?" she demanded. Except . . . she'd known him but a handful of days, yet knew enough that Hugh Savage wasn't a man who'd go back on his word. Not without reason.

Hugh dragged a hand through his hair. "No. That's not what this . . . is."

Understanding dawned. "It's because of your partners, then."

His mouth tautened, blanching the skin at the corners of his lips so the scars there stood out. "My partners have taken exception with your being here."

She waited for him to say something more than that.

Yet still found herself waiting several moments later as it became abundantly clear he intended to say nothing else about the pair, and it spoke to Hugh Savage's loyalty.

"Your partners won't allow you to use the arena as you see fit?" Annoyance swirled. "Who are *they* that they'd expect you to answer to them?"

A muscle rippled along his jaw. "You don't know anything about it, and it's not your business either way."

That crisp deliverance only further roused curiosity and frustration at the peculiar relationship Hugh had with his partners.

"You worry so much about what they say?" she asked.

"Those men saved me," he snapped, and then the color leached from his features, draining his skin to the pale white of his scars. He immediately went tight-lipped, and she knew no matter whether or how much she pressed, he'd reveal nothing more than that. And she'd not ask or force him to.

Even as I yearn to know what monsters are his . . .

It was a reminder that they were more alike than he would ever know, or believe.

"Just because someone saves you doesn't mean you owe them a blind allegiance, Hugh," she said gently, and rested a hand at his sleeve.

The muscles bunched under her touch, but he didn't pull away, and she took heart in that. "Let us . . . for now focus on finding a place to complete my lessons, and when we're done, you can go back to pleasing your partners."

She almost felt guilty about that challenge. Almost. But desperate times and all that called for even underhanded tactics.

Almost.

"I'm a minority shareowner of this place."

"So . . . you believe if you went against their wishes and continued my lessons here, they'd . . . turn you out?" What a lonely existence his was, and proud as he was, he'd likely end the discussion if he caught a hint of the sadness that took root. He'd see it only as pity and would never welcome such a sentiment. As such, she kept her features in a mask to match his own.

"I know I'm not in a position to anger my partners or act in my own interests," he said in a tone that marked an end to that discussion. "If you expect to receive your lessons, it isn't going to happen here."

Did he think to be done with her because of his surly partners? That she'd balk at the possibility of finding another place where they could meet?

Lila began to pace. Fact: his surly co-proprietors had cut short her lessons here. Fact: she and Hugh were now presented with the impossible task of finding a place to train. A place where they could work without being noticed.

Her pacing grew frantic. It certainly couldn't be Sylvia's. Even if there weren't the matter of a household of underfoot servants, Lila couldn't very well train inside her sister's home. It was one thing for Lila to learn how to fight. It was an altogether different one to bring that into her sister's household.

She stopped so abruptly her skirts snapped wildly about her. A smile spread on her cheeks. "Very well . . ." Lila left that there to dangle.

"What?" he asked warily.

"You said we must meet somewhere else, and I've a place."

A short while later, after a hackney ride on to her brother's household, closed up during Clara's confinement, and looked after by the remaining servants, Lila disembarked.

Hugh lingered in the carriage before joining her on the pavement. "What is this?" he asked from the corner of his mouth as she paid the driver.

"We needed a place to train, and I know of a vacant residence." Drawing her cloak closer, Lila peered about the still-empty streets that she'd grown up on. At this early hour, the fashionable sets always slept on. She'd once kept those same hours.

Not waiting to see whether he followed, she started on down Adam's Row. Hugh instantly fell into step alongside her. Together, they wound their way along the alleys intersecting with some of London's wealthiest townhouses. She'd learned—and benefited from—the fact that members of the *ton* wouldn't ever dare be found in those rodent-infested pathways traversed by servants and chimney sweeps.

Hugh, a man more than a foot taller than her, moved with grace, melding with the shadows as one born to them.

They reached the former servants' entrance, and Lila pressed the handle and stepped inside the darkened space.

It was a moment before Lila registered she stood alone in the narrow hall. She cast a questioning look back to where Hugh hovered outside still.

His features were set in a mask, his gaze wary as he ducked his head in and peered around. And for one agonizing moment she expected he'd turn about and walk off . . . reneging on this plan she'd hatched. On the training he'd promised to provide.

And then he stepped inside. Reaching behind him, he drew the panel closed.

Lila's heart pounded wildly, and that erratic knocking had nothing to do with the fact that she danced with the danger of discovery, here in her brother's townhouse, and everything to do with their closeness in these impossibly small quarters.

Hugh caught the sides of her hood and pushed it, baring her face.

Butterflies swarmed as they invariably did because of this man.

He lowered his head close, and her eyelashes fluttered closed as she lifted her lips to meet his, as everything was forgotten: the reason for their being here. The lessons she needed. All she knew was a familiar wanting for this man . . .

Except Hugh brought his mouth close to her ear, so close that as he spoke, his lips brushed the sensitive flesh. "You must be desperate to brave invading some fine nob's home and commandeering that space for your own lessons."

"Determined," she whispered, angling her neck back so that she might squarely meet his gaze. His piercing eyes that threatened to free her of her every secret continued to wreak havoc on her heart's rhythm. She'd been desperate when she'd sought him out. Eager to learn and help those she loved. Lila shed her cloak and let it fall to the floor. "Desperation has nothing to do with us being here." And desperation was something she knew a good deal about.

⌘

There'd been any number of times when Hugh had been awed and intrigued by Lila: the moment he'd spied her through the window. The following morn when she'd shown up, pressing him for lessons. When she'd faced down his partners.

This, however, this was the moment that would be how he forever remembered her.

Lila gathered up her cloak, folded it, and cleared a space on the dusty floor for a makeshift five-foot, narrow ring. She seated herself in the middle of the floor and proceeded to remove her boots until she was barefoot.

Clever woman.

She'd sense enough to mask her steps and avoid notice.

When she someday left and he wondered about the woman he'd once called Flittermouse, he'd think of her as she'd been, leading him on through London as if she were the princess of these streets and as capable at picking locks as she was at bending a man to her will.

It only raised further questions about Lila March, this mystery of a woman.

And God help him for the weak bastard his partners accused him of being; Hugh was hard-pressed to not be wholly enthralled by Lila's ingenuity and stealth—and her commitment to the lessons. Even as he hated fighting and had, at first, been wholly opposed to instructing her, she'd a resolve born of reasons she didn't want to share. Yet from an intuition that came from his time on the streets, he well knew something dark had driven her into his life. He could no more abandon her than he could quit the partners who'd rescued him.

As if feeling his stare, Lila set her boots along the wall and looked up. "What is it?" she whispered, a defensive little edge creeping into her dulcet contralto.

"*This* is what you've found for us?"

An adorable little frown pulled her lips down. "And just why shouldn't it be conducive?" she countered, climbing to her feet. She lifted her gloveless, scarred fingers up one at a time as she spoke, ticking each item off on her list. "One, you tasked me with finding a place, and I did. Two, I trust a person should be prepared to maneuver about even in small quarters."

He glanced around. The quarters she'd found them were decidedly small. "Is there a three?"

She swatted his arm. "Three, you're wasting the little time we have with one another."

"Consider me wary about finding myself hanged by some nobleman because I've gone and broken into his house."

"*I've* broken into it," she reminded him, pride layered into her voice.

Hugh scrubbed a hand down his face and stifled a laugh. "Damn if you aren't the only one who'd find pride in breaking into a nobleman's household." And mayhap he was all the way mad, for he found himself shrugging out of his jacket and laying it atop her cloak. "What is this place?"

He didn't imagine the long beat of silence between his question and her answer.

"Some years ago, the lord who lives here issued a redesign," she said sotto voce. "He was the earl who was reported to have been fleeced by a builder. To cut costs and maximize his earnings, the builder constructed new halls around the old ones, creating this." She gestured around. "Hidden passages."

That familiarity with Polite Society only served as a reminder that Lila March was a woman knowledgeable of this world. That she was a mystery. How did a woman become familiar with this end of society? That was . . . if she wasn't part of it. And coward that he was, Hugh didn't want to explore her connections or his misgivings.

Hugh motioned her over. "In ancient Asia, they denoted two styles of fight: hard and soft."

"I'd think all styles would be hard," she said as she rejoined him.

"It refers to how forcefully a defender counters the force of an attack in armed or unarmed fighting."

He backed up several steps and then held his palms up for her to remain where she was. "The hard technique is going to require greater strength for a successful execution; however, it is the mechanics which matter most. If you want to shatter a leg?" Hugh demonstrated a low kick, just landing a breath away from colliding with her knee. "You come at your opponent forcefully, without restraint, and land your blow."

She gasped and jumped back a step. Her shoulder collided with the wall in a damning echo.

They both went motionless, and Hugh waited for the lord's staff to descend.

When discovery didn't come, he urged her over. "Your turn."

Without hesitation, Lila came forward.

"Now, kicking, just as throwing a punch, is an art form. Get yourself into a boxing stance." When she had herself slightly hunched over and her hands close to her face, he guided her fists up a tad. "In terms of fighting, everything always comes back to boxing," he murmured. "Bring your knee toward you and stomp forward, and then bring it quickly back."

Lila shifted her weight onto her left leg and stumbled slightly.

Lila cursed and caught herself against him to keep herself upright.

"It's all right," he said softly. "It's new."

Just as this idea of him as an instructor was all foreign. "Knee toward your chest, like this"—he demonstrated the stance in slow motion—"and shift so the foot you're standing on pivots slightly away. Try again."

Lila got herself into her fighting stance, and then went through the movements of her side kick. Her plait slapped over her shoulders as she brought her leg sweeping out to the side and nearly collided with the wall.

She gave him a questioning look.

"Better." And it had been. "But you've got your leg fully extended on the kick, and you're locking it, here." He touched the back of her knee and instantly regretted it. Of their own volition, his fingers lingered there on her leg, the thin breeches she wore the only barrier between him and her actual skin.

Sweat beaded his brow, that perspiration having absolutely nothing to do with the lesson.

"I-is there a problem?" she whispered, casting a glance down at him.

Yes, there were all number of problems. Every last one of them stemming from his desire for this woman.

Hugh abruptly yanked his hand back. *Focus.* "No," he lied, and hastened to put some space between them and get back to the lesson. He kicked his leg out once more at the empty air. "It's going to be awkward until you practice the rhythm. Eventually, when you have it down, the quicker you move, the easier you'll find it is to maintain your balance."

They worked in silence, with Lila practicing several more side kicks.

He peered at her in the darkened corridor, taking in her efforts. She moved with a zeal, an eagerness to learn, and yet he'd also witnessed firsthand the perils of overexcited fighters. It made them careless, and even as averse as he was to training anyone on how to fight, he'd sooner chop off a limb than send Lila March out into the world ill-prepared to fight— should she need it. "Let me help you find the feel of it." Hugh positioned himself behind her; the cramped quarters heightened their bodies' closeness. The blood thickened in his veins. And whatever lesson he'd intended escaped him. He palmed the curve of her hip in an unwitting caress.

Her breath rasped . . . was it desire? Her exertions?

Or mayhap that was his own raggedly drawn breath?

He should release her, but even if the fine lord who lived here had come upon them, Hugh still wouldn't have been able to let Lila go. To break this connection.

❧

Lila had been wrong.

She couldn't handle lessons with Hugh Savage.

Only, it wasn't for the reasons she'd initially believed. Reasons that had stemmed from her own weakness and the demons that held her in chains.

Rather, it was him, Hugh Savage, the man.

Her pulse knocked around wildly.

"It's your hips that give you power," he said, his voice slightly hoarsened, and the feminine part of her that reveled in her womanhood thrilled at the discovery that he was as moved as she was by their nearness. That this desire that flared to life wasn't one-sided. That triumph proved short lived as Hugh guided her leg up and out so that it was stretched but not overextended. And the only things keeping her balanced in this unsettled moment were the hands he had on her.

He was once more all business, so that she might have imagined that evidence of his passion.

"When you stomp, you have to think of your power coming from your hips and not your legs. Kick," he instructed, and then as she did, as if to hammer home his point, he tipped her hips. She bit the inside of her cheek. "That's just one way to take your opponent down with a kick."

Lila glanced back over at him. "And the o-others?"

Hugh did a search of their space. "You wouldn't use them in here . . . or any close quarters such as these. Adapting to your space is a key element of fighting." He returned his gaze to hers, and the air came alive. His fingers curved almost reflexively into her hips, sinking into the flesh.

She briefly closed her eyes. She wanted his hands elsewhere. Everywhere.

Lila felt his breath, a cool sough against her neck, and leaned into him, laying her back against his chest. Angling her neck, she lifted her mouth to his.

With a guttural groan, Hugh claimed her lips, and she melted against him.

He was there to catch her. Turning her violently about so they faced one another, Hugh guided her against the wall, anchoring her there.

Their mouths met in a fiery explosion of desire, and she turned herself happily over to it, surrendering to him.

There was nothing tender about this kiss. He parted her lips, and she eagerly let him in. They engaged in a dance with their tongues so primitive it bordered on violence. But it was a violence of the greatest kind. One that left her feeling alive and sizzling inside.

Hugh wedged a leg between hers. She moaned into his mouth and moved against the solid muscle of his thigh. There was a delicious friction, and Lila rocked against him in time to the thrust and parry of his tongue. The pressure at her core built to an agonizing degree, and she increased that scandalous undulating.

They were wicked little gyrations that should have shocked or horrified her, but not with Hugh. Everything with him, every moment before and up to this very one now, was free of censure or shame or regret.

He shifted his mouth from hers, and she whimpered at the loss . . . But he placed his lips against her neck, suckling and teasing at the place where her pulse hammered.

Lila cried out.

Hugh softly cursed and covered her mouth lightly with his fingers.

But it was too late.

"What was that?"

And just like that, Lila's heart pounded for altogether different reasons. That distant but distinct voice of one of the maids rent through the moment.

Lila and Hugh both went motionless.

Removing his hand from her mouth, Hugh raised a fingertip to his lips, urging her to silence, and she struggled to rein in the rasp of her breath.

"Every morning, you insist you hear something in there," one of the parlor maids was saying.

Lila searched her mind, and placed that voice: Ava.

"Ain't natural, it is," the other girl . . . Mary . . . said defensively. "Closing in those halls. Keeping something in there, they are."

"Ghosts, they be," the other girl teased, and then dissolved into a flurry of laughter.

"Well, if you're so certain they ain't, Ava," Mary insisted, "you go have a look and find out for yourself."

Horror clutched at Lila's throat, and she took a step toward the doorway out.

Hugh caught her to him, keeping her in place beside him.

"Wh-what was that?" Ava croaked.

There was a beat of silence, and then the girls took off running in the opposite direction.

The footsteps retreated until they faded altogether and the only sound was that of Lila and Hugh's mingled breathing.

"Well known, indeed," he said in barely discernible tones against her ear.

Yes, her family's failed construction project was information that had fascinated the *ton* for some time before other gossip had taken its place.

"This isn't going to work," he whispered.

Her heart dipped. This was where it came, then—the rejection he'd been so insistent on giving her at their first meeting.

"We'll have to meet someplace else," he went on in that same hushed voice. "Someplace where we aren't going to find ourselves hanged for being there."

"And do you have a place in mind?" she returned, matching his quiet tones.

"My apartments."

It took a moment for those two words to sink in.

He'd invited her to . . .

He arched a brow. "That is, unless you have a problem meeting in my apartments?"

It had nothing to do with the location, and everything to do with the fact that they'd be alone. In his household, where there'd be none of her family or their servants on the fringes, one wrong move away from discovering Lila and all she was up to. "No. I've no problem," she lied.

Meeting in the privacy of his home could only be dangerous.

And yet she proved as reckless as she'd been at Manchester, for she found herself eager for tomorrow, when she'd join Hugh Savage in his apartments—alone.

Chapter 13

He'd not thought she'd show.

The following morning as he unlocked the oak door of his East London apartments and found Lila standing on his stoop, he accepted the young woman's resolve to continue her lessons and their arrangement.

Of course, he should have already gathered enough about her spirit and determination to know she'd never turn tail and run.

And now? Now, she was here.

She smiled. "Good morning, Hugh."

And with the same command of every moment and exchange, Lila stepped past him and made her way inside.

He gave the collar of his jacket a hard pull.

No one had ever stepped inside his apartments, and for the simple fact: there was no one in his life. The extent of his friendship with Maynard and Bragger was really just their partnership. Aside from the club and the ties that bound them to their past, Hugh had no dealings with them. Which was, in short, the way of their world. There weren't really friendships or families; there was just taking what one could from another and offering up whatever skills one had in return. Men and women of the rookeries operated under a system of barter, where it always came down to the services they could exchange.

Lila glanced back, a question in her eyes, and he forced his feet to move, entering more slowly behind her.

Now, as the silent Lila March swept inside the cramped, largely empty quarters he called home, he was needlessly reminded of how little he possessed in this world.

And yet, for as sparse as the four rooms in this place were, it may as well have been a palace when compared with the places he'd called home since he was just a young orphan in the rookeries.

Lila looked around the quarters, and it was a reminder to him that he didn't know where she came from or what her world looked like. But there was only one certainty on which he'd stake his life in that moment: her residence didn't and wouldn't ever look like this.

"Is there a problem?" he asked coolly as he pushed the door closed behind them.

"No," she murmured, that clever gaze that missed nothing moving through the room to the pair of mismatched upholstered armchairs in desperate need of reupholstering. The Irish Fools Chair tucked under the table.

Her eyes stayed on the folded, dark-oak drop leaf table. That small piece, where he took his meals and reviewed his work for Savage's Fight Society, merely highlighted that Hugh's was a place for one.

Which was simply as it had been and would always be, but her seeing that solitary state to his existence? It left him feeling exposed in ways he'd never been.

"This is where you live," she said wistfully.

"Did you expect more?" The question came more sharply than he intended.

Lila, however, merely lifted her shoulders in a casual little shrug. "I just thought you might keep rooms at your business."

He gave her a look. "How many proprietors sleep at their places of work?"

"I . . ." She scrunched her nose up. "I don't know. I . . . suppose I've never given much thought to it." Lila strolled around the room, pausing beside the modified clevy shelf. That shelving, usually placed over a fireplace, that he'd constructed himself out of scraps he'd recovered in the streets, was as out of place where it hung as the mismatched cups and plates and wooden carvings it held.

Shame, the same emotion to haunt him since his return from fighting in the King's Army, found a familiar place in his belly. He was reminded all over again of how little he had, and how much more he needed. It was also why, had it not been for Maynard and Bragger, he'd not even have this place that was a palace for all that it provided him. Shelter from the constant London rain. Walls to keep out those even more desperate than he, who were all too willing and eager to stick a blade in the stomach of those sleeping in the streets, all in the name of survival.

He watched her as she touched a gloved fingertip down the wood he'd carved in a way that had given it a twisted ropelike effect. "It is lovely," she murmured.

Hugh shifted back and forth on his feet. He'd been wrong; he'd felt exposed before. Now, her touching his things, that crude shelf he'd constructed, left him splayed open.

Lila glanced back, and he made himself still.

Her eyes widened slightly. "You made this, didn't you?" She'd already whipped her focus back to the shelving.

"I didn't say that."

"You didn't need to," she said, not taking her gaze from the article.

Whittling had been something he'd used as a distraction during his time in the King's Army. In between battles, to give his mind and fingers something to do, something that didn't involve more blood on his hands, he'd find sticks or branches and carve objects out of them. And upon his return? It had been a skill he'd had no luck putting to use to earn coin. Because there'd been no money to go around to hire anyone, even the soldiers newly returned from war.

Lila picked up a small carved horse; she ran her thumb along the enormous mane that brushed the sideswept tail he'd given the imagined creature, and then she looked to the wood collection of mares and stallions settled upon the shelving.

"They're magnificent," she praised with such a reverent awe for something he'd done. For something that wasn't the brute force he meted out in an arena or on a street corner, and some of the tension at her seeing his life, in this way, left him.

He dropped a shoulder into the wall and watched as she looked at his things. As she picked her way through each and every item on that shelf, she made little *oohing* and *ahhing* sounds to herself.

A grin tugged his lips up.

She stole another glance his way, this one distracted, as if she'd been so absorbed in her study that she'd forgotten his presence. "How long does it take you?"

"It depends." On which memories were haunting him at a given time. On how desperate his need to escape. "Some longer than others."

"This one, then?" She held a pair of small birds aloft; they fit perfectly into her palm. With their carved beaks down as if they were nestling the thick fabric of her work gloves, the pair of mourning doves looked as though they pecked at her hand.

He lifted one shoulder in a shrug. "Hours, perhaps? When I . . . carve . . . I don't think of much of anything. I just . . . feel the wood and focus on whatever it is that I'm creating."

Lila stilled, but for her palm that trembled slightly and set the mourning doves shaking. As if they were creatures who'd come to life and fluttered in her hand. "It is an escape."

Hugh instantly went tight-lipped. He'd shared more than he wished. More than he should. Something about this woman, something perilous and dangerous, made it entirely too easy to open himself up to her.

Except he needn't have worried about more probing on her part. She'd returned her attention to his collection, exchanging out the doves for a dark wood stallion.

She was an oddity, this one.

For all the ways in which she asked intimate questions about his past . . . and himself, she also possessed an innate ability to know when he didn't wish to say more.

And she honored that.

Perhaps that was what made it so very easy for him to converse with her. Perhaps that was why he'd not fought her when she returned and asked him for lessons, and why he defied his partners' wishes even now in bringing her here.

"Do you keep horses, Hugh?"

Keep horses? "No." Aside from the horse he'd ridden in battle, and the one loyal mount he'd purchased when he had enough funds to do so, there'd never been a collection of anything—let alone prized horseflesh. "Not a collection. Just one." The great chestnut mount flashed to his mind. He'd been closer to his horse than any person in the whole of his existence. His chest spasmed with a pain that would always be there. For a loyal steed cut down too soon in a battle that'd won them nothing. That'd succeeded only in watering the earth with the blood of the innocent. His skin burnt with the heat of Lila's gaze upon him; it probed and pierced. He cleared the emotion from his throat. "I've just always had an . . . appreciation for them as creatures," he finished woodenly. Restless, fearing more questions, along with this wave of emotion he didn't need to feel, he pushed away from the wall. "We should get started," he said, dragging the fools chair to the side of the room.

"What was his name?"

"Hmm?" He curled his fingers around the side of his half table.

"Your horse." Setting down the wood figurine, she hurried over and caught the other side of his table. "What was his name?"

"Her name. She was a mare. I called her Winfred." He waved off her effort to help carry the table. "I can see to it."

"I'm perfectly capable of helping." Her eyes twinkled. "At least half."

Together, they set to work carrying the mismatched furniture, depositing each piece alongside the front wall, until they'd formed a row that framed the lone window which looked out at the dangerous streets below.

Thinking better of it, Hugh caught the shutters and brought them closed.

"Winfred is an odd choice for a mare."

"Aye, that it is." And yet, it'd seemed somehow right for her. "She was a wonderful, loyal mount. Fearless." And in the ultimate betrayal, she'd been cut down, not when they fought Boney's forces, but on what should have been peaceful fields of Manchester. "Her name meant *friend of peace.*" Bitterness brought his lips curling into a sneer, while rage and grief, potent as they'd been that day at Peterloo, burnt like acid in his mouth.

"What happened to her?"

"She . . ." *had a blade thrust into her side.* Screamed her agony, that high-pitched wail penetrating the cacophony of men, women, and children being cut down around him. Sweat slicked his body, leaving him first hot, then cold. Until he managed to right his breathing and return to the moment. "She died." The details of Winfred's end and that day at Manchester weren't topics for one like Lila March. Hugh reached for the work stool in the middle of the room, but Lila rested her hand on his, stopping him.

"I'm so sorry," she said, giving a light squeeze, in the first-ever meaningful contact he'd had with any woman. With any person.

Emotion stabbed at his throat, and he gave an uneven nod. "Thank you."

Together, in silence, they finished shifting the furniture about the room.

He'd not talked about Winfred to anyone. In fact, he'd not thought of her in at least two years. Nay, he'd not let himself think of her, and that day that he'd failed her in the name of honor. So why did he share that detail with Lila now?

And what was more . . . why did it feel so natural to do so?

Mayhap it was because after almost thirty-three years of keeping himself closed off from the world . . . protecting himself from all people, he'd tired of this constant need to be on guard. And Lila was the one person with whom he could relax those barriers without fear of being destroyed for that weakness.

Catching the last article, Hugh lifted the bench, a dilapidated piece he'd found and kept for carving, over his head and positioned it atop the half table. "Now, let's begin."

Chapter 14

Lila was in Hugh Savage's apartments.

Her joining him at his household, in the dangerous streets of East London, had it been discovered, would have seen her forgotten name dragged out by Polite Society, who was always eager for a scandal.

Once, she'd cared about protecting her reputation. She'd thought it mattered enough that she'd been furtive in her acts of rebellion.

Of all the bad that had come from Peterloo, she'd developed something she'd been without prior to that day—perspective.

She was here with Hugh Savage because she wanted to be.

Today, something had shifted. It wasn't just about learning skills with which to defend herself and those she loved, but rather a need to know about Hugh.

And here in his apartments, he'd revealed so much about himself, filling her with a greater need to know this man who was a mystery.

"Pay attention," he chided, all business. As if their earlier exchange about Winfred and his carvings had never happened.

Hugh, however, appeared completely unaffected.

"I am." Which was, of course, a lie. She *should* be thinking about everything she had to learn about fighting and looking after her family. Instead, she'd been thinking of Hugh Savage and how she wished to know—

He arched an eyebrow, snapping her out of her musings.

"Stances," she blurted, recalling the day's lesson.

He wiped a hand over his face. "I'm not asking you to tell me, Lila. I'm asking you to do it."

Focus.

But then mayhap it had been far easier engaging in woolgathering about him and the wickedness that was also so very wonderful in them being together. Easier than focusing on the fact that he was now asking her . . . expecting her to do something with her legs.

Hugh gave her a pointed look.

In the end, she made one desperate bid for more time. "Perhaps you might show me again?" It'd been something she'd not truly thought through when she'd decided to appeal to him and seek out lessons.

The fact that she'd have to use her body in ways that were foreign, and likely now impossible with her leg.

Muttering to himself, Hugh got himself into position, demonstrating the fighter's form. "Mendoza's preferred stance was feet forward, body inclined forward, and hands up together." His body pitched as it was, his powerful weight over his knees, he moved like an ancient Roman warrior preparing for battle with only one outcome certain—his win in that great arena.

He moved with a grace she'd not even possessed when her body had been whole prior to Peterloo.

"Lila?" he said impatiently.

"Why are you teaching me other people's stances?" Exasperation pulled that question from her. Of course, she was only delaying the inevitable. She knew it, and also knew she'd have to put herself—and all her weaknesses—on full display before him. But she wasn't ready. Not yet. "Shouldn't people . . ." She cleared her throat and presented her palms up. "Shouldn't I develop a style specific to me? Perhaps something more like . . . this . . ." Keeping her body perfectly erect, she put the weight over her favored leg.

He laughed. A single, sharp bark that sent her belly fluttering, and she almost forgot he was really just laughing at her. Almost.

Bristling, Lila let her arms fall. "What?"

"Stop stalling." How was he able to read her after such a short time knowing one another? "Hands together," he ordered, bringing her fists close. "You've never fought," he went on to explain, "and so there're different ways to hold yourself and carry your body . . . Stop tucking your thumb," he said, interjecting pointers while they talked. "That'll get it broken."

"Seems like it would protect th—" Her words ended on a gasp as Hugh took one of her curled hands, his palm over hers callused and hard . . . and strong. And the sheer heat of it scorched her from within.

"If you keep your thumb tucked inside like so"—he coaxed her palm open, and it unfurled reflexively under that tender caress—"when you hit your target, there's no question . . . you will break the digit."

Something shifted. The air came alive, hissing and popping with the tension pouring between them as it had yesterday morn. He stroked his own thumb along her knuckles.

Her body trembled and curved reflexively toward him.

"Make sure your thumb is tucked below your curled fingers," he said softly. "That way it is out of the way of the impact." He abruptly ceased his stroking; his finger remained on that slight curve from where the bone had never properly healed. "It's been broken."

As it was a statement, she opted to give him nothing more than silence.

He gave her a quizzical look.

"Is that a question?" She smiled in a bid to stave him off.

Hugh scowled, and then lifting her left hand close to his eyes, he inspected her fingers.

Tamping down a sigh, Lila stared at his head bent over her hands as he studied them. She should have expected that she'd never be one to possess one of those flirty, distracting smiles better suited to the innocent debutantes, fresh on the market with hope in their hearts. He looked up. "You broke two fingers."

"Yes." She held her right hand aloft. "And one on this hand," she said in a bid to avoid another examination of the hideous appendages. The breaks had been so bad she'd thought to never again play the pianoforte, but then, after Peterloo, when she'd ordered the curtains drawn and locked herself away in darkened chambers, she'd not even wanted to survive. The idea of playing any instrument had been a secondary preference to death.

She braced for his pity. That hated emotion she was invariably met with by all: the servants, her family.

Only . . .

His gaze sharpened on her face. "How?" There was a guttural, raw quality to that utterance.

Lila's heart did a little dance, for missing was pity, and in its place was a thinly constrained fury.

"And here I thought you didn't want to know anything about my past, Mr. Savage," she softly reminded him. And if she shared that with him? Her past would define her yet again, and every stolen moment of an existence outside of Peterloo would be gone. And she didn't want this place, and this man, to become linked in any way to those parts of her.

Hugh motioned her back to the middle of the room. "Back to it."

Back to it . . .

Three perfunctory words, all businesslike in nature, that gave Lila precisely what she'd wished for—freedom from any more questions.

So how to account for this unexpected rush of disappointment?

It is because you want to know the secrets Hugh Savage clings tight to, and you wish he had a like desire to learn about you, in turn . . .

"Mendoza's style," he commanded, walking a circle around her, and she struggled with the unfamiliarity of the movements as she got herself into that fighting stance. The muscles all down her left leg strained at the foreign motions she now put her body through. Hugh tapped her left elbow, guiding it into the proper position. "We're going to stay here so you can feel how to move. First, where is your target?"

What was he saying? Knees bent as they were, she struggled to focus on his questions or directives or really anything he was saying. "I don't have a target," she muttered. She couldn't maintain this position. Not for long.

"Find one. That's the first rule of fighting."

And she used his instructions as the break she so desperately needed. Lila came out of position and wiped moisture from her forehead. "Actually, I believe you have now given three first rules." How very good it felt to again tease someone. Or it would have, had the intended recipient responded with a grin or a chuckle, or at the very least, not a dark scowl.

"I've given you three rules because you don't even have the basic fundamentals of fighting. Now, identify your target."

"I won't." *I can't.* Not in the position he needed her to assume.

Hugh closed his eyes, and his lips moved in what had the whisperings of a prayer.

And given everything she'd gathered about the surly fighter, the last thing she'd taken him for was a praying man.

Opening his eyes, he tried again. "You require one. Even if it's just an imagined one while you're throwing at the air." He came to stand opposite her. "Now, bring your arms up."

That was the easier of the tasks.

"Not like that," he corrected. "If the thumb is on the inside when you . . ." He went to grasp her forearm, but she stepped out of his reach. "What *now*?"

"I'm not looking to hit *anyone*." Because it was important for her lessons that he know what her intentions and goals were.

Hugh wiped his hands up and down his face. "You asked for lessons," he began again, as if trying to make sense of some riddle.

"I don't want to hurt anyone, Hugh." Not unless she absolutely had to.

He folded his arms. "You're not making sense," he said bluntly.

Taking a breath, she tried again. "I only want to know how to properly defend myself and others should"—*we*—"they need it."

There were several beats of silence. "Isn't it the same thing?"

"No." But how to explain it? Particularly to a man who'd built a reputation off fighting in the name of coin and profit. She wandered off, her gaze on the faint slash of light that had managed to creep through Hugh's shutters. "I'm willing to fight . . . if I need to."

If her sister or nephew or mother or sister-in-law . . . or brother found themselves at risk.

If someone stronger, bigger, or more panicked had Lila in a hold she needed to escape from.

My God, please let me go . . . I can't breathe . . . Pleeeeease . . .

She sucked in a deep breath, trying to fill her lungs with air, as if in doing so, she might give that gift over to the girl she'd been, crushed by a delirious mother who'd scrabbled and clawed at everyone around them, all in the name of freedom and survival.

Could she hurt someone? The metal clang of sabres sluicing through the air rang in her mind.

Where do you think you're going . . . ?

Lila pressed her three middle fingers against the scar down the middle of her forehead.

Men, women . . . children. Babes. They'd all fled. They'd not fought. Surviving had been their only goal, and on that day on St. Peter's Field, it had been a shared one amongst the masses. And yet, even fleeing as they had, there'd been men who'd gleefully cut them down, men who'd sliced the breast off a woman and left her rib cage hanging open. And that violence, that ugliness, was the world she'd retreated from, and the one she wished to protect herself from. And until Hugh's words here, she'd failed to truly consider that sometimes a person couldn't free themselves . . . without fighting. Without risking harm to others. Feeling Hugh's eyes on her, she made herself turn back, facing him, and owned her decision. "I want to learn to fight. And if that means learning to fight aggressively so that I can keep myself and the ones I love safe? Then that is what I want"—*need*—"to do."

Lila March had suffered broken fingers.

Three of them.

Which, in the scheme of what Hugh had inflicted, suffered, or witnessed, may as well have been as insignificant as a sprain. He'd become immune to other people's suffering, emotionally deadened to the sight of violence.

Only to find from the slight angling of her once wounded digits, he wasn't as impervious as he'd believed.

The woman was a conundrum wrapped in a mystery and, because of it, the last thing he could afford. His entire existence centered around secrets and sins and crimes. Whatever ghosts belonged to her, whatever it was that had made her seek him out, belonged to her.

"Close your eyes." She hesitated a moment, and then she swept impossibly long lashes down until they lay as a blanket upon her pale cheeks. It was a detail he shouldn't notice, and yet as he instructed her, he remained riveted by that beautifully lush fringe. "Find your target," he murmured. "See one. In your mind. Who is the person?"

Color slipped from her already pale cheeks, and her perfectly even, pearl-white teeth caught her lower lip, but not before he caught the way that flesh trembled.

She gave a juddering nod. "I have one," she said, her voice cryptic.

And he'd wager his lifelong vow of revenge against his oppressors that her mind's eye had drawn forth the one responsible for her fingers.

Rage licked at his senses, an all-too-familiar, vicious hungering to take apart the coward who'd put his hands upon her. It was an unexpectedly volatile response to this woman. A weakness he'd not permitted since Bragger's sister, Valerie, the youngest of their group, whom they'd protected . . . whom he'd vowed to protect . . . and failed.

Perhaps that was why he found himself, if not liking Lila March, liking her presence. That being with her wasn't about the arena that had become the center of his existence. It wasn't about the need for revenge. Or the young woman Hugh had failed. It was why he'd not sent Lila away again after that first night, and why he'd fought his partners on her being here. In being with her and assisting her, for the first time in his life, he wasn't connected with a person through the Fight Society.

And what he'd never counted on . . . what he'd never expected was just how welcome that was.

And in that, a betrayal, just as Bragger had charged.

Lila struggled to open her eyes. "Hugh?" she asked, a question in her voice.

Shoving aside the needling of guilt, he focused on the lesson. "You know what"—*who*—"your target is?"

"I do," she said, this time with an automaticity that left no doubt that she'd settled on a secret opponent to square off against. And for reasons he couldn't understand, Hugh wanted the man's name. He wanted to know who had hurt her. What exactly accounted for her having sought out one such as Hugh.

"You don't intend to strike unless someone strikes first. Mendoza didn't enter the fighting scene like any fancy gentleman just swapping punches. His was a defensive style. When people came at him"—Hugh danced left—"he'd sidestep." He gestured with open palms at his chest. "Throw a punch."

She hesitated a moment, but then surprisingly complied.

In one motion, Hugh spun out of her reach, ducked, and then lifted his left arm to block her blow. Sweat formed at his brow, and he lifted his forearm to wipe back the perspiration before it dripped and blinded him. "Because of all his sidestepping and ducking, he was considered a coward."

"It seems more that he was a man intent on surviving."

Hugh pointed a finger at her. "Precisely. That's why his style is what you're going to learn. Mendoza was small, shorter than most of his opponents. He was also far heavier. As such, he had to develop a strategy to compensate for his size." He took her chin in his hand, angling her face up to his. "What you need to remember is that it's the same thing, Lila," he said. "Fighting and self-defense . . . You can't disentwine them from one another."

"You're wrong." Fire flared in her eyes. "It's entirely possible. Furthermore, I don't want to learn just one technique, I want to learn everything there is about . . . what you do."

"You think I can teach you different skill sets that you might pull out of your reticule, depending on what circumstances arise. But that isn't how fighting works. You think you can prepare, but you don't know what manner of attack you'll face—from the fighter opposite you in the ring, or the attack from behind. You don't know when some bastard is going to come at you from the shadows with a dagger. Or if a *friend* will turn a pistol on you."

"Is that what happened to you?" she asked softly.

He stiffened. He'd said too much.

"Aye," he said. One key takeaway from living in Covent Garden was that even those one believed to be loyal could turn, and for reasons one could never fully anticipate or prepare for. "That's what happened to me." That, and some stories that would have sent her running off in horror, surely never to be seen 'round the rookeries again. For if she knew about him and what had really transpired in these parts, one certainty remained—she'd not be taking lessons from Hugh Savage like he was the fancy boy, Gentleman Jackson.

"And who taught you how to fight, Hugh?"

He'd taught himself. Every hook, jab, or feint had been learned squaring off against an opponent, with the ultimate prize at the end of each match his life.

They'd moved, however, into territories wholly off-limits. Hugh tensed his mouth. "No questions," he reminded her. Striding into the middle of the arena, he motioned her over.

"I'd hardly call it a question about your past. Why, is it really any different from learning about Mr. Mendoza or Mr. Jackson?"

Aye, it was. Because formal pugilism approved by society was an altogether different thing from the death matches Hugh had taken part in. "It's different," he said cryptically in a bid to stave off more of her rambling.

Only, obstinate as always, she'd not be deterred. "Why? Because you were born in the rookeries? Because you have fought on the streets while they have academies in Mayfair?"

That insistence, that absolute naivete, confirmed not for the first time that she was a woman who'd been born a world away from these parts. And yet the derision he'd first greeted her with . . . did not come. Because whatever accounted for the darkness in her clear brown eyes marked her one as haunted as anyone else in Covent Garden.

He lowered his face close to hers. "Do you always ask this many questions?"

"Actually, I don't." Her gaze grew sad and shifted past his shoulder. "There was a time when I was garrulous and inquisitive, but I've not been either of those things . . . in so long, with anybody." Her eyes slid back to his. "Until you."

Unnerved by that rawness of her emotion and her absolute lack of artifice, he yanked at his collar. "It's just me who inspires you to talk nonstop?" he muttered.

"Yes," she said softly. "I suppose you can say that. With you, it is somehow . . ."—*different*—"different," she finished, her thoughts unnervingly in tune with his. "You don't tiptoe around me." It was one of the first real clues she'd offered into her life. "You're real and honest."

Those four words managed to kill whatever this moment was that had existed between them.

Hugh chuckled, the sound rusty and cold to his own ears. "That'd be the first in my bloody lifetime that any fool had made that accusation." The only thing honest about him was the power behind each blow he'd thrown. He'd stolen, killed, and maimed, all in the name of survival, and he didn't want that life anymore.

Just as he'd wanted a way out as a boy fighting in the rookeries, he was scrabbling for that same elusive gift even now.

Only to find himself saddled with a woman wholly determined to immerse herself in the very life he despised.

"It's true," she said.

He snorted. "That's naive of you."

"Is it?"

His jaw rippled. "I'm not a good man, Lila March." She'd be a goddamned fool to see him as anything other than the ruthless bastard he was.

Lila looked at him a long while before responding. "I can't determine whether you're trying to convince me or yourself."

His entire body recoiled under that charge. He snapped, "I know exactly what I am." And yet this woman, this stranger, presumed to know him better than he did himself? Hers was an arrogance better fitting those masked lords who'd requested meetings with him and the other fighters before their matches.

But as Bragger had rightly pointed out . . . what do you really know about Lila March anyway?

"I know you've told me exactly what you think of me at every turn," she went on, fearless and bold in her challenge. "I know you've been teaching me, even though you didn't want to." Her eyes caught and held his. "Even though others don't approve of my being here."

"You'd make me out to be something more than I am," he said emotionlessly. *A savior.* "I'm not looking to be anyone's savior, Lila March." He was useless where others were concerned.

She paled. "That's not what I was saying. I'm not—"

"And certainly not yours," he hissed.

And if he'd been another man, the honorable one she sought to make him into, there'd have been guilt or pain at the effect his words had on her; she'd the look of one whose pup had been kicked.

A man couldn't be a savior when all he had was the blood of countless men and boys on his hands. It didn't matter that it had been as a bare-knuckle fighter whose life depended upon it . . . or as a soldier on the Continent. His sins were his sins.

"Charge the field . . . charge the field . . ."

Hugh briefly closed his eyes, warding off the memory. Willing it back. And ultimately triumphing over that abyss.

He forced his eyes open. "It's the lie you want, Lila. You want to convince yourself that I'm somehow above the violence and evil. That you are above it. But the truth is? It's part of you. It's part of all of us." Hugh had come to that realization of what the world was—what *he* was—long, long ago.

Her heart-shaped features spasmed. "You are *wrong.*" That denial came as though ripped from her chest.

His lips curled up in a cynical twist. "I'm not wrong about anything, Lila March." Lords. Ladies. Street thugs and rats. Gentlemen in uniforms. They all possessed a primal savagery that couldn't be erased from who they were. Proof stood in the men, women, and children who fought, and the spectators who came to watch. "Do you need me to give you examples of my evil?"

She shook her head. "Stop."

"Do you want me to tell you how every morning I wake up, I look at numbers I had inked into my skin to remind me of my sins? Because I was a fighter. Because that's all I'll ever be." Rage ravaged his voice.

Stop talking.

Why are you talking? Why are you saying these things to her, this woman?

But God help him, it was as though some damned torrent had been ripped open, and he couldn't stem its tide.

"Do you want me to tell you how many men I've killed?"

"S-stop." Her lower lip trembled, and he cursed the vicious ache in his chest that he'd revealed himself exactly as he was to her. And it only fueled his fury with her for making him feel emotion. With himself for feeling anything.

His chest heaved, rising and falling fast and hard from the emotion whipping through him. "I'm no kindhearted gent, carving up wood statues that you think are adorable. I'm a monster carving that wood up to try and distract myself from the memories of my evil. You'd do well to steer clear of me. I'm no good. I'm certainly not the type of man you should be around." And grabbing her shoulders, he claimed her mouth hard and showed her exactly what manner of man he was.

Chapter 15

Lila knew what fear was.

More importantly, she'd learned the art of it: what it felt like as peril danced in the air, there to devour the unsuspecting. Not so very long ago, she'd been the unsuspecting one.

Not any longer.

As such, every lesson learned on the fields of Manchester left her with but one word for this moment: *flee*. Run from the volatility of Hugh Savage's embrace.

For this kiss? This was nothing like the one that had come the day before.

And she knew only one thing of any certainty in this moment: there'd never be anything like it ever again.

Yesterday's embrace had been born of pure passion.

This, Hugh's mouth on hers, devouring as it did, was one of pure savagery. The rawest and realest and most primal of emotions, and she knew she should be horrified. She knew from the emotion shaking his voice that he sought to horrify her. But God help her, she knew only that she wanted more of him and this wild display of desire.

Lila gripped his shirtfront, curling her fingers into the harsh linen, a fabric no gentleman would wear, and preferring the feel of it for its realness. It was as real as the man who bent her body to his, like he couldn't get enough of her. Like he sought to devour her.

And she wished to be devoured by him.

Because with him, in his arms, there were no monsters. There was no pain. There were no memories but the new ones she made with him.

Pressing herself into him, she went on tiptoe and met the angry slash of his hard lips on hers.

An animalistic growl—his? Hers? Both of theirs—filtered around the bare room; it melded with their harsh breathing and created an erotic echo that only fueled her desire.

Hugh filled his hands with her buttocks, molding his palms to that flesh and bringing her close so she could feel the hard, heated length of him even through the fabric of their trousers, like steel against her, and then he began to roll his hips. Undulating so that his shaft rocked slowly against her belly.

She moaned and gave silent thanks for the absence of skirts that allowed her to feel almost everything.

She'd been correct. Men did want to keep ladies trapped in their skirts. *This* was why women were made to suffer the miseries of chemises and voluminous skirts. To protect their virtue.

Or perhaps it was to punish them because of all the pleasures that those garments interceded with.

"Hugh." She moaned his name, a plea for more.

And he used that parting to his advantage, his tongue delving inside, branding that pink flesh as his own. And he needn't have worried, because it was all his. She was all his. In this moment.

Mayhap, forever.

Terror tugged at her mind, and she forced it back, refusing to surrender to anything but simply feeling.

Her legs weakened under her, and with a primitive growl, Hugh drew her more tightly to him.

He deepened the kiss. Teasing with his tongue. Taunting her with the promise of more, and tormenting her for it.

He trailed his hands down the curve of her hips, like one memorizing each curve and line of her, and then bringing his palms up between them, he cupped her breasts.

The air exploded from her lips on an eternal hiss of pure desire.

"I'm no gentleman," he rasped between kisses. "I'm not honorable, and I'm certainly not respectable. You won't ever get anything good from me, Lila March, because there's nothing good to give." And then making himself out as the absolute liar he was, he drew her shirt off, exposing her to the chilled air and his gaze, and then closed his mouth over the peak of one breast.

"Hughhhh." She tangled her fingers in his hair and anchored him there. Pressed her cheek against the top of his head as he laved that sensitive tip, suckling her.

Desire pooled between her legs and sent her hips into a rocking motion as old as time.

There was no thinking. There was no right or wrong or proper. And most important of all? There were no demons. It was just the two of them. And she knew what she wanted . . . what she'd never forgive herself if she didn't know: this man. In every way.

He shifted his attention over to the previously neglected breast and worshipped at that flesh.

Until she was weeping and crying out his name.

Then he stopped, his hot breath fanning her bare skin, a sough upon flesh that he'd set aflame.

As he lifted his head, his burning gaze met hers. "Run now and be free, Flittermouse, because this is your last chance." There was a dare there, in his eyes and in his words, and if he thought to scare her off by the power of his desire, he knew her not at all.

But then, you are more strangers than anything . . .

That voice of logic had no pull over the passion searing her veins.

Curling a palm around his nape, she brought herself up on her toes and kissed him.

He stiffened, and then a low groan shook his chest, its thrum and reverberations pulsing within her like the incessant, rhythmic beat of a drum.

Gathering her under her knees, Hugh swept her into his arms and started across the room . . .

He could have carried her anywhere, and she would have gone gladly with him in this moment because with her pulse hammering away in her ears, and her body afire as it was, she well understood the temptation in that apple Eve had abandoned all for.

Lila slid fingers through his lush black curls, relishing that luxuriant softness against her palms.

Hugh stopped, and for an unbearable moment she thought he intended to stop this . . . and whatever magic she yearned to know beyond it.

Only . . .

He carefully set her down upon a poster bed. The mattress was lumpy. The sheets coarse and cold. And she'd change nothing about this moment. And yet . . . reservations glinted in his eyes.

Shoving herself up onto her elbows, she peered at him through heavy lashes. "I want you, Hugh. I want this. And I don't . . ."

No other words were needed.

Groaning, he came over her, framing her body with his larger, broader one. His lips were on hers.

And then they were everywhere.

A whispery sigh slipped out as he moved his mouth down the column of her neck, placing worshipping kisses, wicked little love bites, as he suckled that flesh where her pulse pounded for him and his mastery over her body.

"You are so beautiful," he rasped against her skin, and she bit her lower lip to keep from crying out.

Then his words registered. Followed by the slight tug of her trousers as he freed her from them, exposing her and the truth that she wasn't really the beauty he took her for.

Her heart thudded sickeningly as she exploded upright. "D-don't," she gasped out.

But it was too late.

He froze, his entire muscle-hewn frame turning to stone in her arms.

Because he'd seen her secret and now knew the truth.

And she, who'd survived hell on earth, found herself fighting off tears.

Batting at his shoulders, she tried to shove him off and break herself free. "Stop."

Except he wasn't doing anything, which was what made for the agony sweeping through her, great big waves of misery beating against her, battering her with a reminder of all the ways in which she was flawed.

And then, he stood up.

A tear slipped free. Followed by another. And another. As this time, she couldn't stem the flow.

For she'd not believed there could be anything worse than his horror at the wicked scar down the length of her left leg.

But this? His rejection? Landed like a physical blow to her chest.

"This is why you weren't getting into the stances," he said quietly. "The reason you were stalling."

She nodded, but unsteady as it was, unsteady as *she* was, it came as more of a sideways shake of her head. Of course, even in a moment of passion, he'd have full command of reason to put together the sham she'd failed to pull off in the room they'd just cleared.

Hugh sat on the edge of the narrow mattress, angled with his back to her, and she gave thanks that she couldn't see his face. The disgust. Nay, what was worse, what she could not see from this man—pity. He stretched a hand out and lightly ran his callused fingers over her leg. She recoiled, curling into herself, but there was no escape as he stroked his three middle digits from her knee down the length of her calf, where some soldier had marked her with his sabre, leaving that scar as a reminder.

As if the memories and nightmares hadn't been token enough of that day.

Nay, she'd had to bear some physical imprint that she had to see day in and day out, so she could always recall the day the world had turned upside down.

Hugh traced his index finger along the puckered flesh. "You're beautiful."

"I know what I am," she said, directing her gaze over the top of his magnificent curls. Even his hair was deucedly perfect.

"You think this somehow makes you less beautiful?" His low murmur resonated in the quiet. Sliding onto a knee, with a tenderness that threatened to shatter Lila, he ever so gently gathered her leg in his hand, as if it were . . . as if *she* were, in fact, the person of beauty he spoke of.

And everything within her that had spent the past nine years hating her flawed mind and body wanted to scream for him to release her, but the part of her that had yearned more to be seen and be touched reveled at the glide of his fingers along her leg.

Sweeping, delicate glides of his fingers. He moved them in slow, smooth arcs over that puckered flesh.

Collapsing back onto her elbows, Lila trembled as his caress eased the tension within her.

Hugh lowered his mouth, and her breath caught in anticipation as he brought his lips closer and kissed her leg.

And she'd now been wrong *two* times before. Each kiss had felt more special than the other, and yet still there was nothing that could ever compare with this brush of his hard, perfectly formed lips upon her marred skin, bringing her eyes shut once more as his kiss penetrated through the ugliness of Peterloo and pierced her soul. A shuddery little sigh spilled from her lips.

"Look at me, Lila March." His was a harsh, graveled command, more captivating for the coarse roughness of that order. She brought her gaze to his. "Don't you ever doubt your beauty." His eyes pierced her. "I forbid it."

I forbid it.

Who could imagine those three words strung together should snap free a piece of her heart for this man so arrogant as to issue that command?

Climbing to his feet, Hugh pulled his shirt out from the waistband of his trousers and tossed it aside, and just as the sight of him had knocked the breath from her lungs that day in his fighting arena, she found the earth kicked out from under her once more.

Beautiful.

That word had been created with this man and his perfectly formed physique in mind. He wore the scars and ink upon his frame like an artist's canvas.

"You are magnificent." She exhaled those latter four syllables.

He chuckled, and resting a knee on the edge of the bed, he curved his body toward hers. "This from the same woman with but a mark upon her leg."

And her head. "This is different."

Hugh captured her left leg and angled it about his waist, so that his scarred forearm kissed her scarred flesh. "*This?* Is the same, Lila."

This is the same.

And with those words, she at last understood her connection to Hugh Savage.

They were the same in so many ways.

Whatever secrets they carried had shaped them both; their lives had left them scarred, and somehow, from two entirely different worlds, they'd found one another.

Lila wound her fingers through his, twining her slightly bent digits with his flawless ones, and then drew them over the mark at the center of her forehead. "Beautiful together," she whispered.

Passion darkened the sapphire of his eyes. Releasing her leg, he hurriedly shucked off his trousers; he kicked them aside, and her breath hitched.

He was masculine beauty personified: his stomach was all taut, ridged muscles . . . and in ways that would have horrified any proper lady of the *ton*, she dropped her gaze, unapologetic in her study of him.

Oh, my.

Had she spoken aloud? Everything beyond the rapid cadence of her heart was jumbled.

His length jutted out, hard, springing from a nest of midnight curls.

Da Vinci and Michelangelo had been liars in their craft; men in all Hugh's naked splendor should be captured and carved only as Hugh Savage stood before her, alive and breathtaking with his rampant sex arced, that rigid length pressed against the flat of his belly.

She brushed her fingers over him.

Hugh exhaled a hiss through his teeth.

She lifted her gaze. The muscles of his face were strained; his eyes clenched. His was a look between pleasure and pain.

Emboldened, Lila stroked his manhood, steel under her fingers that fair burnt to the touch.

He groaned and caught her hand.

Through heavy lids, Lila peered up inquiringly.

"I need you."

His words, a hoarse entreaty, jolted through her, liquefying her.

He, this powerful, unrepentant man, wanted her.

Cupping her nape, Hugh angled her head, availing himself of her mouth, and she gave freely that which he sought. They tangled with their tongues, the taste of him, honey and chocolate and so unexpectedly sweet, only fueling her fascination with this man and her hungering for him. Eyes closed, she gave herself over to the stroke of his tongue against hers, a burning lash whose singe she welcomed.

She'd given up on the dream of passion for herself. And marriage and anything that she'd once coveted, like the secret gifts they were to innocent young ladies.

Only to find herself blessedly whole as a woman.

In her passions. In her ability to take that which she wanted. In what she now chose.

Him.

Hugh guided her down, and the unevenly filled mattress met her back. And she welcomed the sharp reminder that this moment was real. And yearned for it to go on forever.

"What have you done to me, Lila March?" he breathed against her breast. Several curls toppled over his brow, gentling him.

With fingers that shook, she brushed those luxuriant tresses back. The stubborn coils immediately sprang into their previous position of defiance. "The same thing you've done to me, Hugh Savage . . ."

Chapter 16

Over the years, Hugh had taken lovers.

Those relationships had all been based on an animalistic lust. There had been a mutual goal, and when sated, he'd always parted ways without feeling anything more than that momentary satisfaction. His partners had also been pleasured but had gone their way with coins.

This woman . . . everything with this woman and about this woman was different.

In a short time, she'd slipped into his life, and nothing had been—or would ever be—the same. As such, he should be terrified out of his damned mind, and there'd be time enough for that after, but for now, for now, there was this urgency for her.

He flicked his tongue over the tip of her left breast, until Lila gave him just one word—his name. "Hugh." It slipped out. Over and over. An entreaty. A wish. A demand. One that stripped away all evil and darkness from his name and left him before her, only a man. A man besieged by hunger for this woman in his arms.

And lust flared.

In answer, he slipped a hand between her legs and cupped the damp black curls of her mound.

Lila's hips shot out from under her as she lifted into him. Sweat glistened on her brow, and with her eyes clenched as if in the deepest concentration, she rocked in time to the glide of his finger in her moist channel. Hugh slipped another inside, wringing a shuddery gasp from Lila.

"I've never felt like this."

It was impossible for him to say who was speaking in that moment.

His heart drummed, pounding against his chest as he stroked her.

He lifted his gaze and found her biting at her lower lip and, from under heavy lids, watching him as he touched her.

"Please," she whispered, her voice pitched, and by the frantic rise and fall of her hips, she was close. So close.

Hugh's breath came in sharp, agitated bursts as he positioned himself between her legs. To that perfect place he wished to be and would have sold what was left of his black soul for a chance to know.

Lila immediately folded her arms around him, and he clenched his eyes at the intimacy of that embrace. It'd never been like this. Ever. It never would be again with any other woman. He slid himself inside slowly, her tight channel gripping him in a pleasure-pain so deep his body ached from the restraint he showed. When all he wanted was to plunge hard and deep, over and over again.

He stopped.

No.

Bloody hell, no.

He'd known, and yet not wanted to think about or accept the fact that she was an innocent and he didn't bed virgins and—

Lila took his face between his hands, forcing his eyes open.

Through the haze of desire in her eyes, she glowered fiercely back. "If you stop now, I swear I'm going to put together every last bare-knuckle lesson you've given me, you great lummox. I'm a grown woman, capable of knowing what or who I want. And who I want? Is y—"

Hugh consumed the remainder of that profession with his lips, sliding his tongue inside to duel with this woman, fiery in all she did. Fierce and proud, and there wasn't another like her.

And as she keened softly into his mouth, shifting her hips in a bid to be closer, Hugh thrust home.

Gasping against his lips, Lila stiffened. Her entire body went rigid in his arms.

He breathed hard and kept himself absolutely still. Refusing everything within him that hungered to move. As he confronted yet another mark of his brutality.

"I'm so sorry," he said, placing a kiss at the corner of her temple. "I wouldn't hurt you for anything." His gut twisted. And yet, he had.

"*Shh.*" Stretching those long, graceful fingers up, Lila brushed them through his hair, stroking him as if he were the one who'd suffered hurt and she wished to drive it back.

Had there ever been anyone who'd felt that way for him?

In the immediacy of that silent question came an equally swift answer—no.

There was no one. And there'd never be anyone.

But for now, there was this . . . and there was her.

And he'd wring every undeserved joy and pleasure he could from this moment.

Hugh ran his lips down the column of her throat, continuing that trail lower to a pebbled pink nipple. Drawing that bud between his lips, he suckled lightly until Lila's breath quickened and her hips began to again move. And still he continued worshipping that flesh, until her soft, incoherent cries spilled around his room. He found her once more with his fingers and felt her entire body tense under his.

And then he began to move slowly inside her. Her sopping, tight channel slicked the way, drawing him in.

"Lila," he groaned, thrusting now. Lunge-retreat. Lunge-retreat. And as his hungering built, he was capable of only her name, again and again. Over and over. "Lila. Lila."

She matched the rhythm he'd set for them. "Hugh, please," she cried, lifting her hips wildly. Wrapping her arms about him, she clung tight, and that fueled his desire, pushing him higher to that blissful edge of surcease.

And then Lila froze, her eyes went wide, and she screamed her release.

His pace grew frenzied.

Sweat trickled down his face, but Lila brushed that moisture back, the tenderness of her touch shutting his eyes, and he concentrated on the climax he was building toward.

He was so close.

And then he joined her.

Tossing his head back, Hugh bellowed, his voice booming around the rafters as he spilled himself onto Lila's belly.

With a great gasping breath, he came down over her, catching himself on his elbows to keep from crushing her.

Their breath came sharply in alike little spurts as they just clung to one another. Time melted away, and he was happy to see it go.

Sometime later, Hugh rolled onto his side, and grabbing his shirt from the floor, he proceeded to clean the trace of seed from her stomach, then wiped himself.

Resting on her side, Lila watched him through languid eyes; a soft blush pinkened her cheeks and reminded him that she'd been a virgin. And he'd been the one whom she'd chosen to give that gift to.

An undeserving blackguard, a past killer of both innocents and evil alike. And yet, right now? He couldn't care that he was unworthy. He only knew he was grateful that she'd chosen him.

A moth to the damned flame, Hugh looked back and went absolutely stock still.

Propped up on an elbow, Lila had rescued a small carved piece from his nightstand and now examined it.

And as she ran the tip of one finger along the great expanse of the creature's wings, every muscle in Hugh's chest grew tight at what her too-clever mind would piece together, for there could be no doubting that *she* would see the subject of his carving for precisely what it was.

Lila shifted her focus over to him, and Hugh immediately returned to tidying himself.

"It is beautiful," she whispered, turning the bat over in her hands.

He grunted. "It's not quite done."

"It is perfect."

"I still need to carve out his left ear."

"It is *perfect*, Hugh," she said with a greater insistence.

Joining her on the bed, Hugh took her mouth under his, and Lila melted into his embrace. There was nothing frantic or rushed or hurried about this kiss, but rather, a tender joining.

After he broke the kiss, Hugh lay back down beside her and drew her against him. "Who are you, Lila March?" He placed a lingering kiss at her temple.

Setting the flittermouse back where it'd previously rested, Lila angled her head to look at him. "I thought you didn't want to know anything about me."

"I was wrong. Indulge me."

Some of the light in her eyes dimmed. "What do you want to know?"

Everything. "Tell me something no one knows about you."

She drummed her fingertips on his chest, beating a little staccato against one of the tattoos he'd received as a young fighter in the streets. "Well, I sing and play pianoforte, and have since I was a small girl." A mischievous little sparkle flickered in those fathomless brown depths, and she lowered her voice to a naughty whisper. "I sing tavern ditties."

He barked with laughter. "What?" he asked when he could speak through his amusement.

She grinned and went on to sing, tipping her head in time to the up-tempo beat.

She's a lady of pleasure, she's a lady of joy
And she has no illusions of grandeur
You can get what you want when your money's up front
She's a sailor-lad's port in a storm
A sailor-lad's port in a storm.

She broke down, laughing with him. "My mother would be scandalized."

It was a clue as to her origins. Of course, between her speech and the way with which she moved and carried herself, she was no woman of the rookeries. A merchant's daughter, perhaps?

Either way, someone better than his sort.

"And your brother?"

She snorted. "Equally scandalized."

"Just the one, then?"

"Just . . ." Her brow puckered as she flipped onto her side, matching him in repose so that they faced one another. "Are you looking for information about my family?"

He should have known better than to think her anything less than astute enough to gather what he'd intended.

Slipping her fingers into his, she joined their hands in a hold so very natural that heat spread throughout his chest. "You might have just asked. My brother is Henry. He's stuffy and proper and boring."

"In short, nothing like his sister." A woman who, with her fierce displays of spirit and sharp wit, had put him under some kind of siren's spell.

"Well, he *was* those things. He's not them any longer. I've not painted him in the favorable light he deserves. He's devoted and loving. He married a former performer and courtesan, and she's had a thawing effect on him."

"Ah."

She drummed her fingertips along the top of his hand. "Let's see. I also have a sister, who was widowed." Some of the happiness faded from her eyes, and that distracted tapping of her fingers slowed to a stop. "Her late husband was killed in a fighting match."

Suddenly, it made sense. The reason she'd sought him out. And her admission, it also served as an unnecessary reminder of the perils that came in fighting. "I . . . see." How easily a man's life could be snuffed out with nothing more than a tap to the temple. How many men had he witnessed fall as Lila's brother-in-law had? How many times had he been on the other end of those lethal blows? His stomach muscles contracted. "And you still sought me out?"

"Because I still say there can be some good in fighting, Hugh." She spoke with a confidence of one who believed what she spoke. How naive she was. Had he ever been that innocent? He'd wager his very life not.

"You're wrong on that score." Over the top of her head, his gaze tunneled on the bayonet propped behind his bedroom door. "Be it for sport or survival, there's nothing good in it."

"What of you?" Propping her chin on his chest, Lila shimmied up until they were at eye level.

"What of me?" he asked, stalling for time.

"What about your family?"

He stroked a small circle over the small of her bare back, and she arched into his touch like a contented cat. "I was an orphan." *Am?* Did that state ever truly change for one who'd never had a family? "I've no remembrances of any parents." Likely, he was some bastard-born son to a whore on the streets. "There were no brothers or sisters," he said matter-of-factly. "The closest I have is Bragger and Maynard."

Sadness glimmered in her eyes, and he shifted on the uneven mattress. He didn't want her damned pity. He didn't want anyone's. In a bid to cut off any further questioning, he closed his eyes and attempted to steal some rest.

"Your partners," she said quietly, refusing to leave him to that silence.

"Aye."

"The same men who were ordering you about."

He stiffened.

"I'm not passing judgment, Hugh," she said quickly. "It's just . . . True family and friends, they don't go issuing directives."

"I never claimed they were family or friends," he said tersely, discomfited by the sudden shift into a topic he'd no wish to speak of.

"Precisely." Lila sat up in bed, and a pink blush crept from her shoulders all the way to her cheeks. She gathered a sheet and drew it close, concealing her nakedness. "Who are they to make determinations about what you should and should not do with your time?"

"I found us an alternate arrangement," he said between his teeth.

"That's not what I'm talking about." She paused. "Not really." She laid a hand on him. "I'm merely saying that you deserve more."

She's wrong . . .

He deserved nothing for the life he lived . . . Frustration rippled through him. At her insinuating—nay, at her pointedly stating—his weakness before his partners. "We each answer to one another in terms of business decisions. Everything is voted on." Hugh, however, hadn't ever had an equal say . . . His voice had counted only when Maynard and Bragger were in disagreement on decisions. And yet he had some say. Far more than he surely deserved for having fled years earlier.

"Very well." She sank back over her heels. "On what grounds did they wish me gone?"

Hugh stared overhead at the cracked plaster. She'd not let this go. "You're a distraction." Lila pinched his arm, forcing his gaze back to her. "Ouch."

"Do you see me as a distraction?"

Yes. She was the siren tempting those galleons out to sea and battering those hopeless souls against ragged rocks. Hugh hooded his eyes. "We're here, aren't we?"

Her blush deepened. "By your own account, these are the hours you don't work."

Aye, but she didn't know of all the time he'd spent consumed with thoughts of her. It was an admission he'd never make.

"As such, I'd expect you don't have to defend how you spend that time."

How easily she spoke of him being worthy, this woman who was so very clearly of the gentry . . . And when she spoke as she did now, he could almost convince himself that he was worthy. Which was foolish. He'd never be more than he was . . . and she'd never be with a street fighter. Not long term. Not in any way that was truly meaningful. His patience snapped. "What would you have me say, Lila? Do you want me to tell you how as small boys we were made to fight like animals?"

The color leached from her cheeks.

"How some fine lords ran a ring, and we were the draw?" *Stop talking. Why are you revealing these pieces of your past?* And yet, he couldn't keep them back. Mayhap it was because he'd rather kill whatever this connection was between them. "How fighting wasn't enough. The fancy nobs only wanted more violence. More bloodshed." His chest hurt from the force of his breathing. It had to be that and not emotion. He didn't feel. Not anymore. "Until they made us fight death matches."

Lila's lips quivered. "Oh, God."

No, there'd been no Almighty above, only a Devil in the dark.

He gripped her hard by the shoulders, his fingers digging into the soft flesh. "Or would you rather just know that I'd planned to let myself be killed to be free of it all?"

He'd said it . . . aloud . . . for the first time.

Hugh abruptly released her, his horror stamped in her face, but for altogether different reasons. He'd shared too much. Why was he saying these things? To her. Why was he laying himself bare and open? He wanted to throw up. To run from his past and who he was, and this woman who'd made him share more of himself than he'd ever shared with anyone.

A tear spiraled down her cheek. "I didn't—"

"What?" he thundered. "You didn't think that kids were sold and used to fight to the death? All for the amusements and pleasures of perverse men." Lila pressed a fist against a quivering mouth, and that evidence of her sadness sent his fury ratcheting. A rusty, empty chuckle shook his chest. "And do you know who I thought of the night I escaped? I thought of myself. I didn't think of Bragger or Maynard." Or of Angus, or even the girl, Valerie. "The moment I had the chance to break free, I fled and didn't give a single fucking thought to the boys and girls I left behind."

He closed his eyes. There'd been Bragger's small sister. A bloody little girl, and Hugh had just snuck off with the coins he'd traded his soul for, like some Judas Iscariot. And where had he eventually gone instead after wandering the streets? Bitterness pulled the words from his throat. To fight Boney's forces. A good, honorable English lad, using every coin he could for commission. His heart thundered. Hugh opened his eyes and stared blankly at the crude armoire that housed that hated crimson uniform. A token to always remember who he was and all he'd done.

"My babe . . . please help . . . she's just a babe . . ."

He inhaled through his nose, hearing that mother's screams. Her pleas. Only to be cut down by another honorable member of the 15th Hussars.

Lila stared back, stricken . . . and still so very silent.

Coming onto his knees so that his body mirrored hers, he stuck his face close to Lila's. She angled slightly away, but Hugh caught her chin hard between his fingers, keeping her close. "You think me somehow less because I ceded to my partners' request—"

"No," she said hoarsely. "I don't—"

"You ask me why I'm loyal to those men and ask why I'd respect their orders? Years after I'd betrayed them, when I didn't have so much as a piece of weevil-infested, moldy bread to put in my belly, Maynard and Bragger provided me with food. They gave me a place to live. They offered me work." Even as he abhorred it. And that was a debt he'd pay. It was why ultimately, if—when—they called for it, he'd fight. "Bragger and Maynard are no family. What we are, are men with shared aspirations, and that's enough." Wasn't it? That was the best a person could hope for in the rookeries, and that's what he'd found. He scraped his gaze over the delicate planes of her face. And he certainly wasn't going to break that vow for a woman who'd shaken his world this past week. As it was, she'd already left him weak. Hugh abruptly released her and swung his legs over the side of the bed to leave . . . when silken palms came to rest on his shoulders, delicate and soft, and yet they still managed to anchor him to the edge of his lumpy mattress.

He felt the press of his coarse sheet slide against his back, and then that barrier was gone so that his and Lila's heated skin touched.

Lila touched her lips against his neck. "I don't think those things about you, Hugh," she whispered, her breath fanning his skin and bringing his eyes closed. "I believe you're a man of honor."

He opened his eyes once more, looking to where his uniform hung, hidden. "Men of honor don't abandon people in need," he said, his tones deadened by life. Honorable men didn't storm fields filled with innocent men, women, and children, whose only crime had been coming out to advocate for more, only to be set fleeing from the government's oppression.

Lila leaned over his shoulder so their eyes met. "Honorable men don't ask other men to pay a price for kindness shown, Hugh," she said gently. "Your partners, they'd have you fight. They'd hold you to whatever rules they set . . . That isn't a true relationship, Hugh."

He stiffened. Her meaning was clear . . . And yet he'd not allowed himself to think of the fact that Bragger and Maynard had exploited him. Because what did that say that Hugh had allowed them to, in the name of that unpaid debt?

Is it truly a debt that can ever be paid, though?

Lila continued speaking, her quiet murmurings cutting across that tumult. "You spoke of shared hopes with your partners. What are they, Hugh?"

"Hopes," he echoed. A finer, prettier word than *aspirations*. Because *hope* was a word that still meant something for the innocent, who still hadn't been fully jaded by the harsh reality that was life. "Financial security so that there's food in our stomachs and"—he gestured to the cracked ceiling—"a roof over our heads. Power, so that others bent on taking to grow their own wealth and influence don't think to infringe on our territory."

She moved her gaze over his face. "You don't think of anything more for yourself."

Peace. Hugh wanted only peace. With her questioning, however, she drove home the fact of the differences between them, and those questions about her and her past and how she'd come into his life surfaced. Who was she that she didn't know the same fears that dogged everyone born to this side of England? "That is the way one who lives in the rookeries goes through it. People don't live here, Lila. If they're lucky, they survive, and then they die." Unnerved, he eased out of her arms and lay down.

She immediately joined him, sliding against his side. "You deserve more than simply surviving."

Hugh caught her fingers and drew them to his lips. "I wouldn't even know what more than that *is*, Lila."

Liar. You do know. It's her. With Lila, he saw what it was to have a person to talk to and tease. And it scared him out of his everlasting mind. Just as he knew, for all the blood on his hands, he deserved nothing.

This time, she didn't press him further. They remained wrapped in one another's arms, and closing his eyes, Hugh slept.

"Ya bluidy monster. Yar a monster, the lot of ya. May ya rot fuir wot yu've done this day."

His heart hammering, Hugh's eyes shot open. The heavy sound of silence rang in the air.

He was here. In London. In his apartments.

And then he recalled . . .

Turning his head, he found Lila.

At some point, she'd risen, dressed, and plaited her hair. He rubbed at sleep-tired eyes. So much for the soldier's senses that had saved him. Now, she sat perched on the edge of a moth-eaten armchair, and there was something so very wrong in this woman sitting in that seating he'd recovered from the streets years earlier.

Lila reached for one of her boots. As if she felt his eyes on her, she looked over; that abrupt movement sent her dark braid bouncing against her shoulder. "You're awake."

She sounded happy to see him.

Had anyone felt that sentiment for him? Ever?

"So are you," he said gruffly, glancing pointedly at her feet.

She followed his stare, and color splashed her cheeks. "I have to leave."

Of course she did.

And soon he had to return to Savage's and get on with the day's work, dealing with a business he despised.

And he was filled with the keenest of regrets. Swinging his legs over the side of the bed, Hugh stood and made his way over to a washbasin he'd set out that morn. After washing himself, he went about collecting a change of garments.

All the while, Lila resumed strapping her laces. There was an intimacy to the moment, the both of them going about dressing, comfortable in the silence between them.

But then, what had taken place here in his apartments had been a level of intimacy he'd never known or ever thought to know with another person. And he was loath for it to end. For when it did . . . what were they, really? Just two strangers content with their secrets, whose time together was finite. And in the ultimate mark of irony, he and Lila March were joined by the thing he despised most.

After they'd both dressed, Hugh and Lila faced one another. "I have to go."

"You said as much."

She glided over, and then like a loving wife might a husband, she smoothed her palms down the lapels of the jacket he'd donned. "What if I said I was dawdling because I didn't want to leave?"

Stay. His heart thumped extra hard. For that was the word on his lips, and yet as she'd pointed out, they couldn't stay here pretending anymore. He had his work, and she . . .

Where does she go when she leaves you for the morn?

"I'd say we both know we have to split ways eventually." He spoke of the inevitability of their parting.

Did he imagine the sadness that glimmered in her eyes? "Yes," she agreed, and let her arms fall to her side.

Hugh held out a hand. "Come on."

She stared a long while at his callused palm. "Where are we going?"

Annoyance stirred. Did she think he'd simply send her on through the rookeries without knowing she'd found her way safely back? "We'll find you a hackney."

This time, after she'd drawn her hood up into place, Lila placed her palm in his and allowed Hugh to lead her outside.

East London had already come alive; the streets were overflowing with vendors hawking their wares and small children weaving amongst the crowds in a bid for work to be found. As they walked, he felt the press of Lila's body against his. Stealing a glance down, he caught a glimpse of her face from within her hood.

Her cheeks stood out, pale. But it was the sheer panic emanating from within her eyes that gave him pause. She was terrified. "Here," he said, leading her onward.

Lila, however, gave no indication that she'd heard him.

Catching sight of their approach, one of the drivers jumped down.

Hugh fished a purse out from inside his jacket. "See the young woman on her way. Any harm befalls her, I'll end you." He proffered that promise as casually as he did the coins he turned over to Lila.

The balding man blanched.

"Don't pay him a pence until you're deposited where you need to be."

Lila remained absolutely motionless, her focus on the crowds of people behind them.

"Lila?" Hugh quietly urged. "Lila," he repeated more insistently, managing to snap her free from whatever trance she was in.

Blinking slowly, she looked to him as if she'd forgotten him, as if she were seeing him for the first time. "Hugh?"

Bloody hell.

Drawing the door open, he helped her up. "You'll be fine," he promised. "I won't ever be far."

And he was staggered by how very much he wanted that vow to hold true for moments beyond this one.

Hugh stepped away, and a short while later, Lila's carriage sprang into motion.

And she was gone.

Chapter 17

Following Peterloo, when Lila had returned home, carried in by servants and deposited in the confines of her four-poster bed, she'd lain on her back and simply stared at the garish pink wallpaper that adorned her walls.

In the immediate aftermath, amidst the silence and solitariness, of all there'd been to think on . . . she'd reflected upon . . . her hands.

Given how very close she'd come to losing her life, and because of it, never again seeing her family, her hands had been the oddest of things to dwell on.

More specifically, she had pondered how much she'd failed to properly appreciate her hands when they'd been whole. She'd not thought about what gifts they were capable of . . . the chords they could pluck into hauntingly beautiful medleys. She'd failed to appreciate the feel of her older sister's hand twined with hers, their perfectly formed digits perfectly interlocked.

Nor had she understood that hands were, in fact, the carriers of memories. Each protuberance and bend contained within their imperfect lines remembered horrors.

She'd come to dislike her fingers.

Nay, in all honesty, she despised them.

Oh, they weren't her only scars. She bore the bayonet's mark upon her leg, and the ragged line left by a spur down the middle of her forehead. But she could avoid mirrors and forget that her face had been transformed. And the ugly mark upon her leg could be hidden under skirts and chemises—or, as she'd recently learned, by trousers.

After she dressed each day, she was spared from staring at and remembering all the ways she was broken and all the nightmares she carried.

But her fingers she couldn't hide. Even the leather gloves she donned curved about those bent fingers, reminding her when she didn't need to be.

And the whole of her now small world noticed, too: her mother and brother, who could not bring themselves to look at the twisted digits. And Sylvia had gone out of her way to pretend that she didn't see them.

Seated at the pianoforte in her sister's music room, Lila studied them now, seeing in them new memories.

Those she'd made this day with Hugh.

Lifting them close to better inspect them in the dim lighting, she scrunched her brow.

They remained the *same* slightly crooked digits they'd been that morn, but today, she'd used them differently, freely. She'd used them to learn and defend herself, and then after, she'd stroked Hugh Savage with these same broken fingers. And he'd not been at all repulsed.

Today, for the first time in the whole of her life, in his arms, she'd felt . . . beautiful.

Not almost beautiful.

But rather, Hugh had helped Lila see that for all the ways in which her body and mind were scarred, she was still very much a woman.

And he'd desired her.

In his apartments, in his rooms, she'd learned what it was to be desired.

Her body heated, not with embarrassment for her boldness but from desire that stirred to life inside her once more at the memory of that morning.

Only, had it been mere hours ago when her life had changed? When everything had changed?

She'd had the first taste of being in control. It was a sentiment she wasn't entirely sure she'd ever truly known. Not even before Peterloo. As a girl, and then as a young woman, she hadn't ever been one to openly defy her mother. All Lila's acts of defiance and boldness had been secret, furtive acts . . . like the decision to visit St. Peter's Field in Manchester that August day.

But it was not thoughts of fighting and survival and her own reawakening that gripped her still—it was him. Each day she saw him brought them closer to the end of their time together. For that was a certainty. That moment inevitable.

And I'm not ready for it . . .

Lila depressed a single key.

The sad, slightly off-pitch note hovered in the cavernous music room.

And when Hugh had noted her fingers? He'd not looked at her as if she were some circus-show oddity. There hadn't been horror or disgust or sadness . . . only rage. But for her?

Before today she would have said it impossible. They barely knew one another, and he barely liked her . . . if at all.

Lila pressed another key.

And what would he say if he discovered you're a lady of the peerage? Do you think he'd still bring you back to his apartments or offer lessons if he knew the station divide between you?

"It matters not," she whispered into the quiet.

"Who are you talking to?"

Lila whipped about.

Her sister stood in the doorway.

"No one," she said, that sudden interruption sending her heart racing. "Myself. I was talking to myself."

Frowning, Sylvia joined her.

There was a lengthy beat of silence. *She knows.* She knew Lila had been sneaking off to learn how to fight. And it was like a kick to the gut in being reminded all over that in her quest to learn how to protect herself, she'd also kept this secret from her sister.

Sylvia drew a folded note from inside the pocket of her thick cotton wrapper. "This came for you."

"What . . . ?" Her words trailed off as Sylvia held out a note. One written in a familiar, flourishing hand.

Annalee.

And unlike so many other notes she'd rejected in the past, this one she made herself take.

As she slid her finger under the crimson seal, Lila felt her sister's eyes taking in her every move.

> Dearest Lila,
>
> How I miss you! I have heard whisperings that you might join your sister, Sylvia, at the Pleasure Ball, and it is my hope that you will be there. And if you intend to take part in the festivities, why don't we shop for our dresses as we once did? Oh, the fun we had in those long-ago days.
>
> Your dearest and best friend,
> Annalee

Lila refolded the note.

"I take it she is making another appeal to see you," Sylvia murmured.

Lila gave a hesitant nod.

"It might do you good to see her again," her sister went on. "It might do the *both* of you good."

Lila toyed with the edges of the letter. "We're such different people now." Annalee was free and alive, and Lila was . . . well, Lila. Preferring the shadows and entering the living only under duress.

Her sister wrapped an arm around her shoulders and lightly squeezed. "Ah, but how much better the world is when we interact with people who are different from us."

Lila's heart clenched as thoughts of Hugh flitted in.

She again looked at the note. "Perhaps . . . I will reach out to her."

Sylvia's cheeks dimpled from the depth of her own smile. "I think that is a wonderful idea." Suddenly, her brow dipped. "What is this?"

Lila followed Sylvia's stare, and her stomach lurched as Sylvia picked up the carved flittermouse resting there. "It is a bat," she said without conviction.

Bemused, Sylvia turned the special piece over in her hands. "Wherever did you find it?"

"I . . . I just found it in one of the rooms?"

"Hmm." Sylvia returned the bat to its place. "It is . . . lovely. If curious." Yes, curious. And also stolen. It wasn't the first frisson of guilt over pocketing Hugh's work that morn. She'd return it. She would. She was grateful when Sylvia said nothing more of it and made for the doorway. Suddenly, her sister stopped. "Lila? I'll have you know, I have dearly loved having you here with me and Vallen." Emotion hoarsened her sister's voice. "It has been more welcome than you can know."

After she'd gone, Lila picked up the flittermouse. Her sister spoke of Lila remaining on, and even as she was grateful that Sylvia had welcomed her into her home and wished to have her near . . . this was still not Lila's life. She reverently stroked the bat's unfinished ear, this beautiful masterpiece whittled by Hugh. This piece he'd created because of her. Or about her. Either way, there'd been some thought of her as he'd made it. And what did that say about him and her? About them, together?

The carved bat slipped from her fingers, hitting the keys and setting loose a lone G-sharp that blared loudly in the otherwise silent room.

Unblinking, Lila stared at the dark-brown wood creature, now prone upon the stark white-and-black keyboard.

Together? Her . . . with Hugh?

Where had that idea come from?

She . . . she couldn't be together with Hugh.

Nor has he given any indication that he so much as wants more with you. More than that which you already shared this morn.

Nay, the best—and most—she could hope for was their remaining time together. Not because of his past or of any rank that divided them, but because she was too broken for *anyone*.

As if mocking her with that truth, the staccato beat of a drum pounded in the far distance of her mind and memories, joined by the light, airy whistle of flutes as she was transported back to a sun-filled summer's day. Lila let her hands move, plying that familiar tune.

> Hark now the drums beat up again
> For all true soldier gentlemen . . .

Her lips twisted around the lie in the lyrics, and she stumbled over her words. *True soldier gentlemen.* Nothing true or noble about any one of them that day. With their fine crimson uniforms and gold buttons, how very romantic they'd all seemed to the girl she'd been. Lila let her fingers fly.

> So let us list and march I say
> And go over the hills and far away.

She struck the keys hard as she played and sang.

> 'Tis volunteers shall win the day . . .

Her voice grew more and more pitched as she sang. *Volunteers. Cobblers, bakers, and candlestick makers. Men who were neighbors.*

Over the hills and far away . . .

Lila ground her fingers into the ivory and black keys, until the tips of the digits were numb and aching, and she welcomed the discomfort.

Because the discomfort was naught compared with the pain they'd once known, and still, far muted, the pain that came from the memories.

Come gentlemen that have a mind
To serve a queen that's good and kind—

Her voice shook. *Good and kind.* There'd been nothing kind about king or queen that day.

Come 'list and enter in to pay . . .

How many men and women had been betrayed by the Crown? Hugh's visage slid forward. How many were there like Hugh—good, honorable men, who dwelled in East London, forgotten? Reliant upon undeserving men like Bragger and Maynard?

Lila's fingers slid on the keyboard, sending up a discordant melody.

Her heart pounded in her breast. Of course. That was it. This was the answer, not for her . . . but for so many.

She'd been so focused on equipping herself with the skills to defend and protect those she loved, and yet . . . there were so many. Women. Men. Children. People of all origins, who were in need of the very same skills. And how many on the fields of Manchester, had they possessed those abilities, would have been able to break themselves free from a merciless crowd that hellish August day?

Hugh's words came exploding through her frantic musings.

"That is the way one who lives in the rookeries goes through it. People don't live here, Lila. If they're lucky, they survive, and then they die."

They survived . . . *if* they had the skills Hugh did.

And it was as she'd said to him: he deserved far more than simply *surviving*. He'd insisted he didn't know what "more" was.

"I wouldn't even know what more than that is, Lila."

Her heart beat faster. She could help ensure that so many were provided the ability to defend themselves.

A giddy lightness suffused her breast. It was the answer for her . . . *and* Hugh.

If she had someone such as him beside her, working, someone who knew what it was to run a business, particularly one that involved bare-knuckle fighting . . . and someone who'd been immersed in that world the whole of his life, then all of what she hoped to craft would be possible.

Excitement pulsed in her veins, and leaning over the keyboard, she grabbed a pencil and proceeded to record a flurry of notes.

Hugh was the one she'd gone to for lessons so that she might protect those she loved, but it was *his* business. It was his world, and one she was unfamiliar with.

All along, Hugh proved the answer.

Nor was her vision entirely self-serving. With his skill and talents and knowledge, he deserved to be heard and not made to be a silent partner in any arrangement. Working together, they might create something which had never been done.

In time, she could and would learn from him, but he was the one who could help Lila make that dream a reality. He would not be a minority partner, but an equ—

A slight whisper of air whooshed. "What a patriotic lass you are."

Startled, her elbows collided with the keyboard, adding a jumbled discord to the room. Lila gasped, that sound swallowed by a hard, heavy hand.

She twisted and shuddered, but the person at her back had an unrelenting hold upon her.

I cannot breathe . . .

It was happening . . . again.

She was being crushed. The boot pressing her into the earth as people stepped over her and on her sucked the breath from her lungs, and she struggled to get air.

Tears blurring her eyes, Lila bucked wildly.

"Quiet."

Quiet.

It was a single word at odds with the pandemonium unfolding around her in the fields. But it was just one word. That didn't fit. There was supposed to be a sea of sound, cries and gunshots and the roar of the crowd, the thundering of feet and horses' hooves as they set chase.

Her body slowed its thrashing as she slogged her way through the panic to make sense of the incongruities.

There was only one voice.

Think. Think.

Lila struggled to get a grasp on what was real around her.

If she were in St. Peter's Field, there would be a swell of more than fifty thousand. That crowd's roar hovered only as an echo in her mind . . .

The erratic thudding of her pulse slowed a fraction.

Nay, there wasn't a crowd.

There was one man.

And a voice so very familiar.

Hugh!

"I'm going to move my hand from your mouth," he murmured against her ear.

Relief left her giddy, and she strangled on a giggle.

"You don't want to make me regret that decision, my lady."

Lila collapsed, the life drained from her muscles, and her legs failed her. She fell into the pianoforte and worked to pull precious air into her lungs. And when she could at last get proper breath, she looked up and managed but one word. "Hugh," she whispered, needing to hear her voice, to believe it was Hugh and not some bloodthirsty yeoman with a glistening sabre and silly square, feathered hat. "You're here."

Relief weighted her eyes closed, and she let it sweep through her, chasing off the panic of Peterloo. That relief was as real and vivid and beautiful as it had been the day someone had foisted her over the brick wall in Manchester and she'd been plucked to freedom by the men and women waiting at the base. Lila's body trembled. Not with fear. She didn't fear Hugh. Not this man . . .

This man, who was here.

At her sister's townhouse.

In Mayfair?

Oh, bloody hell.

Lila's stomach dropped, and she forced herself to open her eyes, and all that lightness went black, and she faltered.

For she didn't know *this* man.

Oh, it was Hugh Savage. One could never dare confuse the powerful figure before her with another.

"You're . . . here," she said for a second time as the implications of that penetrated the fog of fear.

"Aye."

That was it. A tacit, one-word confirmation, coated in steel, layered with rage.

Hugh was here, but as she'd never before seen him. Not even in the first days they'd known one another, when she'd defied him and his wishes, had he oozed this palpable rage, the kind that oozed from a person's frame and threatened to torch one for the crime of just being close.

His eyes formed razor slits that cut and brought her slowly to her feet.

And those primitive instincts that had been dulled long ago but honed in St. Peter's Field sent one word ricocheting around her mind. *Run . . .*

She feinted left.

Lila made it no farther than a foot past him before Hugh had an arm wrapped about her waist.

Just like that, she was transported to St. Peter's Field all over again.

She was the girl on the grass.

Or rather, one of the thousands of them.

Throwing the fist this very man had taught her, Lila opened her mouth to scream, but all sound was robbed by the weight of his palm.

"I'm not happy with you," he said, and it was the evenness of his tone that managed to ease some of the fear that he intended to kill her here, now. That, and for the weight of his hand, there was still a tenderness to the hold he had on her. "Can I move it?"

Lila gave a jerky nod, her head bobbing wildly of its own volition. For the hungering to be in control of her breathing, she'd have traded him her soul if he'd asked for it.

The moment he released her, she rushed to put the pianoforte bench between them. With his stealth and agility, it was a flimsy protection. He could crush her in a heartbeat and be gone before anyone ever found her.

He wouldn't. Not the one who'd made love to her so passionately and touched her so tenderly.

And yet . . .

Rage tightened his features, from the hard corners of his unforgiving mouth to the blue of his eyes that had gone near obsidian.

And then . . . he smiled. A glacial grin that sucked any heat from the room.

This was bad. This was bad, indeed.

Chapter 18

Of course, he'd known by her speech and ways and familiarity with these parts of London that she was of a station far beyond his. But having it confirmed here and now, in this place, made that divide so much more vast.

And she'd not told him. Nay, she'd not trusted enough to share the truth of her origins with him . . . when he'd let her deeply into his life. Far more than he had any person before her.

Or ever would again.

Lila March lived in Mayfair.

And she was a lady.

Those lies of omission should be the source of the rage battering away at him.

Instead, it wasn't only what she'd failed to share . . . it was how much she'd been unwilling to when he'd given her every part of himself.

Nearly every part, a taunting voice reminded. *Not Peterloo . . .*

And yet he'd laid his black soul bare, and all the while she'd withheld *every* part of herself.

He resisted the urge to laugh with bitterness.

Hugh skimmed his gaze over the gleaming wood instruments, all neatly arranged in a half circle upon the parquetry floor. Why, the pianoforte she stood near was worth more than any of Hugh's collective scavenged items. And where it hadn't mattered earlier that morn that he'd had nothing, now he was reminded once more of the sparsity of his existence. That he was still the same poor soldier, begging for work and forced back into a world of fighting—different battles from the ones he'd fought on the Continent, but battles nonetheless.

To give his restless legs the outlet they craved, Hugh took a slow turn about the music room. The music room he could fit his entire four-room apartments into, four times comfortably. He fought the urge to throw his head back and give himself over to the cynical laugh asking to be set free.

Only there could be no doubting in a house such as this one that there'd be servants upon him in an instant, and the only future he'd have after this night would be a trip to first Newgate and then the gallows.

The primal goal of self-preservation that had guided his existence brought him across the room, and he turned the locks on the double doors with a rapid *click-click*.

All the while, he felt Lila's gaze on him, following his every movement.

"You followed me?"

"I followed you to be sure you made it home safely," he said tightly, and her eyes filled with such tenderness and awe a dull flush settled into his cheeks.

She'd made something romantic of his following her.

But then, you did set out after her to be sure she didn't come to any harm. It wasn't that you were sneaking after her.

Her heart met her eyes. "Oh," she whispered as if he'd handed her the most beautiful of compliments. "Thank you?"

He yanked at his collar. "Are you thanking me?"

"No?"

Except it was another question, and an erratic laugh escaped him. "Bloody hell, Lila." He paused as a new, horrifying thought crept in. "Is Lila March even your name?"

"It is," she spoke quietly, without hesitation, verifying she'd at least given him the truth of her name.

His stomach sick, Hugh looked around. "And this place?" Though "palace" would have been a more apt choice of words. "Do you live here?"

She shook her head, and some of the tension eased.

"This is my sister's residence."

Hell.

"The widow whose husband was killed by a fighter?"

She gave a nod. "Her name is Sylvia. And her husband was killed at Gentleman Jackson's. I'm merely staying here until my brother returns from the country." There was a slight pause. "Henry is an earl."

An earl? Hugh, with his impoverished past and, at best, tenuous present and future—they couldn't be any more different. And he hated the depth and truth of that divide. He despised that she was part of that same lot of people who'd taken advantage of him since he'd been born, and used him for their pleasures.

Unable to look at her lest she see the tumult of emotion, all his own self-loathing and frustration with circumstances he'd never had a hope of changing, Hugh looked at the snow-white keys she'd been expertly plying when he'd entered . . . the flittermouse she'd made off with resting there. As if the crude carving somehow mattered. Which was preposterous. For that would have to mean that he somehow mattered to her beyond the lessons she'd asked him for.

The moon's glow bathed her cheeks in light. "I am so very glad you are here, Hugh," she said softly, and his foolish heart jumped.

"Oh?"

Lila collected a book from the pianoforte.

When he still made no move, Lila pressed him. "Take it." Still, there was a reluctance to her words, a woman surrendering secrets that she wasn't altogether certain she wished to share. And it was why he wanted the book most. Because from the moment he'd spied her outside the windows of his arena, he'd been incurably fascinated by her.

Not taking his eyes from her face, Hugh tugged the book from her fingers.

"An idea came to me, Hugh," she said eagerly when he still didn't bring himself to look at her words written there. "Read it." A command that required he look at those pages in order to have the answers he sought.

He flipped open the cover.

Pages filled with words that looked like they'd been written in haste, barely legible, so difficult to decipher that it took a moment to register them . . . or what he was reading. And then he did. Oh, God, he did.

With hands that shook, he snapped the book closed hard, and dropped it as if burnt.

His mouth went sour, like he'd sucked down a pint of vinegar. Feeling like he was going to toss the contents of his stomach right there on her gleaming hardwood floors, Hugh moved. Needing to put some space between them. Needing to sort through his thoughts. And this revelation.

But she'd not allow him that.

There was the softest whir of skirts, and the groan of a lone loose floorboard as she came over to him. "I don't know why I didn't think of it sooner," she chattered, excitement punctuating her every word. "There're so many who will benefit from learning how to fight. This is what I hope to do. Create a fight society."

A fight society . . .

That name from his past, resurrected by the only person who'd brought light into his life.

Grabbing another one of those notepads, she flipped it open and gestured wildly at those pages as she spoke. "I know it's not the most conventional of ideas, and yet, it is . . ."

Her words all became a jumbled blur of excitement and joy, phrases drifted in and out of focus, and with his spare hand, he briefly dug his fingertips into the right side of his temple.

"It can be something so wonderful, Hugh." She smiled, dimpling both cheeks. Her dream was his nightmare. Spreading the venom that was this ruthless world, and poisoning more with the sin of fighting. "And tonight, it occurred to me . . . what I truly want."

"What is that?" he asked hollowly.

"For us to embark on this venture together."

Embark on this venture? She spoke about it as if she were suggesting Hugh and Lila together begin a grand journey to some far-off land.

"We would be true partners, each with an equal share in the running of the society. You'd be an equal." At last, she stopped talking.

An equal. It was what he'd craved with Savage's . . . a voice in the overall running of the business. Now, she offered him that *opportunity*. A similar proposal to the one made to Hugh when Bragger and Maynard had rescued him from poverty and helped him overcome his reservations about reentering the fighting world.

And in the end? Bragger and Maynard had exploited him, making him fight for money, just as he'd been exploited as a boy.

Just as Lila would do. In the end, fighting was all about the money to be earned.

Lila stood there, all bright-eyed eagerness. Thinking she'd just handed him a gift greater than the king's crown, no doubt. "You're surprised?" she asked when he still didn't speak.

As such, something was expected of him here. In the end, he managed nothing more than a dumb echo. "It can be something *wonderful . . . ?*"

And her eyes lit as he'd only ever seen them once, earlier that morn when she'd been coming undone in his arms and in his bed.

Only, it turned out she was not finished. "I know what your concerns are, Hugh."

Did she?

"But this? This will not infringe on what you and your partners have created. Ours will cater to men and women, and there won't be matches." She chewed at her lower lip. "That is, not *paid* matches. Sparring will of course be required, as the people coming will do so to learn." Lila settled a soft hand on his sleeve, and all his muscles went rigid. "Won't you say something?"

Furious energy brought him whipping about to face her. "All along this is what you've been doing? This is what you intend to do?"

⌘

Just before Hugh had revealed himself, Lila had allowed herself to be swept away with the idea of pursuing her venture, not alone, but with Hugh at her side.

In the moments leading up to his arrival, all the planning and pieces had at last come together. There'd not been time between to consider what Hugh's reaction would be to her proposal.

But had there been, it certainly wouldn't have been . . . this.

This stilted silence.

In her years of reclusiveness, she'd lost much about the nuances in conversation, the subtleties of speaking, as she'd come to think of it. Double meanings. Hidden ones. But she was not so ignorant that she failed to hear the disappointment . . . and worse . . . the scathing disapproval that scraped Hugh's words as he spoke.

He hated her idea.

And she hated that it hurt so much that he hated it.

Unable to meet his flinty stare, Lila fiddled with the notepad, giving her fingers some task with which to occupy them. "Of course, it's entirely in the earliest stages. There's much to be done in terms of . . . well, everything really."

Stop rambling.

It was a silent order she'd never thought to issue herself again.

Alas, the well had sprung open, and she couldn't stop it from pouring out.

"I didn't originally intend to create a business, but it just came to me. And a partnership with you just . . . feels right." Everything with him felt right.

Say something, she silently implored.

The tick of the fruitwood tall case clock, however, proved the only response. That and Hugh's silence.

"Isn't that your way?" He dusted a single finger down the lace of her puffed sleeve, and she resisted the urge to move. Not because she feared his touch, but because she hungered for it still. "The way of the nobility and ruling elite." Derision coated his words. Her body, however, didn't care that he hated her. It only knew the same man who trailed that distracted finger down the slit in her night wrapper had awakened her to a passion that would never be enough.

"I know what it is to mistrust," she tried, attempting to make him see that they were more alike than different.

He scoffed, and his hand fell to his side. "You decided I wouldn't give you what you wanted . . . and so you just took it. Because that is your way." His pointed, cold gaze landed on the flittermouse.

Curling her toes into the bottoms of her feet, she grabbed that beloved carving and handed it over.

"For the love of God, Lila, it isn't about the blasted flittermouse." He hissed through his teeth. "It isn't even about the fact that you're a damned earl's sister. This"—he slashed a hand at her notes—"this is what I care about."

She edged her chin up. "You saw the benefit in teaching *me* how to fight."

"Yes," he hissed. "But not so you could go about teaching others."

"I don't know why you can't see there is good in this idea, Hugh. If you read what I intend for us—"

A hiss exploded from between his clenched teeth. "I read your damned notes, Lila."

Lila briefly studied the tips of her bare toes. What had she expected? That he'd not be horrified at the prospect of her, a woman, entering into the world he inhabited? Unwilling to be deterred, she tried again to make him see reason. "The world of fighting is good enough for you and your partners, so why should it be different for me?"

He cursed roundly. "This has nothing to do with the fact that you're a woman."

"Doesn't it, Hugh?" Wasn't that what it always boiled down to amongst society, and of every station? There was the view of what was men's work and what was women's, and never were women permitted those same freedoms and opportunities. "If I'd come to you as a man intending to make a life in the fighting world, would you have this same response?" After all, he'd agreed to work with his partners, who were undeserving of him.

"I would," he said unequivocally. With one hand, he snapped the book shut, the angry little snap sounding like a gunshot in the quiet. "This isn't about your gender, Lila. It does, however, have everything to do with the fact that you see fighting as a sport. When it's not. It's only violence and bloodshed, and you'd see its propagation."

"And yet, it's a world fine enough for you to be part of?"

He paled. And she immediately longed to call the words back because she didn't want to hurt him. But she also wanted him to understand and believe in her vision, and be a part of it with her.

"I'm not different in what I do," he said quietly. "I despise fighting, and yet I don't have a choice, Lila. While you?" He came close, his hand coming up, and her heart pounded in eager anticipation of his light caress, but he only held her book up between them. "You don't have to, and yet you're choosing to."

That's what he believed. He couldn't see past the end of what he did to the other side of what she intended. What her goals were. "I'm not looking to spread love for it as a sport."

Hugh took her by the shoulders, his fingers digging lightly into the softness of her arms, and brought his face close to hers. "It is the same damned thing. Even as innocuous as you make it sound, a fight club is never going to be innocent. That is what you, with your privileged life, could never understand."

Her lower lip trembled. "You don't know anything about me or my circumstances."

"I know you were likely born with a team of nursemaids and had the finest of cradles with the softest of mattresses, and that you've lived a life of luxury."

She bit down hard on her still-shaking lip. He was right, and yet at the same time, he knew nothing about her. "My life has not been the perfect one you think."

His gaze slid to the scar down the middle of her forehead, and the need to look away from Hugh and his scrutiny was a physical one.

"No," he murmured, touching a finger to that hated scar. "I don't think your life is perfect. Regardless of station, I don't believe any of us are free from strife. But at the end of the day, Lila? Where are you?" Hugh spread his arms wide. "You close the doors to your palace, and even as you might have your own demons, you still don't have to worry about where you'll rest your head for the night or whether you've the funds to maintain apartments that can't even keep the damned rain out." He dropped those long, magnificent limbs back to his sides.

Lila's feet may as well have sprung roots and kept her fixed to the cold, hard floor.

For Hugh spoke of a world she knew not at all. His world.

The one that the men and women and children had been assembled on St. Peter's Field to protest, asking for more.

And as for Lila that day? She'd been perched atop a well-sprigged curricle, with her pretty parasol up to shield her until-then-unblemished skin from the hot summer sun. She and Annalee had watched on as if that gathering of people there to air their grievances had been no different from the performers at Drury Lane, putting on a grand stage production.

And shame licked away at her insides. For even having witnessed all she had, she still hadn't gotten it. Not truly.

She'd been fixed on her own suffering and the perils she'd faced . . . But she'd been just one of fifty thousand souls. Fifty thousand people who, following the massacre, had gone back home to empty bellies.

She struggled to swallow past the wad of shame stuck in her throat.

Hugh, however, wouldn't leave her to that staggering and humbling realization.

He angled his head lower, bringing their eyes into alignment. Nearly seven inches past five feet, she'd never been one to feel small in the presence of most men. Hugh Savage had been the only one to make her feel short. "You knew how I felt about fighting."

"You said you didn't want me sending people to you."

He gave her a hard look, and she forced the remainder of that directive out. "You weren't interested in turning out more fighters."

"And now that is *exactly* what you intend to do, Lila."

Her patience snapped. "You're making it out to be something bad because of your past experiences with fighting," she cried softly, and when her voice echoed from the high ceilings in response, she froze, fearing that servants would be at the door in a moment. When no one came rushing, she took a deep breath, and when she again spoke, she lowered her voice. "You can't allow yourself to see that this might be different. That it *will* be."

He gave his head a sad shake. "Anything connected to fighting will only ever be evil."

Lila took his hands in hers and squeezed them hard. "But that is what brought me to you in the first place."

A sound of exasperation escaped him, and he wrenched away, tugging free. "That was different."

"Why?" she challenged. "You took me on as a student, thinking I was nothing more than a poor, defenseless female." Yes, she was that, too, but she'd been determined to be more than the woman afraid at every turn. "Maybe you saw my scarred forehead and assumed I wanted to protect myself from a cruel husband."

A muscle tensed along the hard, unforgiving line of his chiseled jaw. So she was right on the mark.

Lila swept closer. "You assumed I was just a woman, Hugh. You couldn't imagine that I could possibly be there for more."

A sad smile twisted his lips. "This isn't more," he said, gesturing again to those plans she'd devoted herself to. Plans that she'd finally found a purpose in.

And now, he'd simply cut that out from under her.

Hugh stuck a finger up near her nose, that same finger that had so expertly awakened her body to pleasure now turned on her in chastisement. "You are why I don't deal with the nobility, Lila March. Aside from the patronage they bring to my establishment, and the money they bring with it . . . because nothing about the peerage is to be trusted. And you only proved that."

She couldn't afford to let guilt get in her way. What she sought to do was bigger than this man's opinion.

So why was she still filled with the horrible need to cry? "I would never exploit you," she whispered. Her soul hurt that he could even think that.

He flashed a sad smile. "Lila, just the idea of a fight society does. You're suggesting we take my training techniques, something that is mine when so little is, and you'd use them for your own."

Lila flinched. He was right. Shame rooted around her belly, and she briefly shut her eyes.

"Look at me."

And she could no more have ignored that command than she could have ordered her heart to cease beating.

"I don't care that you were . . . are . . . a lady," he said flatly. "I may be bastard born and raised on the streets, but I'm not the fool you take me for."

Stricken, Lila stared up at him. "That isn't what I b-believe." She clutched a hand to her throat. "I wouldn't ever think that of you." She'd come to only respect him. Lila reached for him, but he brushed back her hand, that rejection hitting like a lance to the chest.

"I knew even with your worn boots that from the dresses you wore to the way you talked, you weren't from the rookeries and likely a lady born. But this"—he gestured to her books—"this I cared about. This is what would have made me turn you out on your pretty arse and send you on to Gentleman Jackson's. Instead, you tricked me with the intention of stealing lessons that you'd pass on to others."

"I didn't intend to start this venture," she entreated. "The idea of it . . . of us, doing this, only just came to me."

Only, he didn't hear her.

Hugh's fingers cupped her cheek in a mockery of a lover's caress; his work-hardened hands, callused from life and fighting, turned her face so their eyes met; his stare was one that compelled her to run and hide and also to never look away from him. That heavy blue with a rim of black around it, the sky before a storm. But then, every moment with Hugh Savage had been like chasing and trying to bottle lightning. "*That* is why I don't deal with the nobility. They have soft lives and know nothing about surviving. They don't care about the suffering around them. They don't care about how the other half struggles. All they care about is themselves." Each word was a lash. "And you only proved that, Lila." He gave his head a sad shake. "You intended to take something from me that I didn't wish to give, Lila March. Stealing it as surely as a thief picks a pocket."

She stood here, as entranced by him as she'd been from the moment she'd seen him outside Savage's. And he seemed to feel nothing more than a keen loathing. Sentiments she was entirely deserving of, and yet, knowing that did nothing to chase away the ache of regret. "I'm sorry. You deserve better than I've treated you, and far more than your partners have ever given you."

He blinked, her words clearly not what he'd been expecting, and it sent hope springing to her breast.

For mayhap if she shared what had brought her to him, then he might understand, and . . .

Then you'll become Peterloo to the last person to only see and know you as Lila March . . .

She didn't want him that way. She didn't want to use pity to erase his fury or explain away her lies.

And yet, she wanted him to understand more . . .

In the end, the decision was taken from her.

There came the distinct tread of quick footfalls. As one, she and Hugh looked to the door.

"Lila?" Her sister's voice reached through the panel. "Is everything all right? A servant thought she heard you cry out." The handle jiggled. "Lila?" her sister repeated, a greater urgency in that question.

Her heart lurched. *Bloody hell.* "I'm fine. I . . . I was singing."

"Will you open the door?"

"In a moment." Looking back at the man before her, Lila tipped her chin up. "I'm sorry, Hugh," she repeated, this time in hushed tones meant solely for his ears. "But I'm not going to change my course. There is nothing wrong in what I intend. There is only right, and if you weren't so blinded by your hatred for what you do, you'd see that, too."

And the moment the last word left her mouth, Lila knew she'd lost him.

His features hardened, transforming those chiseled planes into a mask she didn't recognize.

"I'll have mine for the lessons you stole," he whispered. "We're not done."

It was a vow that sent shivers down her spine.

Lila blinked, and there was a rush of air.

And when she opened her eyes, he was gone.

Chapter 19

He'd been a fool—a bloody fool.

He'd trusted, when life's hardest, first lesson dealt to a boy in the rough streets of the Dials was to trust no one. Against his best judgment, against all logic and reason, and worse . . . he'd done so against the wishes of the two men to whom he owed his unfaltering loyalty.

And all because he'd had a fleeting moment of pity, a desire to help a woman who'd so desperately sought his aid.

She'd sought it so badly that she'd gone and lied to him.

Ruthless was what they were. Lords, ladies, fine gents. They thought nothing of taking from those outside their social sphere, mowing them down even to get what they wanted.

Storming through the doors of the empty arena, he found his partners in the middle of the ring, conversing with an unfamiliar stranger.

Well dressed, the burly man looked as comfortable as Hugh expected he'd feel in those miserable garments.

Hugh ground his teeth together hard enough to send ripples of pain up his jaw. He didn't want to deal with talks of Dooley or the Fight Society. Tomorrow he'd recommit himself to the plan his friends had for their earliest tormentors. Not now. Now, he wanted the privacy of his modest rooms, where he could think on the fact that Lila March was in fact *Lady* Lila March, a woman determined to turn out fighters.

He choked on a harsh laugh.

She, the same woman who'd trembled outside his damned window and gone pale at the crowds of the rookeries, wished to start an arena of her own.

I'm sorry, Hugh . . . But I'm not going to change my course. There is nothing wrong in what I intend. There is only right, and if you weren't so blinded by your hatred for what you do, you'd see that, too . . .

Her non-apology played again in his mind, as it had on a loop during his return from Mayfair.

The gall of her. And worse, the gall of him for feeling this damned awe and wonder at her pride and resolve.

And she wanted you to be part of it.

Hugh had nearly reached the stairway to his offices when Bragger lifted a hand, motioning him over.

Damn it.

"Not now."

"It involves you," his partner called back.

There was to be no peace this day. Hugh shifted course and made his way to the trio.

"This is Connor Steele," Maynard said by way of introduction. "'e's a detective." His partner caught Hugh's eye. "'ired 'im loike ya suggested, to 'elp foind Dooley."

Bloody fantastic. The last thing he wanted to focus on at the moment was Dooley and their still-unknown tormentors.

"'e's got information. A name."

Names meant a step closer to vengeance. It was the closure his partners required, and the only attempt Hugh had at putting his past behind him. And with both came a path to their having retribution.

Connor Steele's eyes lingered on Hugh's scarred face. "I've uncovered information. Details about those with rumored links to—"

"Rumors," Hugh said tersely. "I'm not acting on rumors." As it was, destroying a life would be on his soul. To err and have it be the wrong man? He'd be slaughtering an innocent all over again. "If you'll excuse me?" He started past the group.

"I'm not the manner of detective who'd provide information that wasn't in some way backed up," Steele said, forcing Hugh to stop. "You can be assured, any names I've brought forward are credible."

Either way, the men who'd been served up to Maynard and Bragger were as good as guilty and would be dealt with.

And Hugh would be expected to play a part in that.

Even now, the other men scoured through whatever folio the detective had placed in their hands, their gazes flying over the information Steele had brought them.

"Why don't we do this, Steele?" Hugh's upper lip peeled back in a reflexive sneer. "When you have concrete evidence linking Dooley to the guilty parties, then bring us that."

"That is actually one of the reasons I'm here," the relentless man said with a gravity that managed to bring Maynard's and Bragger's attention from their reading. "I've come across details regarding Dooley's connections to a man named Mac Diggory."

Hugh shuttered his expression. Dead several years now, the man's evil influence lived on still.

Connor Steele moved his gaze over Hugh's face. "I trust that name means something to you, Mr. Savage?"

The notorious gang leader had had his hands in every venture, every criminal ring. "That name means something to every boy or girl who's grown up in the streets of London."

"Aye, that much is true." Something sparked in Steele's eyes, a flash of pain, a glint of one who knew and spoke from experience. By his dress and fine talk, he'd found his way out and remained an outsider not to be trusted. "I'd ask for a word alone with you, Mr. Savage," he said, not even bothering to ask for confirmation on Hugh's name.

It wasn't a question. The resolute angle of the gentleman's jawline indicated he was a man who had no intention of going anywhere.

"You have five minutes." Turning on his heel, Hugh led the way to the abovestairs offices he kept.

The moment he closed the door, Steele was already digging around in the satchel on his arm. "Several years ago, I learned of an underground ring that involved the kidnapping of children."

Hugh stiffened. "I don't know anything of that." For all the black crimes and blood on his hands, taking boys and girls was not amongst his many sins.

"No, I don't expect you do," the other man murmured, motioning to a nearby chair. "May I?"

Hugh grunted. "Please. Should I ring for pastries and tea?"

Setting his bag down at his side, the other man rested a thick folder on his lap. "I trust you are familiar with Diggory's predilection for those born to the peerage. Mostly boys, and a handful of girls, whom he had snatched from their families and absorbed as part of his elite gang of children."

Yes, there'd been rumors that had become widespread truths not long after the bastard had died. "And what does this have to do with me?" he asked impatiently.

"Many years ago, a young child, a marquess, found himself orphaned. After his parents' tragic and untimely deaths, Cannon Hewitt McCade found himself a ward of the Earl of Kent, brother to his late mother, the Duchess of Wingate. Kent was impoverished. In deep. There was no vice he'd not spend his money on." Withdrawing a sheet from his folder, the detective held it out for him.

Hugh walked across the stained floor, the boards groaning and creaking under his weight. He collected the sheet and read through the small biography about the peculiar subject of their discussion.

He felt Steele's assessing stare on him and lowered the page. "He was never a patron here." Hugh well knew the records of every man who'd set foot inside the arena doors since he'd begun working here, and the time before it. "Our crowd tends to largely be the merchant class and street roughs, with some noblemen added to our client list. If you're looking for him, you're wasting your time." He handed back the sheet. "Look somewhere else."

Steele made no move to take it. "That isn't why I asked. Kent was good friends with his sister's brother-in-law through marriage, a Lord Dudley Nesbitt. Both men have since died."

Hugh stole a glance at the clock over Steele's shoulder. "I have business to see to, and I still am failing to see why I should care about—"

"I'm getting there. If you'll bear with me a bit longer?" the detective asked. "A plan was hatched between Nesbitt and Kent. One that would see Nesbitt named duke and Kent's debt forgiven, but it involved the child . . ." Sadness flickered in the other man's eyes and was instantly gone, mayhap a mere play of the shadows. "The Marquess of Pemberton."

He stared long at Hugh, as if that name should mean something.

Hugh racked his brain. Only there was nothing he recognized. No hint of familiarity.

"They claimed the child died and held an elaborate service."

Hugh glanced briefly at the clock. "And . . . I trust he was not . . ." The other man's time was nearly up, and yet he'd insist on filling Hugh's ears with information about some fine lords he knew nothing of?

"No." That glimmer was back in Steele's eyes. "He was very much alive. Kent had the idea to sell the boy to Diggory, for a profit. The child, however, proved an exceptional fighter. Diggory saw there could be greater uses to him."

Ah, this was how it all intersected, then. Even so, Hugh had nothing to contribute. "And this child?"

"He was purchased for a hefty coin by a man named Dooley. The one you and your partners tasked me with finding information on."

An odd hum buzzed in Hugh's ears. He found himself walking around his desk and taking a seat. "Dooley," he repeated. That bastard who'd reemerged, whom his partners were eager to end, and Hugh?

Hugh had less of a stomach for that deserved revenge. Only to have it all come rushing back with the detailed telling of another boy whose innocence had been lost. A nobleman's child, who'd have no chance or hope at survival. And as rage pumped through his veins, he was reminded all over again that a killer was what he was and would always be. "What became of the boy?"

The detective gave him another long, sad look, and when he spoke, he did so in grave tones. "That boy . . . was . . . *is* . . . you, Your Grace."

Hugh froze.

That boy . . . was him?

He burst out laughing. Him, a goddamned duke? As if the far-fetched tale, better suited to a child's story than actual fact, were real? He tossed the sheet across the desk at the other man. "You had me there for a moment. Up through Dooley, I was very nearly with you."

"I trust this comes as a shock," Steele went on, remarkably straight-faced, and the first hint of unease spilled around inside Hugh. "It always is."

The other man was serious.

He scoffed. The other man was off his head, is what he was. "And these gentlemen"—by Connor Steele's account, thieves and kidnappers— "simply divulged all of this to you?"

"No. My records of Mac Diggory's child street gang contained your name. But I wouldn't have pieced together your connection to your title. Nesbitt summoned me. He revealed what had become of you. On his deathbed, he left a note detailing the . . . story."

Hugh clenched his jaw. And a story was all it was. Because what was the alternative? That he, who'd spent his life fighting and killing, had been born to a different fate, one different from the ruthless path he'd led? Done with his company, Hugh shoved to his feet and gestured to the door. "I don't know what game you play, but we're done here."

Steele made no attempt to leave. "This isn't a game," the other man said quietly. "And you are well within your rights and reason to question my presence here." The detective stood. "However, I'll leave this file, your file, so you can have some time to look through it."

Hugh resisted the urge to snort. This tale, if nothing else, had provided a diversion from his last meeting with Lila March.

When Hugh made no move to take Steele's papers, the detective set them down on the desk. "I will allow you some time to process this discovery; however, there is the matter of the title and estates, which will require your attention, Your Grace."

Your Grace.

"The only business I care to speak about is what you were paid to seek out," Hugh snapped.

"Of course. I trusted it important that I share the details surrounding your origins first. With regard to the other matter, the name I've linked to Dooley is a nobleman by the name of Prendergast."

Again, Hugh searched his mind. The name also meant nothing.

"It's common knowledge that Prendergast has an affinity for boxing. The gentleman's son was killed at Gentleman Jackson's."

Hugh sat straighter in his chair.

Steele knew. It was there in his eyes before he even began his next sentence.

"The widow is the sister of a woman who has been seen coming 'round your arena."

Lila.

His gut clenched.

What in hell . . . ?

Steele cleared his throat. "I do not believe there is any clear link between the young ladies and the marquess."

It was too much. "Get the hell out," Hugh said tiredly.

After he'd packed up his belongings, Steele made his way to the door, then turned back. "Someone I know and love very deeply was herself a victim of Mac Diggory's cruelty. I've made it my life's goal to find those who've been wronged by him and help set their circumstances to rights. That is the only reason I'm here. I left my card at the top of the folder. I am at your service when you are ready to speak."

With that, the other man let himself out of the room.

Hugh stared blankly at the folder, at the fine card tucked there with the other man's name at the center of it. Yanking it out, he turned the small ivory rectangle over in his hand. Connor Steele had come here and just expected Hugh to believe . . . he'd been born a damned duke. What bloody rubbish.

There was a sharp knock at the door. "We're done," he called, and his partners filed in.

"Wot'd 'e want?" Bragger asked without preamble.

He hesitated. "He came here with an unbelievable story."

Hooking his right foot around the bottom of Hugh's chair, Maynard dragged it out. "Ya recommended we 'ire a detective."

"Hire a different one," Hugh muttered, reclaiming his seat.

Bragger's eyes remained locked on the file. Always in possession of more restraint than their third partner, he seated himself on the edge of Hugh's desk. "What'd 'e want?"

The pair wouldn't relent, and by Steele's admission, he'd be back. "He claims I'm some Lost Lord or other." He opened the notepad containing the names of fighters to be paired for the next week's matches. As he perused those names, Hugh went on. "Steele says Mac Diggory was responsible for taking children of the peerage and positioning them in his gangs."

The expected guffaws and laughter didn't come.

Glancing up from his work, Hugh caught the serious set to both men's features. "Surely you aren't believing the damned story?" More silence met his question. "It's bullshite. All of it."

Maynard merely rubbed at his chin. "But wot if it's not?"

Hugh's back went up. "It's bloody impossible," he clipped out, determined to return to his work.

The other man slammed a hand down in the middle of Hugh's folder. "If it's not, 'owever, this would grant ya entry into the *ton*."

His partners exchanged a look, and it was the moment Hugh knew he was forgotten. "We ain't goin' to get close to Prendergast . . . But a foine duke with a place in Polite Society?"

Surely they weren't suggesting . . . ? "You aren't saying you *believe* him?"

"And wot reason would 'e 'ave to lie?" Bragger countered. "The man's a detective, and if 'e's to be believed, 'e's given you an entry that we've been missing." As one, they stared at the folder Steele had left behind. "At least read it."

"This can be our chance," Maynard said, an eager light in his eyes. "Places loike Black's."

"White's," Hugh corrected, but Maynard simply continued on.

"Or the homes of fancy lords; they've always been off-limits to us."

Their thirst for vengeance had consumed them in ways that hadn't yet devoured Hugh. Maynard and Bragger only ever had their eyes on an end to those who'd abused them and used them. It'd been why they'd acted before properly thinking on the best way to handle Dooley. It's why, even now, they were desperate to believe a fanciful tale that put Hugh at the center of it as a fine lord . . . a duke, no less.

Maynard held Hugh's gaze. "Ya'd get answers as a duke that we'll never get 'ere."

Hugh gestured to the matches he'd been coordinating. "And what of my work here?"

Maynard shrugged. "Got on well enough with the two of us. It will be an adjustment, but one we'll do foine with. Plus, look at all the money we 'ave from yar dukedom."

Matter-of-factly spoken, those words would never be construed as deliberately cutting, and yet even so, they landed a mark square in his chest. How easily they'd cut him loose, while also thinking they had a claim to his fortune. But then he'd never had a place he belonged. From his earliest days in the rookeries to the fields of the Peninsular War, and on to Waterloo and Peterloo, Hugh hadn't fit with any of those roles. Not truly.

This, Savage's, was the closest he'd been or had ever come.

And now they'd speak of his leaving as casually as they did their coordination of the fight schedule.

With reluctant fingers, Hugh made himself pick up the heavy folder left behind by Steele.

"At least consider it," Bragger murmured. His pale-yellow eyes lit, giving the fighter an unstable look. "Consider the access we'd 'ave."

After the pair had quit the offices, Hugh studied the heavy leather folder on his lap.

His partners saw only a means to have the revenge they'd spent the whole of their lives fighting for. It blinded them to the implausibility of Steele's tale.

But what if it is true . . . ? What if you are a duke and can at last get the answers you and your partners seek? It would be a debt paid to Maynard and Bragger, who'd plucked him from the streets and given him a new beginning.

And mayhap he was as desperate as Bragger and Maynard, for flipping the file open, Hugh began to read.

Chapter 20

THE LONDON INQUISITOR

Society has quite lost its patience with tales of Lost
Lords and Lost Heirs. Too many questions have and
should be raised as to how one can even be so very
certain that these gentlemen returning from the dead
are, in fact, the men whom they claim to be. As such,
it is this person's opinion that from this point forward,
all such claims not be outright rejected, necessarily,
but extreme caution paid to those men who find their
circumstances so changed . . .

M. Fairpoint

In the span of one moment to the next, Hugh Savage—now Cannon
Hewitt McCade—had gone from being not even an owner of the apartments he'd called home and the minority shareholder of a bare-knuckle
arena to one of the wealthiest men in the kingdom.

Ascending to the title of 7th Duke of Wingate had seen him with
the second-oldest title in the peerage, and the third richest.

Among that wealth included holdings in London, Wales, Somerset,
Ireland, Scotland, and . . . Manchester. Which was undoubtedly fate's

way of jeering Hugh as undeserving for that sudden change in fortune. The landholdings included everything from a Grosvenor Square mansion to sweeping estates of three hundred—and, in several cases, more—acres of property.

And in the ultimate irony, with everything he now had, it still had proven not enough to secure an invitation to the most attended ball in London.

Hugh tossed down the morning paper, and it hit the far corner of his recently inherited desk with a *thwack*.

At least not to Polite Society. Polite Society, who'd no intention of allowing an outsider amongst their ranks.

In fairness? Hugh had little interest in being part of that world. Had it not been for Dooley and the questions swirling around the highbrow perpetrators, Hugh would have grabbed himself a map, determined which inherited property was the farthest from this world, and found his way there already.

"Run," he whispered into the offices that had once belonged to the man who'd been his father.

Clasping his hands together, he rested his chin atop them. At some point, a servant had supplanted the portrait thirty feet opposite the desk of Lord Dudley Nesbitt and his two children with another set of strangers: this one, a finely dressed, hand-holding pair with a boy of two very deliberately positioned between them. The artist had captured an intimate family moment. With one leg jutted out, the curly-headed, dark-haired boy had been caught midflight. All the while, he looked adoringly back at the parents, who stared down lovingly. The father had a hand upon the child's small shoulder to keep him grounded so the artist might freeze that joyous family moment in time.

Unblinking, Hugh stared at that child upon the canvas.

Nay, not *that child. Me.*

It was Hugh, inked in oil and preserved there from a long-ago moment in time.

The evidence was there in the curls and the birthmark at the corner of his right lower lip.

And yet the painting may as well have been a work of fiction. One of those books that adorned the thousand-title library Hugh had also seen reverted back to his ownership.

Only one piece of him truly existed on that canvas—his leg. The one bent slightly, poised for flight.

That was what he'd intended to do in the rendering. For that was what he'd always done. The artist had cleverly captured that greatest of flaws amongst his character. He'd always cut ties and run. Apparently, that deficit had always been there, a part of him. It had existed when he'd been the finely dressed, well-cared-for child, fleeing the parents who'd loved him.

Just as he'd left the gang of child fighters without so much as a backward glance.

It was why, even as everything in him didn't want what was to come when the last of his tormentors was found—more blood on his hands—he'd an obligation to do this. To see it through.

A commotion rumbled outside his offices, the indistinct mutterings and heavy footfalls that grew increasingly sharp in clarity.

"His Grace is not receiving visitors."

Bragger and Maynard shouldered past the butler. The poor young man, even after seven visits from the London street toughs, had the look of one about to either cry or run off in terror whenever they came 'round.

And as Hugh could be honest, at least with himself, he found himself welcoming their absence. Eager for the conclusion of their relationship when his debt was at last paid and he no longer owed them.

"Not receiving visitors, are ya?" Maynard dragged the scroll-backed mahogany-and-beech wingback chair closer to Hugh's desk and plopped his large frame down. Lifting up the gossip column there, he waved it. "'ardly seems the way to go making the connections we need."

It spoke to the other man's naivete that they still expected Hugh should—or rather, would—be received by the *ton*.

"I assure you, those who've been coming around aren't the ones who are of any use to us," he said, settling back in his chair. Reporters, busybodies, people looking to make coin or earn currency in the form of gossip about the Lost Lord. But none of the manner of guests he, Bragger, and Maynard had use of.

Growling, Bragger stalked a path before the mahogany desk, the polished French wood gleaming. "The bloody fuckers." He slammed an open palm down on the shellacked surface. "Yar a damned duke."

If his partners hadn't already gleaned from being used by the upper classes for sport and then abandoned and completely forgotten that there was no place for their sort in Polite Society, they weren't ever going to learn. "I'm a duke who has lived on the streets." And what was more, in Hugh they saw the possibility of having their own wealth, prestige, and future yanked out from under them, as had been the case with Nesbitt. "I'm not one of them."

"They can't just not include ya." The relentless Bragger spoke to himself, a man so consumed that he failed to see the obvious truth— Hugh wasn't going to provide the entry they required.

"There's Steele," Hugh put forward, and that stopped Bragger in his tracks.

"Wot of 'im?" Maynard asked for the pair now staring bullishly back at Hugh.

"Steele ain't going to let us 'ave our piece," Bragger spat. "'e got us the name. We don't need anything else from 'im. We'll foind the proof we need."

Nay, the honorable and respected investigator wasn't one who'd blindly look the other way while they cut a man down. Therefore, Hugh would be the one they sent in to secure some scraps of evidence . . . and then they'd destroy him.

As Bragger resumed pacing, Maynard read through the most recent newspaper story about Hugh.

His gut churned . . . This was what his life had become. From one no one knew anything about, to one everyone whispered and read about.

But they wrote of his life as they knew it. They wondered after it.

They didn't know any of his story, and it was a reminder of the loyalty he owed his partners. They could have sold him out long ago for the small fortune they'd likely have made by handing over sordid details about Hugh's past. But they hadn't.

Except, they weren't the only ones he'd shared parts of himself with.

Lila's face flashed to his mind's eye.

It was just one of so many times that she'd slipped into his thoughts.

There couldn't be a future with her. Even if he was a titled duke and was suitable for one of her station. Even if he wished it could be different between them. Because when he was done with Maynard and Bragger, he'd be free of fighting. At last, he could set it behind him and begin anew. And Lila? She'd only be satisfied bringing to life the vision she'd had of that very world he sought escape from.

A memory trickled in.

The bright, excited glimmer in her eyes as she'd shared her dream.

He couldn't live like that. Not anymore. Not even for or with her. Not and remain intact as a person.

Bragger stopped abruptly. "We don't 'ave a choice."

Warning bells clamored and clanged at the back of Hugh's mind.

"The lady," his partner went on. "She's got connections to the family."

Hugh was already shaking his head. "I said I wasn't going to have dealings with her."

Maynard wagged a finger. "Uh-uh. Ya said ya didn't need her to get yarself an invitation into the marquess's 'ousehold. But ya 'aven't 'ad any luck."

"She's our entry in." Eagerness made Bragger sloppy as he fished around inside his jacket. Withdrawing all-too-familiar notes they'd each received from Steele, Bragger slapped it down between them. "She can get ya into Prendergast's. Foind out wot 'e knows about Valerie and then . . ." The retired fighter made a slashing gesture across his throat.

"Honorable men don't ask other men to pay a price for kindness shown, Hugh . . . Your partners, they'd have you fight . . . They'd hold you to whatever rules they set . . . That isn't a true relationship, Hugh . . ."

Lila's insistent words whispered through the latest request his partners had put to him. And yet as much as he loathed the violent plans they had, if he were to abandon them, then he'd be no different from every other nobleman. Men . . . and women . . . who took what they needed and set them loose. "You think we'll simply enter their homes, find their armbands and their masks, and what then?" Hugh's somber voice managed to at last penetrate the other man's excitement.

"'ang 'im with them," Maynard volunteered, not so much as missing a beat.

More violence. Violence met with violence.

"And you think we'll escape all notice."

"Nay, they'll trace it clear back to ya. Ain't goin' to be 'ard for them. Yar a duke. Oi expect ya'll be just foine." Bragger spoke without inflection.

And it was then the truth slammed into him . . . Bragger . . . Maynard . . . they had no intention of coming out alive when this was done. They'd accepted they couldn't simply off a noble and escape mercy at the hands of the Crown.

"It'll be worth it," Maynard murmured, his eyes haunted. Hunted.

And not for the first time, Hugh wondered at what hell had come in his absence. For each year of the Fight Society, there'd been an increasing violence and viciousness. When he'd been cutting down men in the fields of battle, what miseries had his partners known? Guilt, an all-too-familiar sentiment where these men were concerned, threatened to overwhelm him.

Restless, Hugh stood and walked a path to the sideboard.

He reached for the nearest bottle and then froze. His eyes took in the half-empty crystal decanter of brandy. Spirits he himself had never consumed but instead had been drunk by another. One responsible for Hugh's kidnapping, and the reason he'd found himself tormented by his own demons. Beholden to the two men behind him. Fury lent a tremble to his limbs, and he returned the decanter to its place.

He settled himself at the edge of the sideboard. "Do you truly believe those men kept any link to what they were involved in?"

"Those armbands were trophies," Bragger said with a confidence surely born of desperation, a need to trust that there was some way to link those men to their crimes . . . to the three of them.

To Bragger's lost sister.

"And we the spoils," Maynard murmured. Grimacing, the burly man gave his head a shake. And coming out of his seat, he crossed to Hugh and took the bottle Hugh had passed over. On his walk back, he yanked the stopper off and drank deeply from the bottle.

"And you believe they're going to keep them in plain sight?" Hugh asked after Maynard sat. In fact, as he'd said before, it was foolish to think they'd kept them in the first place.

"Nah." Bragger held a hand out for the bottle Maynard had pilfered. The other man immediately gave it up. "Oi believe yar gonna 'ave to 'unt for them. And *that* is why ya need to get into their 'ouseholds." As Bragger availed himself of a long swallow, Hugh stared on at his two partners.

They were determined. They saw Lila as the way in, and they'd not relent.

And he'd be reminded all over that he wanted a woman he had no place wanting.

And when he was done, when his use of her was complete, he'd have to walk away all over again.

This time, without sparing a glance for the spirits previously touched by the man who'd destroyed his life, Hugh grabbed a bottle and a glass and carried them to his desk. After he'd sat, he tried one more time. "I already told you. I don't want to have any more dealings with the woman."

"*Pfft.*" Maynard scoffed. "*Now*, ya don't?" He motioned to Bragger for the brandy. "When she moight actually be of service to us?"

This was different.

Before it had been about just being with her. A woman who, in a handful of days, he'd come to admire. Who'd made him laugh, and teased him, and spoken of him as though he was far more than the street trash he was.

But that had been then.

When Hugh *hadn't* known her intentions or plans, or the fact that a future with her wasn't possible.

And yet he'd sold his soul before. Put himself and his needs and interests first, without giving a damn for any of the other boys and girls. And he could not do that. Not again.

Pouring himself a large drink, Hugh downed the contents in one long, slow, fiery swallow. With a grimace, he set his glass down.

"I'll do it," he said quietly, catching the pleased look his partners shared.

And he could not shake himself of the feeling that he was making another perilous mistake all over again.

Chapter 21

THE LONDON INQUISITOR

Though the Duke of Wingate has been located, not much information about what happened to him has been learned . . . And let there be no mistake: that is all Polite Society cares about . . . How safe is it, really, to trust a man with Cannon McCade, the Duke of Wingate's, reputation?

M. Fairpoint

It had happened.

Sylvia had found her way back to the living.

With the modiste she'd summoned and three girls flitting about the room, layering fabric to Sylvia's frame, readying her costume for the grand masquerade, Lila's sister chattered on.

"And the Town has given him the cut direct."

And on.

"Can you imagine the gall?"

And on.

Actually, she could very well imagine it. *"Mmm."* That obscure response from Lila, who sat off in the corner of the parlor, was enough for Sylvia, who proceeded to prattle on about society's sick fascination with the latest Lost Lord.

It didn't matter that, with her head in her notebook for the better part of her sister's ramblings, Lila hadn't been following whatever gossip so occupied her sister. Just as it didn't matter who the "him" in question was.

It was a universal truth well known that Polite Society would sooner give a person perishing of thirst a cut direct than a cup of water. It was a fact Lila had learned all too well when she'd disappeared from Polite Society, and the *ton* gossip had buzzed with wonderings of her whereabouts, answering their own questions with invented, salacious rumors.

As such, given the Town's sick fascination and reporting on their family, why would Sylvia ever bother with any gossip printed about another?

Sylvia clapped her hands once, and the army of girls fluttering about immediately ceased.

"We really need to consider your costume soon, Lila, if you still intend to join me?" her sister asked.

Lila's stomach clenched. She still planned on accompanying Sylvia. Hugh had taught Lila *some* skills should she be required to defend herself or her sister. *It isn't enough . . .* She forced the misgivings back. "I do. I will . . . just not now," she said, and gave thanks when her sister didn't press the matter further. Lila would be there for that riotous affair . . . for Sylvia.

While the seamstresses helped Sylvia into her garments and tidied up, Lila skimmed through the pages of her notebook. Not long ago, she'd also been as focused as her sister on the tale of stolen children.

Now, through the chattering of her sister's gossip, all she could think about was how those worries had brought Hugh into her life.

Lila trailed her fingers along the top page. This was the particular one Hugh had last held in his hands as he'd railed at her vision and then disappeared like a specter whom she'd merely conjured of her own lonely company.

"You are why I don't deal with the nobility, Lila March. Aside from the patronage they bring to my establishment, and the money they bring with it . . . because nothing about the peerage is to be trusted. And you only proved that . . ."

A painful little ache struck her heart.

Liar—it wasn't a little one.

It was a great big, gaping pain . . . because she missed him. Because she hated that he despised her. And just as much, she hated that he'd looked with disdain upon a future that had fueled her these past weeks, enlivening her where she'd previously been deadened inside.

And in the greatest twist of irony, he'd been the one person who'd made her feel whole again. He'd reminded her what it was to feel, and in ways she'd never felt before.

And how little he'd thought of her. How ill his opinion. And how easily he'd simply cut her out of his life.

What did you expect? You knew him but a handful of days. You made more out of those moments than ever could have mattered to him.

And she'd also given herself to Hugh Savage, and the memory of their embrace was the only gift she retained of their time together.

After the small army of seamstresses had filed from the room, Sylvia sprawled into the seat across from Lila and grabbed for the newspaper she'd been reading from before her dressmaking session.

"All very scandalous, isn't it?" Sylvia murmured. "A kidnapped duke. Can one even imagine . . . losing one's ch-child?" Her voice broke.

From over the top of her notes, Lila stared at that makeshift screen made by the latest edition of *The London Inquisitor*. And for the first time since she'd left Hugh, a pang struck for reasons unrelated to him or their tumultuous parting, or the altogether brief imagining she'd had of him and her together, creating a fight society. This time, it was the thought of a lost child. "The poor boy," Lila murmured softly to herself.

"Something has finally managed to capture your attention," Sylvia said. "Why do you believe I've been absorbed in this every day? Because I *like* gossip?" She brought the paper back up before her face. "He's a man grown now," she clarified. "But that doesn't make any of this less sad. All the lost years. All the lost love. The questions about his past." She angrily lowered those pages once more, wrinkling them in her tight grip. "And all the while, all anyone worries after is whether their own titles are safe? Or whether they'll have to relinquish estates, and wealth, and prestige? *Pfft.*"

Footsteps interrupted Sylvia's telling, and Lila and her sister looked to the front of the parlor.

The young nursemaid, Pamela, came forward with Vallen in her arms. "The master has awakened from his nap, my lady."

"I see that." Sylvia tossed down her papers, the gossip forgotten. And her eyes lit as she jumped to her feet and accepted the precious babe from the nursemaid. "There you are, my prince." Dismissing the maid, Sylvia claimed a spot on the floor, and then stretching out on her back in a way that would have scandalized their mother, she held Vallen up. "I cannot even imagine," Lila's sister said distantly, lost in her own thoughts. "To lose one's child."

"Don't think of it," Lila said automatically. It was a feat she herself had become adept at, burying unwanted memories. Oh, they were still there, but it was a matter of learning how to shut them out before they . . .

"And why should we not think of it?" her sister shot back. Sylvia struggled up into a seated position. "This isn't just gossip. By the news-papers, all the *ton* is concerned about is mysterious, lost heirs coming back from the dead and taking that which is *theirs*." Fire flashed in her soft blue eyes, sparking more emotion in them than Lila recalled since before her brother-in-law's tragic death. "That's all these papers write about and worry after. There was an earl, and now a duke. They'd shut their doors to this man because they see him as a threat to their claims. Shut them out, and keep one's power. Disgusting, the lot of them."

Vallen wailed, and Sylvia immediately adjusted her hold upon the babe, smoothing his back and whispering away his upset until he'd settled comfortably into her arms.

Lila couldn't share the same surprise her sister did. She'd learned long ago who the peerage truly was.

Despite her noble upbringing, she'd witnessed firsthand the lengths to which those in power would go to keep the masses down. In their hungering to keep that power, they'd even step upon the backs of the ladies who made up their ranks. And because of it, she didn't want a bloody thing to do with them. She didn't want to reenter their world, as her family was so eager for her to do. As Sylvia herself wished to. Not just because of her fear, but rather for the plain reason that she didn't want to be part of that ruthless existence.

Lila knew now that the ease which she'd felt in the rookeries, and in paying her visit more than two years ago to Clara in East London, had been a product of her feeling a greater comfort amongst those strangers.

Even as Hugh had seen Lila as an outsider, there was an honesty in being with him and being part of a place so raw that a person didn't have to live in the glittering world of the *ton*, iced in a veneer of false civility. And ironically, it was a world Hugh had taken relish in reminding her she didn't belong to.

Another set of footfalls came, the firm military-march ones very much belonging to Sylvia's butler, Mansfield.

Mansfield, who was always composed and in perfect control, filled the doorway, his cheeks flushed.

"Good afternoon, Mansf—"

"You have a visitor, my lady," he blurted.

"A . . . visitor?" From where she knelt on the floor with Vallen, her elder sister set a small wood horse to rocking. The baby erupted into a great big giggle that proved contagious, and Lila found herself smiling. "My mother, brother, and his wife are not due back—"

"Ahem. It is not the dowager countess or His Lordship. And . . . it is not for you, my lady, but rather"—Mansfield homed his gaze in on Lila—"for *you*."

Annalee.

"You should see her," Sylvia murmured, following Lila's thoughts.

The butler cleared his throat. "If I may? It is not Lady Annalee." Coming forward with a silver tray in hand, he held that gleaming article before Lila. No one aside from Annalee visited her. She'd been removed from society so long that her name had ceased to be mentioned in the gossip columns, a detail she'd overheard her mother giving thanks for some years back.

Feeling her sister's eyes on her, Lila reached reluctant fingers toward an ivory card on the tray.

She puzzled her brow. The Duke of Wingate? Lila stared at the thick calling card emblazoned with the unfamiliar name. "I don't know a Duke of Wingate."

Her sister jerked herself upright. "The Duke of Wingate?" she squeaked. Setting Vallen down, Sylvia all but crawled on her knees over to the gossip columns. She frantically whipped paper after paper aside, flipping through, and then grabbed one. "The Duke of Wingate," she whispered, jabbing at the pages.

Lila gave her head a shake. "It doesn't change that I do not—"

"I've only been speaking to you about the gentleman for the better part of the morning, Lila." Her sister caught her hand and gave it a firm squeeze. "The Lost Lord," she mouthed.

"What . . . I . . . What business would he have with me?" To be precise, she didn't know any dukes. She didn't know any gentlemen . . . or any man. There'd been but one . . . Feeling her sister's penetrating stare, Lila said once more, "I don't know him."

"Of course you don't." Sylvia stood and scooped up her son. "You don't go anywhere that you might know him."

Lila blinked. Did she imagine a double meaning to her sister's words?

Wholly focused on the babe, however, Sylvia gave no hint of knowing.

Either way, it mattered not. Mansfield was mistaken. Lila didn't deal in the living.

She concentrated on the servant. "Please explain to His Grace that he has me mistaken for another."

Mansfield instantly proffered a wax-sealed note. "His Grace asked that I give you this."

Her intrigue deepening, Lila took the missive. Sliding a finger under the crimson seal, she broke the wax and unfolded it.

> Flittermouse,
>   I've come to call.

She gasped.

The letter fluttered from her fingers and landed at her lap.

"Lila?" her sister asked, concern in her tone. "What is it?"

Everything.

Her heart hammered.

It couldn't be.

And yet . . . those words? They couldn't belong to any man but the one who'd slipped out of her sister's household a fortnight ago.

Fourteen long days it had been since she'd seen him. And her heart knocked extra hard at the prospect of again seeing him—even if it was under duplicitous origins. Even as she'd been scorched by his disdain and fury.

Smoothing her features, she very deliberately refolded the page. "Where have you shown the . . . gentleman?" How was her voice so even?

"I've shown His Grace to the parlor," the butler said.

"His Grace," she repeated back dumbly. It was impossible, and yet her sister's servants would never question a visit from a proper duke. A notorious fighter, they would. A fighter who'd trailed his hands over her body as he'd schooled her on the most lethal blows to land. Guilt sluiced through Lila, and she studiously avoided looking at her sister. "Thank you, Mansfield."

The butler turned to go, but stopped as his mistress came to her feet.

"Surely you're not thinking to actually meet him, Lila? The man is a stranger to you." Not allowing Lila so much as a chance to respond, she spoke to the head servant. "Mansfield, see the gentleman out."

Mansfield bowed. "As you wish—"

"No."

Lila's quiet utterance froze the servant, and the poor butler, who ever aimed to please, wore a pained expression on his heavily wrinkled face.

Sylvia looked at her in confusion. "What are you *thinking*?"

"I'm thinking to meet with the gentleman and see what reason he has come," she said with a calm that belied her sister's frantic tone.

Sylvia grabbed the copy of *The London Inquisitor* she'd been reading from out of Vallen's hands, and giggling as if they played a game, the boy stretched fingers toward it.

"We know nothing of him," Sylvia said, furiously shaking those pages, and her babbling son made another grab for the prize. "You know nothing other than he is unwelcome by society."

Lila arched a brow. "And now you'd suggest I shouldn't see him because of that past?"

Her sister blushed. "I didn't say that."

"No, but you may as well have." That was what the world had been for Hugh. Her sister's words, the reason he'd rightfully judged the *ton*. "For you're just not explicitly stating what you think of a Lost Lord showing up here." This was what Hugh had spoken of. This was why he despised a world she herself also abhorred. "You'll say you feel regret for how the world has treated this gentleman, and mayhap even believe that . . . but the moment you're expected to have dealings with him, you'll treat him the same way as the rest of the world."

"It's not me he wants to have dealings with," Sylvia cried out, "but you."

Lila, whom the world sought to protect.

Vallen began to cry. "My-My-My."

"*Shh*, dear angel. Here." She wiggled the gossip column as a prize, and the babe's tears instantly gave way to excited cooing. "Very well," Lila's sister went on. "If you insist on meeting him, I intend to join you."

Sylvia would insist on joining her. Lila, still the youngest March, being coddled and protected. And for how long had Lila herself allowed her family that role? But then, after her return from Manchester, with her refusal to leave their household in London, hadn't she all but thrust them into the roles of caregivers? "No, you're not, Sylvia," she said as her sister started for one of the bell pulls. She'd allowed them to play nursemaids long enough. "I'm meeting him alone."

"But—"

"I don't require a chaperone. I'm capable of handling this . . . on my own." A feat she'd never believed she'd be capable of again.

Vallen continued to slap at the pages of *The London Inquisitor* with both hands, hopelessly wrinkling and ruining those damnable words about the Lost Lord and other poor subjects of that rubbish paper.

Indecision flared in Sylvia's eyes, and then she reluctantly moved her focus to Mansfield. "That will be all."

He bowed and, as if fearing he'd find himself once more in the middle of a debate between the two ladies, rushed off with a speed better suited to a man ten years his junior. "He's going to find out," Sylvia said when Lila started for the doorway.

"Of course he will." She'd used to care more than she ought about her family's opinion of her and her actions. It's why she'd lied to them about attending St. Peter's Field. Just as she lied to them in failing to speak of her aspirations. Pausing, she looked back.

Worry bled from Sylvia's eyes. "Henry will have my head," she whispered.

"He won't." He was in the country, absorbed with the birth of his first babe. "But . . . if"—*when*—"he finds out, is it really his place either way to make a determination about what decision you or I should make?" Henry had accepted his wife as a proprietress. Why should he not support his sisters in whatever decisions they made?

Sylvia wrinkled her nose, and then stopped her frantic twisting of her perfect, unbroken digits. "No, I suppose, when you put it that way."

With her first real smile since that morning in Hugh's East London apartments, Lila walked the remaining length of the ivory Aubusson carpet with measured steps. Once in the hall, she hastened her steps.

He is here.

How she'd missed him. Despite his palpable fury and the anger he'd directed at her that night he'd stolen off, she'd missed him and their exchanges. And simply being herself with him . . . another person.

Perhaps he'd had a chance to think about what she'd proposed and wished to partner with her.

Or mayhap it was even more than that, and he longed for her, as she'd him.

Lila quickened her strides, the brisk pace she'd set sending her noisy muslin skirts whipping about her ankles.

As she neared the Gold Parlor, she made herself slow her steps, then paused until her breathing was even. All the while her belly danced in an eager anticipation.

Lila stepped into the doorway, and with his back to her, she took a moment to drink her fill of him.

He was stylishly clad in a navy-blue frock coat, his garments bearing no resemblance to the ones he'd worn when they'd last been together. The fine wool, however, drew taut across his broad back, accentuating each muscle. Back when she'd taken part in a Season, gentlemen had padded their garments in order to craft a pretense of muscle.

Her heartbeat gave her chest a drubbing.

For there was nothing illusory in the powerful figure before her.

And here she'd believed it impossible that Hugh Savage could be any more spellbinding than he'd been in his bare shirtsleeves.

How very wrong she'd been.

Suddenly, he turned.

"Good morn . . ." Her greeting withered upon her lips, taking her smile with it.

For on the heels of giddy joy born of the letter Mansfield had handed her, reality reared its ugly head.

He smiled. Only his smile was colder. Harder. Much as it had been when he'd come upon her outside his arena, and not in the days following. Just a few they'd had together. "Hullo, Flittermouse," he purred.

That latter word bore only a distant hint of the endearment it had once been on his lips.

He wanted something.

Of course he did. Hadn't he said as much at their last parting? Back when he'd made it abundantly clear that he'd no wish to ever again see her? And why was he introducing himself . . . as the Duke of Wingate?

As if he'd followed her very thoughts, he began a slow walk toward her, that same languid movement of a panther on the prowl, and as he homed that flinty stare in on her, she commiserated with what it was to be one's quarry.

Her stomach dropped, and she took an instinctual step away from him.

In the end, she was granted a brief reprieve.

Her maid appeared in the doorway.

"Adelle, would you please bring us a tray of tea," she said without taking her gaze from Hugh.

Not missing a beat, the girl dipped a curtsy, turned on her heel, and left Lila and Hugh alone once more.

"Ah, tea." He resumed his predatory stroll. "How very polite of you."

His would never be confused as being a compliment.

Her cheeks heated. "I was doing it so that we might have time alone with which to speak." She lifted a thin, perfectly arched eyebrow. "Unless this is a social visit and you care to speak freely in front of a servant?"

"No. This is no social visit, Lila."

And she hated that her heart sank at the rapidity of that confirmation. At how desperately she'd wanted him to be here. For her.

Which was foolish in the extreme. Even if she'd wanted a life with him, half a person as she was, she'd never be whole enough for him . . . or any man.

He continued stalking forward with those sleek strides, and for a sliver of an instant, she considered the path to freedom just beyond her shoulder.

That heartbeat's hesitation cost her that escape.

Hugh shot a hand out, wringing a gasp from her.

With a faintly jeering grin, one that said he'd detected her fear of him in that moment and mocked her for it, he wordlessly pushed the door closed. His near-obsidian gaze pinned Lila to her spot as he turned the lock.

Click.

Odd, how a single twist of a latch could send one's heart threatening to crash through her chest.

He won't hurt you. He never has before. Even as angry as he'd been at his last visit, he'd only ever behaved honorably.

Those assurances did little to still the uneven hammering of her pulse. "Y-you cannot lock the door." She winced. That was what she'd said?

"But . . . I just did." A smile ghosted his lips, that aloof, detached one that had greeted her the day she'd managed to secure his tutelage. It was a smile, but it was one she'd never mistake as warm or full of mirth. Or even *any* mirth. And this—he'd been fully transparent in his ill opinion of her a fortnight ago—being reminded of it all over again landed the same devastating strike to her chest.

She took a deep breath. "What I should have said is that it is not proper."

"I'm not much concerned with propriety." He placed his lips close to her ear, and her breath hitched faintly, but enough that she heard it, which meant that he'd also detected it, and had there been any doubt, his lips curved more at the corners, confirming as much. "And given that you sought me out in the rookeries and asked for bare-knuckle lessons"—each word he spoke brought his mouth against that sensitive shell, brushing it in an unintended kiss that still managed to make her belly flutter—"I'd say you aren't much worried about it, either."

That sent her careening back to the moment. *"Shh,"* she ordered, pressing a fingertip against his lips. "Why are you here, Hugh?"

"As in, how did a street rat gain entrance to your household? Easy enough. I used the front door." He grinned. "This time."

She frowned. "I don't think of you that way, Hugh."

The harsh set to his mouth called her a liar. That same mouth that had so lovingly explored and caressed her, awakening her body to a passion she'd never imagined she could feel. And that he believed she could feel that way hurt worse than any insult he could have hurled.

"Regardless, my circumstances have"—lifting his left hand, he gave a small wave, revealing the bloodred ruby signet upon his littlest finger—"changed."

"I don't understand." She stared, transfixed by the gold mounted stone. Its heinous shade of crimson, the same hue as after her leg had been splayed open by a bayonet, leaving her blood spilled into the already soaked fields of Manchester.

"I trust it's difficult. Most of the *ton* is having a hard-enough time with the idea of an interloper swooping in to reclaim a lost title."

Those words managed to snap her from her reverie. "What?" How was it possible for a mind to race and stall all at the same time, alternating between speeding thoughts and absolute paralysis of reason? He straightened, and oddly she, who moments ago had craved distance between them, wanted to call him back when he left her side.

Hugh perched himself along the rolled arm of the Biedermeier sofa. "According to reports, I'm the Lost Lord, the Duke of Wingate."

"Are you playing some manner of game with me?" she demanded sharply, striding over to where he lounged so casually upon her sister's sofa.

"I assure you, this is no game."

And it was fantastical and impossible to believe, but as Lila peered at the implacable planes of his face, taking in the serious set to his eyes, she rocked back on her heels. Hugh was the Lost Lord. The one whose name filled the gossip pages. She pressed her eyes closed and recalled every detail he'd shared, the suffering he'd known. "My God."

"More the Devil's work," he said with an empty mirth, and her chest tightened.

Lila touched his gloveless hand.

Hugh glanced down and then, in a tangible rejection, pulled back. His rejection hit like a fist to the belly, and Lila let her palm fall useless to her side. "Why are you here?" she repeated quietly. Why, if he'd no wish to be here . . . or, worse, with her?

He smiled coldly. "Why, I've come to collect."

Chapter 22

Certain things had come naturally to Hugh.

Fighting. Fighting had come to him with a shameful ease.

Fighting of all sorts: With his fists. With a sword, a dagger, a bayonet, a musket.

Crafting wood sculptures from nothing.

Surviving in the dead of the coldest London winters without so much as a pence to his name.

But this?

Being here in Mayfair amongst the glittering world of London's preeminent bluebloods? Hugh was entirely out of his element.

Oh, he had been with Lila March before. Many times. He'd even been in this damned palace of a household.

But then, he'd been slipping inside windows and sneaking down halls with a furtiveness that had also come easy to him. It was walking through the front doors which had proven the greater challenge.

Now? Now he was a man stuck between two worlds, not truly belonging to either. He'd figured out how to dress the part, and he dwelled in an even grander residence than the king. Only to feel at sea over how to be in this world.

Unsettled, and loath that she might see, Hugh strolled a circle around the parlor, walking the perimeter of the sculpted floral Aubusson rug.

"You've come to collect," she repeated back carefully, edging away from him, wandering around a fully sprung seat with an upholstered back, finer than any bed he'd ever slept in.

And his annoyance proved greater at the hint she'd hide than the fact of his actual circumstances. "Aye. As promised, I'd have payment for my lessons."

Because he'd no choice.

She was quieter than she'd been fourteen days earlier. Somber. Grave. And he found himself missing and mourning the spirited woman who'd challenged him at every turn.

"What do you want?" she whispered. She thought she'd drive this exchange? He'd no intention of ceding any upper hand to Lila March. Alas, she wasn't a woman who'd ever surrender an inch. Her shoulders back, she marched to the door, turned the lock, and then drew the panel open. "If you don't intend to say what this is about . . . ?"

The maid reappeared, carrying a powder-blue-and-gold, seven-piece tea tray. As she laid it upon the table nearest Lila, Lila was once again the composed, in-command, perfect lady.

How had he failed to see as much?

From the proud squaring of her shoulders to the graceful, gliding quality to her every step, she bore the mark of a lady.

As if she felt his stare, Lila glanced over the top of her maid's head, and their gazes collided.

"Might you see to pastries, after all?" Lila murmured.

"Yes, my lady." The young maid dropped a curtsy and then rushed off once more.

The moment she'd gone, Lila closed the door behind her.

"How clever. You've managed to secure us more time alone together."

"I have, but toying with me as you are, you're squandering each moment."

Touché.

Getting 'round to the reason of his visit, Hugh fished a folded clipping from his pocket and crossed over to her. God, how he despised this. Needing her help. Needing anyone's help. Nothing had ever been without difficulty where Hugh was concerned. As such, he'd not known why he'd have expected that finding himself a duke overnight would have proven any different.

Lila stared at the page a moment before taking the snippet from his hands. It was just a paragraph from *The Times*, but for the study and attention she gave it, it may as well have been the King James Bible.

"Lord Prendergast is hosting a masquerade. It is my understanding that your sister is a relation to the gentleman."

She continued to stare at the page.

At last, Lila looked up and attempted to hand over the scrap. "I'm not certain what you are asking of me."

"I'd like to gain entry to the marquess's ball; however, Polite Society has been anything but polite for one of their Lost Lords," he explained. And once he was part of this world, Hugh would have entry to the marquess's household. The monsters of his past would be brought to justice, and he'd be able to move forward. To set aside the life he'd lived.

Lila refolded the page, creasing it along the distinct line. "And you think I might somehow provide you with that?"

"No." He dropped a shoulder against the elaborate trim of the doorway. "I *know* you can." A respectable lady, born the sister of an earl, and having another sister who was a countess herself, she'd have a secure place in that world. "If we are perceived as a couple." He nodded at the sheet she still held. "Then I trust Prendergast would have to issue an invitation. We can begin today."

"Begin what, exactly?"

"Establishing a connection so that I can gain the same entry your family has."

"What?" she croaked. "Now? B-but . . . s-surely you can't . . . ," she sputtered, and that stammering would have been endearing if it hadn't been a product of her horror at the prospect of the two of them together. "*We* can't . . ."

"Oh, I assure you, we can and we will." Impatient, Hugh consulted a gold timepiece, another newly inherited bauble that, if sold, could have fed him during the longest, coldest year of his life in the rookeries.

Panic lit her eyes. "I didn't even receive the full instruction you promised, Hugh. We only met four days. You cannot hold me to"—she held the snippet up—"these terms."

And there she was. The spirited minx, bold and fearless once more. *Or is it simply her desire to avoid being seen about with you before her world that accounts for her determination?* After all, every meeting between them had taken place in secret, cloaked in shadows.

He set his jaw. "Those are the terms, Lila. Those are the people I'm expecting you to make me respectable before." Hugh shrugged. "I really don't care how you manage it, Lila. Just that you do. But you're a most resourceful flittermouse." Hugh reached for the door handle.

She emitted a little squeak and intercepted his attempt, catching his hand. "Stop! Can we come to a *different* arrangement?"

Briefly distracted by those satin-soft fingers covering his scarred ones, he looked upon them and was brought back to the morning they'd made love. "A different one?" He stroked a knuckle along the smooth curve of her jaw. "This is nonnegotiable, love. Though . . . I am tempted." Hugh left that there as the suggestion it was.

She gasped and slapped his hand away.

Distant footfalls echoed in the hall, indicating the approach of her maid. Ever a proper lady, Lila anticipated that arrival, drawing the panel open, and Hugh took up a place in the corner of the room, needing to regain control of his thoughts and emotions. What was it about this woman that made him feel more than he'd ever felt? More than he'd ever believed himself capable of?

The servant appeared with another platter in hand, a silver one that gleamed bright around its edges, while the interior had been artfully crafted into a display of colorful miniature cakes and tarts done in different preserves. Baked goods he'd salivated over at shop windows as a boy, that were now being presented to him as a guest to this noblewoman's household.

His nape prickled, and he forced his eyes away from the refreshments.

Lila murmured something to the servant, and the young maid dipped a curtsy and backed out of the room. After she'd gone, leaving Hugh and Lila alone, silence hung in the air, broken only by the hum of quiet and the distant, muffled rumble of carriages out the floor-to-ceiling windows that lined the room. Those sounds muted by the drawn curtains.

She proved braver and bolder than him once more, speaking first. "Why is it so important to you that you attend Lady Prendergast's masquerade?"

He hooded his eyes, but Lila was already shaking her head. "I've a right to know."

"No, you don't," he said flatly. She'd lost all rights with her lies of omissions and future intentions.

"Is she in some way connected to . . . your past?"

God, she was as tenacious as she was clever.

"And if I said she was, would you express your shocked disbelief that a peer could be connected to such atrocities?" he taunted.

Except the saddest of smiles ghosted her lips. "I'd say in return that nothing about any gentleman could surprise me."

Unnerved by that response, which was as cryptic as it was unexpected, Hugh tapped his leg. "Well?"

"I'll help secure your entry to Polite Society, Hugh." Joining him, she pressed the newspaper clipping into his hand, forcing him to take it. "I'll see that my family opens doors previously closed to you." There was a "but" there. He waited for it . . . and when it did not come, he pressed her for more.

"You'll speak to your brother on my behalf, then."

"As soon as he returns, you have my word."

Bloody hell. So that was how she'd been able to sneak about . . . and why she resided with her sister. "When?" Neither he nor Maynard nor Bragger could begin to find the information they sought without the entry Lila and her family provided.

"He's not due to return for several weeks."

His brow shot up. "Several weeks." Time they didn't have. Soon details of his past and his connections to Savage's would be dug up, and all those lords involved in the Fight Society would see Hugh barred from their households. "That is insufficient."

"My sister-in-law has just delivered their child, Hugh."

"No."

Her lips dipped at the corners. "I assure you, she has."

He swiped a hand over his face, and despite himself, despite the struggle of being back here with her, a rusty chuckle shook his chest. "I'm not disputing the birth of the babe."

Understanding filled her clear gaze. "You were speaking of the time-line of my brother's return."

"I was," he said, his expression deadpan.

"I . . . see . . ."

A stilted awkwardness hung in the air.

"In the meantime, you and I can begin our . . ."

She stared at him, a question in her eyes. "Our *what?*"

He bounced on the balls of his feet, riddled with the same energy that coursed through him before a match. "I'll court you. It will lend an air of believability to our conn—" *connection.*

Lila collapsed into a paroxysm of coughing, her cheeks turning florid, and she opened her mouth as if trying to speak through her fit. She held an arm out.

He thumped her hard between the shoulder blades.

"*Wh-what?*" she at last managed to strangle out.

"I believe you call it a 'courtship'?" he drawled. "And here, given your tendency of dashing around the rookeries, enlisting aid from a fighter, I'd have thought the courtship of a duke would be mundane."

She'd no intention of joining him out and being seen with him. It was there in her eyes.

As a boy, in exchange for coin, he'd wiped dung from the boots of lofty lords. He'd returned from war a grown man with his hand out, still begging for funds from anyone who could spare it. None of those shames felt anything like this rejection. "*Tsk. Tsk.* Nothing to say?" he taunted.

"I'm not joining you."

"Anywhere?"

She shook her head. "Well, the masquerade . . . I will be there."

He flicked the snow-white lace that dripped from her yellow sleeve. "Too good to be seen about with the Devil Duke." As society had taken to writing of him in their shite gossip columns.

Indignation blazed in her eyes, and she slapped his hand away. "My, what an ill opinion you have of me."

For a moment he thought he might have actually seen hurt there.

She clasped her hands behind her back, but not before he caught the slight shaking of those digits. "I don't . . . take part in *ton* functions."

He narrowed his eyes. "Isn't that what ladies *do*?"

"Most," she said calmly. "I don't." Her gaze dipped to the floor.

He waited for her to say something more.

But she offered him only her silence.

Hugh set his jaw. She'd not help him in this. This, his one opportunity to repay a debt to Bragger and Maynard . . . and every last child he'd failed the moment he stepped away and attempted to make a life for himself.

Regardless, she represented the surest way to gain, if not acceptance, entry to households. "Well, I've information for you, Lila March." Hugh drew the pair of leather fawn riding gloves from his jacket and tugged them on. "Now you do. I'm afraid I'm unable to remain for refreshments but look forward to our outing tomorrow."

"But—"

"Ten o'clock tomorrow morning. Be ready."

With that, he headed for the door.

"Hugh, I can't accompany you." His legs ground to a stop mid-stride, and he slowly wheeled back to face her. She turned up a shaking palm. "I don't go outside."

He waited for her to say something more. And she didn't. A muscle ticked at the corner of his eye. "With me." *A common street rat. A fighter. A murderer . . .*

"No. I . . ." Lila scrabbled with her skirts before catching his gaze on those frenetic movements, and she stopped herself. "I don't go out," she repeated, the same meaning, the words slightly different, but their message the same.

His mind tried to slog through exactly what it was she was saying. He scoffed. "You've visited me and—"

"In the morn." Her quiet murmur vibrated in the thick air.

And then a memory trickled in. Of the day he'd put her in a hired hack, the terror that had brimmed in her eyes as she'd scoured the bustling streets. And his earlier confidence, the internalization that this had been all about him, wavered.

Drawing back her shoulders, she looked him square in the eyes. "I'm a recluse."

Chapter 23

Lila's mouth went dry.

She'd told him.

Because she'd needed to. Only, she'd owed him the truth before this. And it should have come not because he'd put a request to her that she could never fulfill. He'd spoken of his struggles and suffering, and all the while, Lila had kept her demons close, shutting Hugh out.

Now, the one thing he sought . . . The one repayment he'd ask was the one she couldn't give. And as such, he needed to know. He deserved those answers more than she deserved the secrecy that protected her pride.

But how she hated that he had been the one person to see her for more than her past . . . that a man who'd been wholly unconnected to those darkest days should now see her and that day as one.

He turned his left hand up slightly at his side. The hand now holding that newspaper article. "I don't . . ." He shook his head.

Restless, Lila wandered over to the gilded wooden pedestal table. The pale-yellow urn overflowing with flowers infused the air with a sweet scent. Closing her eyes, she drew in a breath and let that floral smell fill her nostrils, one that harkened back to the country and open fields and land she'd sought to avoid. When she opened her eyes, the crimson flowers her sister filled the household with met her gaze. Of their own volition, her fingers reached for one of those stems, plucked free of its thorns, and brought it close to her face.

God, how she despised that color.

In it she saw only blood, and fields slicked with that sanguine flow of life . . . and death.

With her fingers shaking, Lila returned the bloom to the water, to the center of the arrangement, interspersed with pink, ivory, and white roses. She fiddled with the flower . . . several moments? An hour? A lifetime? As she sought to right her thoughts and searched where to begin, time had ceased to make any sense.

But then time hadn't really meant anything in so long.

There'd been no obligations, no commitments. No gatherings or places she'd promised to be. Until Hugh. Hugh had brought order and thought back into her life, had required her to be human again, and to do things that living people did—to honor appointments, to engage in discussion. To think.

To feel.

She felt his presence there. Silent and unmoving as he was, he remained all-powerful in his presence.

She continued to search for a way to begin, and finding there'd never be any perfection in this because there'd been no perfection in that day, she settled on the easiest place to start.

"Do you have any remembrances of being outside London?" she quietly asked.

He gave her a look, and then slowly shook his head. "Not in . . . a long time."

"I don't think your life is perfect. Regardless of station, I don't believe any of us are free from strife. But at the end of the day, Lila? . . . You close the doors to your palace, and even as you might have your own demons, you still don't have to worry about where you'll rest your head for the night or whether you've the funds to maintain apartments that can't even keep the damned rain out."

Her heart tugged, and her mind recalled that she wasn't the only one who'd suffered. That in all he'd lost, he'd known far greater struggles, and that infused a strength into her. One that she'd been so very much without, and for so very long.

"I've always hated London. The streets are crowded. The air is thicker. The clouds even heavier. But in the countryside?" She pressed her eyes briefly closed and let the remembrances back in . . . not of Manchester, but of Kent in all its glorious purity. A wistful smile caught on her lips. "There are days when there is nothing but blue sky. Blues of every shade, a pale blue in the morn, dusted with orange as the sun starts its climb . . . and at noontime, it's just this glorious azure. So very bright that it's impossible to feel anything but joy and a need to lie back and simply stare up at a canvas stretched as far as the eye might see in every direction of that endless blanket of blue." Her words came faster as she spoke. "And in the dead of night, the sky is never truly black but more a shade of indigo, flecked with so many stars, visible, that it all but turns the sky silver." Invariably another shade traipsed across her reminiscences, the memory that ushered in a different sky . . . and another familiar landscape. This one a pale blue, dappled with the errant clouds of amorphous shape, clouds that had done nothing to soften the glare of the sun's rays.

And despite the memory of warmth, then, and in her sister's parlor, a chill went through her, bringing up the gooseflesh on her arms.

She opened her eyes.

At some point, Hugh had abandoned his spot behind her. He'd moved to the other side of the floral arrangement, keeping just those vibrant blooms between them. His magnificent black lashes hooded but didn't conceal those entrancing, nearly obsidian eyes that he now had fixed upon her. She felt his gaze as sure as if he touched her.

And she clung to that illusory connection.

"And the summer," she whispered. "Oh, how very glorious it is then." She hugged her arms around her middle in a bid for warmth.

In a need for closeness, even if it was the forlornness of her own hold. "The days are so very warm in the summer, Hugh. That heat awakens you, but where you cannot bring yourself to care because it's just more time you get to spend with the summer's day." And it was wholly selfish, extolling that beauty when he should have known only the darkness of London. But then, the dark was everywhere. Lila squeezed herself more tightly, her fingers curled into the soft flesh of her upper arms. "I hate the country now." The vitriol and hate that pulled that admission out of her had once scared her. She'd come, in time, to accept that new raw, cynical part of who she was now.

Restive, she yanked the red rose angrily from the vase, costing the bloom several petals; they rained down about her like satin teardrops.

A hand covered hers—Hugh's. Large and reassuring and warm, and so very much alive. Lila stared at the little scars and marks upon him, feeling an even greater connection for the imperfections they both carried. He didn't offer any words, just his touch, and that was enough. "Nearly nine years ago, I was visiting my friend, and there promised to be a grand gathering of people, and I confess . . ." She bit her lower lip. "I didn't truly know anything about what the gathering represented. What it meant, or what the significance was. It was just a gathering to me." A sob caught in her throat. "God, what a self-indulgent, uninformed, supercilious person I was." That day had meant so much to the people who'd assembled there. People not unlike Hugh, who'd known strife and oppression from the government who didn't care for them.

"You would have been a girl," he said quietly, speaking the first words since she'd begun her telling.

"Eighteen, Hugh. Not so young."

"But not so very old, either."

She held his gaze. "And at eighteen, did you consider yourself a boy?"

His eyes went dark. "It's different, Lila."

"It's not," she insisted. "Not at all. Don't use age to wash away my mistakes." She thumped a fist against her chest. "That lack of awareness . . . that was my fault. I had every opportunity to be enlightened." And she'd not been. "I'd been the lady reading fanciful romantic books." Ones where love triumphed and damsels found happily-ever-afters with knights or reformed scoundrels. "All the while? I remained ignorant as to the plight of those outside the exalted ranks of the peerage."

Needing to move, needing to escape but not allowing herself the coward's way this time, she strode out from behind the table and began to pace. "My friend didn't want to go. She didn't see what the furor was over." Lila dug her fingers hard against her temples in a contradictory need to both bring those memories forward and tamp them down. "Why couldn't we go fish?" Because Annalee had loved to cast a line at her family's river. "Why couldn't we go spend the day at the swing?" Hung between two tall pines over that same river, they'd loved to soar over those smooth waters before jumping off and in. To the shame and horror of Annalee's mother and self-indulgent father. "We didn't do either of those things she exceedingly wished to do." *Why?* "Wh-why?" Her voice broke, and she shook her head with sadness, self-disgust . . . and the all-too-familiar sentiment—regret.

Hugh brushed his roughened palm down the curve of her cheek in a caress she didn't deserve. And selfish as she'd always been, she took of that warmth he offered. He didn't put questions to her. He didn't urge her on in her telling. He just offered her patience and an ability to freely share, as she would. And how very wonderful it felt. After all these years of not talking about that day to anyone, for the pain that came in the recounting, there was a peace in unburdening herself of all those details.

Tortured, Lila lifted her eyes to his. "Ultimately, Annalee? She always went along with whatever scrape I'd put forward." The rumble within the crowd, like distant thunder, growing increasingly close echoed in her mind. "Just as she did that morn." She spoke softly to herself of the friend who out of cowardice Lila didn't allow herself to think about. Except when the guilt was strongest. Except when the nightmares were darkest.

〰

Hugh had killed men.

Many of them.

The first had been for hire, a price to be paid for his freedom. The rest? A number so many that in the heart of battle, he'd not even bothered tracking because he'd been so very consumed with just living.

As such, having taken life, having lived a perilous life . . . he'd never considered himself a coward.

Until this very moment with Lila.

For in this instant, he didn't want her story. He didn't want to know what accounted for the heartbreak in her eyes.

Because it was easier to keep the world to strict, definable facts: she was Lady Lila March, the woman who'd tricked him out of lessons, all with the intention of building a fight society. And he, a man who'd disavowed spreading any further violence.

That was simple and clear. Just as when he'd set out to pay her a call and put his demands to her, his request had been clear in his mind: enlist her help, secure the information he needed, and then part ways with her once again.

But knowing more . . . nay, knowing what ghosts were responsible for the fear that so often sparked in her eyes, or the haunted desolateness there even now, left the world a blend of all those millions of shades of blues she'd so poetically spoken of.

Whatever she'd say would alter . . . everything. It would add a layer of understanding to her and all that had shaped her . . . And once discovered, it would forever alter how he saw her . . . and more terrifying for it, his every dealing with her.

As such, he should urge her to silence. Remind her that theirs was an arrangement and nothing more.

And yet he could no sooner do that than he could again willingly take another person's life.

"What happened?" he asked in a low voice.

Lila stopped midpace; she stared at him with wide, wildly blinking eyes as if she'd forgotten his presence. As if she'd only ever really been speaking to herself.

"I told her it would be grand fun. I brought her 'round with talk of how very exciting it was. Nothing ever happened in Tameside." A panicky little uncontrollable giggle bubbled past her lips, and he balled his hands, wanting to quash the pain responsible for it. Missing her mirth and only just realizing in the moment that he'd never truly heard her laughter. He'd had only her smiles and hated that he'd not known both. Suddenly, she stopped, a distant, vacant look in her eyes. "Tameside. We would always jest about it. A place so calm, it was in its name." She pressed a hand down the middle of her face, obscuring the lightning bolt scar at the center of her forehead, then covering her right cheek. "That day, it wasn't fun. And it wasn't grand," she whispered in hollowed-out tones of death.

Ones he knew all too well . . . from Waterloo . . . from Peterloo . . . from every battle that had come before those darkest ones.

The cold of her telling iced the room, and left him chilled from the inside out.

"It was nothing more than a croft. Just this enormous field that had been cleared but for a pile of brushwood that had been stacked at its end. I remember as we rode in on our curricle, looking at that pile." She blinked slowly, a careful downward-and-then-upward flicker of her glorious dark lashes, as if she was seeing that field in her mind's eye, and Hugh was dragged unwittingly back to the last one he himself had stepped upon. "It was as though it'd been tucked in the corner because there'd not been time enough to clear that, too." She'd become lost in her details, painting in vivid strokes that day that haunted her. "The pile sat there, an afterthought. I wondered, why had they left it? Was it simply forgotten? Had they run out of time? It is an odd detail to recollect all these years later, isn't it?" she asked softly, looking to Hugh.

She sought confirmation. As to whether he was listening, or whether he wished to continue hearing her tale, but either way, where moments before he'd been coward enough to want to run from whatever her telling was, now, he wished to hear it. So that he might better understand this woman and her demons. For then, mayhap he might understand what had brought her into his life and what now drove that dark vision she had for her future. "There is no understanding why the mind remembers the moments it does, Lila," he finally murmured. Resurrected from the ashes of trauma came the oddest remembrances, peppered in.

"Yes." Lila nodded, and then they were not two people at odds over their opposing goals but joined by a shared—but different—struggle. As if she'd found some strength in that, Lila's shoulders came back, and she was speaking in even tones. "People had come from all over Greater Manchester to hear him. An esteemed politician . . ."

It took a moment for her words to register.

"Who?" he asked hoarsely, needing confirmation. But not wanting it, either. Now wishing he'd urged her to silence earlier. Please let him have misheard both . . . all . . . of what she said. Because the alternative was—

"The orator, Henry Hunt, but I'd not even heard of him, either," she said softly, mistaking his desperate query for ignorance of the gentleman in question's identity. "I didn't know what he'd come to speak of that day . . ."

Greater Manchester . . .

The orator . . .

And as Lila continued her quiet murmurings, Hugh saw her mouth as it moved, but he could not pick his way through what she was saying. To register the implications . . .

There was only a humming.

It buzzed and whined in his ears.

Not unlike the confusing blend of discordant nonsound that had come in the dead of battle on the fields of Brussels.

Or . . . *Peterloo* . . .

Nay. He shook his head slowly, but she kept on talking. Words slid in and out of focus.

"St. Peter's Field . . . thousands and thousands . . ."

Hugh briefly squeezed his eyes shut, but her recounting didn't cease.

Oh, God.

Peterloo.

She'd been there. She'd been there. She'd lived that hell. She wore her scars of that day . . . invisible and visible.

His stomach revolted.

Please stop. Please stop talking. It was a mantra and a plea, echoing over and over in his head.

"There were so many people," she was saying, and because he was undeserving of escape from this . . . from what he'd done and what she'd suffered because of it, the sound of her voice came roaring back with all the power of cannon fire upon a silent field as she spoke; there was only a crisp clarity. One where he heard each word. Each word that landed sharper and harder than any blow he'd ever been dealt as a bare-knuckle fighter. "There were"—*babes*—"children and babies. And"—*innocent men and women*—"innocent men and women."

She spoke to everything he knew to have been true that day . . . because it was a shared accounting. Only that day, they'd been at opposite ends. Until they hadn't. Until he'd realized what the King's Army had asked, and he'd gone against those commands.

It wouldn't matter to her.

Nor should it.

All that did matter was that he'd been there, charging a field before realizing the truth . . .

"Where were you?" He didn't recognize that graveled voice as his own. "That day . . . at St. Peter's Field." Every place had been fraught with danger, but had she been by the wall, she would have been one of the first to be hauled over . . .

"We had to be close to the front." Lila sank her teeth into her lower lip. "Near the privileged guests. Near *The Times* and other papers."

An agonized, animalistic sound, one he couldn't stop, climbed his throat and choked him on his own sorrow.

"It all went so bad, so quickly. There were yells. I'll never forget them. In the heart of it, I didn't understand what was happening. But then the yeomanry charged." Her words came rapid-fire. "Men, cutting down their neighbors. They called their names, Hugh. They called their names," she repeated, her voice creeping up an octave. "It was . . . personal to them. Our curricle was being buffeted at both sides, and we found ourselves knocked to the ground. We held hands for a moment, and then we were separated."

Hugh shifted on his feet, that slight restless movement all that kept him grounded to the Aubusson carpet, and also kept him from fleeing. "How did you get out?" Gutless as he was, he needed to get to the end of the telling, to the moment she'd broken free.

"I thought I wouldn't," she whispered. "The crowd . . . you couldn't even move. People stood shoulder to shoulder, we were all pressed together." Her breath came hard and fast, her eyes frenzied. She was there. He knew it, because he was there. Not just now in her telling . . . but always.

Hugh rested a hand on her right shoulder and angled her body toward his. And it was as if she found peace and comfort from their bodies' nearness.

Would she still feel that way were she to discover you are the monster of her nightmares . . . ?

That voice jeered and mocked him, and he proved his evil still, because even knowing she'd despise him, he held her anyway.

When Lila had managed to calm, she drew away, just enough that she could meet his gaze, but close enough that her chest brushed his still. "Then, they called"—*the 15th*—"the soldiers. It was this odd . . . suspension of time." She spoke in subdued tones. "It was like . . ." She shook her head. "This great . . ."

"Wave." In his mind, he saw the roll of the crowd as they surged forward and then back as there was no surcease.

She nodded. "Yes. It was this wave of bodies. I could see the cavalry's confusion." He'd been the cavalry. He swallowed spasmodically, trying to keep the bile from climbing. "How could man and horse break through that mass of human beings? They raised their sabres high." Her eyes distant once more, she lifted her right arm, mimicking the soldiers' movements. "As if that would manage to break the crowd. And they cut their w-way through. W-we held our hands up. P-pleading."

Someone moaned.

Was it him? Or her?

Nothing made sense any longer.

Nothing ever would again.

Tears glazed her eyes, the first he'd ever seen her cry, and he would have taken his old sabre and slashed himself to keep her from this pain. "Stand fast." She sobbed and promptly pressed a fist against her mouth to bury that sound. "Everywhere, people were shouting, 'They are riding upon us. Shame. Break. *Breakkkk.*'"

Those screams and cries that would haunt him until he drew his last breath, she heard, too. All along, since their first meeting, he'd believed them so very different, only to realize in this moment . . . their nightmare was a shared one, the both of them more alike than he'd have ever believed.

Pressure weighted his chest, restricting his airflow so he could manage nothing more than sharp little sporadic bursts of shaky inhalations and exhalations.

With his thumb, Hugh wiped at the crystalline trails that wound down her cheeks. Only there were more that just took their place.

"Everyone dispersed," she said in a deadened voice. "There was a wall . . ." Hugh stared blankly over the top of dark curls to the drawn floral curtains that kept out the full force of the sun. He'd been at that high stone fixture. How close they'd been to one another that day; had hers been one of the hands he'd touched, then, when people managed to break free . . . ? Had she been one of those cursing and spitting at him, and running the other way, toward danger, out of fear that he'd cut the men and women at the wall down? "When I managed to break free, I fell . . ."

Darkness crept across his vision, briefly blinding, as he saw her on the ground as frantic spectators fled . . . *trampling her. No. "Lilaaa,"* he groaned. He could manage nothing more than that, just her name.

"People stepped on me. Crushing me." She clawed at the neckline of her gown. "I couldn't breathe. People ran over me. Eventually, I realized they'd stomped all over my hand." He looked blankly down. *Her broken fingers.* "I was so sure I'd die there, and I just recall thinking . . . this is what the end is. This is what it is like to die. Someone's boot scraped over my head." Her shaking fingers crept up to that scar at her forehead. "Someone hauled me to my feet. I don't know who he was. And I felt this overwhelming relief, but then he had this crazed look in his eyes, and he was holding on to me, and I couldn't get him to release me." Lila exhaled a long, slow breath between her compressed lips. "Someone jolted us, and I fell free. But then I was being pushed forward and then thrown over a wall." Her shoulders moved up and down in a little shrug. "And then it was over."

And then it was over.

How simply she spoke about a day in time that had been in no way simple.

He stood immobile, paralyzed by her telling.

Fearing that if he moved, he'd splinter apart and break off into nothing.

And in that instant? It was a fate he preferred to the thought of her that day . . . and him . . . the guilty party whom she'd run from. When she'd only ever come to him for help.

Clasping her hands as in prayer, she concentrated on those white-knuckled digits. "Please, don't look at me like that," she whispered.

Groaning, he reached for her and drew her into his arms. Even as he'd no right. Because he was the one responsible for her suffering.

He held her close, his heart pounding so hard in his chest she surely felt that organ's beat against her ear. And he just held her close. Not wanting to ever let her go, and also knowing he could never truly have her. It was the same fact he'd walked into this household with that morn, and when he left, the truth would still hold, but for entirely different reasons.

Now, he understood her . . .

And in a way, he wished he didn't.

With one arm, he held her close. Hugh pressed a hard kiss against her temple. "I'm sorry. I'm so sorry." For everything. For more than she knew. For more than he could ever confess to her.

Lila edged herself back, and he grieved over even that slight divide. "That's not why I told you this," she said, her tone short. "I told you so you might understand. I cannot go out in crowds. Not the way you need me to. I'm trying . . . for my sister." Her words grew almost frantic, tripping over the others. "So I can be with her at an event she feels she needs to attend. But the unpredictability of all this? I can't be who you are asking me to be with Polite Society."

"It is fine." It wasn't. A sheen of sweat rose on his skin, leaving his body clammy. For it would never be fine again. "I . . ." *I'm going to be ill.* Hugh fought his body's tremble, for he couldn't let her feel that weakness.

He couldn't do this any longer, maintain this calm before her. She was far stronger than he was. He, whose legs trembled and were very near collapse.

Hugh abruptly set her from him, retreating three steps.

Did he imagine her stricken eyes?

"Hugh, there's . . . one more thing."

How can there be? His mind screamed and raged. "Yes?" And how was his voice so steady? Empty and hollow . . . but even.

She darted her tongue out, running it along the seam of her lips. "That wasn't the only reason I told you."

He froze. And for one macabre moment, he thought she knew. Knew that he was one of those soldiers who'd charged—

"I wanted you to understand why I sought you out when I asked you to teach me how to fight." *Oh, God.* It was a prayer . . . a prayer to a God he'd never believed in, but Hugh was desperate enough, anguished enough, to make that appeal. Lila lifted her gaze to his. "I want to create a fight society not because I appreciate violence. But rather I appreciate what happens when one isn't prepared for violence."

He had to leave. He had to run.

And yet he couldn't.

Mayhap this was his hell.

Satan had at last come to collect for Hugh, having sold his soul long ago in the name of survival, and this was to be the punishment expected of him.

Lila had been . . . at Peterloo.

It was an impossibility. Ladies weren't supposed to have been there, and yet . . . that day? Everyone had.

Men, women . . . children. Little babes.

And her. Lila March had been there, too.

He felt her eyes on him. Sad eyes. The ones that were haunted, that had often glimmered with happiness but had also revealed fear . . . and pain.

Because that was what anyone and everyone who'd been on St. Peter's Field had walked away with . . . if they'd been fortunate enough as to walk away.

I'm going to be ill . . .

This was where he was to say something. Where he should have said something moments ago. "I have to go," he said hoarsely, and dropping an unsteady bow, Hugh rushed from the room, poltroon that he was.

Hugh didn't know how he made it home. He recalled nothing of the ride from Lila's Mayfair residence to his own. He only distantly registered handing over the reins of his mount to a waiting servant. But as he climbed the stairs and strode through the door, ignoring the butler's deferential greeting, he was aware of nothing but the sickening thud of his pulse. It pounded away in his ears. Knocking away. Much as it had in the middle of a fight, or when he'd been running through the fields of Manchester in pursuit of people who'd not deserved to be chased.

Oh, God.

Hugh threw the door to his chambers wide and stumbled into the room.

His valet turned in surprise. "Your—?"

"Get out," he rasped, and the liveried servant paled, then dashed past him.

The moment the young man had gone, Hugh slammed the door hard.

Panting, out of breath, he stumbled across the room to the pitcher of water set out before the mirror. Gripping hard the side of the washbasin, he stared at his whitened visage. His body was hot and cold. With his hands wildly shaking, he poured water into the basin and splashed it over his face. That trembling, however, made his movements sloppy, and he soaked the fabric of his jacket.

He was going soft. He'd always struggled with the memories of Peterloo, but at last he'd succumbed to them. Because of the comfortable life he'd turned himself over to.

He buried his head in the wide porcelain bowl and remained frozen there. Until his lungs screamed and strained. And even with the water making the sounds beyond a muted blur, her voice . . . her telling . . . echoed as clear as when she'd spoken it that morning.

When his chest felt on the verge of bursting, Hugh wrenched himself upright, sending water spraying over the mahogany floor.

He concentrated on breathing, locking his gaze on himself in the beveled mirror. Water dripped down his face, running down his cheeks, like the crystal tears Lila had silently shed.

"It all went so bad, so quickly. There were yells. I'll never forget them. In the heart of it, I didn't understand what was happening. But then the yeomanry charged . . . Men, cutting down their neighbors. They called their names, Hugh. They called their names . . ."

His chest moved rapidly, in a jerky, painful rhythm.

Breathe. Breathe. Breathe.

His efforts proved futile.

Retching, he scrambled for the chamber pot. Finding it in time, he threw up. Emptying the contents of his stomach over and over again, until there was only bile and his sides ached from the force of his heaving.

Every muscle in his legs failed him.

Hugh slid to the floor at the foot of his bed, and setting his chamber pot beside him, he simply sat there. Until the morning sky gave way to dusk, and the ink-black night shoved away all hint of light, blanketing London in darkness.

All these years, he'd been consumed with himself. From the moment he'd fled the Fight Society and abandoned the closest to friends and family he'd ever recalled in life, to that fateful day at Peterloo, the thought had been about himself . . . and surviving . . . and never again perpetuating violence against anyone. But it had always been about Hugh—escaping and breaking the chains of the nightmares he carried.

Until now.

Lila and her happiness mattered more.

Lila, who could only bring herself to comfortably stalk in the shadows while still fearing the sunlight.

And in that moment, he resolved to help her find that which she wished, even if it cost him the last parts of his soul, and then he'd do what needed to be done—he'd leave her and this life behind.

For there could be no doubting that if she discovered the truth of him and his past? All that warmth and tenderness in her gaze whenever she looked upon him would die . . . and he could not bear it if that happened.

Nay, he'd attempt to give her back the gifts that had been taken from her. And after he did, he'd do the only other thing he could do . . . he'd leave.

Chapter 24

Sprawled on her temporary bed in her sister's guest chambers, Lila stared up at the floral mural overhead.

Flowers, which her sister so loved she'd adorned every carpet, corner, and console with arrangements. Be they real, or paintings, or embroideries.

As a girl, Lila had hated the nights. In the dark, the shadows would twist and bend into monsters in her mind. So that she'd lain there with the coverlet drawn to her mouth, scanning her spacious chambers for the one that would pounce.

It wasn't until a bright sunny day at Peterloo that she'd come to appreciate the dark for the gift it was. It allowed a person an ability to stay concealed. In the dead of night, most of the world slept. There weren't crowds. No crush of bodies that could consume a person at an unexpected onslaught of danger.

It was why she'd been able to venture out amongst the living once more.

These past weeks—nay, the time in which she'd known Hugh—there hadn't been that fear.

Oh, the memories were there. They always would be.

But when she was with him, the monsters had been quieted, and she'd become any other woman—unafraid, challenging another person, talking with them . . . and knowing passion.

Tiring of those flowers overhead, Lila flipped onto her side and proceeded to pluck at the rose adorned in lace upon the white coverlet.

He'd not come.

Of course, it shouldn't have been any manner of surprise. After the speed with which he'd left her, everything had bespoke horror and said it would be the last she'd ever see him. But last night, when sleep hadn't come, it'd had nothing to do with memories of Peterloo. Nay, it was as though after revealing all to Hugh, she'd purged those darkest of demons, and all she'd been left with was an eager anticipation of seeing him again that morn.

"No doubt he pities you," she whispered. Because she was broken. Because Hugh, as a man of honor, would undoubtedly feel guilt over pressing her for a return favor now that he'd gathered the truth.

With a sound of frustration, she stretched a fist out and punched the pillow next to her.

A soft rap came at the door, and hope brought Lila springing up from her repose. "Come in," she called, unable to still the hopeful quiver in her voice.

The panel slipped open, and her sister entered.

"Sylvia," she greeted dumbly. Her heart fell.

Not her servant. Not any servant who'd come to inform Lila that there was once more a guest.

"No need to appear so thrilled with my visit," Sylvia drawled, pushing the panel shut.

"I'm sorry. Forgive me. I was . . ."

"Expecting another?" her far-too-insightful sister finished for her.

"No." She'd been hoping for another, which wasn't altogether the same.

"You're a horrible liar, Lila March." Sylvia joined her, drawing herself up onto the edge of the mattress alongside Lila. "You always have been."

"And you always saw too much, Sylvia March."

"Nay, not March," her sister said, sadness layered within that amendment. "Caufield. Sylvia Caufield," she murmured to herself. With a sigh, Sylvia drew herself higher onto the mattress and sat tailor-style, with both legs folded toward her body and crossed at the ankles.

Lila matched her sister in repose so that they faced one another. With their dark muslin skirts rucked up about them, squaring off as they were, the moment may as well have been taken from their youth, back before life had gone and broken their hearts, leaving them forever changed.

"Well?" her sister pressed.

"Well, what?"

"Well, it is just . . . I have been very absorbed with Vallen and . . . and . . ." With her grief. Sylvia didn't finish that thought. Nor did she need to. It was as real as spoken. "I'm not, however, a ninny."

"I don't know what you're on about." Lila fought the urge to shift under her sister's pointed gaze.

Sylvia snorted. "Don't you?" Her elder sister rested a hand on Lila's. "Surely you don't think I'm so naive as to believe it a mere matter of chance that a gentleman paid a call to my household, looking for you . . . in error?"

Actually, she'd rather hoped her sister hadn't overthought Hugh's presence there yesterday.

"Given the fact that you sought out Clara, the only logical conclusion is at some point, you've snuck around and had some interactions with the gentleman . . . who just so happened to be society's latest Lost Lord."

Damn her sister for that intuitiveness. And yet at this moment, Lila couldn't bring herself to share the details by which she'd first sought out Hugh . . . because Sylvia would never understand and would see Hugh in only the worst light and by the gossip her sister had been reading aloud—a horrendous light he was undeserving of.

"He wasn't a lord when I met him," she finally brought herself to confide. "He was just a man from East London, and . . . I was just a woman." Lila drew her knees to her chest and looped her arms about them. "And he didn't treat me at all different because of Peterloo." She didn't stumble over the mention of that day as she had every other time before. In speaking to Hugh yesterday, and in sharing all those details aloud about the hell of that day, it was as though there'd been a cathartic release, a breaking of chains. "Of course, he didn't know about Manchester," she added softly to herself. "I told him yesterday."

Her sister was silent for a long moment. "What happened?"

He ran. "He listened." He'd held her. "And then he left."

"And . . . you wished he'd returned today."

Lila bit her lower lip. "And I wish he'd returned." For when she was with Hugh, she was whole in ways where she'd only been fragments of her former self. "But he was different after he learned." Just as everyone was, when they discovered about Lila's time at Peterloo.

"Why was he here?"

Lila blinked at the unexpectedness of that question . . . and then recalled what Hugh had shared—Sylvia's father-in-law. "He wanted me to help ease his entry into Polite Society." Specifically, he'd wanted Lila to secure him an invitation to the Marquess of Prendergast's annual ball. There could be only one explanation as to the gentleman whom Hugh believed responsible in some way for his suffering and that of so many others.

"And . . . you don't wish to help him?" her sister ventured.

"I don't think I'm capable of helping him," she corrected. "Not to the extent he needs me." That was ultimately what it came down to. Despite the shared connection between Lila's family and the marquess's, she'd wished to help. Regardless of his connection to Sylvia's late husband, if Prendergast was responsible of wrongdoing, he should be brought to justice. None of those details, however, could Lila burden her bereaved sister with. "I hate crowds." A panicky laugh built in her throat. "I don't even like the sunlight anymore."

"Well, it is a good thing we reside in England, where the sun is as rare a commodity as our mother's smiles," her sister drawled, startling a laugh from Lila.

Sylvia joined in.

When they'd settled into a comfortable silence, Lila squeezed her sister's hand. "Thank you."

Sylvia blushed. "Oh, hush. I'm your elder sister. Elder sisters have a responsibility for cheering up their younger ones."

And what of the responsibilities of younger ones?

Shame filled her. "I should have been there for you, Sylvia."

Her sister made a sound of protest. "Stop. You are here, aren't you?"

But even Lila's coming to stay with her sister had been a product of her not wanting to retire to the country. "That's not enough," she said insistently. Lila had been so consumed in her own pain and past and suffering, how much had she truly been there—as her sister needed? "Upon Norman's death, you deserved more from me, as a sister and as a friend."

A little sheen glazed Sylvia's eyes at the mere mention of her husband's name. What pain her sister must have known. And how very self-absorbed Lila had been. From those first tragic days of Norman's death to the discovery that she'd been with child . . . to the delivery of that child. Lila had been locked away, too afraid, using that fear as an excuse as to why she couldn't be there for those she loved. Just as she'd used it as a shield when Hugh had come to her yesterday and sought her help . . .

"There'll always be room enough in life for regrets, I've learned," Sylvia said in a soft voice. "What I've come to also learn is that we have today and can make it better than yesterday." Her sister held her arms open, much the way she had when Lila had found herself met with a stern scolding by their parents and governesses for some mischief or another she'd gotten herself into.

Lila hugged her sister. "I'm sorry."

"*Tsk. Tsk.* Listen to your big sister," she said when they drew apart. "There's no place for regrets. There is a place, however, for both of us to make new beginnings. Even if there'll always be pain and sadness there, there can be joy, too."

There can be joy, too . . .

"Do you know," Lila began in muted tones, "when I sought out Clara, I believed music represented my path back to the living." A wistful smile tugged at her lips as she thought about the night she'd put her request to the other woman. The courage it had taken Lila to leave and seek the former madam out. The hope she'd found in being there. "I will always love singing and playing the pianoforte." Since she'd been a small girl, she'd lost herself in the strains of song. "I saw both as the key to my happiness." Lila looked squarely at her sister. "And then I realized . . ."

"What?"

"It isn't music or song that truly fills a soul. Oh, they are pastimes I will forever enjoy, but my life these past nine years has been empty because of the absence of family or friends." And she'd not realized just how very large the void had been . . . and how very much she'd missed laughing and loving and conversing and . . . simply existing amongst the world.

Hugh had shown her that.

"Does this discovery have something to do with your duke . . . and the reason for your sadness . . . ?"

Lila sucked in a long, slow breath. "It does." Because when she again imagined a life for herself, it was one with Hugh in it.

I love him.

"You love him."

Shock held her immobile.

She loved him. She loved him for being a man of convictions. For being loyal, and for not having treated her as though she were a fragile flower to be tucked away and protected and—

Lila's breath came in sharp, sporadic bursts.

Sylvia joined her. "Love leaves a person with that feeling, doesn't it?" her sister murmured, stroking her back. "Alternately giddy and wanting to toss one's biscuits."

Aye, that it did. "There could be far worse things than falling in love." *Like losing one's only love . . .*

Those words hung in the air as true as if they'd been spoken.

"Either way, he's not come around."

A knock split the quiet.

"Enter," Sylvia called.

Lila's maid ducked her head inside. "Forgive me, His Grace, the Duke of Wingate? He's called for Lady Lila." Lila's heart bumped around her chest, and she sat up straighter.

He is here . . .

Adelle nodded, confirming Lila had voiced her disbelief aloud.

"Aye. I took the liberty of showing him to the Gold Parlor." When neither lady spoke, Adelle looked between them with a question in her eyes. "Should I not have done that?"

Both sisters exclaimed as one: "No!"

"That is, yes," Sylvia said quickly. "That is fine. See that refreshments are readied."

"Yes, my lady." Dropping a curtsy, Adelle pulled the panel shut and took her leave.

Sylvia was immediately on her feet. "He is here."

He'd come.

Lila's heart lifted. Even as he'd made a hasty exit yesterday, he'd not been scared away. As if Hugh Savage were a man to be scared of anything . . .

Grabbing Lila's hand, Sylvia pulled her forward, dragging her up. "Come now. Despite your thoughts he wouldn't be here, he is. Now run along and greet him."

Lila hurried to the door.

"Oh, and Lila?"

She paused with her fingers on the handle.

"Perhaps . . . you and His Grace? You might help one another."

Perhaps they could . . .

Lila found her way to the Gold Parlor. He stood precisely as he'd been yesterday. Attired in dark garments and with his hands clasped behind him, the moment may as well have been frozen in time yesterday, before she'd shared . . . everything.

His muscles strained, rippling along his broad back.

And as he turned, she braced for that same cold smile, further confirmation she'd stepped into the past.

He smiled. "Hullo, Lila."

Her heart pattered at an uneven clip. It was a smile, but one as she'd never before seen it. Soft and tender.

She wet her lips. "I thought . . . you might not come."

"Of course I'd be here."

Of course.

And then she remembered.

His request. Her repayment.

"Oh . . ."

Because what else was there to say?

She pulled the panel closed behind her and leaned against the oak for support. "I understand why you've come."

His lashes dipped. "Do you?" he murmured, slipping closer.

She nodded, her head knocking awkwardly against the door. "The marquess . . ." Mindful of her maid, who lingered outside the room, Lila took care to withhold the identifying name.

Hugh stopped before her. "That's not why I've come."

Lila frowned. It wasn't?

"It isn't," he said softly. "I've come to see you."

⌘

Hugh had come to see her.

For reasons that had nothing to do with the Marquess of Prendergast, or probing for information on the part of Maynard and Bragger. Rather, it had been only about seeing her.

"Me?" Lila blurted. "For what purpose if not . . ." Her gaze slid to the door. "If not . . . that?"

She was suspicious of him and his motives. But then, after he'd called her out a fortnight earlier about her intentions and met her plans and confidence with only disgust and disdain, what other opinion should she have come to?

And guilt around this woman, an altogether increasingly familiar and ragged sentiment, took root in his chest again.

Bouncing on the balls of his feet, Hugh looked around him. "My earliest recollections in life all revolve around the one thing I was trained to do—fight. There was no family." He grimaced. "At least, not one that I remember," he added softly. No matter how he strained or struggled to call forth some happy remembrances of the people who'd given him life, there was only . . . emptiness there.

Restless, he wandered the same path he'd traveled in this room yesterday. Except those cheerful blooms woven within the carpet merely brought him back to what she'd revealed . . . what she'd shared.

Hugh found a spot at the drawn chintz curtains.

With his hands tightly clenched at his back, he stared out to the bustling streets beyond those panes. "The children fighters were not friends. It didn't make sense to have relationships."

There was a noisy *whish* of her skirts. "They were . . . discouraged?" The floorboards groaned under the slight depression of her weight as she walked, and then he felt her there. At his shoulder.

"We, the fighters, that is, learned not to bother with them. After all, what kind of relationship can one truly have with a boy . . . or girl . . . he'll be expected to pummel bloody in a bare-knuckle match? How can one punch a friend in the face or . . . inflict any other hurt upon them? But we weren't people to them, and well, we didn't come to see ourselves as people, either."

Lila remained silent. And that allowed him to continue his telling. A telling that wasn't intended to be about him, yet could not be separated from what he shared. "We were kept locked up."

"Hugh." She breathed his name on a soft exhale.

He winced, not wanting her pity, and understanding her outrage yesterday when she'd believed he'd turned that emotion on her.

"And the moment I escaped . . . when I slipped free . . . I vowed to never again be caged in by walls. I lived outdoors because when I was inside, it all came back: being imprisoned, being robbed of the ability to move. Having no freedom." It was why following the drum had represented the path of escape. Only to find too late that the 15th Hussars would also come to be the ties that bound him. Pulling the curtain back the tiniest fraction so he had a wider view of the street scenes below, he went on. "Whenever I was indoors, I could not separate the past from the present. Every suffering, every fear came rushing back . . ." Hugh looked over his shoulder to where she stood, close.

Lila dampened her lips as understanding glimmered in her revealing eyes.

She understood, then. Of course she did. There wasn't a cleverer one than Lila March.

"What did you do?"

"I was trapped between my fears and that which was better for me . . . having safety from the elements . . . and from the most ruthless on the streets who'd tried to stick a knife between my ribs for nothing more than to rob me of the only thing I had in the world: a tattered shirt and trousers." Hugh released the curtain, and it fluttered back into place, sending shadows dancing from the sunlight. "As long as I couldn't step foot inside, my past . . ." He balled his hands as Dooley's face flashed to his mind. "Those responsible for hurting me, they would triumph. And I'd survived. It wasn't much of a life by any standards, and yet it was mine, and I'd be damned if I let them have anything more over me than they'd already had."

"I want to help you—"

"That isn't why I've come," he interrupted her.

The course of their relationship had always been transactional. He didn't want that to be the case with her. Not any longer.

Lila moved closer to him, erasing the little distance left, until they both looked out through that two-inch crack in the curtains. "Why are you here?"

Reaching inside his jacket, he fished out a small notebook and handed it over.

Not taking her eyes from his, Lila accepted it. "What is this?" she asked warily.

As she opened the small book, over her shoulder, Hugh studied his sloppy scrawl, so very different from the elegant, graceful strokes of her own hand. Had he lived the life he'd been born to, he would have possessed an ability to fluently read and speak French. *Combattre la société.*" As it was, looking at his phonetic attempts at the spelling, he felt heat slap his cheeks.

She glanced down at the book. "What of it . . . ?"

"I want to help you."

Lila's body went whipcord straight, her spine jerking erect. "I'm afraid I am not following you, Hugh."

"You spoke of creating an establishment where people were . . . are trained to fight." As he spoke, Lila slowly flipped through those pages he'd pored over last evening. Working without rest, the only break he'd taken had been when he'd bathed and changed into new garments . . . before coming here. And as much as each word he'd written had felt like a betrayal of his goals and beliefs where combat—of any sort—was concerned, to have failed to provide her with the help she'd come to him seeking would have been a greater betrayal to Lila. And that, he'd discovered in a way that terrified him out of his bloody mind, mattered far more. "I've put together essential details for you to understand about bare-knuckle boxing, and other important ones as you organize your business," he said when still she said nothing.

He made himself stop talking as Lila flipped through those pages he'd painstakingly recorded until his hands had cramped and ached, and still he'd written anyway.

"But . . . you disapprove of fighting of any sort. Has that . . . some-how changed?"

Lila didn't even deign to lift her head from those pages he'd written all night long.

"It . . . has not."

She offered him only more of her silence.

Hugh shifted his weight back and forth over his legs. Of all the questions she might have asked, or comments she might have made about the gift he'd given, that particular one had not been imagined. And it also spoke to how small a person he was that he'd expected she would, if not be grateful, at least be enthused by what he'd assembled. Anything, really, more than this . . . silence.

At last, Lila snapped the book shut with a punctilious little snap. "No." She held it out.

Frowning, he stared at his notes in her hand. "No, what?" he asked, ignoring the small leather volume in her fingers.

"No, thank you?"

His scowl deepened. Was she jesting? "I wasn't concerned with damned manners."

Lila lifted a single eyebrow. "What were you expecting?" she asked, so very placid in her query.

He tried again. "I don't understand. I thought this was what you wanted?" He'd forever recall the light in her eyes as she'd prattled on about her vision.

"*This* is," she confirmed. "But I don't *want* your notes, Hugh. I don't want your lessons or suggestions or . . . any of it. Not when you've been clear how you feel about fighting." And as if she'd been burnt by his book—the one he'd given to her—she dropped it in the center of an inlaid table.

"But . . ." Confusion. Embarrassment. Regret. They all swirled, searching for supremacy at Lila's pointed rejection. To give his hands something to do, he adjusted the silk white cravat at his throat . . . which served only to highlight once more just how out of his element he was. How he may as well have been moving upon a different planet from Lila March.

As if there'd been any further confirmation needed.

There was a rap at the door.

"Not now, Adelle," Lila called, and the footfalls of the servant outside the door retreated and then faded altogether. Lila looked back to Hugh. "When you came that night, I spoke about us working together because that was what I wanted. I wished to learn from you about how to run a venture you have expertise in. About how to fight and train." She shook her head. "I didn't want your assistance . . . this way."

There was no help for it. He'd never understand women. "What *way*?" he entreated, feeling flipped upside down.

"Born of pity," she cried out. "I don't want your damned pity." Her chest heaved. When she again spoke, she did so in a low voice. "That isn't why I told you . . . what I told you, yesterday. That isn't why I shared Peterloo and every dark moment of that day."

His stomach muscles clenched as they invariably did from the mere thought . . . and now, in this case, the mention of that place.

Lila stomped across the room.

He registered her retreat. Where . . . ?

"Now, I thank you for coming and for offering to do something so hateful to you." She grabbed the door handle and pulled the panel open hard. "However, I must politely decline your request."

Politely and forcefully.

Hugh struggled for a response. None of this had gone as he'd planned. Never, having come here, had he thought she'd reject his offer. He tried again. "I'm offering you what you *want*, Lila. I'll help you with the venture that means so much to you."

Lila's lips turned up in a sad rendering of a smile. "Oh, Hugh. I'd not have you do this. Not when you abhor violence as you do. No, I'd not have you take this on . . . for me."

All he'd ever known was people using him to achieve their own ends. This, someone putting him first, was something completely unfamiliar. Foreign.

And he didn't know what to do or how to respond.

He joined her at the door. "Lila—"

She pressed a fingertip to his lips, silencing him. "Thank you, Hugh. But no," she repeated with greater insistence.

She'd been very firm in her resolve, and in her request that he leave. As such, he should do just that. After all, who was he to force his unwanted company upon her? Particularly, given their shared pasts, since he had no right.

And yet, he couldn't, not as long as she believed pity was what drove him.

Hugh guided the door closed.

Lila stared up at him with questioning eyes.

"Is that what you think, Lila? That I pity you?" he asked, focusing on the earlier part of her rejection.

"Yes. Everyone does."

"Not me. I never felt anything but admiration for you."

Her plump rosebud lips formed a perfect moue of surprise.

How? How did that come as a shock to her?

"Lila March," he murmured, having no right to touch her, and yet he was weak against her pull. Hugh glided his knuckles along the curve of her cheek. "How is it possible you don't have any idea how strong or special you are?"

She trembled. Was it his words? His touch? A combination of both? And yet . . . how could she not know? "The minute you came to me, everything in me said to send you away, and yet you braved the rookeries, alone in the dark, time and time again. You'd not accept anything but my capitulation." And she'd pointed out, rightly, that he'd blindly gone along with his partners' quest of vengeance. And in that she'd proved more honorable, more in control, than he'd ever been in the whole of his life. Hugh brought his fingers to a halt, stopping that slow caress. "What reason would I have to pity you?" He answered his own question. "Because you had the misfortune of being in a place, at a time, when the world was on fire? Because you managed to survive and, from there, have been clawing your way back? Imagining something better for the future?"

She leaned her head back against the door and studied his face, this time with a tenderness radiating from those chocolate depths that he was also undeserving of. "Something you've already said is wrong for the violence it perpetuates."

He would always abhor fighting, but after he'd taken his leave of her yesterday, he'd had only time in which to think about how he'd lived his life and the absolutes he'd held himself to after he'd quit the 15th Hussars.

Someone hauled me to my feet. I don't know who he was. And I felt this overwhelming relief, but then he had this crazed look in his eyes, and he was holding on to me, and I couldn't get him to release me . . .

"You wouldn't be turning out fighters, Lila." Oh, he wasn't any sort of optimist to trust that all the people she equipped with those skills would use them for good, or even strictly defensive purposes. For one could never truly understand or trust another person's motives. However, he now understood what her intentions were. "You would be turning out people skilled in fighting who might use those abilities to defend themselves." Invariably, in her venture there'd be a man . . . or a woman . . . who came to that society she built, learned the art of war, and used it for evil.

And that was the piece he had to separate in his mind in offering her what he did.

Lila tipped her head in that bewitching little way she did, the one that sent her loose curls bouncing about her shoulders. It was a tangible curiosity she'd never been able to quell, and one he hoped she never would attempt to.

That when she married, she'd find a gentleman worthy of her, who supported her and her inquisitive spirit.

And how I wish it could have been me . . .

It was fate, or God, or more likely, Satan below, dancing with delight over Hugh discovering now that he wished there could be a future with Lila.

With her elbows, Lila pushed herself from the door. "Very well." She held her fingers out. "I accept your offer, Hugh."

He stared at those long, slightly crooked digits a moment, and then slid his palm into hers, all the while unable to shake the feeling that he was the Devil on the other end of their arrangement.

Chapter 25

Nearly a week after Lila had accepted Hugh's offer of assistance, he'd visited every day.

Every day, they spent hours closeted away, giving life to the vision that had previously been only jumbled notes on a page.

And now, because of Hugh, *Combattre la Société* was becoming more and more real.

"You cannot do that."

The tables moved to the perimeter of the room, Lila lay sprawled on her stomach with her legs kicked up behind her. Shoulder to shoulder, in like repose, Hugh studied her notebook.

She frowned. "And whyever not?"

"That's"—he jabbed a finger at the paper, his lips moving as he silently counted—"one, two, three, four . . . twelve rooms. That's going to require . . ." His pencil flew frantically over the page as he recorded his calculations. "At least eighteen to twenty feet, which is . . ." His mouth continued moving. "That's over four thousand square feet you're going to require—"

"Yes—"

"*Just* for the areas for practice sessions," he continued over her interruption. "That doesn't include the space required for dress and undress, which is another . . ." Never before had she seen any gentleman so self-possessed and in command of work he did with his own hands.

Her father, her brother, Sylvia's husband—they'd all dealt with their man-of-affairs and solicitors to see to the details that Hugh even now worked through. He scribbled away at the page, and while he tabulated those numbers, Lila found herself studying him. His dark curls, in a perpetual state of rebellion, fell over his brow, his midnight eyebrows formed a single line from his level of concentration . . . and he was so very disarming in his engrossment. "That is another twelve feet by the twelve." He looked over and, at finding her gaze on him, frowned. "Are you paying attention?"

"I am." Only partially.

How very focused he was. "Twelve by twelve rooms would be one hundred and—"

"Forty-four," she finished for him.

Hugh circled that number three times.

Alas, he appeared wholly unimpressed by her computation. "There is the matter of leasing versus purchasing—"

"I would rather purchase."

"Purchasing the size and space you require, in the end of London you require, will cost in the thousands."

She choked. She'd a sizable dowry, but all her funds would go to just the purchase of the establishment. "What of renting, then?"

"Rent is also expensive." Reaching for the folio lying out before them, Hugh dug around before settling on a sheet. He slapped it down between them. "There is the matter of where you're going to rent in London. I expect you'll have your establishment aimed toward the nobility in East London."

She frowned. "What makes you expect that my services will strictly be offered to members of the peerage?"

He paused. "I . . ." He shook his head. "Then, the lower class?"

Lila shoved herself up into a seated position. "I wish to make *Combattre la Société* a place that is open to all—those in the nobility, and men and women outside of it."

She may as well have sprouted a second head for the look he gave her.

"*Both* classes?"

She nodded.

"Together?"

Lila's lips pulled in another frown. "You find that so hard to believe?"

"That lords and ladies will wish to mingle with commoners?" Tossing his pencil down, Hugh sat up and, drawing his knees up, shifted so they faced one another. "I absolutely do. That's not the way of the world."

"You have patrons who come to your arena."

"That's different," he said with a wave of his hand. "Lords have no compunctions in taking their pleasures outside their ranks as long as they're taking part in uncouth activities: wagering, fighting, drinking . . . But what you're proposing doesn't fit within those customs."

"That's . . . a cynical way of looking at the world."

"That is the *true* way of the world," he countered. "It is a common truth that the wealthy ruling elite don't want to rub shoulders with their social inferiors. They see a threat in them. If they're forced to see how the other half lives, it only reminds them of the precarious hold they have on a world rife for rebellion."

Rife for rebellion.

He spoke as one who knew.

He also spoke of a class tension she'd borne witness to with her own eyes. "It doesn't have to be that way," she said softly.

Hugh looked as though he wished to say something more, but then gathered up his notes. "Very well." He'd ceased debating her, but she in no way believed she'd swayed him to her thoughts . . . hopes? "Your establishment for all would best be housed upon Bond Street like Gentleman Jackson's. Based on that . . ." He went to work once again on his forecasting and then stopped. "By my estimates, if you rent a property this size, in this end of London? You are looking at no fewer than one thousand pounds per year. And then there is still the matter of staff to oversee the place. Your trainers. The people who'll clean, which would put you closer to . . . another two thousand pounds, for a grand total of three thousand pounds each year." Hugh circled that final tally.

Lila brightened. "There will be earnings, though."

"Earnings come slowly. Most expect when they begin a business that it will equate with instant revenue. That's not the case. One operates at a loss for many, many months. Sometimes years. And even then, there's the cost of all that goes into the upkeep that makes the road to a high return a very slow one."

He spoke from experience.

And Lila found herself discountenanced by the fact of how ignorant she'd been. Even after Peterloo, and after having witnessed the class struggle with her own eyes, she'd still not had a proper appreciation for how easily life came to those of her station.

She wished to open a business. She wished to purchase a building, and she'd simply assumed she had all the necessary funds to fuel everything that went into her operation. And as he'd sat here, she'd been even more woefully ignorant to all that went into proprietorship . . . and just how costly it all was.

Whereas, Hugh? He, who worked his days and nights, toiling relentlessly, still found himself struggling financially. It was why he'd felt a sense of debt to his partners. It was why he'd not had the luxury of simply challenging them outright. "I have some funds." It seemed somehow wrong to speak of those monies that had come to her through nothing she'd done. Through no accomplishments of her own. Unlike Hugh, who'd worked with his hands to make every last pence to his name.

"Funds?"

"Not enough for all you've outlined here. There is a portion of my dowry, however, that reverts to me should I not wed." And even more were she to marry. Never before had she considered just how unfair those terms were.

"How much?" he asked. There was such a forthrightness to that question that no member of Polite Society would have dared ask. And it was just another reason she appreciated him all the more. For in discussing business, there should be a frank candidness.

"Twelve thousand pounds." That she had access to were she not to marry. Another twelve would come to her if she wed. Which she would not . . .

Unbidden, an image slipped in of her and Hugh, married . . .

He whistled and grabbed the previously discarded notes, reexamining them. "The operational cost will not pose any difficulty; however, having the funds to establish the setup doesn't mean a person can't lose their money by missteps." And it spoke even more to him that he'd not pass judgment on her for simply having been granted that good fortune through her birthright. "And you've a family who supports you in doing what you would with your funding?"

They supported Lila . . . but would that sentiment expand to include her taking on a venture, as Clara had? *Nay. You already know the answer.* She shifted and stole a furtive glance at the covered portrait of Sylvia and Norman. Nor would Henry turn over one pence more when he learned of her intentions. She knew her brother enough to know that. Even changed as he'd been with marriage, he'd not support this endeavor.

Hugh's gaze followed hers to the black bombazine draped over that gilded frame. "They . . . don't know."

How was it possible for a person to know so very much about her that he might predict her very thoughts? "They don't."

"Have you kept your intentions from them because you think they'll disapprove, or because you think they'll attempt to stop you, Lila?" he asked.

She didn't think . . . she knew. "Both."

"Seems like someone as bold and courageous as you would at least be honest with your family about your dreams."

"It is complicated."

"Your brother-in-law was killed in a boxing match at Gentleman Jackson's. Your brother is protective of you because you're a lady, and your mother wouldn't countenance a daughter who operated a business, let alone one that catered to fighting. Do I have the right of it?"

She blushed. "You might have touched on all the key points," she mumbled. Clever as he was, of course he'd make all those accurate suppositions.

Hugh tossed his notepad down at their feet. "None of this is real."

"It is," she said defensively. Lila hurried to recover the discarded notes and drew them protectively close.

"It isn't. Not if it's cloaked in secrecy."

She opened her mouth to argue him on it, but the air stuck in her chest. He was right.

Just as she'd been wrong about so many things.

"I'm sorry."

He looked at her askance. "I don't . . . ?"

"I came at you recently." The day they'd made love. It was a lifetime ago since they'd been in one another's arms . . . and how she missed it. "I judged you"—*and worse*—"I called you out about your commitment to your partners. Some people"—*nay*—"most people aren't afforded the luxury to risk cutting ties." Particularly after the time that had gone into the investment he currently oversaw. "I understand that now."

He set his pencil down and looped his arms about his knees. "You weren't wrong, Lila. I was setting aside principle for profit."

"But your reasons for doing so? They cannot be separated from the decisions that you make." Abandoning her spot, Lila scooted over. "What now?"

He didn't pretend to misunderstand. "Now that I'm a duke of enormous wealth?"

She nodded.

He flashed a sad little smile, one that tugged at every strand of her heart and made her want to draw him into her arms. "You've been right about so much. I . . . deliberately made myself ignore how my partners have treated me. And you've shown me that I'm more than the debt I owe them." His gaze slid past her. "The thing about having one's fortune change overnight, Lila, is that one doesn't truly change. I have a fine townhouse and endless acres and wealth. Obscene amounts of it, and yet in my mind, I'm still the boy locked in his cell. I'm still the child on the corner with his hand out." His gaze grew distant. "I suspect I might always be that boy."

"What of your work?"

"I'm done with the arena," he said automatically. "My days of that are over."

He deserved that. He deserved that choice and freedom of decision. And so much more. So why, selfishly, could she only focus on where he would go . . . ?

"And . . . your partners?"

"I'll still help them."

"Help them find those responsible for wronging you?" she ventured.

He nodded. "Justice is long overdue."

And mayhap it was because she'd come to know this man so well that she could detect the nuances of his speech, the subtle undercurrents of regret and . . . sadness.

She drew closer to him. "You disapprove?"

"I shouldn't." He turned a hand up. "All the people involved, they deserved . . . *deserve* comeuppance. Every last one of them should be made to pay penance."

"Are you saying what you believe you should feel?" she asked cautiously. "Or what you think you are expected to feel?"

Hugh exploded to his feet. "I don't know of anything anymore, Lila. I'm not sure I ever did." He began pacing at a frantic back-and-forth clip before her. He lowered his voice so that, even close as they were, she struggled to hear him. "When I left . . . I sold my soul. I killed a man in the name of freedom."

She went motionless.

He cast a hard look her way. "That's the manner of man that I am," he said almost imploringly, as if he desperately needed her to believe in his evil. As if he sought to convince her of it.

"That's how I secured my freedom. The lengths that I went to." His jaw hardened and ice formed in his eyes. "The manner of lengths they expected us to go to." All the fight seemed to seep from his frame as he sank back onto the floor beside her. Hugh gave his head a bemused shake. "I should want their blood on my hands. I should want it with the same ferocity as my partners, the men who took me in. And yet . . ."

"You don't," she finished for him.

"I don't." His cheeks flushed red, and he dragged an angry hand through his black curls. "What does that say about me?"

And Lila fell in love with him all over again. For not being the man bent on revenge, and for wanting justice, but justice fairly dealt. There was no other man like him. She considered her words for several moments, and then edged closer to him. "Do you know what I believe that says about you, Hugh?"

Hugh gave a small, brusque nod.

"It tells me you're a complex man with many layers to you. You're not some caricature of what society believes a man should be." All-tough, all-knowing, bloodthirsty savages out for revenge against those who'd wronged them. "It says you're a man who is honorable."

Hugh scoffed. "It says that I'm weak. Any person would want revenge."

She covered his hand with hers. "There's greater strength in finding ways within the legal system than being the arbiter of their fate, Hugh."

Hugh looked to their joined hands.

The air came alive between them. As it did whenever they touched . . . or whenever they were close. It had been this way from the moment he'd first come to speak with her outside his arena.

She caught the slide of his throat muscles as he swallowed. The darkening in his eyes. "Lila." Her name fell from his lips like a prayer.

Leaning up, Lila slid her fingers into the tangle of his dark, satiny curls and tasted him once more as she'd wanted to. For so long. Every moment of every day since the one morning they'd made love, she'd yearned for his mouth . . . on hers, on her, everywhere.

Then his hands were on her. Drawing her tight at the waist, he pulled her closer so their bodies touched. And it still wasn't enough.

It would never be enough.

Hugh's lips played with hers. Every bold slash of his lips a tease, a promise for more. And she wanted it all.

For in his arms, she was home.

Chapter 26

Hugh rode his mount through the unfamiliar streets he now called *home* to his Grosvenor Square residence. As he navigated the crowded thoroughfare, the lords and ladies out for their afternoon strolls and affairs stared boldly back.

It wasn't an unfamiliar state he now found himself in: An object of interest. An oddity. Both curiosity and mistrust followed him where he went.

And oddly, he'd never been more at peace.

There'd never be complete peace, but there was a semblance of it. More than he'd ever believed he'd know. More than he'd ever believed himself worthy or deserving of.

Continuing down Park Lane, Lila's words from their earlier meeting stayed with him still.

"It tells me you're a complex man with many layers to you . . . You're not some caricature of what society believes a man should be . . . It says you're a man who is honorable."

Honorable. He rolled those four syllables silently in his head.

All these years, following his time fighting Boney's forces and then Peterloo, he'd fashioned in his mind what that word meant. Ultimately, it had always connected to loyalty and Hugh's making redress for failings in his youth. Only to now realize . . . there'd never be proper penitence. Nothing he ever did or would ever do—for Maynard, for

Bragger, Bragger's sister, Valerie, or any of the other boys and girls he'd left behind—would ever be enough.

The decisions he'd made and would continue to make would bring forth only more regrets and greater degradation, and a continued search for redemption and peace . . . that would not come.

I don't want revenge . . .

He uttered that truth in his mind, owning it, and extraordinarily, there was no shame in that.

For so long, he'd simply gone along with the plan hatched by his partners, out of a sense of debt and obligation for all they'd done for him, when he'd only been faithless, putting himself first. But repayment also didn't mean that he had to trade his soul to appease Maynard and Bragger. Only, he realized now . . . his partners? They wouldn't be content until their foe was dead, and at their hands.

And Hugh didn't want that. Oh, he wanted justice. He wanted Dooley and the rest of them to pay for their sins and crimes. But Hugh didn't want to be the one responsible for meting out that justice.

There were other ways to see justice done.

Lila had helped him realize that.

Now it was a matter of making Bragger and Maynard see as well.

You're a bloody fool if you expect you can do that . . . a voice silently jeered.

Hugh guided his mount, Pax, to a halt outside the redbrick townhouse. Constructed from three units joined together, it ran the length of the street, and though he had lived here now for three weeks, it was still foreign. But then he suspected that would always be the case.

A servant rushed forward to take his reins. "Your Grace." More boy than man, the groom dropped a bow.

"Thank you," he said gruffly, earning the same surprise he usually did from nothing more than an expression of gratitude.

It was a state he understood, being invisible.

But no longer. As he climbed the five stone steps, the double doors of the townhouse already hung open in wait.

Hugh had gone from being unseen by all, to having his every move waited upon. It was a state he didn't think he'd ever become accustomed to.

The ever-dutiful butler stepped aside. "Your Grace," he said sotto voce. "You have guests. Mr. Maynard and Mr. Bragger."

They were here.

It had been more than a week since they'd come around. With the Marquess of Prendergast's annual ball just four days away, they would be here to discuss his search and their plan forward.

"Where?" Hugh asked crisply. Retaining his hold on his leather satchel, he shrugged out of his black cloak and handed it over to the footman hovering at his shoulder.

"I took the liberty of showing them to your office, Your Grace."

Hugh had already started for the long corridor.

They weren't going to be pleased. Nay, they were going to be livid at Hugh's decision. They, however, had only ever known a thirst for revenge. It was all they'd ever know. That sentiment consumed them and would ultimately destroy them.

Hugh reached his offices and instantly found the pair seated at his desk with their legs dropped on that gleaming surface. And something in the sight of that . . . that disrespect in a house that wasn't theirs, on a desk Hugh's own father, the father he'd never recall, had conducted his work at, sent fury rippling through him. He shut the door with a firm click. "I understand you are looking for me," he said coolly as he stalked forward.

Both men dropped their legs to the floor.

"There ya are," Maynard said at his approach. "Been waitin' for ya."

Nor did Hugh believe for one moment they'd only just heard his approach. Raised in the streets as they'd been, they heard everything. Everything.

Bragger pinned a hard, assessing stare on him. "Been gone awhile."

Taking a seat, Hugh set his bag down close to his hand. "Is that a question or an observation?" he returned, and the other man's brows dipped.

Aye, because the last thing Bragger had ever expected or been accustomed to was being challenged outright by Hugh . . . or anyone.

And also for the first time, Bragger backed down. With a little grunt, he nodded at Hugh. "Ya secured yar invitation?"

"Aye." Lila had gotten him an invitation into the marquess's residence.

"And ya know wot ya 'ave to do?"

He knew what they expected him to do. "I understand what you're asking," he said quietly.

Maynard rubbed his hands gleefully. "Bloody comeuppance toime."

Bragger, however, kept his gaze locked on Hugh. "Wot?"

"I cannot do it." Only, that wasn't correct, either. "I won't do it. Not what you intend."

Bragger and Maynard looked at one another. Maynard surged forward, but their other partner held a hand up, quelling him.

"You won't do what?"

"I'll search and retrieve anything in the gentleman's household that links him to the Fight Society, but if I discover anything, it will be turned over to the law. They should be brought to justice, but we shouldn't be the arbiters of their fate."

There was a lengthy silence, and then Maynard slammed a fist down hard on Hugh's desk, where Steele's folder on the Fight Society rested. "Of course we should. That's the way of the streets. And ya? Ya'd simply forget? Forget wot was done to ya? To me." He jabbed a finger at Bragger. "To 'im and 'is sister? And why?" He spread his arms wide. "Because ya got yar fancy loife now. Because ya don't want for anything, so ya forget wot they did and 'ow ya lived."

The other man was entitled to that opinion, and Hugh well understood how he'd found his way there. "I will never forget what was done to any of us . . ." Every punch he'd landed. Every bone he'd broken. Every boy he'd brought to tears of agony and misery. Of the boy he'd killed. "It will be with me always," Hugh said softly. "But this . . ." He motioned to Steele's packet sitting out on his desk. "This isn't going to make any of it go away. Slitting his throat or putting a bullet in Prendergast? All that is going to leave us with is that same evil on our hands." He shook his head. "It makes us no different, no better, than them."

Maynard scoffed. "Ya believe that?"

"I do," Hugh said solemnly.

"Then yar a damned fool."

Hugh had been a fool about so much, but this? This was right. This time, his actions weren't being driven out of a sense of obligation, but rather a moral right.

Bragger sat back in his chair, and with the coiled tension in his frame, no one would ever dare mistake his repose for relaxed. "This is because of the woman."

"Nay," Hugh said automatically. Not directly. "Not in the way you think."

"That's the only way there is to think," Maynard spat. "It's because yar tupping the sister of the bastard's daughter-in-law. Yar only worried about making a scandal for 'er and 'er fancy family."

Hugh refused to take their bait.

"When ya left, ya left without looking back," the other man finally said with his usual quiet restraint. "Everyone knew what ya did. We woke up, ya were gone, and from that moment on, the Fight Society became a gladiatorial ring."

"For you, don't you mean? Finish the question, Savage . . . What is in it for you? . . . Always be in it for yourself."

Every muscle in his stomach seized at the remembrance of Dooley and that day . . . "I will forever regret walking away." For so many reasons: all the men he'd killed in battle. Peterloo. "I'm grateful to you and Maynard for giving me a start." *For saving me.*

"Oi don't want yar gratitude." Bragger spoke quietly. "But Oi did expect ya to do roight for the group." *For once.* That barb may as well have been spoken for the mark it found in Hugh. And yet, too, as Bragger said, "do right by the group" would also be doing that which was wrong . . . again. When that was the only path he'd followed before this one. "Yar the only one of us who's going to get close enough to Prendergast . . . and the evidence we need."

How desperately they clung to the hope that the marquess had kept that incriminating evidence that could be used against him. "It's a chimera. Nothing but a dream." And a dark one at that.

Bragger's eyes darkened, and Hugh knew the very moment the other man had ceased seeing him. "It's as real as Prendergast's crimes. 'e's arrogant. 'e'd never let go of that trophy."

They . . . they'd been the trophy for those lords.

"I've never seen anyone fight like you. You don't sound like a street rat. But you fight like one. You are unique, and that deserves to be protected."

That. He'd not even been a boy or man to Dooley, or if Prendergast was in fact guilty, to him, or any other damned lord.

That all-too-familiar rage sparked to life and fanned the flames of his hatred.

"That is it." A glacial smile iced Bragger's lips. "Yar loike us. Ya 'ate as we 'ate because ya should."

"You take down the Assassin . . . kill him . . . and I'll see you with a significant *prize."*

Hugh balled his hands into tight fists, his nails scraping his callused palms, muting any pain.

"They took ya from this . . . from a family . . . they turned ya into a beast like the rest of us."

"But what if the cage is sprung . . . And what if you've the chance to . . . escape . . ."

Hugh's stomach roiled as the past wove in and out with the present as the other man spoke.

"Learning to 'ate our enemies was the only good to come out of wot 'appened to us. Just as making them pay is the only thing that matters."

Hugh closed his eyes and let himself feel every last wave of hatred as it lapped at him, with each lash reminding him of every pain he'd been made to suffer. Every cruelty he'd been forced to carry out. And God forgive him, he did want Dooley and Prendergast and every last one of that blood lot to pay the price . . . just as they had.

"Come, this is the roight decision," Maynard pressed in cajoling tones. "Do ya think they'd 'ave any compunction about ruining us?"

Hugh opened his eyes, and his gaze locked on Steele's file. "No." They'd have happily destroyed Hugh and anyone else who so much as stood in the way of their pleasures. For those *pleasures* had mattered more than even human life.

Lila's recounting cut across the burning hatred.

"Then, they called . . . the soldiers. It was this odd . . . suspension of time . . . It was this wave of bodies. I could see the cavalry's confusion . . . How could man and horse break through that mass of human beings? They raised their sabres high . . ."

He never again wanted to lift a sabre . . . to anyone.

Let go of that thirst for revenge.

For if they didn't . . . if *Hugh* didn't . . . Dooley and his noble patrons would win. They would, when they'd already taken so very much from Hugh.

Hugh opened his eyes. "Someday, you will find a path forward. One different from this one. One not rife with revenge and the hungering for more bloodshed, more violence. But I'm afraid I cannot bring you Prendergast. Let the law have the information we're in possession of, and let them have him."

Exploding to his feet, Maynard erupted into a litany of black, vile curses. "Yar a bloody coward is what ya are. Ya never 'ad a family, so you don't know anything about loyalty. Ya were always weak, and now that yar a foine toff, yar even more weak now."

"And worse, 'e's turning 'is back on us," Bragger spat.

Maynard sneered. *"Again."*

At last it had been spoken. That barb neither man had thrown out. Until now.

With that Maynard grabbed his folder, marched off, and slammed the door in his wake.

Once, those words Maynard had hurled would have gutted Hugh. Lila had helped him see that fairness wasn't a weakness. Rather, it was a mark of strength. "All these years," Hugh said quietly, "I've been trying to pay a debt to you." One he now knew would never be sufficiently paid. Not to them. "I've been filled with regret for leaving you both behind. But nothing I do will ever be enough. You would have been content to take and take." And if it hadn't been for Lila, Hugh would have continued trying to atone for a decision he'd made as a boy trying to survive.

Bragger jumped to his feet. "Ya want to speak of forgiveness and justice," he said with a calm more eviscerating than had he gone on the attack. "But the truth is? Ya don't know anything about anything. Not really. Ya never 'ad a family. Not that ya remember. Me?" He pounded a fist hard against his chest. "Oi 'ave to think of the sister made to foight." Bragger's voice cracked, and through it, he glared blackly at Hugh, as if blaming him for that rare show of vulnerability. "Oi'm the one who 'as to wonder where she disappeared to after a foight. Which nob took her for 'is pleasures. Or worse . . ." Bragger inhaled slowly and then released his breath.

Hugh remained calm through that explosion of emotion. "I'll get you the information you seek about Valerie. I'll even help you take down the last ringleader—not for revenge, for justice for the victims."

Of which there'd been so many. "But after this? I'm done with you."
And he was done with his past.

A freeing lightness came with that vow.

Bragger's eyes blazed with emotion. "Oi want ya to understand
wot yar turning yar back on. Yar loife. This." He jerked a chin. "It's all
charmed. Ya've got a foine lady yar dancing attendance on. A bloody
mansion. It's all charmed . . . until it's not. And then? Then, yar just
loike us once more. Miserable and alone." Bragger turned quickly on
his heel and, with that ominous warning, left.

Hugh stared after him at the entryway the other man had just
departed through . . . and he considered his former partner's charges.

Ya never 'ad a family . . .

In that, Bragger had been correct. Hugh had been born to a duke
and duchess, but he'd no recollections of them. Whereas Bragger?
Bragger'd known and remembered and would always recall the sister
he'd lost.

And when Hugh left London and the memories here, there'd still
be no family.

A thought slid in . . . of he and Lila and a babe. A girl, like Lila
with her spirit and courage. The hungering for that proved palpable,
a yearning far greater than any hungering for justice. And yet . . . that
could not be. Not with who he was . . . and where he'd been on that
worst day of her life.

And selfish as he was, Hugh intended to steal every moment with
her like the thief he was until he was just as the other man had tossed
in his parting shot—all alone.

Chapter 27

It was the day.

And perhaps that was why, as they worked side by side in her sister's parlor, she was distracted.

Curled on a scroll sofa, Lila tapped her pencil, tip to bottom, against the top of her page; all the while she watched Hugh.

He gave no outward hint that he'd heard that absentminded staccato beat. He remained bent over the latest notes he'd compiled for her future business. His pen flew over the pages, and where he usually spouted detail after detail of what he recorded, now he was silent.

"You are nervous," she said softly, and Hugh paused midscribble.

Hers wasn't really a question as much as a statement. He would venture out into Polite Society . . . despite his aversion for the *ton*, despite the fact that he knew no one at all, he'd do so.

Hugh rubbed at the back of his neck, massaging the muscles there, and she wanted to be the one who eased that tension from him. "I don't get nervous," he said matter-of-factly.

She tossed her notebook down and turned so her back rested against the arm of the sofa, and she faced Hugh at the opposite end. "*Pfft.* Everybody gets nervous about something." Even before she'd discovered the true meaning of fear, there'd been plenty to be disquieted over: Her mother. Mrs. Belden, the dragon at her finishing school. Her Come Out. Her debut at Almack's.

Hugh closed his book but retained a hold on it. "My first fight," he began, momentarily confounding her with that unexpected turn in discourse. "It took place on a back alley in Hog Lane. I take it you've never been to Hog Lane?"

She hesitated, then shook her head. "I saw a sketch in a book once." Even as that admission left her, Lila's cheeks flushed with shame at knowing only from pages that which he'd lived. "Gin Lane, it was called," she finished limply.

Hugh rolled his shoulders. "At Hog Lane, there's lunatics cavorting about the streets. People screaming and chasing them off. All around, people drunk. It's this absolute cacophony," he said, his tone conversational about a hell so vividly described.

But for the impaled babe from that rendering, Hugh perfectly conveyed the squalor and desolation William Hogarth had sketched. "I went from being a common pickpocket for a gang leader to a child fighter. My handler dragged me deeper and deeper into St. Giles." Hugh lifted a shoulder in a shrug. "I couldn't tell you how old I was. Maybe nine . . . ten, perhaps. But I can tell you everything about St. Giles: the sights, the sounds, the smell . . . shite in the air, so thick you choke on your vomit."

And with every word, her heart cracked open and bled all over again for what he'd known. And she would have taken that pain to have eased some of the burden he carried still. "What did they do?" she whispered.

"They pushed me into the ring." The right corner of his eye ticked. A slight but visible indication that the memories haunted him still. "Another boy, one of their best child fighters, came at me. I was expected to fall that day. I was the underdog. All around me there was cheering, and my heart was racing, and all I knew was if I survived that fight, I could survive anything. Hmph," he said softly, a sad smile on his lips. "I couldn't have imagined any hell could be worse than that. And with every day that came and then passed, I realized how damned naive I was in thinking that . . . because every day, in every way, life was worse. And once you understand and accept that, Lila? Nothing else is going to make you nervous again."

With that, as if he'd recounted a cheerful remembrance of his youth and not a story that had ripped apart her very soul, Hugh finished his telling and went back to work.

Restless, needing to give herself something to do, Lila picked up her book and flipped through the pages of notes he'd compiled this week. From layout and design, to the academy she'd create, to the best way to find staff, to the salaries to be paid them, he'd so very effortlessly put it all together for her.

All the while she absently skimmed his writing, Lila considered that story he'd shared—the misery no man, let alone a child, should ever know.

Hugh, the Duke of Wingate, had proven stronger than any person she'd ever known. And outcast as he'd been made by the *ton* through no fault of his own, he'd still go and face them down . . . in an attempt to find information that would see justice.

Could he face down the vipers of Polite Society? From all he'd shared, she'd no doubt that he could and would do anything, and give the world a to-hell-with-you grin for their troubles.

And yet . . . just because he could, didn't mean he should do it alone.

And what was more, she didn't *want* him to.

I want to be there with him . . .

She wanted to be there when he took on the Town, lending her support. She wanted to help him determine whether the answers he sought were in fact there . . . and if they were, she wanted to stand beside him through that, too.

And she could do all those things.

Hugh had shown her that.

Lila snapped her book closed, bringing his attention her way. "Come with me." Balancing their belongings in one arm, she pulled herself to standing.

"Where . . . ?"

Not breaking stride, Lila grabbed him quickly by the hand and led him from the room.

And mayhap it was more a fear of her courage deserting her that prompted the quickness of her steps. But Hugh followed close behind. Wordlessly, they wound through the empty halls until they reached the furthest recesses of Sylvia's townhouse.

Lila paused at the door, and then, gripping the handle, she shoved the doors open a fraction.

A blinding ray of sunshine slashed through that crack, and she blinked rapidly, little black orbs forming behind her eyes from the unaccustomed brightness. She took several moments to accustom herself to that light, and then, pushing the panel wider, she stepped out.

Hugh came to a stop beside her shoulder. "It is . . . magnificent." He spoke in soft, reverent tones.

Lila stared out, seeing it through his eyes. Seeing the grounds with new ones. "It is," she softly acknowledged, to herself as much as to him.

The gardens had long been a haven for her sister. But with the late earl's passing, they'd become a sanctuary . . . the place her sister disappeared to. Also the place Lila had long avoided. "It doesn't look at all a part of London, does it?" she murmured wistfully.

He shook his head, remaining mute, transfixed.

Where stone or gravel should be, there was instead a blanket of emerald-green grass. Lush blackthorns lined a path on both sides, all the way to the back of the enclosed plot. The small trees with their blackish barks were already in full bloom. Abundant as they were, they formed a canopy of creamy white petals.

Lila drew the door closed, shutting them both off from the rest of the world. Clasping her hands behind her, she lay against the panel and tipped her gaze up. "Since Peterloo, I've despised everything green, and anything that recalled memories of the countryside." A pair of goldfinches fluttered and flittered about one another in the air, and she followed their sweet dance as they chirped their late-spring song. Lila didn't take her gaze from them as they soared about, following their entire flight until the two small passerine birds crossed over the high brick wall and disappeared from sight. "It's been so much easier, staying indoors. Coming out at night when the rest of the world sleeps. Only to now realize how very dark it has been in the shadows," she whispered. "I don't want to work indoors anymore. I don't want to be shut away. I don't want to let myself be trapped here in London because I'm afraid of the memories that belong to a different countryside." Her skin tingled with the heat of his eyes on her, and her eyes found his. "I want to work with you . . . in the sunlight, for a change." For when Hugh was here, anything felt possible.

He stilled. "Lila . . ."

She held a shaky hand up, silencing him, needing to get the words out. Not knowing if he intended to deter her, not allowing it either way. "And I want to be with you tonight. At the Marquess of Prendergast's."

⚬⚬⚬

She wanted to attend the Marquess of Prendergast's masquerade.

With him.

He'd never been much with words. In the rookeries, they'd been a commodity without any real value.

Even if he had been in possession of every last right word, in this instance, he'd never have come up with anything.

For all the fear she carried, she'd brave that crowd . . . for him.

Hugh, who wasn't worthy in any way.

"I don't know what to say," he said hoarsely.

Her eyes sparkled. "There's nothing for you to say. I'm not asking you. I'm telling you."

And he laughed. It burst from him. Raw and real and honest, and it felt so very good. Hugh dropped his brow to hers. "Ordering me about still, are you?"

Her smile deepened. "Always."

Always, which implied forever together, an impossibility.

He'd no right to the gift she offered.

None at all.

Tell her. Tell her everything. So that she could take back that offer, and that truth could be between them. He didn't want her there . . . not for him.

And yet, at the same time, she was the only person he wanted beside him . . . for not only the damned masquerade . . . but for everything.

Hugh took her hands and drew them close to his chest, near the place his heart beat. For her. There was only her, and there'd only ever be her.

Her features softened, her lips parted ever so slightly . . . as distracting as this woman had always been. But it was time. It was long past. "Your hands," he said softly, forcing himself to focus on the words, which required a physical effort.

"I don't . . . ?" She stared at him with confused eyes.

"Strengthening your hands is the first part of any training you should learn, or expect of your clients."

Her eyebrows dipped. "Are we fighting?"

"I'm teaching you to fight," he corrected, bringing her hands up. "When you're learning, when you're using them for the first time, some boxers will have you wrap them. Don't. Not until you condition your hands and knuckles." Undoing the buttons of his jacket, Hugh shrugged out of the garment and tossed it onto the grass.

Lila followed its descent. "We're doing this here . . . now?"

They were running out of time. Before he left, he'd see her properly equipped to fight and defend herself. "There's no other place to do it." Not anymore. Not with him now belonging to the aristocracy and destined to leave. "Now, you can't expect to know when you're going to be attacked." It was the first lesson Hugh had learned as a boy in the rookeries. "That's why you have to practice any response so that it becomes intuitive. So that in the heat of battle, you call forth the skill you require to break free or . . ." *kill or maim or hurt . . .*

Lila's fingertips came to rest on his sleeve. "We don't have to do this, Hugh."

She'd be generous in this even now. She'd turn down the lessons she sought, all because she knew precisely how he felt about the art of battle.

He'd never been worthy of her.

"First," he went on, as though she'd not allowed him that reprieve, "know the most vulnerable parts to strike in order to weaken your opponent: The eyes. The nose. The ears. The groin. And then there are other areas . . ." His stomach churned, and he made himself continue through the nausea. "The most lethal place to strike a person is at the base of their skull. Their neck. At your height, if a man has you in a hold . . . it will likely present you with an awkward angle. In the middle of an attack, that will lead to panic. Your two surest places?"

Hugh touched the side of his neck. "And here." He shifted his fingers to the middle of his throat. "These places . . . they're vulnerable. They'll kill a grown man."

It was time.

"Do you remember your stances?"

How long it had been since she'd first come to him . . . to the day when they'd snuck off to his apartments. An entire lifetime may as well have elapsed.

"I do," she said, all business as she got herself into Mendoza's stance.

Hugh walked a slow circle about her, assessing Lila's form, the angle of her arms. "Show me your fists." Even with the time that had passed and the briefness of their lessons, she still managed to perfectly angle her wrists slightly down with her knuckles in front of her fingers.

And even hating fighting as he did, he still could feel only pride at her proficiency.

Hugh brought his arms up. "Now, hit me."

She wavered. Before throwing a punch.

Hugh danced out of her reach and circled around her.

"You're too fast," she said, adjusting the positioning of her fists.

"Align your wrist with your forearms," he instructed. "That will prevent you from accidentally bending it back and breaking it. And in the middle of a fight, your opponent isn't going to slow down because you need it."

Lila came at him again, pushing forward, throwing an impressive right, and then left, jab.

One of her blows bounced off his arm.

She blanched and stopped in her tracks. "I've hurt you."

"You didn't," he assured her as she ran her fingers over his sleeve, probing the muscles. They bunched under her scrutiny, and the air changed. Hugh's chest moved fast, the rapidity of his breathing having nothing to do with his earlier efforts and everything to do with that tender caress.

Hugh lowered his head closer.

Lila glanced up at him through heavy lids. "When we began, I rather thought you were going to kiss me, Your Grace," she whispered.

"I rather prefer kissing you." To anything. It was a gift greater than the air he breathed.

Going on tiptoe, she touched her mouth to his.

Hugh took . . . and gave all at the same time. He nipped and licked at her lips, both savoring and worshipping the plump, formed flesh.

Lila's moan filtered between them, tickling his lips, and he reveled in the unrestrained evidence of her desire.

From somewhere behind them, Hugh registered the click, soft and faint but enough to send a spear of logic through the lust.

Cursing, he wrenched his head back, shattering the kiss, just as the door exploded open.

Hugh had faced danger of all forms, from all men. Never had a single one looked upon him with the same icy, ominous promise of pain and death the way the well-dressed stranger did before him.

The older brother, then.

It was all that made sense, and also it had been long overdue. Given society's repeated speculation and gossip surrounding Hugh's daily visitation to Lila March, the only surprise came in the fact that it had taken the other man this long to return to London.

"H-Henry!" Lila called in a shaky, breathless voice that might have been confused for fear had it not been for the intimate angling of her and Hugh's bodies. Or the flush on her cheeks.

The brother—Henry's—eyes narrowed as he moved a clear, assessing, and smart-as-his- sister's gaze over them. Taking in everything.

Hugh stepped away from Lila and clasped his hands behind him.

"What is going on here?" The earl bit out each syllable.

"We're fighting," she blurted.

Hugh briefly closed his eyes, but not before he caught the way the earl's brows went flying up.

Oh, bloody hell.

Lila tried again. "Uh . . . that is . . . how is Clara and the babe?"

It proved the wrong thing to say.

The earl found his legs. He came stalking over. "How is *Clara*?" The other man's voice crept up a decibel but remained largely restrained, proving the earl to be a man with a remarkable degree of self-control. "How is *Galvin*? My God, Lila, I had to leave them to come for you."

She dropped her arms akimbo. "I don't require you to check on me."

"Don't you?" The earl flicked a frosty stare briefly over Hugh, lingering it on Hugh's shirtsleeves before diverting all his focus back to Lila. "Where the hell is Sylvia?"

"And Sylvia isn't my nursemaid."

"No, but you bloody well need one," the earl snapped.

Hugh took a step closer to Lila. "Have a care," he said on a silken whisper. The other man was entitled to his rage and fury . . . but Hugh would be damned if he turned that emotion on Lila.

The earl's eyebrows snapped together. "Are you *threatening* me?"

"If you don't watch your tone with your sister, then aye, I am."

Color splotched Lord Waterson's cheeks.

Clearing her throat, Lila stepped between them. "Why don't we begin with introductions." Her brother opened his mouth, but Lila was already performing the necessary ones. "Henry, this is Hugh, the Duke of Wingate. Hu—Your Grace, may I present my brother?"

Neither Hugh nor the other gentleman bothered with social niceties.

Every man had a snapping point. It turned out that was the earl's. "Do you truly believe I'm concerned with damned introductions?" Lila's brother thundered.

She flinched. "I know this looks bad . . ."

"Looks bad? *Looooks* bad," the earl repeated, adding several extra syllables to that utterance. He slashed a hand over at Hugh's discarded jacket, lying damningly on the grass.

"I assure you, we were doing nothing improper." The lie slid easily from Hugh's lips, and by the daggers the earl leveled on him, the gentleman was wise enough to spot a lie—even a well-delivered one.

"Oh?" Lila's brother all but purred. "Forgive me if I fail to trust the gentleman is an honorable one."

Something in that accusation, an undercurrent, sent unease tripping up Hugh's spine.

Lila charged over. "How dare you, Henry. Hugh has been only honorable. He has given of himself while asking nothing in return. And I won't have you disparage him." Her chest rose and fell hard from that furious defense that came as though torn from her.

A defense Hugh was undeserving of.

Shame needled around his belly.

From over the top of his sister's head, the earl glared darkly back at Hugh.

He knows.

Of course he didn't. Of course he couldn't. Shut away in the country, how could the other man have gleaned the darkest parts of Hugh's past?

"Then what is he doing here, Lila?"

"Hu—His Grace has been good enough to provide me with instruction."

The greying nobleman rocked on his heels. "Instruction."

Couldn't Lila tell that her brother's increasing echo boded unwell? This was bad. Hugh had felt tension on the eve of battle less thick than this.

Lila drew a deep breath. "I sought out His Grace, asking him to provide me with lessons on fighting."

The earl went absolutely still. "What?"

Finding her voice, Lila hurried to gather up the notebooks she'd carried outside, and handed one of them over to her brother.

"I should leave," Hugh said quietly.

Lila's brother jabbed a finger in his direction. "You're not going anywhere," the earl snapped as he flipped open the top page. He paused. *"Combattre la Société."* He looked up. "What the hell is this?"

Lila frowned. "I've asked Hugh to help me."

"You want to open up a boxing arena?" The earl's bellow frightened several finches from their perches, and those creatures flapped noisily.

Lila winced. "That's not what it is." She turned her hands up, all but pleading with her palms for her brother to understand.

"Then what is it?" her brother demanded.

Floundering for words, Lila looked over to Hugh. There was a plea for help there in her eyes. She still couldn't realize a man like Waterson would never accept his sister dabbling in that world, one so far removed from the opulent one she'd been born to. Still, Hugh sought to give support through his words. "Your sister came to me with the idea of building a place where women and men might come and learn skills which they might need to survive. It's not an arena. It's not even a boxing studio, but rather . . ." And then it finally came to him, what she intended. "It will be a place where people are motivated by a need to learn the art of self-defense." It was something that had never been done in the fighting world. And a use for the sport which Hugh had never considered. "An art of battle not driven by aggression, but rather by a need to protect oneself."

Lila looked to him with so much emotion shining in her eyes, they warmed Hugh all the way through. Tears gleamed in their beautiful dark depths as she gave a slight, appreciative little nod. "Thank you," she mouthed.

Hugh touched a hand to his chest.

The older gentleman, head bent in his book, however, proved singularly unimpressed. He snapped Lila's notes closed. "No."

Lila recoiled. "That is what you'd say . . . ? No?" She didn't allow him a word edgewise. "My God, you are a *hypocrite*. You'll support your wife, but should I or Sylvia dare venture into something outside the peerage, then you'll order us about and forbid us like we're children."

"Do you truly believe I'd support your dealing in . . . in . . . this?" The earl didn't manage to get the words out.

"Yes." Lila edged her chin up. "I believed you would."

"You want to engage in a brutal sport." The earl marched over, stopping just a pace away from Lila. "The same sport that killed your brother-in-law?"

That charge sucked the blood from Lila's face.

"Her efforts and intentions are honorable," Hugh said quietly. By God, he'd be damned ten times to Sunday if he let the pompous earl cut her dream out from under her.

"And you?" The earl shot him a death stare. "You know so very much about honorable? Tell me." He seized a note from inside his cloak and whipped it at Hugh. "Do you really know everything there is to know about His Grace, Lila?"

Oh, God.

Hugh's stomach roiled.

The earl did know.

It was there in the dark eyes that seared all the way through him.

Sweat slicked Hugh's palms, and never more had he wished he favored those leather gloves donned by members of the *ton*.

"I know everything I need to know about him," Lila said with a faith he didn't deserve. With a confidence she'd not ever show if . . . when . . . she discovered the truth.

"Lila," Hugh said in barely audible tones, his voice hoarse to his own ears. "I'd—"

"And do you know, in addition to his time as a fighter, one who killed men in matches, that he also served in the King's Army? His partners were good enough to enlighten me as to the duke's past."

Of course Bragger would have. That betrayal was no less than Hugh deserved.

Lila wavered, and Hugh's eyes briefly slid closed. Unable to see the moment that light and warmth she had for him died.

"I didn't . . ." She alternated a perplexed stare between Hugh and her brother. "I . . . don't need to know anything more."

She didn't need to know anything? Or she didn't want to?

Hugh rather suspected it was the latter. In a moment's time, any and all affection she'd ever felt for him would die, and in its place would be the loathing he deserved but hadn't ever wanted to be around to know. Not from her. Not from this woman. "Lila, I can . . ." *explain.* Hugh's throat worked painfully.

Her eyes pleaded with him to do just that.

Except, he couldn't. And the fury burning from the earl's eyes said he knew as much.

"Did he tell you he was in the 15th Hussars, Lila?"

Lila paled.

She would know what that regiment had been responsible for . . .

Balling his hands into tight fists, Hugh made himself stay motionless as her gaze found him—the shock and disbelief and agony there, each a physical lash greater than the next.

And when next the earl spoke, he did so in gentle tones, proving he wasn't a totally heartless bastard, but rather one who sought to protect his sister above all else. "Did you tell her the rest, Duke?" Henry asked, this query directed not to Lila, but to Hugh.

As it should be.

And he had to be the one to tell her.

"Hugh?"

His name fell from her lips as a question, a desperate one that sought an altogether different truth from the ominous question her brother had given her.

Only he'd convinced himself he'd never have this reckoning with her. That he'd be gone long before she could ever learn the truth about that day they'd been on opposite ends of a battle.

Every muscle in his being seized and clenched. And gutless as he was, Hugh couldn't bring himself to look at her. Instead, he fixated on the point just above her thick brown curls. "I was there." Regret and shame and sorrow clutched at his throat, and he had to swallow several times to get the remainder of that admission out. "After I . . .

fled the Fight Society, I enlisted. I served, fighting Boney's forces, and when I returned, I was eventually stationed in Manchester . . . I was at Peterloo." Except, that wasn't right, either. "I was one of the soldiers at Peterloo."

Lila swayed and caught the tip of a nearby iron armillary sphere to keep herself standing.

"Oh, God."

Who did those words belong to? Were they his or hers? Or perhaps both.

This? This was worse than he'd ever anticipated a pain could be. For now she knew. She knew precisely who he was . . . the monster she'd been so determined to not see. Not the honorable man of convictions and courage that she'd insisted he was.

Hugh dragged both hands through his hair, yanking slightly at the roots, welcoming the sharp sting of pain. Hating that he'd never been the man she'd taken him for.

"The thing about soldiers," he said huskily. "We're conditioned to follow orders. To do as we're commanded. To question is to see one cut down in the thick of b-battle." His voice broke and he coughed, clearing his throat. "Nothing about that day made sense. Even battle-trained as I'd been, even I knew it."

Lila stared at him with stricken eyes.

Everything hurt inside. Every muscle, every organ, every piece of him.

"I didn't know how to tell you," he finally managed, his voice hollow. "I-I'm sorry." He lifted a hand to her, and she stared at his fingers as if they belonged to a stranger. As if she couldn't make sense of any part of him.

And he knew the feeling. Because he didn't know which way was up, down, or in between anymore.

Lila bit down on the quivering flesh of her lower lip.

And it was too much. "Forgive me," Hugh said roughly. "I'm . . . please forgive me. I am so very sorry." And like the hounds of hell were nipping at his heels, he turned . . . and fled.

Chapter 28

Lila's ears rang, muting the quick throbbing beat of her pulse.

Hugh had been there.

He'd been at Peterloo.

Nay, what was worse, what was more . . . he'd been a soldier.

He'd been everything she'd feared that morn and had carried nightmares of since.

Lila hugged herself tightly, trying to slog through the heavy confusion that cloaked her brain. All these years, every last soldier and member of the yeomanry that day had been the Devil incarnate sent down to earth to smite the innocent.

She'd gone into hiding because of the fire they'd set to the world, and been haunted by the ghosts that had risen from those ashes. They'd all existed as monsters in her mind. All of them, together, one and the same, each man in uniform inseparable from the others. They'd been less-than-human beasts, and she'd hated each of them with a burning intensity that she'd feared would one day consume her.

Only to find they weren't all the same. There'd been one man amongst the field of many, whom she'd come to know . . . and care about. Love.

And now, Lila's breath coming in hard and fast sporadic spurts, she was unable to see anything beyond the stricken horror and grief in Hugh's eyes.

For he wasn't those violent soldiers at St. Peter's Field. A man who abhorred fighting and imagined a world without that ruthlessness would never be one lifting his bayonet against innocent men, women, and children.

Unless it was because of what he'd done and what he'd seen . . . and the guilt he carried.

Nothing made sense. None of it.

Digging her fingers sharply against her temple, Lila tried to sort through her brother's revelation . . . and Hugh's flight.

On the other end of her shock came the knowledge that Hugh may have been there that August day . . . but he was not the man he'd been. Whatever he'd done that day, or whatever he'd not done, he'd been as altered as Lila and every other survivor of Peterloo.

For there could be no doubting the emotion that had blazed deep within his eyes.

It is why he left so quick after I shared about my time at Peterloo . . .

And also why he'd agreed to help her, even as her vision ran counter to every principle he held on violence.

Of course.

It all made sense.

It hadn't been, as she'd first suspected, pity that prompted him to help her. Rather, it had been guilt.

"Lila."

It took a moment for that quiet baritone to register.

Unblinking, she looked to her elder brother. Henry, who'd always meant well, and who loved her desperately. Desperately enough that he'd left his wife and new babe and run to London to assure Lila's well-being . . . and had also run off the only man Lila would ever love.

"What have you done?" she whispered.

Confusion deepened the lines of his high, noble brow. "What are you saying?" he asked, confusion heavy in his tone. "Surely you heard . . . this fighter . . ."

"He's not a fighter." It was the only way the world saw Hugh, and the only way he wished to not be viewed.

"That is a hard argument to make, given your own admission that you were sparring when I arrived," he said tightly. "Either way, this man, he's *ruthless*. He's done horrible things. According to his partners—"

"His partners would punish him because he'd not go along with . . ." She pressed her lips firm. She'd not break Hugh's confidence, not even to defend him.

Her brother narrowed his eyes. "Go along with what?"

"It doesn't matter." He'd gone against them . . . what they sought, and in the end, they'd betrayed him to Lila's brother. Nay, they'd never deserved Hugh's loyalty. They may have saved him . . . they may have given him work, but a person needn't sell their soul for those kindnesses shown. Kindness should be given without conditions or strings at the end to be pulled when favors were sought. "His past doesn't matter to me." He'd done everything he'd needed in order to survive.

"Surely you are not saying you are all right with . . . all of this, Lila?" her brother all but begged.

"I am," she said quietly. "Because I love him."

Her brother stumbled back several steps, and she may as well have shot him for the shock in his face.

Lila hugged herself all the tighter. "I love him, and it doesn't matter to me that . . . he was there." Except she had to say it. She had to own that her past and Hugh's had been linked that day . . . even as she'd not realized it until now. "It doesn't matter that he was at Peterloo. It matters who he is now, and who he's shown himself to be—"

"A man who withheld the truth of his involvement that day in Manchester," Henry quietly interrupted, bringing her up short.

Peterloo would always be there. That truth. That day.

But it would matter more if Hugh was not in her life now.

"These past years, Henry, have not been easy. We've known suffering and sorrow and strife." Her eyes went to the jacket Hugh had rushed off and left. Drawn to that small link to him, Lila walked over and rescued it from the ground. The sandalwood scent that clung to it wafted about. "What I've learned, however, is that even with that sadness, we really don't know what it was to be born without influence. We don't know what it is to have no options. And so I'll not judge Hugh for the decisions he made. And it would be wrong for you to pass judgment when you know him not at all."

Footfalls sounded from the back of the garden, and they looked as one. Lila's sister came stumbling through the entryway. "What is going on?" she asked. "I passed His Grace, leaving."

A vise squeezed Lila's heart. Why hadn't she said something? Why had she allowed him to leave? "He didn't . . ."

Sylvia seemed to just then note their brother. "Henry!" She gripped the front of her dress. "Is Clara . . . ?"

"The babe and Clara are both fine."

Confusion in her eyes, her sister looked between Lila and Henry. "What is going on?"

And just then, all the piles of books she and Hugh had been working on lay damningly between Lila and her sister.

"Tell her, Lila," Henry said gravely.

"What is it?" Sylvia demanded when neither sibling rushed to speak.

"I plan to build an establishment where women and men learn to fight," Lila blurted, and with that admission came a lightness in her chest.

Sylvia's mouth parted. Her lips moved several times, as if she were attempting to make words.

"I intend to do it, and I understand if you disapprove. I understand even that my decision will likely bring you pain, but I know this needs to be done. I was a woman once trapped, caught, and clung to by men bigger and stronger."

Tears filled Sylvia's eyes.

Was it the remembrance Lila shared, or the decision Lila had committed herself to? "And I believe fighting doesn't have to be used to hurt, but rather as a means for one to protect oneself."

A pressure eased in acknowledging that which she intended. There wasn't shame to be found in her dream. And at last, owning it, as Hugh had urged, made it . . . real . . . and right.

"I'm sorry if I've disappointed both of you," Lila said softly. "But I need to do this . . . for me." Lila gathered up her and Hugh's work from these past weeks. "If you'll excuse me? I'll see my things are packed."

With that, she left her brother and sister staring after her.

Lila continued forward and didn't stop until she reached the confines of the guest chambers she'd used these past three months. She set her books down and headed for the painted pine armoire. Drawing open the double panels, she fished out her valise from the bottom. She'd been shuffled from household to household—her brother's residence to her sister's. And as a spinster on the shelf, not very many years from thirty, she wanted more than a life with either her brother or sister.

For too long, she'd been so very consumed in hiding that she'd not imagined any kind of existence for herself.

Now, she saw that she wanted not just the business she'd dreamed of but a family, too. She wanted Hugh.

Dropping to a knee, Lila tenderly packed each notebook into the bottom of the valise. When she had the last one in hand, the last he'd worked on and hadn't yet shown her, she paused. Settling onto the floor, Lila opened the small volume and flipped through the pages. She read each word in Hugh's sturdy scrawl until her neck ached and the afternoon sun gave way to darkness. She reached the end of the book. A small folded square fluttered onto her lap.

Puzzling her brow, Lila picked up the paper. Unfolding it, she began to read.

Lila,

I questioned your venture from the moment you confided in me. I hated everything about it. I realize now I didn't *know* anything about it. I didn't understand what you sought to create because there's never been anything quite like it. But then, there is no one in the world like you.

Hugh.

Emotion wadded in her throat, and she stroked her fingers lovingly over the words he'd written and intended to give her.

She wanted a future with Hugh, a home with him.

Knock-Knock-Knock.

Lila stiffened. It had been inevitable. She wouldn't have simply said her piece and that would've been the end of it. Nor was it fair for Lila to expect as much. She'd withheld information from her sister, all the while knowing how Sylvia felt about fighting. And yet Lila had conducted work in her household.

And in that careful omission . . . were you really any different from Hugh?

Knock-Knock-Knock.

Shaken by that realization, she called out. "Enter."

The panel opened a fraction and then widened as her sister stepped inside.

It was the first time she'd shed her widow's weeds. Gloriously attired in robes of burnt orange and red, with gold wings and a gold crown atop her flaxen curls, she was every bit the Phoenix she'd come in as, a young widow risen from the ashes.

Lila stuffed the damning page in her hands into the notebook. "Sylvia," she greeted. She dropped that last volume into the bottom of the valise and then snapped it shut.

Her sister fidgeted with the black diary in her hands. "You've not changed into a costume."

Taken aback, Lila glanced down. "You . . . want me there?"

Tears filled her sister's eyes. "*Of course* I do." She brushed the drops back, and a glimmer shone there. "Would it have stopped you from joining me tonight?"

From the moment she'd learned Sylvia would attend Lady Prendergast's masquerade, she'd resolved to be there. Lila managed a watery smile. "No."

"Good."

Balancing her weight onto her right side, Lila made to struggle to her feet, but her elder sister waved her back into a seated position. Instead, Sylvia joined Lila on the floor. Her makeshift wings knocked awkwardly against the armoire. "You expected I shouldn't understand what your dream was . . . is?" she asked without preamble.

"I . . . thought you might not be able to look past what it is."

"I hate fighting," her sister said, a fire to match her costume flaring in her eyes. Passion drew forth every word from Sylvia's lips. "I hate Gentleman Jackson's and boxing." She drew in an unsteady breath. "But I understand what you wish to create, and more importantly why you wish to do so." Inching over, she took up a spot beside Lila's shoulder. "Since you've spent time with His Grace . . . and learned how to fight, you've been empowered. In ways that music didn't even do for you. As such, I'd not hold your dreams against you because of my nightmares." Sadness traipsed across Sylvia's eyes, and she glanced down at the book in her fingers. "I never understood Norman's deep love for fighting . . . until I did." She held the diary out.

Lila moved her gaze from the cracked and aged leather back to her sister.

Sylvia nodded. "Go on, take it."

Collecting the small volume, Lila opened the book and read through the words written there. All the while her sister spoke. "It began with his family"—*the marquess?*—"and grew . . . because of them."

Lila went absolutely still as the full weight of what she had read slammed into her.

A lone tear wound a trail down Sylvia's pale cheek, and Lila's sister caught that drop and dashed it away. Angling her head away from Lila, she stared off to the opposite side of the room. "I found it the day of the funeral. Entirely by chance. In fact, I don't think I would have come across it otherwise. That morn, I was ill . . . because of the babe, and had to slip away to be sick. I found the marquess rummaging through Norman's desk. He was frantic. The moment I came upon him, he stopped and said something about a special note he wanted to find as a keepsake for his wife, and then rejoined the viewing. After the guests had gone, I scoured Norman's drawers, searching everywhere. There was a hidden panel. I found that." She tipped her chin toward the diary.

Lila read each damning word. An accounting of years of atrocities. And her very soul ached for the nameless victims who were mentioned. For Hugh. Lila stroked her fingers over the faded black ink. Hugh had been one of those children used to fight for the marquess's pleasures. And then the implications set in . . . for her sister. "Oh, Sylvia," she whispered, woefully inadequate with a response. But then even the young woman she'd been before Peterloo would have never had anything for this. "The marquess ran the Fight Society."

"You know of it because of your Hugh."

Lila nodded.

"The moment he came here, I knew who he was. I knew what he was likely asking you, and I wanted you to give him what he needed; and yet, selfishly, I couldn't make myself do it."

Surprise brought Lila's lips into a silent circle. "You knew."

"Selfishly, I've held on to this because . . ." This time, the tears fell freely, and Sylvia let them go unchecked. She shook her head, unable to get the words out. Her sister struggled, and then finally managed to speak. "Then the whole world would know, and I didn't hate it for me as much as I hated it for Vallen." A little sob burst from her sister that Sylvia caught and buried in a fist. "Keep reading. I can't do this unless you don't talk . . ."

Loath to read the remainder of the words there but owing her sister a strength to do so, Lila looked back to her late brother-in-law's diary . . . and she couldn't move.

She squeezed her eyes shut.

"He met her at one of the fights. He saved her. H-he . . . H-he . . ." Sylvia covered her face with her hands and then, after five long seconds, let them fall to her knees. "He loved her," she said quietly, her voice steady. "Her name was . . . is Valerie. She was the one following me and Vallen and Mother that morn. She recently found me and . . . shared about her past with Norman." Grief seized her features. "She apologized and explained that she didn't know about me."

The great love of Sylvia's life, the devoted husband her sister had mourned, all along had loved another. Closing her eyes, Lila wrapped an arm about her elder sister's shoulders and simply held her.

Sylvia rested her head atop Lila's, and for a long while, she said nothing. She simply took the only thing Lila knew to offer—her silent support. "All our money went to her. It went to seeing her cared for and safely hidden so that Norman's father could not bring her back and hurt her. And I want to hate her. I want that desperately." Sylvia sucked in a shuddery breath. "But I can't. I hate him for making me love him on a lie. I hate myself for loving him still."

This was the woman Hugh had spoken of. Bragger's lost sister, Valerie, hadn't been taken, but rather, she'd gone off and stayed hidden. She'd lived a life with Norman.

Lila resumed turning those damning pages that burnt down the illusion of love that Sylvia and Norman had known.

And then she stopped.

Lila read and reread the words there.

"He was going to reveal everything he knew about the Fight Society," her sister murmured. "To be sure that this young woman remained safe . . . and the next day . . ."

Her sister didn't need to finish her thought. Lila knew precisely what had happened that following morn: after an unlucky punch to the head, Norman had died, and her sister had found herself a widow.

Except . . .

"What if it wasn't a mistake, Lila?" Sylvia asked, giving voice to Lila's very suspicions. "What if the marquess had his son punched in such a way that killed him? Is that . . . possible?"

Lila thought of every lesson Hugh had given her, about the lethality of blows. Norman had caught one at the base of his skull: according to Hugh, the most lethal place to strike a person.

"Could the marquess be responsible for his son's death?"

Lila looked down at the notes sprawled on her lap, the damning words recorded by her late brother-in-law. "I believe a person who could organize what the marquess did . . . using children for the perverse pleasures of society, is capable of any manner of cruelty."

Her sister nodded. "That is also the conclusion I drew."

Lila knew but one thing . . . tonight, Hugh would enter the marquess's townhouse and set out in search of information that would link the gentleman to his crimes. Only, he needn't search any further . . . because everything he required rested right here in Lila's lap.

"We need to go to the masquerade." What a perfectly apt and suitable event for a man whose entire life of respectability had been nothing more than a show. He'd been a monster posing as a *gentleman*.

"For Hugh."

Lila nodded. He deserved all the evidence Sylvia had discovered, and peace from his demons at last.

"But . . . did you even find a costume?"

"Of course I did." As much as she'd loathed joining her sister, she'd resolved to do so the moment Sylvia had shared her intentions of attending the masquerade. In each lesson Hugh had provided Lila, she had found strength in her ability to defend herself . . . and those she loved.

It was time to reenter the living.

⁓

Nearly two hours later, on the arm of her sister at the top of the stairway of the Marquess and Marchioness of Prendergast's crowded ballroom, Lila stared down at the crowd below.

Laughter pealed about in a steady stream of waves, the revelers giving voice to their joy and hilarity.

Her palms slick with moisture and perspiration beading her brow, Lila adjusted the small bag she'd incorporated into her costume, and struggled to dredge forth the confidence that had sent her here this night.

"If you would rather leave," Sylvia called loudly over the din, "we can." Her lip peeled back. "I suddenly find myself . . . with less of a taste for being here." Her sister settled her masked stare on a figure garbed as Cleopatra at the center of the festivities, alongside a portly king.

The marquess.

And all the same loathing surely spiraling through Sylvia wound its way through Lila as hatred so deep and dark spilled into her veins.

This was the man who'd hurt Hugh.

Used him for his perverse enjoyment.

Lila tightened her mouth, and through the earlier horror, her strength came roaring back. "I need to be here . . . I want to." And she did.

Hugh. She had to find him. And yet . . . Lila scrabbled with the inside of her cheek. She'd not considered being parted from her sister.

"We'll split up," Sylvia said as they started down the steps. She placed her lips close to Lila's ear. "We have to find him and get your duke out. It's not safe for him here."

"It's not safe for y—"

Sylvia's glare cut her off. "You're not the only one capable of caring for yourself. I'm not the weak one you might take me for."

And then it hit Lila all at once. She'd been so insistent on looking after Sylvia and her nephew that she'd underestimated her sister, and in that, she'd wronged her. "I didn't mean . . ."

"Go," her sister mouthed, and without waiting to see whether Lila complied, she sailed down the remaining stairs and lost herself in the crowd.

Lila hesitated a moment more, and then set off in search of Hugh.

People swarmed all around her, tunneling her vision as sweat coated her skin.

Do not think of it. Focus on Hugh. Focus on finding him . . .

For him, she could do anything.

And yet as she worked her stare over the guests, it felt like the lie it was.

Someone brushed her arm, and she recoiled.

Lila quickened her pace; she knocked into drunken revelers as she went. All the while she searched for him. He was taller than any man she'd ever known, broader and stronger—she could find him in a crowd.

To retreat was to fail.

And yet it was too much. The orchestra's playing reached a dizzying crescendo. The walls were closing in.

Needing air, Lila escaped the crush of bodies and rushed out to the nearest corridor. Her legs gave out from under her, and she sank against the wall. Her chest rose and fell fast and hard, and she focused on breathing.

You thought you could do this . . . but you can't . . .

Tears pricked behind her eyes as she fought off that mocking taunt echoing in her mind.

"It does become easier, the more you go out," a quiet voice murmured, bringing Lila's eyes flying open.

She gasped.

There she stood, attired in an outrageously daring, crimson gown; with layer after layer of red, she'd fashioned herself into a crimson rose.

Annalee drank from a champagne flute.

"Annalee," she said, taken aback.

"Lila."

That was it. Just two words exchanged, their names and nothing more . . . when they'd shared so many memories, both joyous ones and the darkest, ugliest ones. But then what did one say after all these years?

Lila struggled to rise. "I'm sorry I've not—"

Annalee waved her glass about. "Do not. I'm not looking for apologies. I've only ever wanted your friendship."

Emotion stabbed at her breast. "I've not known how to be a friend . . . I've barely known how to get through each day." She smiled wistfully. "How I admire you." How even longer she'd envied her.

Bitterness lent a smile to Annalee's lips. "I'm not one to be admired. I learned I could either stay indoors and let the demons eat me up, or I could live outrageously and dare life to destroy me." *Once more.* Those two words danced unspoken in the silence.

"You *are* thriving." How could Annalee think she wasn't?

Annalee tittered, a drunken little giggle, as she raised her glass in salute. "This isn't thriving. This is living in its basest form."

And while Annalee downed a deep swallow, Lila noted that which had escaped her before now: the other woman's bloodshot eyes. Her slightly slurred speech.

A furious voice came echoing from a nearby corridor, and Lila froze.

"Where is she? We must get her home this instant. She is making a scandal of herself."

Annalee's mother. The ever proper viscountess.

Annalee lifted a finger to her lips.

"She is meeting someone again," the viscountess lamented. "I just know it . . . How dare she behave this way, at Lady Prendergast's?"

"*Shh* . . ." the viscount commanded. "We'll find her, and then we'll . . ."

Neither woman spoke until the pair drew farther away, and then their voices faded altogether.

A small, husky laugh slipped from Annalee; there was a faint desperation . . . and mayhap even madness to it. "How highly they speak of the marchioness. That woman who's engaged in even more wicked pleasures than I." Lila started—what was the other woman *saying* exactly? "Alas, they would never expect that even I, their shameful daughter, find the marchioness ruthless and vile." Her lips quirked as she again hefted her glass. "My apologies. I forgot your familial connections."

Lila waved that apology off. Once upon a lifetime ago, she'd have shared what she'd learned with the woman before her. Perhaps they'd return to that ease . . . someday.

Annalee looked as though she wished to say more. "I should be going," she said softly.

"I should as well." Lila, however, couldn't make herself move.

Annalee had deserved her friendship. This reunion had been long overdue . . . Time had passed, but it was not too late. "I'd like to see you again," Lila blurted.

Her friend's mouth trembled. "I'd like that *verrry* much." She turned to go and then stopped. "Oh, and Lila?"

She stared questioningly at her friend.

"Have a care. The marchioness is ruthless to the extreme. I'd pressed you in the hopes that you would be here so that I might warn you.

She's capable of great evil . . ." With that ominous warning, Annalee slipped off.

She's capable of great evil . . .

Between the marquess's involvement in the Fight Society and his son's murder, it seemed the whole of Norman's family was ruthless.

Lila froze. Her friend's warning held her locked to the floor.

Impossible . . .

Her heart pounded.

But why should it be impossible? Hadn't she spent all these months arguing the capabilities and strength of women?

All this time, she'd simply assumed that Lord Prendergast was the one responsible for his son's death . . . and Hugh's misery.

"I was wrong," she whispered. She and Sylvia had *both* been wrong.

It wasn't the marquess.

It had been the marchioness.

Renewed purpose infused her as Lila set off in search of Hugh.

Chapter 29

This was his hell.

Only, it was the nightmare he'd not known he had.

Standing on the fringe of the Marquess of Prendergast's dance floor, with a sea of masked guests throughout the candlelit ballroom, Hugh was transported back to another time . . . to a different crowd.

One with masked noblemen on the sides, screaming and cheering on the boys and girls scrabbling in the middle of a fancy arena.

And in the ultimate twist of irony, Hugh had come full circle in a way, surrounded by noblemen in disguise. Only this time, he now found himself a lord behind one of those hated satin scraps. Vibrant colors from the excessive articles donned filled every corner and space. Even the servants bearing trays were resplendent in gold robes and gilded crowns to match the golden trays filled with bubbling spirits that they hefted high above their heads.

It was a garish display of opulence and grandiosity, enough to turn an outsider's stomach. All around, men and women waltzed and pranced about, getting drunk off their own frivolousness.

In short, it was nothing less than what Hugh might have expected of an event hosted by one who'd run the Fight Society.

A champagne flute in his fingers so as to blend with the other lords and ladies present, Hugh stared on at the tall, slender figure in the middle of the ballroom. His face concealed, Hugh could make out little of his features. He didn't know what he'd expected . . . some immediate recognition. A telltale hint or sign or mark upon the man's face that he'd been the head of the Fight Society.

Instead, arm-in-arm with a petite woman some twenty years his junior, the man was as much a stranger as every other man here this night.

Just then, the guest Prendergast greeted moved on and the marquess looked out.

And for a moment, Hugh believed the other man saw him standing there, watching him. Knowing Hugh intended to search his lair for any hint of wrongdoing.

But then Lord Prendergast shifted his focus to a portly pair.

So many men and women of all ages, coming here for a night's revelry, almost wicked enough to border on respectability.

He swept his gaze around the room, taking in the outlandish display.

When his partners had asked him to enter the nest of vipers, Hugh had not thought beyond the ultimate outcome: procuring evidence that could link Prendergast and, through him, all the other men responsible for the Fight Society.

His focus had been singular: securing an invitation and then slipping about like the expert thief he'd once been to find that which he wished. Information which Hugh would bring himself to steal, and then justice would be done.

What Hugh hadn't allowed himself to think about was that he'd be surrounded by the many men who'd tossed coin down, betting on him, cheering him on . . . or worse, shouting him down in favor of the boys he'd faced. All the while, those spectators had expected him to maim and kill . . . or to be broken or killed himself.

And there was a peculiar . . . numbness as he lingered his gaze on the older gentlemen with greying or white hair. Were they the same men responsible for Hugh and Bragger and Maynard's hell? Did they even now take their pleasures here, just as they had in the Fight Society?

A voluptuous woman draped in wet silver satin drifted closer. From behind her sharp-beaked owl mask, an invitation blazed from her eyes, and she extended it in the form of painted fingernails that she caressed along the tops of her bosom.

For the first time, grateful for the mask he wore that concealed his disgust, Hugh shook his head.

With a little pout, the fleshy creature instantly turned and shifted her attentions to a more appreciative, agreeable gentleman near her.

The worries he'd carried in invading the marquess's townhouse had been for naught. Prendergast and his guests were so intoxicated and consumed by their pleasures that Hugh could have conducted a formal search of each person present, and they'd have only mistaken his touch for a scandalously bold caress.

Abandoning his glass on the tray of a nearby servant, Hugh set off in search of the marquess's offices.

Using the same furtive steps that had saved him in the ring and in the rookeries, Hugh wound his way along the perimeter of the room and made his way out into the corridors. The gaiety grew muted and muffled the more distance he put between himself and those festivities, until he'd reached the recesses of the marquess's townhouse, so only the faintest of echoes met his ears.

Working his eyes over the empty halls, Hugh kept on alert for lords or ladies, or trysting couples.

Alas, most of the household staff appeared to have been put to use ensuring the pleasures of the guests. Methodically, Hugh cracked open door after door. Well-oiled hinges added not so much as a damning creak to his search. He pressed the handle of the last door in the hall, and froze.

Heavy mahogany paneling lined the walls, that shiny, dark wood a perfect match to the desk that stood at the very center of the room.

Prendergast's offices.

His heart hammered: Was it excitement? Fear that he'd not find any hint of what he sought? A triumph of having at last found his way to the possible answers of his past?

Hugh stiffened. Sensing it before he heard it.

And then it came . . .

From down the opposite corridor, a lone floorboard squeaked a long, damning creak, announcing the visitor before he saw him. A steady tread of just one set of footfalls, not a pair to signal lovers sneaking off for a different night's pleasures.

He'd been followed.

Slipping inside the marquess's office, Hugh pushed the panel a fraction, taking care to not allow so much as an incriminating click. He layered himself along the right side of the entryway, blinking slowly to adjust his vision to the darkened space. Hugh remained absolutely motionless.

His soldier's ears caught the quickening footfalls, swifter and sloppier than they'd been when he'd first detected them.

And then they came to a stop directly outside Prendergast's offices.

Bloody, bloody hell.

Hugh braced, willing the interloper gone.

Instead, the stranger pushed the door open and stepped inside.

The smaller man did a turn, looking slowly around the room . . . when his gaze caught on Hugh.

The stranger opened his mouth to announce both their presences to the world.

With a silent curse, Hugh shot a hand out, muffling that cry, and catching the other man lightly by the throat, Hugh pressed him against the wall . . .

A sharp heel came up, unexpectedly, catching Hugh in the right kneecap.

A hiss exploded from between clenched teeth as he hit the floor hard.

Hugh's assailant dealt a swift uppercut to his solar plexus, briefly knocking the air from his lungs, and lights danced behind his eyes.

"Hughhhh?"

And when his vision cleared, horror-filled brown eyes stared back. Very *familiar* horror-filled eyes.

Lila . . . She was here. Attired in the same breeches she'd donned from their earliest time together, she'd now paired with them a fine lawn shirt. Her thick curls had been plaited and tucked under a top hat affixed to her head.

How was she here? "You're here."

She nodded. "I am."

She'd braved the crowds to come . . .

And then it all came rushing back: her brother's return. *Peterloo.*

And Hugh's heart knocked dully in his chest for altogether different reasons. When she remained staring at him with those hopelessly wide eyes, he shoved to his feet. "I see we must retire the name of Flittermouse for you." He'd taught her well.

Giving her head a shake as if she'd been yanked to the present along with him, Lila pressed a fist against her mouth. "My God, I've hurt you."

"Aye, actually you did." He winked in a half-hearted attempt at humor. "You had a good teacher."

The full moon's glow lent light enough to illuminate the glare she shot him. "This is not a matter of jest. I. Hurt. You."

"I'm fine, Lila," he soothed. "I've endured worse." *Far worse.*

Except it proved the wrong thing to say. For resurrected between them were those very darkest memories. The ones her brother had forced out into the light. Yet in fairness, Hugh had owed her the truth long before. It shouldn't have required an intervention from her deservedly outraged brother.

"Why are you here?" he asked in a low voice, mindful that in lurking in the marquess's offices, they both flirted with different forms of danger, the least of which was her ruin. The greater risk being that of their very lives, should their intentions be discovered.

Had it been for him . . . ?

And how desperately he wanted that answer to be yes.

"I needed to see you," she said softly, giving breath to that dream. Stealing a hasty glance at the door, Lila rescued her bag, and fished out a small black book from within. "You don't need to be here. Everything you need . . . is here. My sister discovered it amongst her late husband's belongings."

Wordlessly, he accepted the small diary.

"You were not altogether correct. It was not the marquess who was responsible for the Fight Society." She spoke on a frantic rush, and as he opened the book, his mind struggled to keep up with what she revealed. "It was his wife, the marchioness. *She* is the one responsible for the death of her son because my brother-in-law disapproved and intended to see her brought to justice. There was a woman he . . ." A wave of grief contorted her features. "Loved. A woman who was not my sister, but rather, one by the name of . . . Valerie." Hugh stilled as the weight of her revelation sank in.

He breathed. "Bragger's sister?"

Lila nodded. "She is alive. My sister has met her."

Emotion threatened to drown him—at everything she'd learned . . . at her even being here now. "You came here to share this with me." It was a statement of wonder. She had braved the crowds she'd so avoided over the years . . . for him.

Just not necessarily to *see* him. Rather, to help ensure Hugh was able to do that which was right. It was everything he'd been searching for.

Nay, Lila was.

When Hugh still didn't say anything, Lila spoke in more urgent tones. "Your partners may feel you denied them vengeance, but you have something else you can give them in repayment . . . a gift far greater." Bragger's reunion with the sister he'd loved and lost.

Who'd not really been so very lost, after all.

"I . . . see . . ."

This was the reason she'd come.

Hugh closed the book with a soft click and looked over the aged leather.

"I expected you might . . . be more excited."

All elation he'd felt had come at finding her here with him. And he wanted to be suitably overjoyed at what she'd managed to secure . . . but even justice was empty . . . hollow . . . without Lila in his life. "I am . . . grateful for what you've given me," he finally brought himself to say.

A little frown puckered that space between her brows, wrinkling the bottom of the jagged scar that ended there.

They stared at one another a long while in silence. "You left."

He didn't pretend to misunderstand. "I didn't think there was much point in staying," he said gruffly.

Hurt flashed in the expressive depths of her eyes. "I wasn't a reason to stay?"

His heart found a normal cadence and then accelerated once more. Her charge, that question she leveled at him, suggested she'd wished to see him. But that was impossible . . .

"I saw how you looked at me, Lila. It's how I look at myself." Every morn of every day.

She drifted closer. "Did you take part at Peterloo?" she asked with her usual frankness.

Hugh's eyes slid shut, as that name, her question, ushered in a host of all the darkest nightmares.

"Please, I beg ya . . . Help me, good sir . . ."

And he'd tried. God, how he'd tried. But in just being there, he'd failed. The nameless men, women, and children. And now the one woman whose name he did know. Whose name meant more to him than even his own life. "I was there."

"That's not what I asked," she said before even the last syllable had left his lips.

They'd already held enough from one another. He'd not have partial truths between them. Not anymore. "We'd been positioned away from the fields. When L'Estrange called us for a forward charge, I galloped at those fields just as the rest of the 15th did." He felt her eyes boring into him. "It didn't take long to discover it was an impossibility for anyone to move . . . or that the innocent were under attack." Hugh tightened his hold upon the diary the late earl had discovered. "I attempted to help." His chest hurt from even the retelling of that hated day. "Everywhere I rode, the innocent rushed off and only fell at the hands of another soldier. But I charged the field," he repeated, needing her to hear that. "And I was present." Hugh sighed. "When the dust had settled, I left. I left my mount. And with nothing but my uniform and satchel, marched from Manchester to London, where I started begging again."

Shame squeezed at his insides. At even that ignominy.

"And Bragger and Maynard found you then," she accurately speculated. "It is one of the reasons for your loyalty to them."

Precisely. He managed a nod but could add nothing more to the telling. Because there really was nothing more . . . to say.

Soft fingers covered his, and Hugh started. Her callused fingers, so tender and delicate, felt like . . . absolution.

"You are so much more than that day, Hugh McCade. You are more than you ever will give yourself credit for being. And I love you. I would never hold your being there against you."

There was a buzzing in his ears, and he clung to just one admission: "You love me?"

A little laugh escaped her. "Of course I love you, you daft man. I have loved you since the day you put a cheroot in my fingers and helped me through my nightmares."

A joy so dizzying, so beautiful filled Hugh. "I love you," he rasped. With his spare hand, he cupped her cheek. "I've loved you since you pressed your face against that arena window and refused to take no for an answer. There is no one like you." Hugh claimed Lila's mouth; parting her lips, he swept his tongue inside.

He was home.

Through the thick haze of desire came quiet, delicate footfalls.

Hugh wrenched away and pushed Lila behind him just as the panel was opened.

Oh, bloody hell.

The Marchioness of Prendergast stepped inside. Still wearing her mask and cape, along with the same smile she'd worn for the guests in her receiving line, anyone might have mistaken the lady for an affable one.

"Savage . . . you filthy street bastard." The marchioness spoke in a husky voice. A familiar one that came haunting back from his past. *Kill him, you filthy street bastard.* Hugh's flesh crawled. She shut the door and turned the lock. Surprise briefly flashed in the dowager marchioness's eyes when she caught sight of Lila. "Hello, Lady Lila. An unexpected pleasure finding you here . . . that is, at my ball. Not in my husband's offices. *Tsk. Tsk.* That is not where I'd expected you would or should . . . venture."

He felt the tension in Lila's frame, pulsing, but when she spoke, there was only an evenness, and Hugh found himself falling in love with her all over again.

"Good evening, my lady. It is still . . . all a bit overwhelming, and His Grace was so kind as to escort me from the crowd."

God, how he loved her. She was nimble of mind and had a strength of spirit that would put any other man or woman to shame.

"How very good of him," the marchioness said dryly. She folded her arms. "What a matter of . . . happenstance that you should also have come here with my son's diary."

Lila's eyes went to the book held damningly between Hugh's fingers. He gave a slight shake of his head, willing her to silence. For the evil Lila had encountered on St. Peter's Field . . . she was still too innocent to ever be prepared for the depths of evil that Lady Prendergast was capable of.

"We brought it for you," she blurted.

The lady's eyes narrowed.

Hugh moved . . . a second too late.

Lady Prendergast removed a pistol from her kalasiri. She smiled coldly. "The convenient thing of masquerades is that they're noisy affairs. So many guests. So many distracted servants. So much confusion."

Plenty of covers for the woman to carry out a murder on her grounds.

"You're many things, but you aren't sloppy," Hugh said, slowly bringing his palms up so they framed his face and were in the marchioness's plain sight. "You'd have a deuced difficult time explaining—"

"What?" the marchioness cut in, casually. "That the mad March sister riled the Savage, that fighter society already had every reason to mistrust? And that I should have come upon and intervened . . . *Tsk. Tsk.* Too late. Timing is everything."

"Was it also perfect timing that saw your son killed?"

The silver-haired lady's body coiled like a serpent poised to strike.

"Lila," Hugh warned out of the corner of his mouth.

Alas, she may as well not have heard, for she stalked boldly over to the marchioness. "I know what you did to Norman."

Oh, Christ.

It was a prayer.

Prayers, however, had proven futile before, and they proved to be the same now.

"Not another step, Lady Lila," Lady Prendergast ordered, shifting her pistol so that the barrel was leveled at the center of Lila's chest. The place where her heart beat.

Hugh broke out in a cold sweat; it covered his body.

If anything happened to her, he'd not survive. He'd not want to. There was no life without her in it.

Stop.

Have your wits . . .

Except, how had he managed a sharp focus through every battle and every fight . . . until now? Because living hadn't mattered before her. She mattered above anything.

"I'm the one you have qualms with," Hugh said, diverting the marchioness's attention back over to him. "Your family has shared connections with the March family."

Only a woman who'd killed her own son, all to protect her secrets and her perversity, wasn't a sane person. She had no allegiance to anything but her libertinisms.

From the corner of his eye, Hugh caught Lila creep closer to the dowager marchioness.

Stop. Just stop, he silently screamed, willing her to remain motionless.

But then from the first meeting, Lila March had never done what he'd wanted or expected.

"I should really thank you . . . the both of you. You brought me what I've been searching for," Lady Prendergast said almost conversationally. "You've saved me a trip. The both of—"

The door handle rattled, and all the blood leached from the marchioness's chiseled cheeks.

"Open the door."

Connor Steele?

The investigator's command was muffled.

From behind Lady Prendergast's mask, her eyes bulged before flickering between Lila and Hugh.

"I said, open the door." This time, Steele's voice cut more distinctly through the heavy oak panel.

Hugh's gaze remained trained on the marchioness; the woman was prey, cornered, and there was no more volatile enemy than that.

And in the end, hate flared bright as she found her final target. The dowager marchioness pointed her pistol at Hugh.

He surged forward.

"Ahh!" An ungodly cry burst from the lady as Lila shot the heel of her boot out, catching the older woman in the front of the kneecap, crumpling her leg. The pistol went flying from the dowager marchioness's hands, and the moment it hit the floor, the weapon discharged, emitting a cloud of smoke.

Madness lit her eyes as she unsheathed a dagger from her scanty gold-wrapped kalasiri.

Hugh was upon the woman in a single stride. Wrapping his arm so his forearm was wedged between her chin and chest, he grabbed her shoulder with his dominant hand, and stabilizing his grip, he applied a light pressure.

The woman immediately went limp, and he lowered her to the floor.

Stepping over the woman's prone, unconscious body, Hugh had Lila in his arms. "Are you all right?" he rasped. His heart was never again going to find a normal cadence. "Why did you do that?" he begged, running his hands down her arms, searching for any hint that she'd been hurt. "Why did you *do* that?"

"I-I'm so sorry." She collapsed into his arms and clung hard to his shirtfront. "I'm s-so sorry."

"Sorry." Hugh cupped her cheeks, stroking his palms over them. "My God, what are you sorry for?"

Weeping softly, Lila rested her forehead against his chest. Crying, when she'd only ever tried to restrain her tears; she now let them fall freely, and it sent him into further tumult. "You don't want to u-use violence and—"

He groaned, cutting her off. "Listen to me, Lila March," he said hoarsely. "I will never, *ever* hesitate to do whatever I need to protect you. And I'll carry no regrets. You are all that matters. I love you."

Catching her close, he drew her against him and just held her.

Hugh dimly noted the give of the lock as Steele worked his way inside the room. At his heels were Lila's sister . . . and brother.

Lady Sylvia's cry went up as she rushed forward, and in an instant, Lila was swept from his arms and surrounded by those of her family.

And Hugh fell back, the outsider once more.

From over the top of that familial exchange, Hugh caught Steele's gaze as the investigator knelt beside Lady Prendergast's body.

"She's alive," Hugh said quietly. "Everything you need to see her brought to justice is in that book," he advised the investigator.

It was done.

Chapter 30

Lila had become something of an expert at sneaking.

It was how in the dead of night, when the respectable at last slept and the servants managed to steal their too-few hours of rest, she'd found her way through the servants' kitchens of the unfamiliar townhouse.

Drawing her hood deeper over her face, she crept through opulent halls.

Candlelight streamed from under the small crack at the bottom of the door. Gripping the handle, she went to press the iron latch down and then stopped herself.

Over the past two years, she'd engaged in all manner of bold behaviors: she'd petitioned a former courtesan and madam for music lessons. She'd snuck about the rookeries, requesting bare-knuckle fighting lessons from one of London's most legendary fighters. She'd gone off to that same legendary fighter's apartments.

But this . . . this was altogether different.

Or it felt different.

It isn't. He is the same man, and you are the same woman . . .

And those assurances rolling around her head didn't help.

Inside her gloves, Lila's palms slicked with moisture.

And for a long moment, she considered the even longer path she'd just traveled through the townhouse.

You've already come here . . . Now, say your piece . . .

"Are you going to enter, love? Or do you intend to stay outside my door until the sun rises?"

She gasped, that telltale exhalation echoing damningly around the empty halls. Springing into movement, Lila hurriedly let herself in.

Having changed from the highwayman costume he'd worn just hours ago, he'd donned a white lawn shirt. He'd not bothered with a jacket. And she drank her fill of him. Preferring him in this state of undress. It was how she'd forever see him in her mind. Shoving her hood off, Lila leaned against the door. "How did you know it was me?"

Looping his arms around his head, Hugh reclined in his wingback chair. "I know the cadence of your footsteps."

Lila cocked her head. "Impossible."

"You tread heavier on the forward fall."

"Indeed?"

"Indeed."

Well, there had gone her element of surprise.

"I trust your family doesn't know you're here?"

"You trust correctly on that." Though after she'd been escorted out of the marquess's residence, she'd been altogether certain her siblings intended to stand guard outside her rooms as if she were once more Lila March in need of protecting. Lila pushed herself away from the door and, loosening the clasp at her throat, freed herself of her cloak. "I must confess, I'm disappointed in you, Your Grace."

Hugh grinned. "'Your Grace,' am I?"

"That is your title," she pointed out.

"Aye, it is. You were saying?"

When she reached the opposite side of his desk, she stopped. "I was stating my displeasure."

Hugh let his arms fall. "I believed it was disappointment?"

She planted her palms on the surface of his cluttered desk. "It is now both."

He smoothed his features. "Forgive me. Carry on."

Hmph. He hardly sounded contrite. Lila leaned forward. "You did not come. I expected you would, and . . . you didn't." She straightened. "As such, I was required to take matters into my own hands."

Hugh shoved lazily to his feet, unfurling every last splendid six foot six inches of his magnificent frame. "And is that what I am . . . a matter?"

"Oh, y-yes." Lila's voice wavered as he started a slow, sleek, pantherine stride around the desk. Her mouth went dry. She struggled through a wicked desire for the man before her and found her words. "I came to ask you to marry me."

That managed to bring Hugh up short.

Lila cleared her throat. "I know it is highly unconventional, and I'll have you know I thought good and long about it before I set out this evening, and I surmised that I've not really been conventional in many ways." She wrinkled her nose. "Really any. As such, it seemed entirely appropriate to come, since you did not," she added for good measure, "and tell you how ardently I love you and want a life with you."

Hugh opened his mouth.

"Of course, I also had much time on the way here to consider you might not be amenable to marriage." Lila squinted. Was he . . . smiling? Except, the light cast by the hearth merely sent shadows playing off his face, and it very well may have been nothing more than an illusion. "Because of . . . my other dreams."

"I intended to come," he murmured.

Lila blinked slowly. "You did."

"I did." He resumed his stroll.

"And . . . what did you intend when you came?" she said, her voice breathless.

Hugh stopped, perching himself on the side of his desk, and then reaching for her, he drew her between his legs. "I intended to tell you how ardently and desperately I love you."

"Y-you did?"

He touched his lips to the curve of her jaw, bringing her lashes closed. "I did." Straightening, Hugh moved his mouth in a slow trail, lower, to her nape. "Then I intended to get down"—and he proceeded to drop to a knee, earning a soft gasp from her—"and ask that you be my duchess."

A smile pulled. "Did you?" She slid her fingers through his dark curls and tipped his face up so he looked at her.

He grinned. "Oh, yes. However, I had business to see to."

That was why he'd not come. Which of course made sense. There was the matter of his meeting afterward with Connor Steele, and the marchioness being carted off. There had been reasons enough that he hadn't come.

Hugh stood. "You were the business I had to see to."

A little giggle bubbled up from her throat. "And is that what I am, Your Grace? Business?"

He looked back with a serious set to his features. "It is an important part of who you are. Just one of the many parts I love of you."

Lila's heart fluttered in her chest as she allowed Hugh to pull her into his arms once more and take her mouth in a slow, searing kiss. Before he set her away.

Reaching past Lila, Hugh fetched a sheet and handed it over.

"What is . . . ?" Her words trailed off as she read. Unable to speak, she lifted her gaze to his.

"I would have supported you in whatever dream you had, because of who you are: you are a woman of courage and strength and convictions. I didn't truly understand what you wished to create . . . until tonight." Terror turned his eyes nearly black. "When I saw her . . . with that gun at your chest, I died a thousand deaths, and every one of them would have been preferred to a life without you in it. And then, I understood your vision . . . and I want you to have that."

Tears filled her eyes, blurring his beloved visage, and she blinked frantically in a bid to see the words there.

"I was drafting the paperwork that would see the property in your name. I know you have funds of your own"—he shifted and bounced on the balls of his feet in that endearing telltale gesture of his nervousness—"however, I thought if you had this property, then you'd be able to use all your funds for the operation of—*oomph*."

Lila launched herself against Hugh, toppling him back so they landed atop the desk.

Papers and parchments rained down upon the floor.

"I trust this means you like—"

"I love it," she rasped, kissing him. "I love you," she said when she pulled her mouth from his.

"And I love you, Lila March."

He smiled, a beautiful, sincere grin that dimpled his left cheek and glimmered in his eyes. Lovingly, she stroked her index finger along his lips. How different this smile was than at their first meeting. How different hers was. For so very long, they'd both been trapped by their pasts. Together, they'd found a way out.

And with a giddy laugh, Lila threw her arms about him, kissing him once more.

They were free.

About the Author

Photo © 2016 Kimberly Rocha

Christi Caldwell is the *USA Today* bestselling author of the Lost Lords of London series, the Sinful Brides series, and the Wicked Wallflowers series. She blames novelist Judith McNaught for luring her into the world of historical romance. When Christi was at the University of Connecticut, she began writing her own tales of love—ones where even the most perfect heroes and heroines had imperfections. She learned to enjoy torturing her couples before they earned their well-deserved happily ever after.

Christi lives in southern Connecticut, where she spends her time writing, chasing after her son, and taking care of her twin princesses-in-training. Fans who want to keep up with the latest news and information can sign up for Christi's newsletter at www.ChristiCaldwell.com.